This book should be returned to any branch of the
Lancashire County Library on or before the date

4/17

Lancashire County Library
Bowran Street
Preston PR1 2UX

Lancashire
County Council

www.lancashire.gov.uk/libraries

'Why should I trust you?' Memories of his intimidation on the courtroom steps flooded back.

Adele became aware that she and the tall, broad-shouldered Alex Mikhalis were the focus of interest among the customers of the café. She moved closer to him so she could lower her voice. He moved closer as well. Too close. She felt as if he were taking up all the air, making her heart race, her breath come short.

'I'm a different man,' he said, his expression intent, his dark eyes unreadable as he searched her face.

He *looked* different—that was for sure. Stripped of designer trappings to a raw masculinity that, in spite of her dislike of him, she could not help but appreciate. As for his nature… Leopards didn't change their spots. And there had always been something predatory about him.

She couldn't help the snort of disbelief that escaped her. 'Huh! *You*? As if I'd believe—'

A flash of pain contorted his features, but was gone so quickly she might have thought she'd imagined it if it hadn't made such an impression on her that it stopped her words short. For a long moment she stared up at him. It had been three years since she had faced him on the courtroom steps. He had been through trauma such as she couldn't imagine. Who knew how that might have affected him? Maybe he was telling the truth. Maybe ̲ ̲ ̲ ̲ ̲ ̲ ̲ ̲ ̲ ̲ ̲ ̲ ̲ ̲ ̲ ̲ be their ̲ ̲ ̲ ̲ ̲ ̲ ̲ ̲ ̲ ̲ ̲ ̲ ̲ ing… for

she should consider taking his offer. May...
convenient arrangement would change everyth...
both of them.

CONVENIENTLY
WED TO THE GREEK

BY
KANDY SHEPHERD

MILLS
BOON

HarperCollins
PUBLISHERS
Since 1817

First Published in Great Britain 2017
By Mills & Boon, an imprint of HarperCollins*Publishers*
1 London Bridge Street, London, SE1 9GF

© 2017 Kandy Shepherd

ISBN: 978-0-263-92296-7

23-0517

Our policy is to use papers that are natural, renewable and recyclable products and made from wood grown in sustainable forests. The logging and manufacturing processes conform to the legal environmental regulations of the country of origin.

Printed and bound in Spain
by CPI, Barcelona

Kandy Shepherd swapped a career as a magazine editor for a life writing romance. She lives on a small farm in the Blue Mountains near Sydney, Australia, with her husband, daughter and lots of pets. She believes in love at first sight and real-life romance—they worked for her! Kandy loves to hear from her readers. Visit her at www.kandyshepherd.com.

To Catherine and Keith,
with thanks for introducing me
to the beauty of the Ionian Islands.

CHAPTER ONE

ADELE HUDSON WAS too busy concentrating on the yoga teacher's instructions to take much notice of the late-comer who took a place to her left and unrolled his mat. From the corner of her eye she registered that he was tall, black-haired, and with the lean, athletic body she would expect from a man who did yoga. *Nice.* But that was as far as her interest went.

Until she attempted to balance on one leg, with the other tucked up against her upper inner thigh, in the *vrksasana* or 'tree' pose. It seemed impossible for a beginner. Why had she thought this class was a good idea?

Dell risked a glance to see if the guy next to her was doing any better. He held the pose effortlessly, broad shoulders, narrow hips, tanned muscular arms in perfect alignment. But the shock of recognition as he came into focus made her wobble so badly she had to flail her arms to stay upright.

Alexios Mikhalis. It couldn't be him. Not here in this far-flung spa retreat on the south coast of New South Wales where she had come to find peace. Not now when she so desperately needed to regroup and rethink her suddenly turned upside down life. But a second quick glimpse confirmed his identity, although he looked very different from the last time she had seen him three years ago pummelling her reputation in court. This man had done everything in his power to destroy her career. And very nearly succeeded.

A shiver of dread ran through her—threatening her balance in more ways than one. He was the last person on earth she wanted to encounter. She had more than enough on her mind without having to shore up her defences against him. Quickly Dell looked away, praying her nemesis hadn't recognised her. Tragedy had visited him since they'd last met, but she doubted he would be any less ruthless. Not when it came to her.

'Lengthen up through the crown of your head,' the yoga teacher intoned in her breathy Zen-like voice.

But it was no use. Dell's concentration was shot. *Why was he here?* The more she tried to balance on one shaky leg, the more impossible the pose seemed. How the heck did you lengthen through the crown of your head anyway? In spite of all efforts to stay upright, she tilted sideward, heading for a humiliating yoga wipe-out.

A strong, masculine hand gripped her elbow to steady her. *Him.* 'Whoa there,' came the deep voice others might find attractive but she had only found intimidating and arrogant.

'Th…thank you,' she said, her chin down and her eyes anywhere but at him, pretending to be invisible. But to no avail.

His grip on her arm tightened. *'You,'* he said, drawing out the word so it sounded like an insult.

Dell turned her head to meet his hawk-like glare, those eyes so dark they were nearly black. She tilted her chin upwards and tried without success to keep the quiver from her voice. 'Yes, *me.*'

Her final encounter with him burned in her memory. Outside the courthouse he had stood on the step above her using his superior height to underline the threat in his words. *'The judge might have ruled in your favour but you won't get away with this. I'll make sure of that.'*

In spite of his loss since then, she had no doubt he still meant every word.

'What are you doing here?' His famously handsome face contorted into a frown.

'Apart from attempting to learn yoga?' she asked with the nervous laugh that insisted on popping out when she felt under pressure. 'Resting, relaxing, those things you do when you come to a health spa.' She didn't dare add *reviewing this new resort.*

This was the tycoon hotelier who had chosen to do battle with her. She was the food critic who had dared to publish a critical review of the most established restaurant in his empire. He'd sued the newspaper that had employed her for an insane amount of money and lost.

Alex Mikhalis had not liked losing. That he was a winner was part of the ethos he'd built up around him—the hospitality mogul who launched nightclubs and restaurants that instantly became Sydney's go-to venues, wiped out his competitors and made him multiple millions. *'Playboy Tycoon with the Magic Touch'*— her own newspaper had headlined a profile on him not long before her disputed review.

After the scene on the courtroom steps, she'd been careful to stay out of his way. Then he'd disappeared from the social scene that had been his playground.

Even the most intrepid of her journalist colleagues hadn't been able to find him. *And here he was.*

'You've hunted me down,' he said.

'I did no such thing,' she said. 'Why would I—?'

'Please, *silence.*' The yoga instructor's tone was now not so Zen-like.

'Let's take this outside,' he said in a deep undertone, maintaining his grip on her elbow.

Dell would have liked to shake off his hand, then place her hands on his chest and shove him away from her. But she was a guest at the spa—here at the owner's invitation—and she didn't want to cause any kind of disruption.

'Sorry,' she mouthed to the instructor as she let herself be led out of the room, grateful in a way not to have to try any more of those ridiculously difficult poses.

With the door to the yoga room shut behind them, Dell took the lead to one of the small guest lounges scattered through the resort. Simple white leather chairs were grouped around a low table. It faced full-length glass windows that looked east to a view of the Pacific Ocean, dazzling blue in the autumn morning sun filtered through graceful Australian eucalypts.

Now she did shake off his arm. 'What was that all about?'

'My right to privacy,' he said, tight-lipped.

Dell was struck again by how different the tycoon looked. No wonder she hadn't immediately recognised him. Back then he'd been a style leader, designer clothes, a fashionable short beard, hair tied into a man bun—though not in court—flamboyant in an intensely masculine way. She'd often wondered what his image had masked. Now he was more boot camp than boutique—strong jaw clean shaven, thick dark hair cropped short, pumped muscles emphasised by grey sweat pants and a white singlet. Stripped bare. And even more compelling. Just her type in fact—if he had been anyone but him.

'And I impinged on your privacy how?' she asked. 'By taking a yoga class that you happened to join? I had no idea you were here.'

'Your newspaper sent you to track me down.' It was a statement, not a question.

'No. It didn't.' The fact she no longer worked for the paper was none of his concern. 'I'm a food writer, not an investigative journalist.'

His mouth twisted. 'Does that matter? To the media I make good copy. No matter how hard I've worked to keep off the radar since…since…'

He seemed unable to choke out the words. She noticed tight lines around his mouth, a few silver hairs in the dark black of his hair near his temples. He was thirty-two, three years older than her, yet there was something immeasurably weary etched on his face.

Another shiver ran up Dell's spine. How did she deal with this? This wealthy, powerful man had been her adversary. *He had threatened her with revenge.* She was convinced his attack on her newspaper had led in part to her losing her job. But how could she hold a grudge after what he had endured?

'I know,' she said, aware her words were completely inadequate. Just a few months after his unsuccessful court case against her, his fiancée had been taken hostage by a crazed gunman in one of his city restaurants. She hadn't come out alive. His grief, his anger, his pain had been front-page news. Until he had disappeared.

Wordlessly, he nodded.

'I'm so sorry,' she said. 'I…wanted to let you know that when…when it happened. But we weren't exactly friends. So I didn't. I've always regretted it.'

He made some inarticulate sound and brushed her words away. But she was glad she had finally been able to express her condolences.

She was surprised at the rush of compassion she felt for him at the bleak emptiness of his expression. *He had lost everything.* She didn't know where he had been, why he was back. His colourful and tragic history made him eminently newsworthy. But she wouldn't make a scoop of his secret by selling the story of her encounter with him. In spite of the fact such a story would bring her much-needed dollars.

'Be assured I won't be the one to reveal your whereabouts,' she said. 'Not to my press contacts. Not on my blog. I'm here for the rest of the week. I'll stay right out of your way.'

She left him looking moodily out to the waters of Big Ray beach and had to slow her pace to something less than a scurry. No way did she want this man to think she was running away from him.

In theory, Alex should not have seen Adele Hudson again. The Bay Breeze spa was designed for tranquil contemplation as well as holistic treatments. In the resort's airy white spaces there was room for personal space and privacy.

But only hours after the yoga class he encountered her in the guest lounge, still in her yoga pants and tank top, contemplating the range of herbal teas and chatting animatedly to an older grey-haired woman who was doing the same. He was on the hunt for caffeine so did not back away. Not that he was in the habit of backing away. He'd always thrived on confrontation.

Alex had always regarded the sassy food critic as an adversary—an enemy, even. Back then he had been implacable in protecting every aspect of his business—an attack on it was an attack on *him*. He certainly hadn't registered anything physical about the person he'd seen as intent on undermining his success with her viperish review of his flagship restaurant. Yet now, observing her, he was forced to concede she was an attractive woman. Very attractive. And in spite of their past vendetta, he had seen compassion and understanding in her eyes. Not the pity he loathed.

She wasn't anything like the type of woman he'd used to date—blonde and willowy models or television celebrities who'd looked good on his arm for publicity purposes. Mia had been tall and blonde too. He swallowed hard against the wave of regret and recrimination that hit him as it always did when he thought about his late fiancée and forced himself to focus on the present.

Adele was average height, curvier than any model, with thick auburn hair she'd worn tied back in the yoga class but which now tumbled around her shoulders. She wasn't conventionally pretty—her mouth was too wide, her jaw line rather too assertive for 'pretty'—but she was head-turning in her own, vibrant way. It was her smile he was noticing now—she'd never had cause to smile in his presence. In fact he remembered she'd been rather effective with a snarl when it had come to interacting with him.

Her mouth was wide and generous and she had perfect teeth. When she laughed at something the other woman said her whole face lit up; her eyes laughed too. What colour were they? Green? Hazel? Somewhere in between? The other woman was charmed by that smile. Alex could tell that from where he stood.

Yet when Adele looked up and caught him observing her the smile faded and her face set in cool, polite lines. Her shoulders hunched as if to protect herself from him and her eyes darted past him and to the doorway. Who could blame her for her dislike of him? He wished he could make up to her for the way he'd behaved towards her. As he'd tried to make amends to others he'd damaged by his ruthless, self-centred pursuit of success. Make amends to them because he could never make amends to Mia. Her death hung heavily on his conscience. *His fault.*

He headed towards Adele. She smiled at him. But it was a poor, forced shadow of the smile he'd seen dazzling her companion just seconds before—more a polite stretching of her lips. He found himself wanting to be warmed by the real deal. But not only did he not deserve it from this person he had so relentlessly hounded, it would be pointless.

There was something frozen inside his soul that even the most heartfelt of smiles from a lovely woman could never melt. Something that had started to shut down the day he'd got a phone call from the police to say a psycho had his city restaurant in lockdown and was holding his fiancée hostage with a gun to her head. Something that had formed cold and rock solid when Mia had lost her own life trying to save another's.

'Hello there,' Dell said very politely. Then turned to the woman beside her and gestured towards him. 'We met in the yoga class,' she explained, not mentioning his name by way of introduction.

So she intended to keep her word about maintaining his privacy. He was grateful for that. Alex nodded to the older woman. He did not feel obliged to share anything about himself with strangers—even his name.

He turned to the artful display of teas in small wooden chests. 'This is a fine selection,' he said with genuine interest. He was here to glean information for his new project. A hotel completely different from anything he'd created before. He'd been isolated from the hospitality business in the past years and needed to be on top of the trends. He knew all about partying and decadence—what he sought now was restraint and calm. A different way of doing business. A different *life*.

'Tea has become very fashionable,' Adele said in what seemed a purposely neutral voice, more for the benefit of the other woman rather than any conscious desire to engage in conversation with *him*. 'Not any old teas, naturally. Herbal teas, healing tisanes, special blends. I highly recommend the parsnip, ginger and turmeric blend—organic and vegan, which is a good thing.'

Alex gagged at the thought of it.

But if that was what people wanted at a place like this, it would be up to him to give it to them. Of course Adele would know about what was fashionable in foods and beverages. Her *Dell Dishes* blog attracted an extraordinary number of visitors. Or it had three years ago when he had instructed his lawyers to delve deep into her life with particular reference to her income.

At one stage he had thought about suing her personally as well as via the publishing company that had employed her as a food critic and editor of its restaurant guide. Back then, scrutinising *Dell Dishes*, he hadn't thought she had done enough to monetise her site, to take advantage of the potential appeal to advertisers. Needless to say he hadn't offered her any advice—he'd wanted to bring her down, not help her soar.

'I'll pass on the parsnip tea, thank you,' he said, suppressing a grimace. 'What I want is coffee—strong and black.' He couldn't keep the yearning from his voice.

'No such thing here, I'm afraid,' she said, with a wry expression that he couldn't help but find cute. *Cute*. It was incomprehensible that he should find Adele Hudson *cute*.

He groaned. 'No coffee at all?'

She shook her head. 'Not part of the "clean food" ethos of the spa. You'll have to sneak out to the Bay Bites café. They serve Dolphin Bay's finest coffee. I can personally vouch for it.'

'I might follow up on that.'

His friends the Morgan brothers, Ben and Jesse, had made the once sleepy beachside town of Dolphin Bay into quite a destination with the critically acclaimed Hotel Harbourside, Bay Bites, Bay Books and now the eco-friendly Bay Breeze spa in which Alex had invested in the early stages. It would not be long before he saw a return on his investment.

The new resort was still in its debut phase but had been an immediate success. It had been booked out for Easter a few weeks back. The Morgans had read the market well. In just one day Alex had picked aspects he liked about the operation and ones he didn't think would translate to his new venture. What worked in Australia might not necessarily work in Greece.

'Escaping for coffee is hardly in the spirit of eating clean food.' Adele sounded stern but there was an unexpected gleam of fun in her eyes. Eyes that were green like the olives growing on the island in the Ionian Sea that had once belonged to his ancestors and that he had bought so it once more was owned by a Mikhalis.

He couldn't help his snort of disgust at her comment. 'So does "clean food" mean that all other food is "dirty"? I don't like the idea of that. Especially the traditional Greek foods I grew up on.'

'I think that term is debatable too,' she said. 'I wonder if—?'

Adele's grey-haired companion chose that moment to pick up her cup of herbal tea and make to move away. 'I want to say again how much I love your blog,' she enthused. 'My daughter told me about it. Even my granddaughter is a fan, and she's still at school.'

Adele flushed and looked pleased. As she should—it was no mean feat to have her site appeal to three generations. 'Thank you. I hope I can keep on bringing you more of what you enjoy.'

'You'll do that, I'm sure,' the other woman said. 'In the meantime, I'll leave you two to chat.' She departed but not without a speculative look from Alex to Adele and back to him again.

Alex groaned inwardly. He recognised that gleam in her narrowed eyes. The same matchmaking gleam he'd seen often in the women of his extended Greek family. This particular lady had got completely the wrong end of the stick. He had no romantic interest whatsoever in Adele Hudson. In fact he had no interest in any kind of permanent relationship with any woman—in spite of the pressure from his family to settle down. Not now. Not ever. Not after what he'd endured. Not after what he had *done*.

Besides, Adele was married. Or she had been three years ago. He glanced down at her left hand. *No ring.* So maybe she was no longer married. Not that her marital state was of any interest to him.

Adele had obviously not missed that matchmaking gleam either. When she looked back at him, the undisguised horror in her eyes told him exactly what she thought of the idea of anyone pairing her with *him*.

Alex had taken worse insults in his time. So why did that feel like a kick to the gut? He decided not to linger any longer at the tea station. Or to admit even to himself that he would like lovely Adele Hudson to look at him with something other than extreme distaste.

CHAPTER TWO

THE NEXT TIME Alex saw Adele Hudson he'd beaten
her to their mutual destination—the dolphin-themed
Bay Bites café that overlooked the picturesque harbour of Dolphin Bay. The café was buzzing with the
hum of conversation, the aromas of fresh baking—
and that indefinable feeling of a successful business.
Alex missed being 'hands on' in his own restaurants
so much it ached. That world was what had driven him
since he'd been a teenager. Even before that. As a child
he'd spent some of his happiest hours in his grandfather's restaurant.

Here he could sense the goodwill of the customers, the seamless teamwork of the staff. All was as he
liked it to be in his own establishments. And Adele
had been right, the café did have excellent coffee. He
was sitting at a table near the window, savouring his
second espresso, when he looked up to see her heading his way, pedalling one of the bicycles Bay Breeze
provided for guests.

She cycled energetically, a woman on a mission to
get somewhere quickly. Her face was flushed from ex-
ertion as she got off and slid the bike onto a rack outside the café. She took off her bike helmet and shook

out her auburn hair with a gesture of unconscious grace. Her hair glinted with copper highlights in the morning sunlight, dazzling him.

This woman was nothing to him but an old adversary. Yet Alex found it difficult to look away from her fresh beauty. Since he'd been living in Greece, getting back to basics with his family there, he felt as if he were seeing life through new eyes. He was certainly seeing something different in Adele Hudson. Or maybe it had always been there and he'd been so intent on revenge he hadn't noticed. There was something vibrant and uncontrived about her, dressed in white shorts and a simple white top, white sneakers and with a small multicoloured backpack. She radiated energy and good health, her face open and welcome to new experience.

Alex didn't alert her to his presence; she'd notice him soon enough. When she did, her first reaction on catching sight of him was out-and-out dismay, quickly covered up by another forced smile. Again he felt that kick in the gut—quite unjustifiably considering how he'd treated her in the past.

She stopped by his table and he got up to greet her, glad she hadn't just walked by with a cursory nod. 'So you took my advice,' she said. Her flushed cheeks made her eyes seem even greener. Her hair was tousled around her face.

'Yes,' he said. 'I become a raging beast without my coffee.'

It was a bad choice of words. The look that flashed across her eyes told him she found the *beast* label only too appropriate. And that not only did she dislike him, but it seemed she also might fear him.

A jolt of remorse hit him. That was not the reaction

he ever wanted from a woman. He thought back to the court case. There'd been some kind of confrontation outside on the day the judge had handed down his decision—although surely nothing to make her frightened of him.

'I'm not partial to raging beasts,' she said. *Beasts like you* were the words she left unspoken but he understand as well as if she had shouted them.

Against all his own legal advice he'd gone after her and the major Sydney newspaper that had published her review. He'd been furious at her criticism of Athina, his first important restaurant—the one that had launched him as a serious contender on the competitive Sydney market. He'd had a lot to prove when he'd closed his grandfather's original traditional Greek restaurant and reopened with something cutting-edge fashionable. The risk had paid off—and success after success had followed. And then she'd published a bad review of Athina, detailing how the prices had gone up and the quality gone down, along with the levels of service. It had seemed like a personal assault.

So much had happened to him since then. His fury at her review now seemed disproportionate—a major overreaction to what the court had found to be fair comment. In light of what had happened during the hostage scenario and its aftermath it seemed insignificant. She had nothing to fear from him. Not now.

He looked directly at her. 'I told you this beast has been tamed,' he said gruffly. It was as much an explanation as he felt able to give her. He didn't share with anyone how he'd had to claw his way out of the abyss.

But her brow furrowed. 'Tamed by the coffee?'

She didn't get what he meant. But he had no intention of spelling out the bigger picture for her. How devastated he'd been by Mia's death. The train wreck his life had become. He'd been a broken man, unable to deal with the public spotlight on him—the spotlight he'd once courted. There had only been the pain, the loss, the unrelenting guilt.

His father had intervened, packed him up and sent him back to the Greek village his grandfather had left long ago to emigrate to Australia. At first, Alex had deeply resented his exile. But the distance and the return to his family's roots had given him a painfully gained new perspective and self-knowledge. He'd discovered he hadn't much liked the man he'd become in Sydney.

The presence of Adele Hudson was like an arrow piercing his armour, reminding him of how invincible he'd thought himself to be back then when he'd been flying so high, how agonising his crash into the shadows. He forced his voice to sound steady and impartial. 'The magical powers of caffeine,' he said. 'Can I order you a coffee?'

Adele gave him a look through narrowed eyes that let him know she realised there was something more to his words that she hadn't grasped. But didn't care to pursue. She peered towards the back of the café to the door that led to the kitchen. 'No, thank you. I've popped in to see Lizzie.'

'Lizzie Dumont?'

Jesse's wife was a chef and the driving force behind the exemplary standards of the Morgan eateries. Alex had tried to poach her to work for him on a start-up in Sydney, a traditional French bistro. That was before he'd realised she'd been engaged to Jesse Morgan. That had stopped him. Back then he'd let nothing stop his quest for success—except loyalty to friends and family. That had never been negotiable.

'She's Lizzie Morgan now, well and truly married to Jesse,' Adele said. 'They have a beautiful baby boy, a brother for her daughter Amy.'

'Yes,' he said.

Lizzie had a child from her first marriage. Alex had admired Jesse for taking on a stepchild. Had admired him the more because it wasn't something Alex himself could ever do. His feeling for family and heritage was too deeply ingrained to ever take on another man's child. He would never date a woman who came encumbered.

'Here she is.' Adele waved at a tall woman with curly, pale blonde hair who had pushed her way through the doors from the kitchen.

'Dell! It's so good to see you.' Alex watched as Lizzie swept Adele up in a hug. 'It's been too long. We've got so much to catch up on.'

'We certainly do,' said Adele, giving Lizzie the full benefit of her dazzling smile. Politely, she turned to include him in the conversation. *No smile for him.* 'Lizzie, I think you know Alex Mik—'

'Of course I do,' Lizzie said. She greeted him with a hug and kisses on both cheeks. 'He's a good friend of Jesse's. When we heard he was going to be in Sydney we invited him down to Bay Breeze. Long time, no see, Alex.' Her smile dimmed and her voice softened. 'Are you okay?'

He nodded. 'As okay as I can be,' he said. 'I've appreciated the support from you and Jesse. It means a lot.' He didn't want to talk about his loss any further.

Displaying vulnerability clashed with all the ideals of manhood that had been imbued in him by his family. 'I didn't know you two knew each other,' he said. How much did Lizzie know of his history with Adele? No doubt he'd been painted as an ogre of the first order. *A beast.*

Lizzie beamed. 'Dell was one of our first customers. Her glowing reviews of Bay Bites helped put us on the map. The bonus was we became friends. Though we don't see each other as much as we'd like.'

Adele studiously avoided his eyes, obviously uncomfortable at the mention of her good reviews when she'd given Athina such a stinker. The court case had ensured she'd never reviewed his newer ventures, never put them 'on the map'.

'I've always loved this part of the world,' she said. 'And Bay Breeze is the icing on the cake. I love what you guys have done with it, Lizzie. The building, the fit-out, the food. The timing is perfect. Stress and burnout are endemic today. Offering this kind of retreat in such an awesome natural setting is just what a particular lucrative market is looking for.'

Had she read his mind? She could have been quoting him on the pitch for his new luxury boutique resort.

As she chatted with Lizzie, Alex was surprised at how much Adele knew about the hospitality business. She was both perceptive and canny. She understood how success came from meeting people's needs but also about anticipating them. Giving them what they didn't know they wanted until it was offered to them, all new and shiny. Knowing your customer through and through. Being open to change and nimble enough to adapt to it.

The strength of Bay Breeze she had pinpointed was on track with what he wanted for his new venue. It wasn't often he met someone who was so in tune with how he thought about the business. Although that was perhaps not such a surprise when in the past he'd surrounded himself with too many 'yes' men.

'So what are your plans for life after the newspaper?' Lizzie asked her.

Adele frowned at Lizzie with what was obviously a warning. Alex realised she didn't want him to hear that. Which made him determined not to miss a word.

'What do you mean?' he asked.

Lizzie sounded outraged. 'That darn newspaper fired Dell. Booted her out with a cheque in lieu of notice.'

Adele glared at her friend for spilling the beans.

'Is that true?' he asked Adele. 'You've lost your job?'

She shrugged. But he could see it was an effort for her to sound casual about such a blow. Especially in front of him. 'Budget cuts, they said. It…it was a shock.'

'Because of the court case?' Regret churned in him. How much damage had he caused for something that now seemed unimportant?

She didn't meet his eye. 'No. That was three years ago. Although I was never popular with management afterwards. Being sued wasn't regarded as a highlight of my résumé.'

He frowned. 'What will you do?' He felt a shaft of shame at what he had put her through. Although he had felt totally in the right at the time.

Alex expected a snarl and a rejoinder to mind his own business. But she couldn't mask the panic in her eyes. 'I don't know yet. They only gave me the boot a week ago. But I've got options.'

'Of course you have,' said loyal Lizzie. 'Publicity and marketing among them. That would be a logical move for you.'

Adele nodded to her friend. 'Yes, I've thought of that,' she said. 'And I can freelance. It will also allow me to give my blog more attention.'

Alex doubted she could make enough to live on from that blog, in spite of the number of readers it attracted. Unless she'd made big strides with attracting advertising since he'd last looked at *Dell Dishes*.

'Your husband?' he asked after some hesitation. He was sure there'd been a husband.

Her mouth twisted. 'Divorced.' Her chin tilted upward. 'In any case, I don't depend on a man to support me.'

He wouldn't have expected any other response from the feisty food critic. 'Do you have children?'

Something he couldn't read darkened her eyes. She shook her head.

'Then come and work for me.' The words escaped his mouth before he'd had time to think about them. But some of his best decisions had been made on impulse.

Dell looked up at Alex Mikhalis, the man she regarded as the devil incarnate. He towered over her, darkly formidable in black jeans and a black T-shirt that made no secret of his strength, his impressive muscles.

'Did you just offer me a job?' She couldn't keep the disbelief from her voice. From behind her, she heard Lizzie gasp.

'I did,' he said gruffly.

'Why would you do that?'

'You need a job. I need help with a new venture. Your understanding of hospitality is impressive. You have skills in PR and publicity.'

Entitled and arrogant, he so obviously expected an instant 'yes'. But it would not be forthcoming from her. She sympathised with his personal loss. That didn't mean she wanted to work with him. Especially not to be under his control as an employee.

She couldn't think of anything worse.

'I appreciate the offer,' she said. 'But I can't possibly accept. I suspect you know why.'

His legal team had undermined her credibility at every opportunity. Even though her newspaper had won the case, she had come out of it bruised and battered with her reputation intact but shredded around the edges. Even three years later she felt it had influenced her employer into 'letting her go'. And that was apart from the stress it had put on her marriage.

He scowled. 'I want to make amends.'

Alex Mikhalis make amends? To her? She frowned. 'Is this some kind of trick?'

'No tricks,' he said. His voice was deep, assured, confident. Yet did nothing to reassure her.

'I find that difficult to believe. You...you threatened me. Told me you would get even.' He made her so nervous it was difficult to get her words out. She had heard the rumours of how effectively he had brought down his business opponents. But she would not let him sense her fear.

'That was a different time and place. There is no threat.'

'Why should I trust you?' Memories of his intimidation on the courtroom steps flooded back.

Dell became aware that she and the tall, broad-shouldered man were the focus of interest among the customers of the café. She moved closer to him so she could lower her voice. He moved closer as well. *Too close.* She felt as if he were taking up all the air, making her heart race, her breath come short.

'I'm a different man,' he said, his expression intent, dark eyes unreadable as he searched her face.

He *looked* different, that was for sure. Stripped of designer trappings to a raw masculinity that, in spite of her dislike of him, she could not help but appreciate. As for his nature? Leopards didn't change their spots. And there had always been something predatory about him.

She couldn't help the snort of disbelief that escaped her. 'Huh! You? As if I believe—'

A flash of pain contorted his features but was gone so quickly she might have imagined it if it hadn't made such an impression on her that it stopped her words short. For a long moment she stared up at him. It had been three years since she had faced him on the courtroom steps. He had been through trauma like she couldn't imagine. Who knew how that might have affected him? Maybe he was telling the truth.

She felt a gentle tap on her arm and turned, dazed, to see Lizzie. 'Perhaps you should consider this offer,' her friend said quietly. Her eyes gave her a silent message. *You have debts.*

Dell was only too aware of the debts she had run up during her marriage and that had become her responsibility. Lizzie always gave her wise counsel. Her

friend would be horrified if she knew the decision she
had made just the week before she had lost her job. If
it paid off, she might need a job more than ever. And
with so many people reviewing restaurants online for
free, she felt the newspaper editor had been telling
the truth when he'd told her that her role was redun-
dant. Job offers weren't exactly flooding her inbox. She
forced herself to take a deep, calming breath.

Then turned back to face Alex. 'Why do you want
to make amends?' she said. 'And what makes you think
we could work together? I'm a writer, not a restaura-
teur.'

'I'll answer both your questions with one reply,' he
said. 'Every criticism you made about my restaurant
Athina was true. My manager was systematically de-
frauding me. Your judgement was spot on. I should
have taken your review as a warning instead of taking you to court.'

'Oh,' was all she was able to choke out. Alex Mikhalis admitting he was *wrong*?

A ghost of a smile lifted the corners of his mouth.
She was more used to seeing him glare and scowl at
her. The effect was disconcerting. A devil undoubtedly.
But a fiendishly handsome devil. For the first time she
saw a hint of the legendary charisma that had propelled
him to such heights in a people-pleasing business.

'I've shocked you speechless,' he said.

'I admit it. I'm stunned. After all that…that angst.
When did you find out?'

'When I slipped back into Sydney for the review of
the police handling of the siege,' he said, now without
any trace of a smile.

Dell nodded, unable to find the words to say anything about what must have been such a terrible time in his life. The saga had made headlines in the media for weeks. 'From my memory, the manager was your friend,' she said instead.

'Yes,' he said simply.

How betrayed he must have felt on top of everything else he'd had to endure.

'Perhaps if I had been an investigative reporter I might have discovered that,' she said.

'I wouldn't have believed you. Everything in your review pointed that way. I just didn't see it.'

'Didn't *want* to see it, perhaps,' she said.

He paused, then the words came slowly. 'I… I'm sorry, Adele.'

Alex Mikhalis *apologising*? After all this man had put her through?

She thought again about all *he* had been through since. Realised she was intrigued at the thought of what project he might be working on now. And that it wasn't healthy to hold a grudge or wise to refuse an apparently sincere apology. Especially when she really needed a job. Lizzie was right. She should consider this.

'Dell,' she said. 'Please call me Dell. Adele is my newspaper byline, the name on my birth certificate.' She looked up at him. 'Tell me more about this job.'

CHAPTER THREE

ALEX DIDN'T KNOW why it had suddenly become so important that Adele Hudson—Dell—accept his impromptu job offer. But he didn't question it. Much of his success in business had come from following his instinct and he'd learned not to ignore its prompts.

Dell could be just the person he needed to help him launch his new project. The project he needed to get him back on track with life.

Mentally, he checked off the skills she brought to the table. Without a doubt she was good with words—a huge asset for launching into a new market. Another strength was she saw the hospitality industry through the eyes of the customer while at the same understanding how the business side operated. Her blog gave her an international view with access to readers all around the world. On top of that, she was smart and perceptive.

Her review of Athina had raised red flags he should have heeded. His traitorous so-called friend had been doing illicit deals with suppliers and siphoning off funds to a private bank account. He would have saved himself a good deal of money if he hadn't let pride and anger blind him to the truth of what she had observed.

Since he'd been back living in the land of his ancestors he had thought a lot about the Ancient Greek concept of fate. Was it his selfishness or fate that had put Mia in his city restaurant when a sociopath had decided to make a deadly statement? Could it be that fate had brought Dell back into his life? Right at the time when he needed help to launch something different and she was in need of a job? At a time when he was growing weary of punishing himself for something that had been out of his control.

Dell looked up at him, her green eyes direct. 'What exactly does the job entail?' she asked.

Fact was, there wasn't a job vacancy as such. He would create a role for her.

Alex looked around the café, filling up now as lunchtime approached. Lizzie had left them to return to the kitchen. 'We need to go somewhere more private where we can talk.'

Dell nodded with immediate understanding. 'What about the harbour front?' she said.

He put cash on the table to cover both his coffee and a very generous tip. 'Good idea.'

He followed her out of the café. She looked good in shorts with her slender legs and shapely behind. In fact she was downright sexy. How had he not noticed that sensuous sway before? Alex forced his gaze away. *This was about business.*

He walked with her past the adjoining bookstore towards a lookout with a view across the stone-walled harbour with its array of fishing and pleasure craft. The scene was in some ways reminiscent of the fishing village his Greek ancestors came from, in others completely different.

He'd been born and grown up in Australia and

thought of himself as Australian. But his Greek heritage was calling to him. He was back here just for a quick visit to help celebrate his father's sixtieth birthday and to take a look at Bay Breeze. Greece was where he wanted to be right now. He didn't think he could ever live back in Sydney again. Not with the memories and regrets that assaulted him at every turn.

'No one will overhear us here,' Dell said when they reached the lookout. 'Fire away.'

He looked around to be sure. His success hadn't come about by sharing his strategies. 'I would usually require you to sign a confidentiality agreement before discussing a new project.'

She shrugged. 'I'm good with that. Just tell me where to sign.'

Through his dealings with her as an adversary he'd also come to a grudging admiration of her honesty. According to the judge, her review had been scrupulously within the boundary of fair comment. And his lawyers had been unable to dig up even a skerrick of dirt on her.

'I wasn't expecting this, so I don't have an agreement with me,' he said.

'You can trust me,' she said. 'I'm good at keeping secrets.'

He had been accused of being a ruthless and cynical businessman—never taking anyone on trust. Yet instinct told him he could talk to this woman without his plans being broadcast where they shouldn't.

Still…he hadn't changed *that* much. 'I'll email a document to you when I'm back at the resort.'

'Of course,' she said with a tinge of impatience. 'I'll sign it straight away. But right now I'm dying of curiosity about the role you have in mind for me.'

Alex leaned back against the railing. 'I'm not at Bay Breeze for the yoga and the parsnip tea,' he said.

Dell's green eyes danced with amusement. 'I kind of got that,' she said.

'I'm a stakeholder and I wanted to see what my investment has got me. The more I'm involved, the more I like the well-being concept. It seems right for the times.' And for *his* time.

'You want to start a similar kind of resort?'

He nodded. 'It's already under way. On a private island. Upscale. Exclusive. To appeal to the top end of the market. But my experience is all in restaurants and nightclubs. A resort is something different and challenging. I need some help.' Alex had to force out the final words. He never found it easy to admit he needed help in anything. Had always seen it as a weakness.

'That's where I come in?'

He nodded. 'But I don't have a job description for the role. I wasn't expecting someone like you to come along at this stage.'

'You mean you're making the job up as you go along?'

She was direct. There was another thing he'd found interesting about Dell during their legal stoush. He added another, less tangible asset to the list of her attributes. *He would enjoy working with her.*

'Yeah. I am. Which is good for you as I can shape the role to your talents. I have input from top designers and consultants for the building and fit-out. I've got my key hospitality staff on contract. But I want someone to work with me on fine-tuning the offer to guests and with the publicity. Establishing an exclusive well-being resort on a private island is something different for me.'

'That is quite a challenge,' she said.

'Yes,' he said. And a much-needed distraction. He'd go crazy if he didn't throw himself into a big, all-consuming project.

He'd thought he could walk away from his business. The business he blamed for Mia's death. She'd been a chef in one of his restaurants when he'd met her. There had been a strict company rule against fraternising between staff in his businesses. He'd instigated it and he'd broken it when he'd become beguiled by Mia. They'd been living together—her pushing for marriage, he putting it off—when the chef at his busiest city lunchtime venue had been injured in an accident on the way to work. Mia was having a rostered day off. Alex had pulled rank and insisted she go into work that day to replace the chef. He could not take that memory out again, to pick and prod at it, a wound that would never heal.

Since he'd been away, he'd discreetly sold off his Sydney venues one by one. All except Athina. He couldn't bear to let his inheritance from his grandfather go. Financially he never needed to work again. But he *had* to work. He hadn't realised how much his work had defined him until he hadn't had it to occupy himself day after lonely day.

Dell's auburn brows drew together in a frown. 'Why me? There must be more experienced people around who would jump at the chance to work with you on such a project.'

He didn't want to mention fate or kismet or whatever it was that had sent her here. The hunch that made him think she was what he needed right now. 'But it's you I want. And you need a job.'

'The role does interest me,' she said cautiously. 'Although I'd want to keep my blog. It's important to me.'

'I see your blog as an asset, complementary to your work with me,' he said. 'You could utilise it for soft publicity, along with social media.'

She nodded. 'I'll consider that.'

'I'm thinking the title of Publicity Director,' he said. He named a handsome salary.

She blinked. 'That definitely interests me,' she said.

'I pay well and expect utmost commitment in return.'

'I have no issue with that,' she said. 'I've been described more than once as a workaholic.'

Her mouth set in a rigid line and he wondered if it was the ex-husband who had criticised her. He remembered wondering why he hadn't been at court to support his wife during the case. 'Truth is, if I get really involved, the line between work and interest blurs,' she said.

As it always had with him. 'I think you'll find this interesting,' he said. 'The project is under way but the best is yet to come. You'd be coming on board at an exciting time. I want to open in June.'

Her eyes widened. 'It's already April. Isn't that leaving it late?'

'Agree. It's cutting it fine. I won't expect full occupancy until next year.'

'When would you want me to start?' she asked. He could sense her simmering excitement. 'Because I'm firing with ideas already.'

'A week. Two weeks max.'

She smiled. 'I could do that.' That big embracing smile was finally aimed at him. For a moment, he had to close his eyes against its dazzle. 'I love the idea of an exclusive private island. Where is it? North of Sydney? Queensland? South Australia?'

He shook his head. 'Greece.'

'*Greece?* I... I wasn't expecting that.'

Alex had expected her to react with excitement. Not a clouding of her eyes and a disappointed turn down of her mouth. He frowned.

'My island of Kosmima is in northern Greece where my ancestors come from. Where I've been living with my Greek family since I left Australia. The most beautiful private island in the Ionian Sea. I'm sure you would love it.'

Of course she would love it.

Dell had always wanted to visit Greece. It had held a fascination for her since she'd studied ancient history at school. The mythology. The history. The ancient buildings. She wanted to climb the Acropolis in Athens to see the Parthenon. To visit the picturesque islands with their whitewashed buildings and blue roofs. There was nowhere in the world she wanted to visit more than Greece.

But travel had long been off the cards. She'd committed young to her high-school boyfriend and been caught up in mortgages and marriage to a man who hadn't had an ounce of wanderlust in him. She'd travelled some with her parents and longed to travel more. Even to live abroad one day.

But there was something else she'd wanted more.

Wanted so desperately she'd put all her other dreams on hold to pursue it.

'I…assumed the job was in Australia,' she said.

He shook his head. 'No new venues in Australia for the foreseeable future. Europe is where I want to be. But I'd like a fellow Australian on board with me. Someone who knows about my businesses here, understands how things operate. In other words, you.'

So this was how it felt when big dreams collided.

Dell swallowed hard against the pain of her disappointment. 'I'm very sorry, but I'm going to have to say no to your job offer. I can't possibly go to Greece.'

His dark eyebrows rose in disbelief. She had knocked back what anyone might term a dream job. *Her* dream job. She suspected Alex wasn't used to people saying no to him. But there was disappointment too in those black eyes. He had created a role just for her, tailored to her skills. She was grateful for the confidence he had put in her ability.

But she couldn't tell him why she had to turn down the most enticing offer she was ever likely to get. Why she couldn't be far away from home. That there was a chance she might be pregnant.

CHAPTER FOUR

When Dell had been a little girl and people asked her what she wanted to be when she grew up, she had always replied she wanted to be a mummy. They had laughed and asked what else, but she had stubbornly stood her ground.

She didn't know why, as heaven knew her mother hadn't been particularly maternal. And her father had verged on the indifferent. Both her parents had been—still were—research scientists for multinational pharmaceutical companies. She suspected they would have been happy to stop at the one child, her older brother, and when she'd come along when he'd been five she'd been more of an inconvenience than a joy. Her brother was of a scientific bent like her parents. She, while as intelligent, had broader interests they didn't share or understand.

As a child, Dell had loved her dolls, her kitten, her books and food. Her mother was a haphazard cook and by the time she was twelve Dell had been cooking for the family. It became a passion.

At the insistence of her parents, she had completed a degree in food science. A future in the laboratory of a major grocery manufacturer beckoned. Instead, to the horror of her parents, after graduation she went straight to work as an editorial assistant on a suburban newspaper. She showed a flair for restaurant reviewing and articles about food and lifestyle and her career went on from there.

At twenty-two, she married Neil, her high-school boyfriend. He supported her in her desire to become a mother. That was when her plans derailed. In spite of their most energetic efforts, pregnancy didn't happen. At age twenty-seven they started IVF. The procedure was painful and disruptive. The hormone treatments sent her emotions soaring and plunging. The joy went out of her love-life. But three expensive IVF procedures didn't result in pregnancy. Just debt.

Then Neil had walked out on her.

Growing up, Dell had often felt like a fluffy, colourful changeling of a chick popped into the nest of sleek, clever hawks who had never got over their surprise in finding her there. She had become adept at putting on a happy face when she'd felt misunderstood and unhappy.

The end of her marriage had come from left field and she'd been devastated. She'd loved Neil and had thought she'd be married for ever. She shared her tears with a few close friends but presented that smiling, fluffy-chick face to the world.

Being suddenly single came as a shock. She'd been part of a couple for so long she didn't know how to deal with dating. After a series of disastrous encounters she'd given up on the idea of meeting another man. Work became her solace as she tried to deal with the death of her big dream. Accepted that, if IVF hadn't worked, she wasn't likely to ever be a mother.

Then just weeks ago the fertility clinic had called

to ask what she wanted them to do with the remaining embryo she had stored with them.

Dell knew she should have told them she was divorced. That her ex-husband was in another relationship. But they didn't ask and she didn't tell. She'd undergone the fourth procedure the week before she'd been fired. All her other attempts at IVF had failed. She hadn't held out any real hope for this time. But she'd felt compelled to grab at that one final chance.

Now, the day after her meeting with Alex Mikhalis, Dell lay back on her cool white bed at Bay Breeze racked by the cramps that had always heralded failure. She took in a great, gasping sob then stayed absolutely still, desperately willing that implant to stay put. Her baby. But a visit to the bathroom confirmed blood. She'd failed again.

She would never be a mother.

Dell stood at the window for a long time staring sightlessly out to the view of the sea. Her hand rested on her flat, flat stomach. There was nothing for her here. No job. No man. No close family. Just parents who, if she left the country, would wave her good-bye without thinking to ask why she was going. Her friends were starting families and moving into a life cycle she couldn't share. She hadn't told anyone about this last desperate effort to conceive so there was no one to share her grief. But she did have all her cyber friends on her blog. She had to put on her fluffy-chick face and move on.

Without thinking any further, she picked up the house phone and called through to Alex Mikhalis's room. She braced herself to leave a message and was shocked when he answered. Somehow she found the words to ask could she have a meeting with him. His tone was abrupt as he told her to be quick—he was packing to head back to Sydney.

Dell had no chance to change. Or apply make-up. Just pushed her hair into place in front of the mirror and slicked on some lip gloss. Yoga pants were *de rigueur* in a place like this anyway. He wouldn't expect to see her in a business suit and heels.

He answered the door to his room. 'Yes?' he said, his voice deep and gruff and more than a touch forbidding.

For a long moment Dell hesitated on the threshold. He towered over her, in black trousers and a charcoal-grey shirt looking every inch the formidable tycoon. Half of the buttons on his shirt were left open, as if he'd been fastening them when she'd sounded the buzzer on his door. It left bare a triangle of olive skin and a hint of dark chest hair on an impressively muscled chest.

Her heart started to beat double-quick time and she felt so shaky at the knees she had to clutch at the doorframe for support. Not because she was nervous about approaching him. Or feared what kind of a boss he might be. No. It was because her long-dormant libido had flared suddenly back into life at the sight of him—those dark eyes, the proud nose, the strong jaw newly shaven but already shadowing with growth. *He was hot.*

Dell swallowed against a suddenly dry mouth. This unwelcome surge of sensual awareness could complicate things. She was beginning to rethink his devil incarnate status. But who knew if he was sincere about having changed? After all, she'd seen him at his intimidating worst on those courtroom steps. She had to take him on trust but be cautious. That did not mean fancying the pants off him.

Eyes off the gorgeous man, Dell.

He stepped back and she could see his bag half packed on his bed. Perhaps he was headed to Greece and she would never see him again. This could be her only chance.

She forced her lips into a smile, the wobble at the edge betraying her attempt to be both nonchalant and professional. And not let him guess the turmoil of her senses evoked by his half-dressed state. 'Your job offer?' she said.

He nodded.

'Can…can a person change her mind?'

Alex stared at Dell. What had happened? Thinly disguised anguish showed in the set of her jaw, the pallor of her face, her red-rimmed eyes. The expression in her eyes was sad rather than sparkling. But as she met his gaze, her cheeks flushed pink high on her cheekbones, her chin rose resolutely and he wondered if he'd imagined it.

'I'd like to accept the job.' She hesitated. There was an edge to her voice that made him believe he had not imagined her distress. 'That is, if the position is still on offer.'

Alex had been gutted when she'd turned him down. Disappointed out of all proportion. And stunned that he'd been so shaken. Because of course she'd been right. Whisper a word in a recruitment agent's ear and he'd be inundated with qualified people ready to take up the job with him. Why Dell Hudson? Because it was her and only her he'd wanted. He'd had no intention of taking her 'no' as final. In fact he'd been planning strategies aimed at getting a 'yes' from her.

Once he'd made up his mind about something it was difficult to budge him. It was a trait he had inherited from his stubborn grandfather. No one else would do but *her*. Was it his tried and tested gut feel telling him that? Or something else? It was nothing to do with the fact he found her attractive. That was totally beside the point. He did not date employees. Never, ever after what had happened with Mia.

'Why did you change your mind?' he asked Dell.

She took a deep breath, which emphasised the curve of her breasts outlined by her tight-fitting tank top. How had he never noticed how sexy she was? He forced his eyes upward to catch the nuances of her expression rather than the curves of her shapely body.

'A…sudden change of circumstances,' she said. 'Something…something personal.'

'Problems with a guy?' he asked. Over the years he'd learned to deal with the personal dramas of female staff. Not that it ever got easier.

She shook her head and again he caught that glimpse of sadness in her eyes. 'No. I'm one hundred per cent single. And intending to stay that way. I'm free to devote my time entirely to my work with you.'

'Good,' he said. He didn't want to hear the details of her marriage breakup. Or any bust-ups that came afterwards. That was none of his concern. This was about a job. Nothing more.

Although he found it very difficult to believe she was single by choice.

'I don't let my personal life impinge on my work,' she said. 'I want your job and I want to go to Greece.'

'You're sure about that? You're not going to change your mind again?'

She took another distracting deep breath. 'I'm very sure.'

He allowed himself a smile, knowing that it was tinged with triumph. Reached out to shake her hand. 'When can you be ready to fly to Athens?'

CHAPTER FIVE

SHE WAS IN GREECE, working for Alex Mikhalis!

It had all happened so fast Dell still felt a little dizzy that, just two weeks after her wobbly encounter with him in the yoga room, the man who had been her adversary— the man she had loathed—was her boss.

So far so good. It had been a long, tedious trip to get here even in the comfort of the business-class seats he had booked for her—twenty-three hours to Athens alone. Then another short flight to the small airport at Preveza in north-western Greece.

Too excited to be jet-lagged, she staggered out into the sunshine expecting to find a sign with her name on it held up by a taxi driver. But her new boss was there to meet her. Tall and imposing, he stood out among the people waiting for passengers. He waved to get her attention.

Dell's breath caught and her heart started hammering. It was the first time she'd seen Alex since that meeting in his room at Bay Breeze. For a moment she was too stunned to say anything. Not just because her reawakened senses jumped to alert at how Greek-god-handsome he looked in stone linen trousers and a collarless white linen shirt. But because she wasn't sure

what rules applied to their changed status. It was quite
a leap for her to take from enemy to employee.

'Good flight?' he asked.

'Very good, thank you,' she said, uncertain of what
to call him. He was her employer now but they had history of a kind. 'Er…thank you, Mr Mikhalis.'

His dark eyes widened as if she'd said something
ridiculous, then he laughed. 'That's my father's name,'
he said. 'Alex will do. You're not working for a corpo-
ration here. Just me.'

He held out his hand to take hers in a firm, warm
grip. 'Welcome on board.' His handshake was professional, his tone friendly but impersonal. She would take
her cue from that. And totally repress that little shiver
of awareness that rippled through her at his touch.

'Thank you,' she said. *That was her third 'thank
you'.* Their status might have changed but she wondered if she would ever be able to relax around him.

He went to take her luggage and made a mock groan.
'What on earth have you got in here?'

Her suitcase was stuffed to the limit—she'd had no
real idea of what she'd be facing and had packed for
any occasion. 'Just clothes and…er…shoes.'

'Enough to shoe a centipede by the weight of it,' he
said. But he smiled and she felt some of the tension
leave her shoulders.

'There's snorkelling equipment there too,' she said
a tad defensively. She knew this wouldn't be a regular nine-to-five job but she hoped there'd be leisure
time too.

'The waters around the island are perfect for snorkelling,' he said. 'But the water temperature is still too

cold to swim without a wetsuit. It warms up towards the end of May. I'll swim every day then.'

A vision came from nowhere of him spearing through aqua waters, his hair slicked dark to his head, his body lean and strong and muscular, his skin gilded by shafts of sunlight falling through the water. *This was all kinds of crazy.* She forced the too personal thoughts away and thought sensible work-type thoughts. The *only* kind of thoughts she could allow herself to have about him.

What kind of boss would he be?

He'd had a reputation for being somewhat of a tyrant in Sydney. There were rumours of banks of CCTVs in his most popular venues to ensure he could monitor the staff at all times. Spying on them, according to disgruntled employees. Alex's explanation had been the surveillance was there to ensure drinks weren't being spiked with date rape drugs. She hadn't known who to believe at the time.

She followed him to his car. In Sydney at the time of the trial, he had driven the latest model Italian sports car, as befitted his wealthy, playboy image. Now she was surprised to see a somewhat battered four-by-four. Effortlessly he swung her heavy luggage in the back.

'Next stop is Lefkada,' he said. 'You'll be staying at a villa in the port of Nidri and coming over daily by boat to Kosmima.'

Dell already knew that Kosmima was the small private island he owned and the site of his new resort. 'I can't wait to see it,' she said, avid for more information.

As soon as she was settled in the front seat, she launched into a string of questions. She listened as he explained the size of the island—about one thousand metres by one and a half thousand metres. That it was largely untamed vegetation of cypress and oak and a cultivated olive grove. Past owners had turned old donkey trails into accessible roads. The most recent had put in a helipad.

But his deep sonorous voce had a hypnotic effect. Dell was interested—intensely interested—but she had been awake for more than thirty hours. She only kept her eyes open long enough to leave the airport behind and to cross the causeway that connected Lefkada to the mainland.

She woke up, drowsy, to find the car stationary. For a moment she didn't know where she was. An unfamiliar car. An unfamiliar view through the window. *An unfamiliar man.*

Dell froze, suddenly wide awake. In her sleep she had leaned across from her seat and was snuggled up to Alex Mikhalis's shoulder. Mortified, she snapped her eyes shut again before he realised she was awake. *What to do?* She was aware of a strong, warm body, a spicy masculine scent, his breath stirring her hair—and that she liked it very much. She liked it too much. *He was her boss.*

She pretended to wake with a gasp and scooted across the seat away from him as fast as her bottom would take her. 'I'm so sorry,' she said, aware of the sudden flush staining her cheeks. That short, nervous laugh she was forever trying to control forced its way out. 'How unprofessional of me.'

His eyes met hers, dark, inscrutable, as he searched her face. She swore her heart stopped with the impact of his nearness. *He was gorgeous.* But she could not let herself acknowledge that. This inconvenient attraction had to be stomped on from the start. She needed this job and could not let anything jeopardise it.

He shrugged broad shoulders. 'Jet lag. It happens to the best of us.' But not everyone used their boss's shoulder as a pillow. 'Don't worry about it,' he said as if he'd scarcely noticed her presence. As if it happened all the time.

No doubt he'd been used to women flinging themselves at him. That was, of course, before he'd lost his fiancée, the lovely chef who had worked for him. The story of their tragic romance had been repeated by the press over and over after she'd died. Everywhere he'd looked he must have seen her face. Such an intensity of loss. No wonder he'd escaped the country.

She realised she was doing the same thing. Running from loss of a different kind but painful just the same. Every month she'd been just a day late she'd hoped she was pregnant. Before each IVF procedure she had allowed herself to dream about the baby she would hold in her arms, imagined how he or she would look, thought about names. Then grieved those lost babies who had seemed so real to her. Two pairs of tiny knitted booties, one pink and one blue, had been hidden in a drawer to be taken out and held against her cheek while she dreamed. But not this last failed attempt at IVF. Packing up her possessions to move out of her small rented apartment, she had found the booties and packed them with the clothes she gave away to charity.

'Thank you,' she said. Again. Were *thank you* and *sorry* going to be the key words of this working relationship? *Toughen up, Dell.*

They were parked near a busy harbour. The marina was packed with a flotilla of tall-masted yachts, motor cruisers and smaller craft of all kinds. The waterfront was lined with colourful cafés and restaurants, each fronted by signs proclaiming their specialities. 'This is the port of Nidri,' Alex said.

Dell noticed charter boats and ferries and signs in English and Greek—of which she couldn't understand a word—to the islands of Corfu and Ithaca and Cephalonia. Excitement started to bubble. She really was in Greece. That dream, at least, had come true.

'This is the town where I'm staying?' she said.

'In a villa complex owned by my aunt and uncle. You'll be comfortable there. There are shops, restaurants, lots of night life. My cousin will take you to and from Kosmima by boat.'

'Do you live there too?' she asked. He didn't wear any rings. She hadn't given thought to whether or not he was still single. He could be married for all she knew, he'd done so well to keep out of the gossip columns where he used to be a regular item. A man like him wouldn't be alone—unless by choice.

'I live on Kosmima, by myself,' he said. His tone told her not to ask any more questions.

She might not be an investigative journalist—she came under the category of lifestyle writer—but Dell was consumed with curiosity about how the nightclub prince of Sydney came to be living in this place. How he had kept his whereabouts so secret when he had disappeared from Sydney.

'I'll take you to the villa,' he said. 'We'll have lunch there then you can settle in and get some sleep before you start work tomorrow.'

Dell wanted to protest that she was ready to start work right now but of course that would be ridiculous. Her impromptu nap in his car had proved that. She needed to get out of the jeans she'd worn on the plane, shower and then sleep before she could be of any use to Alex.

She'd been expecting bare cliffs and blinding white buildings accented in bright blue. But Alex explained that landscape was typical of the southern Greek islands. This part of Greece had green, vegetated islands with homes that blended more into the landscape. The Greek blue was there all right but in a more subtle way.

The one-bedroom apartment she was to make her home was in a small complex of attractive white-painted villas with terracotta roofs set around a swimming pool. Tubs of lavender and sweet-scented herbs were placed at every turn. Sad memories would have a hard time following her here.

Her compact apartment was white and breezy with a tiled floor. Dell looked around her in delight. She would be more than comfortable. Even better, her accommodation was part of her salary package. With the generous remuneration Alex had offered her, she hoped she might be able to make a dent in the debt left to her from the IVF. As she showered and then changed into a simple linen dress, she found herself humming and wishing she knew some Greek songs.

New start?

Bring it on.

As soon as Alex's Aunt Penelope and Uncle Stavros had heard he was picking up his new staff member from Australia from the airport, they had insisted he bring her to share a meal with them. The elderly couple lived on site and managed the villas they let out over the summer, one of which he had secured as Dell's accommodation.

They were actually his great aunt and uncle, Penelope being the youngest sister of his grandfather, but no one in the family bothered with that kind of distinction. He hadn't tried to keep track of all the familial layers. It was just enough that his Greek family had welcomed him without judgement when he had arrived, the high flyer from Australia who'd crashed in spectacular manner. Like Icarus of Greek myth he'd melted his wings by flying too high—in Icarus's case to the sun, in his case too much hard living and stress followed by the tragedy with Mia had led to burnout. He'd come here to heal but wasn't sure how he'd ever get his wings back. He hoped the new venture might lead to the growth of new feathers. Because he couldn't stay grounded for ever.

Dell had instantly charmed his aunt and uncle with her winning smile and chatty manner. She seemed to have a gift for making people feel at ease in a natural, unselfconscious way. Even in repose her face looked as if she was on the verge of smiling. Who could help but want to smile back in response? Yet he'd seen her snarl too and knew she could be tough when required. He felt some of the tension relax from his shoulders. It had been the right decision to bring her here. Dell Hudson on his side could be a very good thing.

The table was set up under a pergola that supported a grape vine, its bright new leaves casting welcome shade. Dell's hair flashed bright in the filtered light, her simple blue and white striped dress perfectly appropriate.

It was a typically Greek scene and he marvelled, as

he had many times since he'd got here, how quickly he'd felt at home. During school vacations there had been visits with his parents and two sisters. But once he'd taken over Athina, he hadn't had time to make the obligatory trek to Greece, despite the admonishments of his parents.

'Family is everything,' his grandfather had used to say. But it was only now that Alex really appreciated what he had meant. It wasn't that he didn't value his heritage. Or that he didn't love his family back home. But as he was the much-longed-for son after two daughters, too much pressure and expectation had been put on him. His subsequent rebellion had caused ructions that were only now healing. He felt he'd at last made his peace with his father on his recent visit to Sydney.

Now he tucked into his aunt's splendid cooking— sardines wrapped in vine leaves and herbs; lemon and garlic potatoes; and a sublime eggplant salad. The food was reminiscent of his grandfather's old Athina, not surprising when the recipes had probably been handed down from the same source. Dell chatted and laughed with his aunt and uncle over lunch, as if they were already friends.

'I'm asking your Thia Penelope if I can interview her about her cooking for my blog,' Dell said.

'I am teaching her Greek,' his aunt interjected.

'I'm keen to learn.' Dell smiled at the older lady. 'I've never tasted eggplant cooked as deliciously as this. It's a revelation. That is, if I'm allowed to tell my readers that I'm living in Greece.'

'Why not?' he said, bemused by the fact his aunt

had taken it upon herself to teach his newest employee the language. 'Just don't mention the new venture yet.'

'Sure, this will be a subtle way of leading into it,' she said. 'When the time is right it will be fun to reveal exactly what I'm doing here. Right now I'll say I'm on vacation.'

His aunt beamed, her black eyes almost disappearing into the wrinkles around her eyes. 'She's a clever girl, this one,' she said. As she said it she looked from him to Dell and back again.

There it was again—that matchmaking gleam. Just because he was single and his aunt had ascertained that Dell was single. Even though his aunt knew the story of how Mia had died. How responsible he felt for her death. How he did not want—did not deserve—to have love in his life again.

Dell blushed and looked down at her plate. The speculation must be annoying for her too.

'That she is, Auntie,' he said. 'Which is why I've employed her to work with me on the hotel.' He had to make it clear to his family that his relationship with Dell was strictly a working one. He had to keep reminding himself too.

On the drive from the airport she had got drowsier and drowsier as she'd tried to keep up the conversation through her jet lag. Her responses had dwindled to the odd word in answer to something he'd said minutes before and quite out of context. If he knew her better, he'd tease her about it.

But he would not tease her about the way, when she'd fallen fully asleep, she'd slid across her seat to rest her head on his shoulder. Because instead of pushing her away, as she'd murmured something unintelligible in her sleep he'd smiled and without thinking dropped a light kiss on her head. He'd been without a woman for too long. It was the only explanation for his lapse.

That could not happen again.

CHAPTER SIX

THE NEXT MORNING Dell stood on the expansive front balcony of Alex's new resort building on the private island of Kosmima and looked around her in awe. There wasn't another building in sight—just the jetty that belonged to the island.

Below her, the waters of the Ionian Sea sparkled in myriad tones of turquoise as they lapped on the white sands of the bay. She breathed in air tinged with salt and the scent of wild herbs. The bay was bounded by pale limestone cliffs and hills covered in lush vegetation. The sky was a perfect blue with only the odd cloud scudding across the horizon. She felt almost overcome by the natural beauty of the site as she felt the tension and angst of the last weeks start to melt away.

Her new boss stood beside her—waiting, she suspected, with a degree of impatience for her verdict. She turned to him. 'It's every bit as perfect as you said. Magical.'

Alex nodded slowly. 'I think so too. It makes me believe that people have been feeling the magic for hundreds of years. Thousands, perhaps.'

They stood in silence for a long moment, looking out to sea. Was he, like her, imagining the pageant of

history that must have been played out on and near
these islands?

'Do you know anything about the history of this island?' she asked. 'Any chance it was the site of an ancient Greek temple? That would be useful for publicity.'

'It could also mean Kosmima could be declared as
a site of archaeological significance and business pro-
hibited. So I don't think we'll go there,' he said.

'I hadn't thought of that,' she said. 'Maybe we
should stick to the de-stressing and well-being angle.
Just taking in this view is making me feel relaxed. Although not too relaxed to start work, of course. Tell me
what you need me to do. I'm raring to start.'

'First thing is to inspect the site.'

Dell turned and looked back at the magnificent
white building that sat stepped back into the side of
the hill. It was modern in its simplicity but paid homage
to traditional architecture. 'I expected something only
half constructed but you must be nearly ready to open.'

'On first sight you might think so, but there's still a
way to go before we welcome the first guests in June.
This main building was initially built as a private residence. It was very large, but needed alteration and ad-
ditions to make it fit for the purpose.'

The building was light and airy, luxurious in pale
stone with bleached timber woodwork and marble
floors. Expansive windows took full advantage of the
view, to be shuttered in the colder months. From the
back of the building she could hear the construction
crew who had been here since early morning.

The last thing she wanted to do was remind Alex of
the car journey from the airport. But she couldn't pretend to know important details she had missed while

snoozing. 'In the car yesterday you were telling me about the background of this place. But I… I'm afraid I didn't hear it all.'

'Really?' he said, dark brows raised. 'You don't recall anything?'

'Er… I remember the geographical details.'

'Before you fell asleep, you mean?'

'Yes,' she admitted, unable to meet his eyes.

'Was I so boring?' he said.

'No! Not boring at all.' In fact, she'd never met a man less boring. Who would have thought she might be actually growing to like the man who had been so vile during the court case? A man she'd considered an entitled, arrogant playboy who in the short time she'd known him seemed anything but that.

Now she did look up to find his black eyes gleaming with amusement. 'I soon realised you were drowsing off.'

And falling all over him.

How utterly mortifying. But she would not say the sorry word again. 'I do recall something about a billionaire,' she said. 'I promise I'm over the jet lag and wide awake and listening.'

She followed him into the high-ceilinged living space destined to be the 'silent' room where guests could meditate or just be quiet with their thoughts without interruption. Their voices echoed in the unlived silence.

'There was an older, traditional house on this site when the island was owned by a very wealthy Greek industrialist,' he said. 'He and his family used it as a summer retreat. Some members of my family were tenant farmers on the island. Others were employed as gardeners and caretakers.'

'So there's a personal connection?' She was still looking for angles for publicity.

'Yes,' he said. 'The owner was a benevolent land-lord who, for all the opulence, never forgot his peas-ant roots. There were many good years for my family.' He paused. 'I've only found out all this since I've been living in Greece.'

'I guess it wasn't relevant when you were building your empire in Sydney.'

'Correct,' he said. 'I hardly knew this side of my family. Just my grandfather, my father's father, emi-grated. The rest of the family stayed here. I only vis-ited a few times back with my parents, the last when I was a teenager.'

'So how did you come to buy the island?'

'The Greek owner died and it was left to a nephew in Athens who had no use for it. He sold it to a Rus-sian billionaire who demolished the house to build this summer palace.'

The tone of his voice told her that the transfer of ownership might not have been good news. 'What hap-pened to your family?'

'They were evicted. The new owner wanted utter privacy. The only staff to live on the island were the ones he brought with him. The island is only accessed by sea. He installed a heliport, and armed guards pa-trolled the coastline. The construction crews were escorted on and off the island. Every delivery was scrutinised.'

'That's scary stuff. Was there any real threat?' She

wasn't quite sure how she could work that into a press release.

He shrugged. 'Who knows? The locals were pragmatic. They got used to it. The development brought employment—much needed in Greece as you probably know. The good thing is the guy was passionate about sustainability and brought those organic principals to the new build. That was good for me when I took over.'

'So how did you end up owning the island?'

'The owner decamped with the mega-residence unfinished. No one ever found out why, although as you can imagine there were all sorts of rumours. Then the island went up for sale again.'

'What made you buy it?'

'Impulse.'

'You bought an entire island on *impulse*?'

Of course, he'd been a multimillionaire while he was still in his twenties. Why wouldn't he? And if his past history had anything to do with it, the impulse would pay off in return on investment.

'I've always operated on instinct. It seemed the right thing to do.'

There was an edge to his voice but Dell wasn't sure how deep she should dig into his motives. Escape. Retreat. Heal. Even giving back to the land of his ancestors at a time when investment was desperately needed.

But once they started to generate publicity for his new venue, it would be inevitable his personal tragedy would come to the fore. She would carefully suggest they work with it rather than hope it would stay buried. Perhaps a few carefully negotiated exclusives might be the way to go.

The story of the crazed gunman holding Alex's

lovely fiancée and a number of customers hostage in a robbery gone wrong had travelled around the world. That the handsome hotelier had sought refuge from his grief in the islands of his ancestors and built a resort there would generate good publicity. But she didn't feel ready to raise it with him just yet. She would have to learn to read him first.

As Alex continued his tour Dell continued to be impressed by everything she saw—kitchen, spa treatment areas, guestrooms, an office area with Wi-Fi and computers. When he asked her opinion she gave it honestly. Better to have areas of potential weakness sorted now rather than after the retreat opened. His venues in Sydney had won design awards. This one would no doubt be clocking up some wins too.

'You certainly know your stuff,' she said. 'I realise you've got a ton of experience in Sydney, but it must be very different doing remodelling and a fit-out in a different country. Where did you find the architects and interior designers?'

'That's where having an extended Greek family helps. My cousins in Athens were able to point me to the right people.'

'And furnishings?' Many of the rooms were still bare.

'In the hands of the designers. Most of it is being made to measure and exclusive to this resort. I need to go to Athens next week. I'd like you to come with me.'

'I would be pleased to,' she said. A ripple of excitement ran through her. 'Just one thing. Would it be possible to time it before I have a day off? I'd love to stay in Athens overnight so I could climb the Acropolis and see the Parthenon. It's something I've always wanted to do. Then I'd like to spend some time in the Acropolis Museum. I've heard it's wonderful.'

'It is spectacular,' he said. 'I'm not what you'd call a museum kind of guy. But when you're seeing all the antiquities and then look up to see the Parthenon through the windows it's quite something.'

Alex spoke with pride of the museum. He looked Greek, spoke like an Australian. Yesterday he'd been too well-mannered to speak more than a few words of Greek to his aunt and uncle in front of her. But he had sounded fluent. She wondered what country he now identified with. Again she felt it was too personal for her to ask him. His grief must run very deep to have left everything familiar behind.

The tour ended outside with a beautiful aquamarine swimming pool, landscaped around with palm trees and bougainvillea. 'Was the pool already here?' she asked.

'Yes. It's big for a private residence but not outstanding for a hotel. I considered extending it but—'

'Why bother when you have the sea on the doorstep?' she said.

'Exactly.' He met her eyes and they both smiled at the same time. It wasn't the first time today that they'd finished each other's words. She felt she was in tune with his vision and it gave her confidence that she would be able to do a good job for him. She held his gaze for a moment too long before she hastily switched her focus.

Set well back from the pool and completely private was an elegant pavilion, the design of which, with its columns and pediments, gave more than a nod to classical Greek architecture. 'Was the pool house here, too?'

He nodded. 'It's a self-contained apartment and where I'm living.'

'It looks fabulous.'

Dell wondered if he would show her around his personal residence. She ached with curiosity to see inside where he spent his private time.

But he took her around to the southern side of the building where there were substantial kitchen gardens and a greenhouse full of early tomatoes. Mature fig, pomegranate, fruit and nut trees were planted behind— spring blossom surrendering to new leaves so green they seemed fluorescent. From their size, she assumed the trees had been there since the days of the Greek owner. Maybe longer.

'How wonderful,' she breathed.

'I've employed the gardeners who used to work here. We intend to grow as much fresh produce as possible,' he said.

'I couldn't think of anything better,' she said. 'It's early days for me planning the food, but I really think the core of the food offering should be based on the Mediterranean diet. I mean mainly plant-based from this garden, olive oil from your grove, fish from these waters, white cheese and yogurt—could you keep goats here, chickens?—with lots of fruit. Food like your aunt's baked eggplant based on traditional recipes handed down in your family. Maybe some of the daring new twists to old favourites that you served at Athina. Greek dishes interpreted in an Australian way, which would be a point of difference. Of course you'll also have to cater for allergies and intolerances as well as whatever faddy ways of eating are in fashion. The juice bar is essential, and the fancy teas.' She indicated the vegetable garden with an enthusiastic wave. 'But the heart of it starts here. The locavore movement at its best. It checks the boxes for locally grown and "clean", whatever you like to call it. This resort will be an organic part of this island, not *on* it but *of* it.'

Dell faltered to a halt as she realised she'd held the floor for too long, having scarcely paused for breath. 'Er…that is if you think so too…'

He stood watching her, dark eyes enigmatic, before he broke into a slow smile. 'That's exactly what I think,' he said.

Dell felt as breathless as if she'd run a long race. It seemed she'd passed a test of some sort. After all, he'd acquired her on an impulse too. She kept up to date with food trends. She had a degree in food science, which had covered commercial food preparation. She had critiqued a spectrum of restaurants and resorts in Sydney. But that wouldn't have mattered a flying fig if she hadn't proved herself to be on the same wavelength as Alex when it came to his project.

'That's a relief,' she said. 'I do tend to go on when I'm…passionate about something.'

He smiled again, teeth white against his olive skin, eyes warm. His shirt was open at the neck, rolled up to show tanned forearms. Had a man ever looked better in a white shirt? It would be only too easy to get passionate about *him*.

'Don't ever hold back,' he said. 'I like your enthusiasm. It energises me.'

Passion, energy, his eyes focused on her, his hands—
She couldn't go there.

She took a deep, steadying breath. 'One more thing,' she asked. 'Have you decided on a name for the resort?'

'Pevezzo Athina,' he said without hesitation. '*Pevezzo* in the local dialect means "safe haven". That's what I want it to be: a haven from life's stresses for our guests.'

And for you too, Dell thought.

'Why the name Athina again?' she said. 'In homage to your restaurant in Sydney?' She felt uncomfortable mentioning it, considering their history.

'That restaurant was named by my grandfather after the *taverna* on the adjoining island, Prasinos, which was run by his parents. It's still there. Pappouli left his home for a better life in Australia. The seas here were becoming over-fished and he found it difficult to make a living as a fisherman. He wanted more. I'm named after that grandfather, in the Greek way.'

Dell took up the story. 'So he started Athina restaurant in the city, serving traditional Greek food. It was a great success. First with other migrants like himself and then the Australian business people caught on to how good the food was and it became an institution.'

'You know a lot about it. Of course you do. Because of the—'

'The court case,' she said. No point in avoiding the elephant lurking in the garden.

'What you did not realise—what no one outside our family knew—was how important Athina was to me personally.'

'You defended it so...so fiercely.'

'You mean irrationally?'

'I didn't say that,' she said, her voice dwindling away. But she meant it and he knew it.

'My grandfather came to Australia with nothing, unable to speak more than a few words of English. He ended up successful and prosperous. His kids became professionals—my father is an orthopaedic surgeon, his sister a dermatologist. All thanks to Athina. As a kid, I spent happy times with my *pappouli* and my *yia-yia* at the restaurant. I'd get underfoot in the kitchens, annoy the chefs with questions. Helped out as a waiter as soon as I was old enough.'

'So that's where your interest in restaurants started.' An image of what a dear little boy he must have been flashed into her mind. But she pushed it away. Neil had been dark-haired and dark-eyed—the image of Alex as a child came way too close to what her longed-for babies might have looked like. She had to put that dream behind her.

'I didn't want to be a chef. I wanted to be the boss.' He smiled, an ironic twist of his mouth. 'That's what comes of being the only son in a Greek family. But the pressure was on for me to be a doctor, to keep the migrant dream alive of being upwardly socially mobile. I enrolled in medicine. Loved the social life at uni, the classes were not where I wanted to be. My parents were not happy, to say the least.'

'And your grandfather?'

'Pappouli wasn't happy either. He left Greece and his extended family to better himself. Everyone saw me as going backwards when I dropped out of uni and started work behind a bar. It didn't count that it was at the most fashionable nightclub in Sydney at the time. No one thought it was worth applauding when I became the club's youngest ever manager. I continued to be a great disappointment.'

She knew some of this story. But not the personal insights about his family. Not how his spur to success was proving himself to them. 'If I remember, your grandfather became ill.'

'He had a stroke. I insisted on running the restaurant for him while he was in hospital. Straight away I could see Athina's time was past. It was now in the wrong end of town for a traditional Greek restaurant. The older people who had come for the nostalgia were dying off. The younger punters had moved on. I saw what could be done with it, but of course my hands were tied.'

'Until...' Dell found she couldn't say the words.

'Until my grandfather died and left the restaurant to me. You know the rest.'

Not quite all the rest—much as she ached to know it. But Alex was her boss. Knowing this was relevant to the naming of the resort. His private life continued to be none of her business. 'I see why you want to honour your grandfather. Thank you for sharing that with me.'

She'd believed she and Alex were poles apart. Perhaps they had more in common than she could have dreamed. Both brought up by parents who wanted to impose their ambitions and expectations on their kids. She'd fought those expectations to get where she was. As a result, she remained a disappointment to her parents too. Alex's arrogance and ruthlessness seemed more understandable now. But it seemed he'd paid a price.

She had to fight an impulse to hug him.

'Now I better understand your attitude in court,' she said. Not that she was condoning it.

He sighed. 'It seems a long time ago in a different place. I'm a different person.'

Was he truly? Was she? She remembered how she'd

wondered if he'd worn his public image like a mask. Was she now seeing glimpses of the man behind the mask? Because she liked what she saw.

'I'd rather put it right behind me if we're to work in harmony together,' she said. *In harmony.* She was already using the language that would define this place.

'I've apologised and I hope you have forgiven me,' he said, a little stiffly. 'One day I'll take you to my family's Taverna Athina and you can see where it all started.'

'I'd like that very much.' She realised she was hungry to find out as much as possible about this man who was beginning to take up way too much time in her thoughts.

CHAPTER SEVEN

TWO WEEKS INTO her new job and Dell was loving every minute of it. She and Alex worked so well together she found herself musing that if they had met under different circumstances they might be friends. *More than friends,* her insistent libido reminded her with inconvenient frequency.

Often when she was with him, from nowhere would come a flash of awareness of how heart-thuddingly handsome she found him. When he laughed—and he seemed to laugh more often these days—he threw back his head and there was a hollow in his tanned neck that she felt an insane urge to press her lips against. When they were going through a document or a set of plans, she'd become mesmerised by his hands, imagining how his long, strong fingers might feel on her bare skin.

She treasured the day he'd taken her to Athens for work. The music he'd played in the car on the way to the airport had been the same music she liked. They'd operated with the designers and suppliers like a team— so much so the people thought they'd been working together for years. But on the journey home, when she'd felt overwhelmed by sudden tiredness, she'd been very careful to stay on her side of the car. She didn't trust herself. Sometimes she'd awoken from dreams of him—dreams filled with erotic fantasy.

Every time she realised the way her thoughts were taking her, her redhead's skin would flush. She prayed he didn't notice, because she never saw anything in his reactions to her to indicate *he* might feel in any way the same about *her*.

Although he had never mentioned Mia—not once— she got the impression she'd been the love of his life and no other woman would ever measure up to her.

According to his aunt Penelope, her landlady, there was no woman in his life. Not that Dell had indulged in gossip with her about her nephew, in spite of her curiosity. There was no guarantee it wouldn't reach Alex and she doubted he'd be happy about her speculating on his love life—or lack of it—with his family. Then there was the annoying fact that Aunt Penelope appeared convinced that she and Alex were more than boss and employee. The older woman seemed to think that the more often she subtly mentioned her suspicions, the more likely Dell would cave in and admit it through the course of the conversation.

But no matter how Dell denied it, she could no longer deny the truth to herself—*she was developing a crush on her boss*.

What a cliché—and not one she had thought she would ever find herself caught up in. The anticipation of seeing him brought a frisson of unexpected pleasure to her working day. She found herself taking greater care with the way she dressed. If Alex happened to compliment her on her dress, she would hug the knowledge to herself and make sure she wore something similar the next day. He'd mentioned he liked her perfume—and she had to fight the temptation to douse herself in it. But her secret crush was harmless, she told herself. He would never know.

There was only one flaw in her new life in this Greek paradise—a new susceptibility to seasickness. It was most inconvenient when she was working on an island accessible only by boat.

Every day, Alex's cousin Cristos took her and some of the tradespeople across and back to Kosmimo in his blue-painted converted wooden fishing boat. At first she'd looked forward to it. She'd always been fine on the water, whether sailing on Sydney Harbour with friends or a cruise to Fiji with her parents.

Yet this small boat chugging across calm, clear waters had her gagging with nausea all the way. She'd sat by turns at the front and back of the boat but it was no use. In desperation, she'd got up earlier to catch the construction company's much bigger boat, but it was no different. She had to deal with a niggling nausea until mid-morning. By mid-afternoon she was dreading the return trip for another dose.

It was getting worse. This morning she'd managed to get up the steps from the jetty to the lower levels of the building and into the bathroom just in time. She'd tried eating a bigger breakfast, a smaller breakfast, no breakfast at all, but the outcome was the same.

Afterwards, she splashed cold water on her face. Fixed her make-up to try and conceal the unflattering tinge of green of her skin and brushed back her lank hair from her face. She gripped the edge of the hand basin and practised her fluffy-chick smile in the mirror. The last thing she wanted was for Alex to notice all was not well.

She loved working here with him. However she was aware it was early days yet. Theoretically, she was still on probation although he had told her several times how pleased he was with her job performance. But how could she continue in a job on an island only accessible by boat if she was going to feel like this every day?

Alex finished going through some plans with the plumber who was installing the fittings in the guest bathrooms. A smile of anticipation tugged at the edges of his mouth as he headed back to the office that would become the hotel's administration centre but right now served just for him and Dell. She should be at her desk by now.

He realised the day didn't really start for him until she smiled a 'good morning' greeting. Her warm presence was like the dark Greek coffee that kick-started his day. How had he managed without her?

But as he got to the office he stopped, alarmed. She was leaning on her elbows on the desk, her head resting in her hands in a pose of utter exhaustion. Had she been out last night partying late in the nightclubs of Nidri? Somehow he didn't think so. She wouldn't be so unprofessional to come to work with a hangover.

'Dell, are you okay?'

She looked up, her splayed hands still holding onto her head. 'Alex. I thought you were out the back with the builders,' she said in a voice so shaky it hardly sounded like her. Her face was so pale a smattering of freckles stood out across the bridge of her nose. Make-up was smeared around her eyes. Her wavering smile seemed forced.

'What's wrong?' he asked, fear stabbing him.

He'd become accustomed to her presence in his day. Her smile, her energy, her awesome attitude to work, the way he could fire ideas off her and she'd come back with ideas to counter or complement his own. Whatever he'd directed her to do she'd taken a step further. He'd found himself thanking whatever lucky star had made him turn around to see her in that yoga class. She couldn't be ill. Especially with so much still to do before the hotel would be ready to open. He depended on her. He couldn't imagine his days on the island without his right-hand person. Fate had delivered her to him at just the right time.

He could see what an effort it was for her to force out the words. 'I feel dreadful. The boat. I'm getting seasick. I don't know why as I don't usually suffer from it.'

He frowned. 'But the sea is so calm.'

'I know. The first few days I was fine. But since then it's getting worse.'

'Is Cristos showing off and speeding around? That would make anyone sick.' He'd have words with his cousin if that was the case.

'Not at all, he's very good and taking extra care since I told him I wasn't feeling well.'

Maybe it was her time of the month. Alex knew enough not to suggest it. Two older sisters had trained him well in that regard. Not that he wanted to press for details. 'Are you sure it's the boat? You're living in a new country. It could be the water. Or the food. Maybe you're allergic to something. Eggplant perhaps. You told me you're on a mission to try all the different Greek ways of cooking it and put them on your blog. You could be eating too much.'

'I suppose it could be that.' She looked doubtful.

'Or a stomach flu?'

'I don't think so. But I guess it's a possibility.'

'Then I suggest you go see a doctor as soon as you can. Perhaps you need to get medication for motion sickness. At least until you get more used to the boat. Aunt Penelope will be able to help find an English-speaking doctor in Nidri. I'll take you back in my boat now.' The sooner she sorted this out, the better.

She groaned and put up her hand in protest. 'Thank you but no. I couldn't face getting back into a boat right now. I'll feel better as the day goes on and go back with Cristos this evening as usual.'

'See a doctor tomorrow. I insist. Call and make an appointment this morning. Don't come in to work until you find out what's wrong. If it's serious and you have to take time off work let me know. Whatever the result let me know.'

It was on the tip of his tongue to ask her would she like him to come with her. But that would be overstepping the mark as her employer. It would be appropriate as a friend, and he realised he already thought of her as a friend. The informal nature of their work arrangement had seen a kind of intimacy develop very quickly between them.

If he was honest with himself, he would admit he didn't view her in just a platonic way. He found her very attractive. Not his tall and blonde type, but alluring just the same. Curvy and auburn-haired was growing on him in a major way. He reacted to the sway of her hips in a tight pencil skirt, the tantalising hint of cleavage when she was shoulder to shoulder with him discussing a plan, the wide curves of her mouth. And he delighted in that smile. Always her warm, embracing smile that made him feel better than any other stimulant ever had.

But he forced himself to turn away, to switch off his feelings. He was not ready for another woman in his life. Was not certain he would *ever* be ready. And it was never a good idea to have an affair with a member of his staff.

Next morning, Dell stared across the desk at the doctor, too shocked to comprehend what she was saying. It wasn't the doctor's lightly accented English that was incomprehensible, it was her words. 'You are pregnant, Ms Hudson.'

'You are pregnant.' The three words she had longed almost beyond reason to hear reverberated through her head but the doctor might as well have said them in Greek for all the sense they made. The middle-aged woman had insisted on Dell taking a pregnancy test, routine in cases of unexplained nausea she had said. Dell had muttered to herself about what a waste of time it was. To her utter shock, the test had proved positive. Then the doctor had examined her to confirm the diagnosis.

'But it's impossible for me to be pregnant,' Dell protested. As she explained her history, the doctor took notes.

'I would say that your IVF has been successful,' the doctor said. 'Bleeding in pregnancy is not uncommon. What you experienced could have been caused by implantation or any number of reasons. Have you had other symptoms?'

How Dell had prayed for the symptoms of pregnancy throughout all those years of hoping. Now she was so deeply immersed in her new life she hadn't actually recognised them. The 'seasickness' that was actually morning sickness. The sensitivity of her breasts she'd put down to the havoc IVF had played with her hormones. The tiredness she'd attributed to the long hours in her new job.

'I believe so,' she said slowly, then explained her symptoms to the doctor.

'I'm sure a blood test will confirm your pregnancy,' the doctor said. 'Congratulations.'

Dell's head was reeling. It was too much to take in. This was the best and the worst of news. *A baby at last.* But pregnant by IVF to her ex-husband while she was living in a different country on the other side of the world from home and with a halfway serious crush on another man?

Through a haze of disbelief, she made a further appointment with the doctor. Then walked blindly out into the street.

Nidri was more a boisterous, overgrown village than a town. Dell tripped on the uneven pavement and gave a hysterical little laugh that had a well-dressed woman turn and look at her askance. She steadied herself against the wall of a beauty salon that specialised in tiny fish nibbling the dead skin from people's feet. Moved on to a *fournos* with a tempting display of the most delicious local cookies and pastries. In her shocked, nauseated state the scent of baking did not appeal.

She was struggling to find a foothold in the suddenly turned upside down landscape of her own life. She would have to take step by dazed step to try to negotiate the uncharted new territory. Not at all certain where it would lead her.

Alex. How would she tell him? What would this mean? Almost certainly the end of her dream job. The end of the already remote chance that they could ever be more than friends. She wrapped her arms tightly around herself against the shivers that shuddered through her, even though the warm spring sun shone down on her shoulders.

CHAPTER EIGHT

ALL NIGHT ALEX had been plagued by a nagging concern for Dell. He'd become so concerned that next morning he decided to take his boat across to Nidri so he could check on her. Her ailment had sounded like something more than seasickness. What if she was seriously ill?

His gut clenched at the thought. Dell had become his responsibility. He had talked her into moving to Greece to work with him even though she had been initially reluctant. Now it was up to him to look out for her. He was all she had here. The job had kept her way too busy for her to get out and make friends. He hoped the doctor's diagnosis would be something easily fixed. That *he* could fix for her.

His aunt Penelope had pointed him in the direction to where Dell was seeing the doctor. He stood across the road and waited for her to come out of her appointment. It wasn't a long wait. He caught sight of her immediately, in the short pencil skirt he liked so much and a crisp striped shirt—she had obviously intended to head to work afterwards. Cristos was on call to take her over.

But as he watched her walk away from the doctor's

rooms, Alex wished he'd been somewhere closer. *What the hell was wrong?* She seemed to lurch as if in a daze, tripping on the uneven pavement, righting herself without seeming to realise what she was doing. Finally she stood out of the way in the doorway of a closed souvenir shop and hugged her arms tightly around herself. Her hair shone bright in a shaft of sunlight. Had she been prescribed medication? Was she suffering from a fever? Been given bad news? *She should not be on her own.*

He broke into a run to get to her. Cursing the traffic, he ducked in and out of cars and buses. The delivery guy on a bicycle balancing an enormous flower arrangement shouted at him but he scarcely heard him. *He had to reach her.* 'Dell!'

She looked up, seemed to have trouble focusing, her eyes huge in her wan face, her lovely mouth trembling. Alex was struck by how vulnerable and alone she seemed. How suddenly *frail*.

He felt swept by an almighty urge to protect her, to make her safe. An urge that went beyond the concern of an employer for a member of staff. *He cared for her.* Alex didn't know when or how it had happened, but somehow she had snuck under his defences. All he knew was he wanted to fold her into his arms and tell her everything would be all right because he was there for her.

'Alex,' she said. 'Wh…what are you doing here?' Her eyes darted every which way. As if she'd rather be anywhere but with him right at this moment. As if she was looking for an escape route, not a pair of comforting arms. Especially not *his*.

Alex shoved his hands into his pockets. He forced

his voice to calm, boss-like concern. 'To see if you're all right. Which you're obviously not. What news from the doctor?'

Emotions that he couldn't read flickered across her face. *Secrets she didn't want to share.* People shouldered past them on the narrow pavement. An English couple standing outside a shop loudly discussed the benefits of olive wood salad servers. Motor scooters in dire need of adjustment to their exhaust systems puttered by. 'Can we maybe go somewhere more private?' she said, her voice so low he could scarcely catch it.

'There's a coffee shop just up there,' he said, indicating it with a wave of his arm. 'You look like you could do with Greek coffee, hot and strong.' If it weren't only mid-morning he'd suggest brandy.

She shuddered and swallowed hard. 'Some orange juice, I think.'

'Sure,' he said. 'Whatever you need.' He put his arm around her shoulder to shepherd her in the right direction. Initially she stiffened against his touch, then the rigidity of her body melted. Her curves felt soft and warm against him. Alex tightened his hold to keep her close, liking the feeling he could keep her safe. But as soon as they reached the coffee shop she broke away from him.

He sat her down at a table in a quiet corner. Pushed the juice towards her. Once she'd taken a few sips, she seemed to revive somewhat, although there was still a worrying pallor to her face.

'Thank you,' she said. Her hands cradled around the glass in an effort, he realised, to stop their trembling.

'So what's wrong? Eggplant allergy?'

A hint of a smile—perhaps ten per cent of its full

incandescent power—hovered around the corners of her mouth. 'Not quite,' she said. She met his gaze directly. 'There's no easy way to say this. Turns out the seasickness wasn't that at all. I… I'm pregnant.' She sounded as though she didn't quite believe it, was just trying on the words for size.

Alex reeled back in his chair, too stunned to say anything. Shock at her words mingled with his own disbelief and disappointment. And a sudden bolt of jealousy that she had a man in her life. A man she had denied. 'Did you know about this when you accepted the job with me?'

The words spilled out from her. As if she was trying to explain the situation to herself as well as to him. 'No. It came as a complete shock. I… I thought—hoped— there was a chance, which is why I said no to your offer in the first place. Then…well, then it seemed I wasn't pregnant. But…the evidence that led me to think I wasn't pregnant and could accept your job turned out to be a false alarm. Turns out, though, I am pregnant.'

'You said you didn't have a man in your life. "One hundred per cent single," if I remember correctly.'

'I don't. There hasn't been anyone for a long time.'

He drummed his fingers on the metal top of the table. 'That doesn't make sense.'

'I realise that. It…it's complicated.'

Cynicism welled up and spouted into his words. 'What's complicated about getting a woman pregnant?' He didn't know why his reaction to her news was so sour. Perhaps because he'd started to think of Dell as *his*. Her news made it very clear she had another man in her life. *The father of her child.*

'We all know how it happens.' Had she met a man

since she'd been in Greece? One of his family? His cousin? She'd remarked on several occasions how good-looking Cristos was. He had no right to be furious if that was the case, he had no claim on her, but a black rage consumed him at the thought.

She bit her lower lip. 'In this case, not quite the way you think,' she said with a dull edge to her voice.

'Perhaps you'd better explain.' He made no effort to keep his disillusionment from his voice. One of the things he'd liked most about her was her open face, her apparent honesty. It appeared he'd read her incorrectly.

Dell quailed against Alex's grim expression. He hadn't been able to hide his shock at her revelation. Of course he'd be annoyed, angry even that his newly contracted employee was pregnant. It had been an incredible shock to her, too. But her joy in finally seeing her dream of motherhood in sight overrode everything.

There was no point in telling him anything other than the unembellished truth. She took a steadying breath. 'This baby was conceived by IVF. I'd been undergoing treatment during my marriage.'

Alex's dark brows pulled into an even deeper frown. 'But you're divorced now.'

'Yes,' she said. 'Legally divorced. The marriage is done and dusted.'

'So who is the father?'

'My ex-husband.'

He pushed back in his chair. Slanted his shoulders away from her. It hurt to see him distancing himself. 'I don't get it,' he said.

Dell caught a half-sob in her throat. She'd known this wouldn't be easy. But she hadn't expected it would be this difficult. 'The IVF procedures I had when I was married to Neil didn't work. It was one of the reasons we broke up. Well, not broke up strictly speaking. He left me. I hadn't been expecting it. But he wanted out. He blamed my obsession with having a baby and...and for neglecting him as a husband.'

Alex's eyes narrowed. 'And was that the reason?'

'Looking back, I see it did put the marriage under stress. I always thought having a baby was what we both wanted. But maybe...maybe it was more about me. I'd always wanted to have kids, felt a failure that I couldn't fall pregnant when everyone around me seemed to do it so easily. My life became a roller coaster of alternate anticipation then despair. And with some hormone crazy happening too. Maybe there were cracks in the marriage I just didn't want to see. That it wasn't strong enough to survive the pressure.'

She looked down at her hands, realised abstractedly that the dent from where she'd worn her wedding ring for so long had finally disappeared.

Alex shifted in his chair, obviously uncomfortable. She appreciated this was an awkwardly personal conversation for a boss with his employee. 'That still doesn't enlighten me to how you're pregnant to your ex-husband.'

'It took me a while to pick myself up from the aftermath of my marriage. We'd been dating since high school and—'

'So you'd been with the same guy since high school?' Alex sounded incredulous. She remembered his reputation as a player and a man about town before he'd met the lovely Mia. How tame her own life had been in comparison. But she hadn't wanted it any other way.

She nodded. 'He was nice. Steady. I thought he'd be a good husband and father.'

There hadn't been a lot of fireworks to start and what there had been had eventually fizzled out. But then it hadn't been sizzling sensuality she'd been after. She'd seen Neil as steady and secure and a family man totally unlike her distant father. Had it been enough? For the first time she wondered if sex had become the effort for Neil that it had for her. It had become all about making babies, not making love. She thought about the thrill she felt just being in the same room as Alex. Had she ever felt that way about her ex-husband?

'But he didn't turn out so nice,' Alex said.

Slowly she shook her head. 'To be fair, there must have been wrong on both sides for the marriage to have ended.'

'So how did you manage on your own?'

She shrugged. 'Okay.' Of course it hadn't been okay but she didn't want to admit that to Alex. Of how Neil had screwed her out of her fair share of their assets. How she'd been left with the considerable IVF expense as he'd convinced her it was what she'd wanted, not him. She hadn't been able to understand how he'd turned so nasty until she'd discovered he'd met someone else while they were still married and had moved in with her straight away.

Alex's dark eyes were perceptive. 'Really okay?'

'Not really.' An awkward silence fell between them. But she had no desire to discuss her dating disasters with Alex. That was something she could laugh at with her girlfriends. Not with the only man who had attracted her since—well, pretty well ever.

Alex was the one to break the silence. 'So…back to your pregnancy.'

'The fertility clinic got in touch, asked me what I wanted to do with our last stored embryo.' She implored him with her eyes to understand. 'I'd wanted a baby for so long. Desperately. I saw this as my last chance. At twenty-nine I was running out of time to meet a guy who wanted to get married and have kids. Start again. I told the clinic I wanted to try.'

'What did your ex say?'

Dell found it difficult to meet Alex's eyes. Concentrated instead on the pattern of olives printed on the café placemat. 'Here's where it gets complicated. I didn't tell him.'

'*What?*' His voice made no bones about his disapproval. 'You didn't tell the guy who fathered it?'

She looked up at him again. There was no point in dissembling. 'I know. It was probably wrong. Even immoral.' She leaned over the table towards him. 'But you don't understand what baby hunger feels like. A constant ache. Torture every time you see someone else's baby. When you have to congratulate a friend who's pregnant and all the time you're screaming inside *why not me?*'

'No. I don't understand that,' he said shortly.

'Don't judge me, Alex. I did what I did because I had to grab that one, final chance of achieving the dream of holding my baby in my arms. I didn't hold out any hopes as no attempt had ever worked before. But when the chance was offered to me I had no choice but to take it.'

'Is that why you initially turned down my job offer?'

'Yes. I didn't want to be away from home if by some miracle the treatment worked. It never had before but I kept alive that tiny beam of hope. Until…until it appeared I had failed again. Evidence that it turns out was false.'

'So what does your ex think of this?'

'What? Me being pregnant? I only just found out myself. He doesn't know.'

'When do you intend to tell him?' It was ironic, she thought, that she had told Alex, her boss, before the biological father.

'Not…not yet. The pregnancy is still in its early stages. I… I…may still lose it. I wouldn't want to tell him until I'm more sure. Why go through all that for nothing?'

'You obviously don't anticipate a happy reaction.' Alex's fingers drummed on the table top. Dell resisted the temptation to reach over and still them with her own.

'He's moved on. Married already to the woman he left me for.' Swift, brutal, her ex had put their years together behind him as if they'd never happened.

She'd made the decision to take the embryo without really thinking about Neil. Possibly she'd even justified it by remembering how he'd said she wanted the IVF so much, she could pay the bills for it. Didn't that make the baby hers and hers alone? In her heart she knew that thinking was wrong. Not so much for Neil's sake—though she knew he had a right to know he was going to be a father—but for the baby's sake. Her child deserved to know about his or her other parent. The idea of a baby had seemed so abstract. Now it was beginning to feel real. A little person she hoped she would be bringing into the world. And for whom she bore the entire responsibility. It was both terrifying and exhilarating.

'What do you intend to do?'

'Give you my resignation, along with my sincere apology, if that's what you want. I certainly don't blame you if you do.'

He leaned forward across the table. 'Is that what you want? Legally, I can't fire an employee for being pregnant.' For a moment she saw a flash of her old adversary in the set of his jaw.

'It wouldn't come to that,' she said. 'I... I...' She was going to say *I love working with you* but somehow she couldn't utter the word *love* to him under any circumstance. Not with the knowledge of her secret crush on him throbbing away in her heart. 'I really enjoy working with you and would like to continue. The baby isn't due until after Christmas. I would like to stay here and help you with the launch, then return to Australia at the end of summer, say late August. I need to be back there for the birth.'

He leaned back against the chair. Templed his fingers. 'You're sure you want to do that?'

'Yes. I really want to continue working with you. To...to be part of your awesome project.' *To stay part of his life.*

His expression didn't give away anything. She had no idea what his decision would be. She would accept it either way. But she just hoped he would agree to keep her on.

'With all the hospitality staff I've employed over

the years, I've worked with pregnant women. There's no reason not to keep you on.'

Hope bubbled through her. 'You mean I've still got a job?'

'Yes,' he said.

'You're not just saying that because you'd be breaking some employment code if you asked me to go?'

'No,' he said gruffly. 'I want you to stay. I consider you an…an indispensable part of my team.'

She wanted to fling her arms around his neck to thank him, but knew it would be totally inappropriate. Especially now considering her condition.

'Thank you,' she said. 'I promise I won't let you down.'

'What about your motion sickness?'

'The doctor has given me some strategies to cope with that,' she said. 'No medication, of course.'

'What about the boat ride to and from the island every day? You looked very shaken by it yesterday.'

Her chin tilted up. She wouldn't give him any excuse to renege on his decision. 'I'll just have to grit my teeth and bear it, won't I?' she said. 'This job is really important to me, Alex.' *You are important to me, but I'll never be able to let you know that now.*

'I think there's a better way. You should move onto the island.'

'But…but none of the rooms are ready for occupation,' she said.

'There are two self-contained suites in the pavilion,' he said. 'You'll have to share it with me.'

CHAPTER NINE

How did she deal with this new development?

Sharing an apartment with Alex would be quite the challenge, Dell realised. That afternoon, she followed him as he carried her suitcase across the marble floor of the pavilion into the sumptuous bedroom that was to be hers. She noted that, as he had said, the bedrooms and bathrooms were completely separate—thank heaven.

Growing up, she had shared a bathroom with her brother. And of course she had shared a bathroom with her ex. But she could not even imagine having to share a bathroom with Alex. Not in a room where the occupants spent most of their time naked. Not when her imagination would go crazy thinking about him naked in the same space where *she* was naked. Standing where he stood to shower that tall, broad-shouldered body, twisting to soap his powerful chest and lean, six-pack belly. At least, she assumed he'd have a six-pack belly. He did in those dreams that came to taunt and tantalise her—where he was wearing considerably fewer clothes than he did in real life. She shook her head to clear her thoughts. *Enough.*

She had to stop this crazy fantasising about Alex. It

was never going to happen. She was pregnant and he was *not* okay with it, no matter how much he quoted his employer code of practice. Her pregnancy was an inconvenience to him. There'd never before been a sign he was interested in her as anything other than an employee; there certainly wouldn't be now she was pregnant. She had a thrilling new life ahead of her—mother to her miracle baby—and that life would not include Alex. Once she went back to Australia she doubted he would be anything more than a name on her résumé, her boss on a particularly exciting project.

That new life was not quite the way she had envisaged it for all those years—having the child's father around had been the plan. But she had not the slightest regret about her rash visit to the clinic. In fact the more she thought about it, the happier she became that she had made that reckless choice. *Her baby.* Now she needed to concentrate on doing the best possible job she could do so Alex would not regret keeping her on in a job she still sorely needed. She needed to earn to both pay off her debts and start saving for the baby. Indulging in fantasies about her handsome boss was a time-wasting distraction.

'This bedroom is magnificent,' she said, looking around her at the restful, white room straight out of a glossy interiors magazine. The furniture was sleek and modern, the huge bed piled with expensive linens and pillows. A few carefully chosen paintings hung on the walls, contemporary works she recognised as being by the artist she had visited in Athens with Alex. He had commissioned a series of arresting scenes of the islands for the resort. Nature also provided its own artworks, the windows framed a view of the green hills behind. Tasteful. Private. Peaceful. Well, as peaceful as it could be with *him* in a room just across a corridor. 'It's incredibly luxurious for a pool house,' she said.

'I understand the previous owner lived in it when he flew in to check on the construction of the main house.'

'That makes sense,' she said. 'Is your room the same as this one?'

Why did she say that? She didn't want him to show her his bedroom. To see his bed and imagine him there, his tanned, olive skin against the pale linen sheets, as he sprawled across— She flushed that tell-tale flush but thankfully he still had his back to her. Why was her libido leading her on such a dance? Pregnancy hormones? Or *him*? She didn't need to think about the answer. Fight the unwelcome feeling as she might, she had never felt so attracted to a man.

'Yeah, it's the same,' he said. 'A slightly different colour scheme.' He was more subdued than she'd seen him, closed off, communicating only what he needed to. Possibly he was regretting his offer for her to share the pavilion with him.

What would he think if he could see the scenarios playing in her head, where he played a starring role? Again she flushed, this time with mortification.

She forced herself back to the real world. He was her boss. She was nothing more to him than an employee—valued, she knew, but an underling just the same. Now she felt she had to work even harder, to prove herself to him all over again. Prove that being pregnant was no barrier to performance. She would do well to keep reminding herself of that.

'Thank you, Alex, for this. I think I feel better already knowing I don't have to face that boat trip twice a day. As soon as the sickness abates I can go back to the villa.'

'When you're ready,' he said. 'You can stay here as long as you need to.'

Dell followed him through to the spacious living area and kitchen. Despite her good working relationship with Alex, she felt awkward at the subtle shift between them that being roommates would inevitably bring. She knew she was intruding but at the same time she was very grateful for the offer of such wonderful accommodation on the island. She was happy at the villa but this apartment was the ultimate in opulence. Once the resort was up and going, the pavilion would become exclusive, highly priced accommodation for well-heeled guests. What a treat to stay here in the meantime. She could never afford this level of luxury on her own dime.

'So how do we handle this?' she asked him. 'I'm aware I'm invading your privacy and I'll stay out of your way as much as possible. What do you do about food? Do you cook for yourself or—?' She actually knew a daily housekeeper came over on the construction crew boat every day to cook and clean for him. But she didn't want to admit she'd been snooping into his life.

He told her what she already knew and she pretended it was news to her. 'The housekeeper can leave meals for you, too, if you like,' he said. 'Or you can order what you need to cook your own meals. Just co-ordinate with her when you're likely to need to use the kitchen. There's breakfast stuff in the pantry. Again, order what you need.'

So no shared meals, then. No intimate evenings over

the elegant table set in the loggia overlooking the pool. Not that she'd expected that. Alex made it very clear he put her in the same category as the housekeeper— mere staff.

'I'll leave you to unpack and settle in,' he said. 'Then you can join me in the office. That is, if you feel up to it.' He was bending over backwards to be considerate when she knew he must be cursing the break in their timetable.

'I'm feeling better by the minute, just knowing I don't have to get back into a boat every day.'

He paused. 'I need to go to Athens again day after tomorrow. Will you be able to come?'

'I'll manage,' she said. 'I don't want to miss out.' If she had to nibble on dry crackers and swig lemonade all day to keep the nausea at bay she'd be there.

'We'll have a very full day. Pack for a night away,' he said. 'If you want to see the Acropolis, it might be a good opportunity to get up early and do it before we fly back. I don't know how you'll feel about all the walking and steps involved in getting up to the Parthenon once you're further into your pregnancy. It will get too hot as well.'

'That's very thoughtful of you. I'd love to.' *Why was he being so nice?*

'Good.' He turned on his heel. 'I'll see you in the office. I've got work to catch up on.' The implication being he had lost valuable time attending to her. Dell felt bad about that. She had hours to make up too. She'd work later that evening. Which would make any awkward encounters in the pool house less likely. She would be careful to schedule her meals around his so she did not intrude.

He started to stride away. 'Alex. Before you go. One more thing.'

He turned back to face her.

'Your aunt Penelope…'

'Yes?'

'I got to like her while I was staying in the villa. She's teaching me Greek, you know. And sharing her traditional recipes. My blog fans are loving them.'

'Very nice,' he said dismissively. But Dell felt she had to plough on.

'As I got to know her, I realised that she…well, your aunt Penelope is the disseminator of information to your extended family.'

'Which is your kind way of saying she's an outrageous gossip.'

Dell laughed. 'I wouldn't quite say it like that, but yes.'

Alex laughed too and Dell felt a relaxing of the thread of tension that had become so taut between them since she'd dropped her bombshell back at the café in Nidri.

He might not be so relaxed when he heard what she had to say next. 'Er…with that in mind, do you realise your aunt thinks I'm moving in to the pool house to be with you? I mean, not to share like a roommate, to actually live with you. She's convinced we're lovers.'

'What?' Alex exploded. 'Where the hell did she get that idea from?' His eyes narrowed. 'What did you say to give her that opinion?'

'Nothing. Not a word, I promise you. As far as I'm concerned you're the boss and I'm the employee. You're helping me out because I'm suffering so much from motion sickness it's affecting my efficiency in my job. That's all I told her.'

His face set granite hard. 'It needs to be perfectly clear that there is nothing else whatsoever between us and never could be.' Dell tried not to react to the shard of pain that speared her at his words. She knew that to be the case, but hearing it so vehemently expressed hurt.

'Promnestria.' He spat the Greek word.

'What does that mean?' Dell asked. 'It…er…doesn't sound very pleasant.'

'It means "matchmaker", and I'm using it as a short-cut to express how annoyed I am at the interference from my family—well-meaning as they are. My aunt, and some of the other women, know very well I don't intend ever to marry. Yet they continue to speculate about me and every halfway eligible female who comes my way. And even the entirely unsuitable ones.'

Like me, thought Dell, the shard of pain stabbing deeper.

He cursed some more under his breath. This time she didn't ask for a translation.

'I'm afraid there's more,' she said.

He rolled his eyes heavenward. 'I'm so fond of my aunt but—'

'She also suspects I'm pregnant. I think she recognised the signs I never saw myself. At her age I guess she's seen it all before. I have a feeling she's crowing with delight because she thinks my baby is…is, well, yours.'

The normally eloquent Alex seemed completely lost for words. Dell squirmed in an agony of expectation of his reaction. Suddenly her job didn't seem so secure after all.

When he finally found his voice, it was ominously calm. 'How on earth would she think that?'

Dell shrugged. 'I guess she thought we knew each other in Australia. Put two and two together and came up with completely the wrong answer.'

'What have you told her?' Again she caught a glimpse of her old adversary. Alex seemed as though he was looking for her to slip up in her evidence. Had he really changed? She so wanted to believe he had.

She willed him to believe she was telling the truth. 'Nothing, I assure you. Not about the court case, nothing. I'm here to work, Alex, not to gossip with your family. I mean it.' It was a trap she'd been determined not to fall into, beguiling as Aunt Penelope could be.

'Good,' he said abruptly. But his taut look relaxed and she felt like she was off the witness stand.

'It won't be long before it becomes obvious that I'm pregnant. Should I tell your aunt? And that the baby isn't yours?'

He shook his head. 'My publicity director's personal life is none of their concern. Although in one way you telling them would quell some of the speculation about the reason you've moved in here. People close to me know I would never get involved with a woman carrying another man's child.'

His eyes didn't meet hers as he said that. Dell was relieved. It gave her valuable seconds to hide her surprise. Was that a message for her? She didn't need it spelled out.

'On balance,' he continued, 'your pregnancy is your

business. My family can stay out of it.' Not for one moment would he think she might not want him along.

'I shall hereby resist all hints, innuendos and subtly worded questions,' she said, holding up her hand as if swearing an oath.

'Thank you,' he said. He stilled, his shoulders tensed, his stance braced. 'I can't bear to be the subject of gossip—my private life bandied around as if it's some game. Not after...not after everything that happened. When I couldn't turn around without seeing a paparazzi shot of myself with some journalist analysing my expression and suggesting what I was feeling. Photos of her and me together before...before...' His words faltered to an end in a tortured groan.

Again Dell felt a great rush of compassion for him. She couldn't begin to imagine how she would have dealt with what he had been through, the horror and loss, the immeasurable pain. She ached to put her arms around him and comfort him. But he was her boss and she his employee and he had drawn the line between them. She kept her distance.

'I promise I will not encourage your aunt in any speculation about my personal life or yours. Not that I will be seeing much of her while I'm staying on the island. There's a lot to be done here. I'm going to concentrate my efforts on that.'

'As far as my family is concerned, I suggest we present a united front—your role in helping me with the launch of Pevezzo Athina is why we spend time together,' he said. 'There is nothing else of interest to great-aunts, aunts, cousins and whoever else seems determined to see something else that simply isn't there.'

His tone was businesslike in the extreme, in complete denial of the informal, friendly tone she had become used to. As he spoke, she noticed the shift in the angle of his shoulders away from her, distancing her, re-establishing boundaries.

'Of course,' she said, swallowing against the lump of disappointment that threatened to choke her.

He turned on his heel to head out of the pavilion and towards the main building.

Dell watched him, his stride both powerful and graceful as he walked away, each footstep seeming to determine a new distance between them.

Some of the magic of this special place where she had been so happy seemed to spiral away above him to dissipate in the cloudless blue sky.

CHAPTER TEN

TWO DAYS LATER Alex gritted his teeth as he walked by Dell's bedroom suite. From behind the closed door he could hear the faint splashing of her shower. He could plug his ears to the sound. But he couldn't block his imagination. Images bombarded him of her in there, naked, the water flowing over the creamy skin of her shoulders, her breasts and downwards over the curves of her hips. Was she slowly soaping her body? Did she have her face tilted up towards the jets of water as if she was preparing to receive a kiss?

His kiss.

His wild imaginings were torture. Living with Dell in such close proximity was torture. Even a glass left on the sink with the lipstick outline of her lips on the rim drove him into a frenzy of fantasising about that mouth on his. It was crazy. And totally unlike him.

He'd always been confident with women. To be frank, he'd never had to chase them. From the age of fourteen they'd chased him. And he'd been only too happy to be caught. He'd never gone through that stage of stuttering awkwardness in the presence of a beautiful woman. Until now.

The pressure of denying his attraction to his lovely

employee, totally out of bounds because she was pregnant to another man, was telling on him. To his immense frustration, conversation with her about anything other than work had become awkward, stilted. *Because of him.*

He could tell she was puzzled at his often abrupt tone, at his silences. She made the effort to be her usual friendly self, but with an edge of uncertainty as she became unsure of his reaction. But he seemed incapable of returning to that comfortable working relationship, that easy camaraderie and repartee. Not when he couldn't get her out of his thoughts. Not as a trusted workmate. Or a person he thought could be a friend. But a smart, sensual, very appealing woman. A woman he *desired*.

He wasn't looking for this. He didn't want it. Not when her pregnancy complicated everything. But the feeling wouldn't go away. No matter how many times he plunged into the chilly water of the pool and swam laps until he was exhausted.

When she'd lived at the villa, he could escape to the pavilion. Now her warm presence had invaded his man cave, where he'd been able to retreat with his dark thoughts and memories. In just days, it had become stamped with her personality, even when she wasn't actually there. The sound of her laughter seemed to linger on the empty stillness, tantalising hints of her perfume wafted to greet him, there was Dell food in the fridge.

The enforced intimacy was making him yearn for something more, needs and feelings he had long denied himself because of the guilt that tore him apart over Mia's death. Sharing a house with a woman—if only in the roommate sense—was bringing back painful memories of his late fiancée.

He had been happy dating Mia but she had pressed for more commitment. In fact she had delivered an ultimatum—get engaged or she walked. He had agreed to the engagement, she had agreed to move in. But then it had stalled with his ambivalence about setting a date for the wedding. As their relationship had gone on, he hadn't been certain they had enough in common to build a life together, the kind of committed family life he'd had growing up with his parents and grandparents. Under his playboy, party prince exterior that was what he'd known he'd wanted one day. He still hadn't been certain Mia was the one when he'd sent her to her death.

Dell was so different, in looks, personality, everything. Put both women together and Dell would be overshadowed by Mia's tall, model-perfect looks. He couldn't, *wouldn't* compare them. Yet in his mind he could almost see Dell looking up at the other woman with a wry smile, unleashing her own vibrant beauty in acknowledging Mia's statuesque Scandinavian looks. And Mia would smile back. Mia would have liked her, and Dell would have liked Mia. Polar opposites they might be, but they were both warm, kind people.

Mia had connected with his wild, party animal side. Together they had worked hard and played hard. Dell... Dell was something altogether different. There was a connection with her he had never felt before, a sense of certainty, of continuity. They thought in the same way. He kept coming back to that concept of fate. It was almost as if she'd been sent to him to help redeem and heal him.

And yet it was impossible. He could not get around the fact she was pregnant to another man. Okay, so it was a 'test-tube baby'. He didn't have to torture himself with images of her making love with her ex. Of the baby being a product of an intimate union rather than a laboratory procedure.

But being in Greece only intensified an even deeper connection—the connection to his family and heritage. In a traditional Greek family like he came from, blood was everything. Even generations down the track and in Australia, thousands of miles away from the land of his ancestors, that hadn't changed. His family had liked Mia, but he knew they would have been a whole lot happier if she too had come from a Greek migrant family.

That deeply ingrained sense of family made the concept of taking on another man's child seem alien to him. His attitude was something he couldn't change—it was as much of him as the proud Mikhalis nose that went back through generations of males in his family. He had admired Jesse Morgan for accepting Lizzie's daughter when he had married her. Jesse adored little Amy, had an amicable relationship with the little girl's French father. But taking on another man's child was something Alex could never see himself doing.

He was so lost in his thoughts he started when the door to her room opened and Dell stood in the doorway. He had to force himself not to stare. She was wrapped in a white towelling bathrobe, her hair in damp tendrils around her face, cheeks flushed from the warmth of the shower. The neckline of the robe had fallen open to reveal a hint of cleavage and the smooth top curve of her breasts. Her legs were bare. *Was she naked under there?* He balled his hands by his sides.

'Is everything okay?' she said. 'I'm not late, am I? I got up in plenty of time so we'd get the plane to Athens.'

'It's okay,' he said gruffly, looking at her feet rather than letting his gaze centre on her chest. She had small, well-shaped feet with pink-painted toenails. Lovely from top to toe, came the thought from nowhere.

She frowned. 'It's just I heard you pacing up and down and wondered if—'

'I wasn't pacing,' he said.

'You needed to see me,' she said at the same time, with a small, perplexed frown.

'No,' he said.

'You could have knocked on the door if you did,' she said. 'I'm always there if…if you need me.' Her voice faltered away.

For a long moment their gazes met. For the first time he saw something in her green eyes that kick-started his heart into a violent thudding. An awareness, an unspoken acknowledgement that he was not alone in his feelings. That if he were to pull her into his arms and slide that robe down her shoulders, she would not object.

He took a step backward. Broke that connection with an abrupt turning away from her. 'I'll be out by the pool. Meet me there when you're ready. We've got a lot to get done in Athens.'

The next morning, Dell looked at the computer-generated images on the screen with immense interest. She and Alex were in the architect's studio in the old centre of Athens in a street behind Syntagma Square. From the get-go, Alex had involved her in every aspect of the resort, not just the food, which was her primary area of expertise, and she was fascinated by how the plans had developed.

The designer was showing them on screen realistic images of how the interiors of Pevezzo Athina would look when everything was finished and ready for guests. The images were so detailed Dell could imagine herself walking through the rooms, furnished right down to the flower arrangements on the tables and the towels in the bathrooms.

'Every detail and change we discussed last meeting is there, looking perfect.' *We.* How easily she slipped into referring to herself and Alex as *we.* 'It makes it seem so real, so close to completion.'

She straightened up and in doing so caught Alex's eye. They shared a quick smile of complicity and triumph. They were a team and their team was firing on all cylinders.

Dell felt an overwhelming sense of relief. She'd mourned the loss of the easy feeling between them back at the island. Tortured herself with the thought that maybe he'd become aware of her crush on him and had backed off in discomfort. Perhaps moving in to the pavilion had been a mistake. Living in such close proximity was only making it more difficult—she had to be continually on alert.

She thought she'd kept her feelings carefully hidden, effectively masked. Then there had been a moment yesterday morning at that post-shower encounter when she'd sworn a recognition of mutual want had flashed between them. But the shutters had come down leaving just his inscrutable expression. Had she given herself away? Had she imagined his response?

He'd hardly spoken afterwards. On the journey she had been too busy keeping the nausea at bay to be concerned at the paucity of conversation, the silences that had been anything but comfortable.

But from the first meeting the day before, things had started to ease. Perhaps it was because at their meetings the designers and suppliers treated them as a team they started to behave like one again. She used the word *team* loosely. For all the politeness, for all the acknowledgement of her role as his assistant, the deference was very much to Alex as the boss. He was the person with the money and the authority and the power—the man who owned a private island and was spending a fortune on the services these talented people were providing. While they spoke mainly in English there were times they needed to break into Greek. She listened carefully but could only identify the odd word here and there. Still, that was better than when she'd first arrived, thanks to Aunt Penelope.

'Any other thoughts on the interior design?' Alex asked her now, indicating the CGI.

She shook her head. 'If you're happy, I reckon you can sign off on it.'

'Done,' he said and they again shared a smile.

That smile warmed her. Leaving the island to fly to Athens had been a good move. It marked, she hoped, a return to the working relationship that had bonded them in the first place. In her deepest heart she longed for the impossible, but was content to have their work camaraderie back.

Hands were shaken all round, congratulations and

thanks expressed. Then she and Alex were back out of the office and into the mid-morning busy street. She looked around her avidly trying to soak in as much detail as possible—the historical buildings guarded by soldiers in fabulous traditional uniforms, the shopfronts, what people were wearing, the buzz of it all. One day she would love to spend more time here. Again that feeling of excitement swept through her that she was actually living in Greece. She needed to make the most of it before she went home to Australia. She pushed aside the feelings of sadness that looming return evoked in her. When big dreams collided there was ultimately a casualty.

'That was the last meeting for today,' Alex said. 'Time well spent. Thank you for your contribution.'

He really was a wonderful boss, certainly not the tyrant some had painted him in Sydney. Had his reputation sprung from a resentment of his high standards, envy even? Or had he really changed as he claimed to have done?

'Back to the hotel?' she asked.

After a jam-packed afternoon of meetings, they had spent the previous night in a luxurious hotel not far from Plaka, the oldest and most historical part of Athens. Separate rooms, of course, but on the same floor.

Alex had gone out to a fashionable bar and restaurant in Syntagma with one of his cousins. To her surprise, he had invited her too, though she suspected it was more from good manners than any real desire to have her along. Her presence would only fuel the rumours in his family that she was more than an employee.

But she'd been too exhausted to accept. She did not

want to admit to her bone-deep tiredness as she didn't want to remind him of her pregnancy, or that it could affect her capacity to work. Rather she'd had dinner in her room, looked for a long time at the amazing view of ancient ruins lit up from below and gone to bed very early.

Now he looked at her trim business suit and medium-heeled shoes; her stilettos had been put away until after the baby was born. 'You might want to change before you climb the Acropolis.'

'There's still time before we have to leave for the airport?' The meeting had run a little late.

'Your expedition was built into the schedule.'

'I don't quite understand why you did that, but thank you,' she said, looking up at him.

He didn't meet her eyes. 'It pleases me that you like Greece so much, are learning the language. Visiting one of our most significant historical sites is to be encouraged.'

Dell thought there was rather more to it than that. Remembered he had said he wanted to make amends for the past. But she didn't want to bring up the court case again. It seemed a lifetime ago that they had been enemies.

'I can't wait,' she said. 'I've wanted to see the Parthenon since I was a kid.'

'I chose the hotel for its easy access,' he said. 'We'll make our way through Plaka up onto the Acropolis, right up to the Parthenon and the Temple of Athena.'

It took a moment for the significance of what he'd said to sink in. *'We?'* she asked, her heart suddenly pounding. 'Are you—?'

'Coming with you? Of course.' He spoke with the confident assuredness she found so appealing.

'There's no need, you know. I'm perfectly okay by myself,' she said. Her fingers were mentally crossed that he would not agree.

'I want to come with you, Dell,' he said. His tone, to her delight, brooked no disagreement.

She knew her pleasure at the prospect of his company was beaming from her eyes but she didn't care. For just this few hours she was going to pretend there were no barriers between them and enjoy every second of her time alone with him.

CHAPTER ELEVEN

ALEX WAS GLAD he had booked a late flight back to Preveza. This was to be no cursory trip up to the Acropolis so Dell could check off a tourist 'must-see'. She stopped to examine and exclaim at everything on the walk up the rocky outcrop that towered over the city of Athens, the ancient citadel of the Acropolis that dated back to the fifth century BC. She was the one who filled him in on the dates and facts. Her knowledge of ancient Greek history was impressive, though when he complimented her, she demurred saying it was snippets she remembered from high school. Oh, and a little brushing up on the Internet.

First of the ancient structures to catch her attention was the Herodes open-air amphitheatre, with its semicircular rows of marble seating built in tiers from the stage, built in 161 AD. 'Can you imagine how many people must have been entertained here over the centuries?' she said as, after a long pause for thoughtful contemplation, she snapped photos with her smartphone.

'And continue to do so,' he said. 'There are plays and concerts staged here throughout the summer.'

Her face lit up. 'Really? I would love to attend one. I wouldn't care what it was, just to be here would be the most amazing experience. Please, Alex, can you help me book a performance before I go home?'

Alex paused for a moment too long and the silence fell awkwardly between them. He knew she would have to go back to Sydney for the birth of her baby, but didn't want to think about the gap her loss would leave in his life. Almost as if he didn't acknowledge it, it wouldn't happen. 'Of course,' he said eventually, forcing himself not to sound glum.

As they continued the climb, glimpses of the immense marble columns of the Parthenon above them beckoned. 'There it is!' Dell paused, gawking above her, and tripped over the uneven paving on the pathway. 'I wondered if I would ever get to see it.'

'Careful,' Alex said as he took her elbow to steady her. He intended to keep a grip on her but she flushed and he loosened his hold.

'I'm okay,' she said.

'A woman in your condition isn't supposed to fall,' he said.

'Condition?' she said with a quirk of her auburn brows. 'You make it sound like something medical. Being pregnant is something natural for a woman. Something wonderful.'

'But you've been so ill,' he said, remembering the day he'd seen her in Nidri, how her haggard appearance had shocked him.

'That's just the hormones, the doctor told me. All part of the process of pregnancy. Some women suffer more than others. I don't need to be wrapped in cotton wool.' She looked up at him with a sweet curving of her lips. 'Although I do appreciate your concern. It's very chivalrous of you.'

'So long as you're okay.' Chivalrous? Alex didn't think he'd ever been called that before. Selfish. Inconsiderate. Arrogant. That was what he'd been used to in his past. He tried on the feel of *chivalrous* and liked it, though he really was only doing what came naturally when he was around Dell.

'I'm actually more than okay.' She breathed deeply as she looked around her, at the steep hill wooded in parts with cypress and olive. If you looked closely there were spring flowers in the undergrowth and Alex pointed them out to her. She took a few snaps with her smartphone.

'Thank you,' she said. 'I don't know anything about the plants here. And you never know what can make an interesting blog post.'

'The ten minutes you spent reading the poster on "Vegetation and Flora of the Acropolis" must surely have helped,' he said with a smile.

'Did I spend that long?' she said. 'I'm sorry. I'm fascinated with everything about this place.'

'I like that,' he said. He was learning that Dell was never satisfied with skimming the surface, she had to dig deep, to learn. It was one of the reasons she made such a good employee and why he valued her more each day.

'Being on this ancient ground, I can't help thinking of all the people who have been here before us, all the people who are to come,' she said. 'I'm bearing a new life. It makes me feel connected, part of something much greater.'

A new life? Alex had not thought of her pregnancy in that way, perhaps he hadn't wanted to. He had seen it as an inconvenience, limiting the months she could work for him, blocking the possibility of pursuing his attraction to her. Not as the growth of a new little person who would make Dell a mother. She would be a good mother, he thought. But what about the father? What role would he play in her life? He felt a stab of discomfort at the thought of her ex. He refused to consider it could be jealousy.

Dell placed her hand on her stomach. She was wearing a wearing a white dress of soft cotton that flowed around her body. He realised with a shock that she was probably wearing it because it was looser than what she usually wore. It tied under her breasts with a blue woven tie. He noticed a new curve to her belly. Were her breasts bigger too? A quick glance said they were. Her new curves made her even lovelier.

She must have noticed the direction of his gaze. She smiled. 'I've started to show. Now I'm letting myself really believe I'm having a baby. Did you notice me tugging at my skirt during the meetings today? I tried not to make it obvious, but it's getting very tight.'

'You're happy about that?' he said.

'Really happy,' she said without hesitation. Alex could see from the glow of her face and the joy in her eyes that she meant it. 'The timing isn't the most convenient, I acknowledge that. But I've wanted a baby for so long and this is probably my only chance.'

'What will you do when you go back to Sydney?' he asked.

A little of the glow faded. 'I'll have to fling myself on the mercy of my parents.'

He frowned. 'Wouldn't they be delighted they were going to be grandparents? My sisters both have children. Nothing makes my parents happier than their grandbabies.'

He wondered if they'd given up hope for any grandchildren from him. He had been so busy turning partying into a multimillion-dollar business he hadn't actually thought much about children. He'd always wanted to have kids but it had been filed in the 'one day' category—even with Mia, who had also thought of babies as something for the future.

'From what I've heard about your family, that doesn't surprise me,' she said. 'My parents are very different. They're not really family orientated. We're not close. They'll be shocked at what I've done. I'm just hoping they won't disapprove so much they won't help me.'

'Can't you live on your own? Don't you have your own apartment in Sydney?'

She shook her head. 'I came off the worst in the spoils of divorce. He got the apartment, I got the debts.' Her attempt to sound flippant failed miserably.

'Can you expect support from your ex?'

'No way. I...er... I'm not sure I'll even tell him. He's married again, has a new life. We're not in touch.'

He frowned. 'Doesn't he have a right to know he's going to be a father?'

'I'm not sure that he does,' she said, tight-lipped. Alex could read the *don't go there* signals flashing from her eyes. But the little she gave away made him believe she had reason to be wary of the ex. The guy sounded like a jerk.

'So you'll be going back to Sydney to nothing?'

'That's not quite true. My parents have a large house. Even if simply out of duty I'm sure they'll find room for me and the baby until I get on my feet again. Though to tell you the truth, I'm not looking forward to telling them my news.'

'Your parents don't know you're pregnant?'

'No one does but you, and my doctor in Nidri, of course.' She looked up at him, her eyes huge. 'I've been disappointed so many times. I'm waiting until I'm further down the track before I tell anyone. Just in case.'

Pain shadowed her eyes and he realised how desperately she wanted this pregnancy, how vulnerable it made her and how alone she seemed in the world. He felt angry her parents sounded so distant, that they wouldn't want to help her at such a time. As for the ex, Alex's fists clenched beside him. Again that fierce desire to protect her swept over him. He couldn't bear to think of her struggling on her own. Life could be tough for a lone parent. He knew that from the juggling some of his single-mother staff had had to do to keep an income coming in. How would Dell manage?

This was not his baby. Not his business. But *she* was his business. He had brought her to Greece and she had proved herself tuned to the same wavelength as he was when it came to the business. The plans for the hotel would not be moving along so quickly or so efficiently without her help. He'd have to find a way to give her a substantial bonus before she left his employment. Otherwise, he didn't know how he could help her.

But there was one way he could help her now. He took her hand in his. 'Come on, let's get up to the top. But I'm going to make sure you don't stumble again. You're stuck with my chivalry.'

This time she smiled and didn't pull away. He folded her much smaller hand in his; the answering pressure made him feel inordinately pleased. When they reached a smoother part of the path he didn't let go of her hand.

With each step forward up the hill Dell silently chanted a *what if?* inside her head. What if Alex was holding her hand because he wanted to, not just out of consideration of her pregnant condition? What if they were a genuine couple, linking hands as they always did when they walked together out on a date? What if she were pregnant to a man like him—she couldn't go so far as to fantasise she was actually pregnant to *him*. Then there was the biggest *what if* of them all, one she scarcely dared breathe for fear of jinxing herself: what if she weren't pregnant and she were free to explore her attraction to Alex, to flirt a little, let him know how she felt, act upon it? *What if he felt the same?*

He kept hold of her hand as they reached the top and at last the Parthenon towered above her. The ground was rough, broken stone and marble caused by ongoing repairs and the tramping of thousands—possibly millions—of feet across the ancient land over the centuries. She had to be careful she didn't go over on her ankle.

'Wow, just wow,' she breathed as she gazed up the iconic structure, which no photo or painting could do justice. Built around 432 BC as a temple to worship the Goddess Athena, it had been scarred by attacks and battle over the centuries. Yet its remaining pillars and sculptures still stood overlooking Athens, an imposing edifice to an ancient civilisation.

'You're so lucky to have this as your heritage,' she said with awe.

'It's the world's heritage,' he said, his voice edged with pride.

Dell had long realised how important his Greekness was to Alex. Would he ever go back to Australia? Would she ever see him again after she went back?

For a long time she stood gazing in wonder at the magnificence of the ancient building with its massive columns and pediments achingly beautiful against a clear blue sky. It made it poignant that she was sharing it with Alex—boss, friend, man she longed to be so more than that if things were different.

She looked up at him, so tall and broad-shouldered, handsome in light linen trousers and white shirt, his dark hair longer now than when she'd first seen him at Bay Breeze, curling around his temples. Her heart seemed to flip over. 'Thank you, Alex. I'll never forget this moment, here with you in the land of your ancestors.'

He looked back down at her for a long moment. She could tell by the deepened intensity of his dark eyes that he was going to kiss her and a tremor of anticipation rippled through her. At that moment, it was what she wanted more than anything in the world. She swayed towards him, not breaking the connection of their eyes, her lips parting in expectation of his mouth on hers. And then he was kissing her.

His mouth was firm and warm, a gentle respectful touch asking a question that she answered by tilting her head to better kiss him back. *Bliss.* This was one small dream that was coming true. Dell realised she had closed her eyes and she opened them again, not wanting to miss anything of this—touch, taste, his scent, the sight of his face. She found his eyes intent on hers and she smiled. He smiled back and then kissed her again. They exchanged a series of short, sweet kisses that escalated with a subtle sensuality that left her breathless.

She was dimly aware that they were still standing with the Parthenon behind them, in one of the most public arenas in Athens. But when he pulled her closer into a longer, more intense embrace she forgot where she was. All she was aware of was Alex—the feel of his arms holding her close, her arms twined around his neck, his mouth, his tongue, the fierce strength of his body. Every kiss she'd ever had faded into insignificance. *This*. Alex.

'Bravo!' Good-natured catcalls and cheering broke into the bliss and she realised they had an audience. She doubted anyone knew who Alex was, but there were a lot of smartphones around. Everyone was a potential *paparazzo* these days.

She broke away from the kiss although she couldn't keep the smile from her voice. 'That was probably not a good idea,' she murmured. On one level she meant kissing in public. On another, she meant shifting their relationship to something more personal wasn't either. If, indeed, that was what this had signalled.

'Yes, it wasn't,' he said with rather too much vehemence. The shutters came down over his eyes again, leaving them black and unreadable. He took an abrupt step back and tripped on the uneven ground. Dell had to catch his arm and hold him steady. But she didn't care about his less than romantic reaction. This day could end right now and she would be happy. Alex had kissed her and she would treasure the moment for ever. No matter what might or might not follow.

'Thank you,' he said. Then, his voice hoarse, 'Thank you for rescuing me.'

'All I did was help you keep your balance,' she said.

'You've done that all right,' he said and she realised they were speaking at a deeper level. 'But you've done so much more.' He reached down to trace a line from her cheekbone to the edge of her mouth. His touch sent a shiver of pleasure through her. 'I didn't think I could be attracted to another woman after…after Mia. But you've proved me wrong.'

'Was…was kissing me some kind of experiment?' She tried to mask the hurt in her voice with a light-hearted tone.

His face darkened. 'No. How could you think that? You looked so lovely, so warm and vibrant with laughter in your eyes, I simply couldn't resist you.'

Warmth flooded through her heart, only to chill at his next words. 'Even though I know I should not have done so. Dell, I—'

Her spirits plummeted to somewhere around her shoes. She put a hand up to halt him. 'Please, we still have an audience.'

He glared at the people watching them and they hastily dispersed.

Dell looked around her. 'It's getting hot. Can we find somewhere with some shade?'

Shade was in short supply on the Acropolis. But they managed to find a patch as they headed across to the Temple of Diana. Dell forced a laugh as they seated themselves on one of the large chunks of marble lying around the site. 'Is this marble a part of the Parthenon and an archaeological treasure, or destined to be used in the restoration? I can't believe there's so much marble scattered around the place.'

'The latter I suspect,' Alex said, obviously not interested in talking about marble, perhaps aware she was using it as a stalling tactic. He spoke bluntly. 'Dell, I meant what I said before. I find you very attractive in every way but you're pregnant to another man and that puts you out of bounds.'

'I... I see,' she said, thinking back to her list of *what ifs*. She took a deep steadying breath against a twisting stab of disappointment. 'I appreciate your honesty, understand where you're coming from. A lot of men would probably feel the same way, I imagine. That doesn't stop me from being delighted I'm pregnant.' Her eyes dropped, so did her voice. 'What it does make me feel is regret...regret that maybe we didn't meet at a different time or place.' She looked up at him again. 'For the record, I find you very attractive. I... I like you too, which is a surprise as I used to loathe you.'

His laugh was broken and rough. 'I can't imagine how I could ever have considered you an enemy,' he said.

He went to kiss her again but Dell put her finger across his lips to stop him. 'No. That last kiss—that *first* kiss was perfect. Let's not override it with a kiss of regret and...what might have been.'

She took his hand in hers. 'But please, hold my hand for the rest of the day, because I couldn't bear it if you didn't.'

'As you wish, although I would kiss you with no regret.' He folded her hand into his much bigger one.

She took a deep breath to keep her voice steady. 'When we get back to Kosmimo, I suggest we pretend this never happened. That we agree you're my boss and I'm your assistant. We go back to the status quo, as it can never be anything more than that between us. I... I couldn't bear working with you, sharing the pavilion with you, if it was any other way.' If ever there was a time for her fluffy-chick face, this was it.

But when in defiance of her feeble ban he lifted her hand to his lips and pressed a kiss into the sensitive centre of her palm, she did not object. She could not let a betraying quiver in her voice let him guess she was crying deep down inside her heart.

CHAPTER TWELVE

TRUE TO HER WORD, Dell didn't refer again to their trip to the Acropolis. Alex wasn't sure if he was surprised or relieved at the way she had totally wiped from their agenda their kiss in front of the columns of the Parthenon.

During the week they'd been back, she deftly changed the subject if anything regarding that day threatened to sneak into the conversation. He had even looked on her *Dell Dishes* blog to see what she had posted about her trip to Athens.

She wrote about her climb of the Acropolis and shared food images from the Athens restaurants where they had eaten together. But without a mention of him. *'My companion,'* she referred to when describing her climb. Her neuter-general companion was what he had been relegated to. Common sense told him that was perfectly appropriate. He should appreciate her discretion. It was insane to feel excluded. Not when he was the one who had called the shots.

At the office she was bright, efficient and as totally professional as she should be. As if she had never murmured her pleasure at his kiss with a sweet little hitch to her voice.

It was he who felt unsatisfied. Grumpy. Frustrated. Because just that taste of her lips had awakened a hunger for her. A need. If he could take her to bed and make love to her before she showed any further signs of pregnancy, pretend she wasn't expecting another man's baby, he would. Only he knew it would be the wrong thing to do. For him, for *her*. Because he liked her enough not to want to hurt her. And sex without commitment, whether she was pregnant or not, was not something that Dell would welcome. He sensed that, *knew* that.

Yet how ironic that the further she got into her pregnancy, the more she bloomed and the more beautiful she appeared. He had heard the word *blooming* used to describe expectant women but had never had an idea what it meant. She was still barely showing but she was curvier in the right places, her hair appeared thicker and glossier, her skin glowed and her eyes seemed a brighter shade of green.

On occasion her complexion was greener too. But her morning sickness seemed to be easing. Soon she might be able to handle the daily crossing between Nidri and Kosmima and go back to stay in Aunt Penelope's villa. But she didn't mention it and neither did he.

Alex liked having her in the pavilion, even though she studiously avoided any potential moments of intimacy. Even though it was frustrating knowing she was in the bedroom next to him—each of them all alone in those super-sized beds. Because her presence—her light, quick footsteps on the marble floor, snatches of her voice as she hummed a Greek song his aunt had taught her as she moved around the kitchen—was comforting.

He realised for the first time in a long time he didn't feel lonely. The nightmares about Mia in the clutches of the gunman had abated. Thanks to Dell. He dreaded how empty the rooms would seem when she went back to Australia to have her baby.

He felt like humming himself—although he never did anything so unmanly—as he checked the latest reports from the architects and designers. They were well on track; in fact some of the rooms in the hotel were already just about ready for occupancy. It was pleasing.

Dell had still been in the pavilion earlier this morning as he had headed over to the main building and their shared office. He hadn't enquired about her estimated time to start work. It was likely she wasn't well. Not that she'd let her morning sickness interfere in any way with her work. That added another notch to his admiration of her; he knew how difficult it must be.

This morning he was impatient for her to get to her desk. He wanted to share his exultation that things were going so well. Because she had contributed to it with her keen eye and smart observations. Not to mention her meticulous record-keeping. Another thing that pleased him was her handling of publicity. Her careful drip-feeding of snippets about the launch, her forward-planning of interviews and media site visits were beginning to create the low-level buzz he had hoped for. He had every reason to pay her that bonus—sooner rather than later perhaps.

He looked up from his desk as he heard her footsteps approach, dragging rather than tip-tapping on the marble. Alarmed, he leapt to his feet. Was she ill again?

But when she entered the room Dell looked more distressed than sick. Her face was flushed, high on her cheekbones, her eyes glittered, and her hands were balled into fists. 'Sorry I'm late,' she said, tight-lipped.

'Dell, what's going on?'

'Nothing,' she said.

'That's obviously not true.'

She gave a great sigh that wrenched at him. 'I don't want to bring my personal problems to work.'

'Where else can you take them right now?'

That forced a glimmer of a smile from her. 'Are you sure you want to hear this?'

If it had been anyone other than Dell, he would have beat a hasty retreat. Girl problems were something to be avoided. But she really didn't have anyone else with whom to share her obvious angst. 'Fire away,' he said.

She stood by her desk, feet braced as if steeling herself. 'I just had a horrible, abusive call from my ex-husband, Neil. He's found out that I'm pregnant.'

'How? You said no one else knows but me and your doctor.'

Alex swore he could hear her teeth grinding. 'The stupidest of mix-ups. The fertility clinic sent a letter to me at his address—which was my old address. Seemed they'd sent it to me at my rented apartment and it had been returned, even though I paid for a redirection order on my mail. So they sent it to the previous address they had for me. Needless to say I'm furious at them. And at the darn post office.'

'Your ex opened a letter that was addressed to you?'

'That would be typical—he always thought my business was his business. I... I used to think his controlling ways were because he cared. Boy, did I get to know better towards the end.'

Alex hated to see the bitter twist of her mouth. The

more he heard about her ex, the less he liked him. 'You said he was abusive?'

'Furious. Shouting. Making threats. Said he refused to have anything to do with the baby. That…that the embryo should have been destroyed. That I…that I had no right to take it. That… I was utterly selfish to have done what I did. That I… I wasn't thinking of anyone else but myself.'

'I'm so sorry, Dell. If there's anything I can do—'

'Thank you but, despite how vile he's being, he did have some right to be angry. I don't regret undertaking the procedure but I knew it probably wasn't the right thing to do. We weren't married any more. Circumstances were entirely different.'

Alex wanted to draw her into a hug but he knew it would not be welcome. In spite of all his business expertise he honestly didn't know how he could help her make the best of the complex and unusual situation she found herself in. But his thoughts were racing. He knew a lot of people in Sydney. People who could track down this guy. Keep an eye on Dell's ex. Report back to Alex so he could make sure Dell wasn't under any threat. He worried about her going back to Sydney on her own.

'What else did he have to say?'

'Again and again that he would deny paternity. That being a sperm donor didn't make him a father.'

'Good point. And why would you want him as the father?'

She made a gesture of despair with her hands. 'I guess he has good genes. He's handsome. Intelligent. Good at sport. I used to think he was kind.'

'What does the guy do for a living?'

'He's a civil engineer.'

Alex groaned.

'What was that for?' Dell asked.

'You should have added boring to his list of genetic attributes.'

That elicited a watery smile from Dell. 'I guess I should. He always was a tad on the dull side. But I traded that for security. How did I put up with it for so long?'

'Because you really wanted a kid and you thought he'd be a safe bet?'

'Something like that, I guess,' she said. 'There I was married and living in the suburbs at age twenty-two while you were building up your fortune.'

'Partying was a far less boring profession,' he said. 'But back then you wouldn't have looked at me, would you?'

'Probably not. I was far too prim.'

'Were you really? I find that very difficult to believe. I suspect you're a very passionate woman. When I kissed you I—'

'That's a no-go zone, Alex,' she warned. 'Can we change the subject?'

'Back to your boring, bad-tempered husband?'

That brought another smile. 'If you put it that way. Actually, I think I'll think of him that way from now on—Neil the BBTH.'

'The Boring Bad-Tempered *Ex*-Husband, you mean,' he said.

She giggled. 'Okay, the BBT Ex-H.' He was glad he could make her laugh. The phone call must have been traumatic.

'It's a mouthful. Why not settle on BX, *boring ex*,

for short?' he said. He could think of much worse
things he could call her odious former husband. 'Boring is worse than bad-tempered. We all have our bad-
tempered moments.'

'BX he shall be from now on.' She sobered. 'Deep
down I guess I hoped he might want to have some kind
of contact—for the baby's sake, not mine. Back then he
wanted a child as much as I did. But perhaps he didn't.
Perhaps he's right. Am I being selfish in having this
child on my own? Maybe it's always been about my
need to have a baby.'

'Isn't that how most people decide to have children?
Because they want them?' he asked. 'Not that I know
a lot about it.'

'Perhaps. But that's all beside the point, isn't it? I'm
going to love this baby enough for two parents. There
are worse ways to come into the world than being utterly loved, aren't there?' She sounded in need of reassurance.

'Indeed,' he said. 'Your baby will be lucky to have
a mother like you.'

But a child needed a father. Alex had had his dif-
ferences with his father, but he'd always been there
loving and supporting him. Dell's child would grow
up without that constant male presence. Of course,
she might marry again, meet someone like Jesse Morgan who would be a father to her child. He pulled the
'off' switch on that train of thought. He couldn't bear
to think of Dell with another man. He'd been called
selfish too.

'One last thing the BX told me was that his new wife
was pregnant. Therefore all the problems we had were
my fault.' Her voice broke. 'There was nothing wrong

with him—no, siree—it was *me* who was the failure.
Me who put him through all that. And if I insisted on
going ahead with this pregnancy I'd better get myself
checked out to see if I was actually capable of carrying
a child.' Her last words came out so choked he could
hardly hear them.

Alex could feel a bad-tempered moment of mammoth proportions threatening to erupt. Was there a
hitman among all those contacts in Sydney? He ran
through all the swear words he knew in both English
and Greek. None was strong enough to express his
contempt for Dell's ex-husband.

He gritted his teeth. 'Lucky he's not here because
if he was I'd—'

'Whatever you'd do I'd do worse.'

'Dell, you're better off without that…that jerk. So
is your child.'

'You're absolutely right. In some ways the encounter with him is a relief. I don't have to worry about the
BX ever again.' Dell spat out the initials so they came
out sounding like the worst kind of swear words. She
took a deep, heaving breath. 'I was so worried about
him, now I won't have to worry. If he denies paternity,
that's good too. It might make it easier for me to get
help if that's the case.'

'What do you mean?'

'Back home in Sydney, if I have to apply for a supporting mothers' benefit, I will have to name the father
and try to get support from him—something I never
intended to do, by the way. If I put "father unknown"
it might not make me look very good but I could get
help for a while if needed.'

Anguish that this spirited, warm, intelligent woman

should be in that position tore through him. 'Dell, don't go back to Sydney. Have the baby here. You're entitled to maternity leave. Your job would still be waiting for you. You wouldn't have to beg for help from your parents or the government or anyone else.'

Tears glistened in her green eyes and she scrubbed them away with her finger. It left a smear of black make-up that made her look more woebegone. 'Thank you, Alex. That's incredibly kind of you. I love it here but…but I don't want to give birth to my baby surrounded by strangers. I have to go home, no matter what I might face.'

Alex stared at her for a long moment. *A stranger.* That was all he was to her. *That was all he'd let himself be.* The realisation felt like another giant kick to his gut.

He had to pull himself together, not let her know how her words had affected him. 'The offer is still there,' he said.

'Thank you,' she said again. 'I truly appreciate it.' She squared her shoulders. 'But we have work to do.' She didn't seem to realise she was wringing her hands together. 'Now that we've got personal, it might be time for me to ask you about Mia. I have to know how to spin your story before the media goes off on their own wild tangents. I'm going to fix my face. When I get back I need to talk to you.'

Mia. When would he ever be able to talk about his guilt over what had happened? But if there was anyone he could open up to, it would be Dell.

CHAPTER THIRTEEN

DELL HAD BEEN trying to bring up the story of Alex's late fiancée for some time but she'd never quite found the courage to do so. The stricken look on his face told her no time would be the right time.

'I… I'm sorry if I sounded blunt,' she said. 'But you know the launch of the resort will mean you coming back into the spotlight. As soon as that happens all the stories of the siege and…and Mia's death will be resuscitated. The personal story will always override the business one. I don't need to remind you that the anniversary of the siege is coming up. Let's give the media a story before they go burrowing for one.'

Alex slid both hands through his hair to cradle his head with such an abject look it tore at her heart. 'I knew this was coming,' he said. 'I suppose I can't put it off for longer?'

Dell shook her head. She felt mean forcing him to talk. But this was about helping launch his new venture. 'If we could give an exclusive interview to, say, one of the weekend newspaper magazines we might be able to control it to some degree.'

Alex looked barely capable of standing. 'Why don't

we sit over on the chairs so I can take notes?' she suggested tactfully.

'Sure,' he said.

Once they were seated—him opposite her, so close she had to slant her legs to avoid their knees touching—she decided to conduct this as if it were an interview.

'Alex, I know how difficult this is for you. Well, I don't really have any idea but I'm trying to imagine the unimaginable. I'm aware that Mia was the love of your life and what a tremendous blow it must have been to have lost her under such shocking and public circumstances. After she…she died you disappeared from Sydney. What people will want to know is where you went, why you did so, and how it led to the development of Pevezzo Athina. Try to answer me so we can work out what we tell the media.'

He was silent for a long time. Dell became very aware she might be overstepping the mark. But this was her job, why he had brought her to Greece. She wasn't interviewing Alex her boss, her friend, the man she was in serious danger of falling in love with. This was Alexios Mikhalis, multimillionaire tycoon, ruthless businessman, man who'd led a charmed life until that terrible moment a maniac had walked into his restaurant brandishing a gun and had grabbed Alex's beautiful fiancée as hostage.

The silence was getting uncomfortable before he finally spoke, his words slow and measured. 'As far as the media is concerned, I was so devastated by the tragic loss of my fiancée I decided to get as far away from Sydney as possible. It made sense that I went to Greece, to the place my grandfather came from, where I still had extended family and could remain anonymous. I stayed with my relatives, worked with them on their fishing boats and in their olive groves, even waited tables in the family *taverna*.'

'Getting your hands dirty? Grounding yourself?'

'That's a good way to put it,' he said. 'You could say I found peace in the glorious surroundings and wanted to share it with others. I came up with the concept of a holistic resort where our guests could also find peace.'

Dell scribbled on her notepad, not wanting to meet his eyes, too scared of what she might see there. 'Have you found peace, Alex?'

'I'm still seeking it. I think you know that.'

She looked up. 'Can I say guests can come to heal?' she asked tentatively. 'Like you healed?'

'You can say that,' he said.

Could the scars he bore ever really heal? For the press release she had to take his words at surface value.

'And you bought a private island? The media will be very interested in that.'

'That is a matter of public record, so yes, I should certainly talk about Kosmimo. Not, however, about the most recent owner.'

'What about the island's link to your family?'

'Many years ago, Kosmimo was owned by my ancestors. Circumstances conspired to allow me to buy it back. I will never let the island get out of my family's hands again.'

Dell turned a new page of her notebook. 'Sounds like the perfect sound bite. That will make an excellent story. Especially back in Sydney with the city's obsession with real estate.'

He cracked a half-smile at that. She braced herself

for the next question, knowing it would vanquish his smile. 'Alex, I have to ask about your private life.'

As predicted, his smile tightened into a grim line. 'I have no private life,' he said. 'The media will find nothing titillating about me and other women.'

Unless someone recognised him kissing his assistant on the Acropolis, Dell thought.

'Because you could never find a woman to live up to Mia?'

'You can tell that to the media,' he said. 'But the truth is quite different.' He leaned forward with his hands on his knees so his face was only inches from her. She breathed in the already familiar scent of him. The scent that made her feel giddy with the hopelessness of her crush on him, made even deeper by those kisses on the Acropolis. Kisses she revisited every night in her dreams.

'The truth is only for your ears,' he continued. 'I meant what I said on the Acropolis that day.'

She held her breath not daring to say anything, realising how important this was to him. And perhaps significant to her.

'The truth is I feel so damn guilty I sent Mia to her death that I will never be able to commit to another woman.' His eyes were shadowed with immeasurable sorrow.

Dell gasped. 'But you didn't send her to her death. How could you possibly believe that? The gunman chose your restaurant at random. It was sheer bad luck Mia was there at the time. It could have been any of your staff. It could have been *you*.'

His face darkened in a grimace, his voice was grave

and low. 'You don't know how many times I wished it had been me...'

Dell swallowed hard. She didn't know that she was capable of replying the right way to such a statement. But out of compassion—and her regard for him—she would try. 'Alex, you can't mean that. You cannot punish yourself for something that was completely out of your hands.'

He spoke through gritted teeth. 'It was my fault Mia was there that day. It should have been her day off.'

Dell frowned. 'I don't get it.'

'Here's something you wouldn't have read in the press. I insisted she go in to work when the head chef was injured in an accident. Mia and I argued about that. One argument led to another. Until it ended up where it always ended up. My tardiness in setting a date for the wedding. We hadn't resolved it when she stormed out. Mia went to her death worrying that I didn't really love her. That's what I can't live with.'

Dell realised she had been holding her breath. She let it out in a long sigh. 'Oh, Alex. I'm so sorry.' She reached out and laid her hand on top of his. 'But you were engaged to be married. She would have known you loved her.'

He choked out the words. 'Or suspected that I didn't love her enough.'

'I can't believe that's true.'

He got up from the chair. Started to pace the room. Dell got up too, stood anchored by the edge of her desk. She had long stopped taking notes. These revelations were strictly off the record.

'You have to understand the place I was in at the time I met Mia. Settling down with one woman hadn't been on the agenda. I was growing the business at a relentless pace. One new venture after the other.'

'To prove you could do it, to prove to your family that you'd made the right choices for yourself.'

He stopped his pacing. 'That's perceptive of you. I'd never thought of it that way, but you're right.'

'It left no time for dating?' She knew about the string of glamorous blonde women he had been seen with on any social occasion where a photographer had been present.

'I made it very clear to the women I dated that I was not interested in commitment. I didn't have the time, or the inclination.'

'Then you met Mia.' Their love story had been re-hashed over and over again in the media.

'Mia…she made me change my mind.'

'She was beautiful.' It hurt Dell to talk about the woman who had won his heart and met such a tragic end. But she wanted to understand him. And not just because she needed to for her job. That was the cra-ziness of a crush on a man who wanted nothing to do with you. You wanted to find out everything you could about him. Because that was all you would ever have.

'Mia was beautiful, fun, a super-talented chef and liked to party hard and work hard like I did. I was smitten. I still didn't feel ready to settle down. But if I wanted Mia in my life I had to make a commitment or lose her. Those were her terms.'

'Quite rightly too,' Dell murmured in sudden soli-darity with his late fiancée.

He paused. 'She would have liked you.'

'I think I might have liked her.' Would she have been jealous of Mia? It was a pointless question. Back then she'd been too busy with her marriage and her desire to start a family to even think about another man. No matter how attractive. No matter how unattainable.

'I can tell myself over and over that it was fate she was in the restaurant at the wrong time. But fate had nothing to do with me beginning to question if Mia was the right person to be my lifetime partner. And not being honest enough to tell her.'

'So that's where the guilt comes from,' Dell said slowly. 'But if you don't forgive yourself you'll go crazy. Mia loved you. She wouldn't have wanted you to live your life alone. It's been nearly three years, Alex. Wouldn't she have wanted you to move on?'

'Meeting you showed me I could be attracted to another woman, Dell. I thought that would never happen. You don't want to talk about that day in Athens. But I meant what I said. That doesn't mean I intend to commit to another woman ever again.'

'It's as well I'm out of bounds because of my pregnancy, then,' she said, trying to sound as uninterested as if she were discussing someone else.

For her own self-protection she had to do that. Did he realise how hurtful he sounded? Or was he still so caught up in his grief and guilt he didn't realise that the best thing that could happen to him was to let himself love again? If not with her then with someone else. And when that happened, she wanted to be far, far away.

CHAPTER FOURTEEN

THREE PEOPLE INVITED Dell to the party to celebrate Alex's Aunt Penelope's seventy-fifth birthday on the coming Saturday. Aunt Penelope herself. Alex's cousin Cristos. And then Alex.

Dell had told the first two she would have to check with Alex before she could accept. She hadn't missed their exchange of sly smiles at her words. She had protested that Alex was her boss and she was accountable to him. Aunt Penelope had replied, with a knowing nod, that in Greece the man was always the boss. Dell had decided not to argue with the older woman on that one.

When Alex invited her to the party she told him about the other two. His eyes narrowed at the mention of the invitation from Cristos. Surely he couldn't be jealous of his handsome cousin? She quite liked the little flicker of satisfaction she got from that. Cristos was, in fact, extraordinarily good-looking. But the only man Dell had eyes for was Alex. Much good that it did her.

'The party will be at the original Taverna Athina on Prasinos,' he said. 'Of course you will come. I promised to take you there one day, if you recall.'

'I'm honoured to be invited,' she said. 'But do you

think it's wise, considering the ongoing speculation about us as…well, as a couple?' She laid her hand on her gently rounded belly. 'It's getting harder to conceal my pregnancy.'

'Your pregnancy is your business,' he said. *And nothing to do with me.* Dell sensed his unspoken words. 'You don't owe an explanation to anyone in my family. When it becomes obvious you're expecting you can tell them whatever version of the story behind it you choose.'

'In that case, I happily accept the invitation. All three invitations.'

'But you'll be coming to the party with me,' said Alex.

An imp of mischief prompted Dell's retort. 'But Cristos said he'd take me in his boat.'

Alex glowered down at her. 'You will *not* go in my cousin's boat. You will go in my boat. It's much more comfortable and better for a woman in your—'

'Condition, I know,' she said. 'Of course your boat is far superior to Cristos's boat. Your boat is superior to any other man's boat I know. Not that I know another person who owns a super duper speedboat like yours.' What was lacking in his four-by-four Alex kept on Nidri, and the equally battered van he kept on Kosmimo, was more than made up for in his luxurious streamlined boat.

'You'd better believe it,' he said with a reluctant grin. 'Cristos can transport his grandparents Aunt Penelope and Uncle Stavros to the party.'

'Befitting as she is the guest of honour,' Dell said.

'The party starts in the afternoon and might go on quite late,' he said. 'The *taverna* also has rooms to rent.

I will book one for you so you can stay overnight. If you get tired you can slip away any time.'

'And you?' she said.

'I'll bunk down at my uncle's house. It's where I stayed when I first arrived from Australia. It's on the same street so I won't be far should you need me.'

'I'll be okay,' she said, hoping that was the case. Anyone she had met from his family had been friendly and hospitable, while being subtly—or not so subtly, depending on gender—interested in her relationship with Alex. 'I'm looking forward to it.'

Taverna Athina was set right on the beach at the south-ernmost corner of a delightfully curving bay. The water rippled from sapphire, to the palest aquamarine, to crystal clear lapping up on a beach comprising tiny pale pebbles.

The open-air dining area of the *taverna*—entirely reserved today for the family party—sat right over the water on a dock. A banner was strung from post to post with a message in the Greek alphabet that Dell assumed meant Happy Birthday but Alex explained read *hronia polla*, and was a wish for many more happy years of life.

The *taverna* was painted white with accents of bright blue and tubs of Greek basil at its corners. The effect was friendly and welcoming. Behind the *taverna* was a traditional Greek building with a terracotta-tiled roof. Its idyllic position with the tree-studded hill as background and the water in front made it look as if the restaurant could sail off at any moment.

'That's where you'll be staying,' said Alex, indicating the older building as he helped her off his boat, moored nearby. 'It's humble but comfortable.'

'The *taverna* is charming, Alex,' she said. 'No wonder you were so attached to Athina in Sydney if this was its parentage.'

Greek music, typical of the Ionian Islands, was echoing out onto the beach. 'It's what Tia Penelope likes,' Alex explained.

'I like it too,' said Dell.

She held back as she and Alex got near to the *taverna* entrance, suddenly aware of her ambivalent status as employee and yet friend enough to be invited to a family party. And then there was the persistent speculation about her and Alex as an item.

She need not have worried. As soon as she got inside she was swept up by Aunt Penelope and introduced to the family members she hadn't previously met at either the villa or on Kosmimo. She told herself she was imagining it that the first thing the women did was glance down at her stomach.

As she was being carried away Dell turned to see Alex in animated conversation with a tall older man with steel-grey hair and glasses and an elegantly dressed woman of about the same age who had her arm looped through Alex's as though she could never let him go. Dell had no idea who they were. But even from a distance, she could see Alex bore a distinct resemblance to the man. Perhaps they had come from Athens for the party.

'What are you doing here?' Alex asked his parents, still reeling from his shock at seeing them at the *taverna*. 'I had no idea you were coming.'

'A surprise for Penelope for her birthday,' his father said. 'She says she's getting too old to fly all the way to Australia so we decided to come to her.' His father's voice was husky as if he had a heavy cold. He was getting older now, surely he shouldn't have flown with a cold.

'We wanted to see you, too, catch up with how you're doing,' said his mother.

That made sense. But Alex detected an unfamiliar restraint to the tone of both his parents' voices and wondered. 'Why didn't you tell me?' he said.

'We thought it could be a surprise for you too,' said his mother, unconvincingly to Alex's ears.

'It's certainly that,' said Alex. 'Where are you staying?'

'Here at the *taverna*,' his father replied. 'Where we always stay when we visit the family.'

Alex's father was a highly regarded orthopaedic surgeon back in Sydney, his mother a sports physiotherapist of some renown. They could afford to stay in the best of hotels. Fact was, on Prasinos the two-star Athina was the best hotel. There were luxury villas and houses to be rented but the family would take great offence if his parents stayed anywhere but the family hotel.

'We saw you come in with that lovely red-haired girl Penelope has been telling us about.'

'You mean my assistant, Dell Hudson?' Alex asked, forcing his voice to stay steady.

'Is that all she is?' said his mother, sounding disappointed. 'Penelope led me to believe there was something more between you. You know how much we want you to be happy after Mia and—'

'Dell is a very capable employee, that's all,' Alex said through gritted teeth.

Was his aunt just speculating or did she at some level recognise how attracted he was to Dell? Whatever, he wished she would stop the gossiping. The sideways glances and speculation from the rest of the family were beginning to get uncomfortable. There were handwritten name-cards at each table place. Someone had thought it funny to strike out *Dell Hudson* to be replaced by *Dell Mikhalis*. He had grabbed it and crumpled it into his pocket before Dell could have a chance to see it.

His father frowned. 'Wasn't Adele Hudson the woman who gave Athina that bad review? When you sued the newspaper and lost all that money.'

'Yes,' he said.

'So why are you employing her?' said his mother. 'Is this a case of keeping your friends close and your enemies closer?'

Why was this conversation centring on Dell? 'She's not an enemy. In fact she was right about the falling standards at the restaurant. I employed her because she's really smart and switched on. She's proved to be immensely valuable to me on my new venture.'

'Oh,' said his mother again. Alex gritted his teeth even harder.

He looked over to see Dell helping out by carrying a tray of *meze*, an assortment of Greek appetisers, to the buffet table. Dell was laughing at something Aunt Penelope was saying. Among his mostly dark-haired family she stood out with her bright hair and her strapless dress in multiple shades of blue that reflected the colours of the Ionian Sea. She had never looked lovelier. Alex could see exactly why his mother was looking at her with such interest.

'Would you like to meet Dell?' he asked his parents.

'We would, very much so,' said his father. 'But first we need to tell you something important. News that we ask you not to share yet with the rest of the family. Come outside so we can talk with you in private.'

Dell was enjoying herself immensely. Alex's extended family were so warm and hospitable she hadn't felt once she was an outsider. In fact she had been embraced by them because she was his friend.

A lot of good food and wine was being consumed. No wine for her of course—she hadn't touched a drop since she'd discovered she was pregnant. She realised her abstinence was probably a dead giveaway but came up with an explanation that she was allergic to alcohol. Whether or not she was believed she wasn't sure.

She looked around for Alex. Despite what half the room seemed to think, she wasn't there as Alex's date. Still, it seemed odd that he would leave her so long by herself when he was aware she only knew a handful of people.

Several times she looked around the room but didn't see him. When the older couple he had been speaking with came in by themselves, she went outside to see if she could find him.

Night had fallen and light from the *taverna* spilled out onto the beach. Some distance away, Alex stood by himself on the foreshore staring out to sea. In the semi-darkness he looked solitary and, Dell thought, sad. He had every good reason to be sad in his life but she hoped from their conversation the previous week that he was beginning to come to terms with the tragedy that had brought him to Greece. He appeared so lost in his thoughts he didn't seem aware of her approach.

Softly, Dell called his name. Startled, he turned quickly, too quickly to hide the anguish on his face.

Shocked, Dell hurried to his side. 'Alex. What's wrong? Are you okay?'

Slowly he shook his head. 'Everything is wrong.'

The devastation in his voice shocked her. 'What do you mean?'

'My parents are here. You might have seen me talking to them earlier. A surprise visit, to share some news with me, they said. But the news was to tell me my father has cancer.' His voice broke on the last words.

'Oh, Alex.' After the tragedy he'd endured he didn't deserve this. 'Is it…serious?'

'Cancer of the oesophagus. He's started radiation therapy already. More treatment when he returns to Sydney.' He clenched his fists by his sides. 'Dad is a doctor. Yet when he started having difficulty swallowing he didn't realise it could be something bad. By the time he sought help the cancer was established. There…there's a good chance he won't make it.'

Dell put her hand on his arm. 'I'm so, so sorry. Is there anything I can do to help?'

'Actually there is,' he said.

'Just tell me, fire away,' she said.

'My father told me his greatest wish is to see his only son married before he…before he dies. My mother wants it too.'

Dell gasped. 'How can I help you with that? Find you a bride?' Her words were flippant but she couldn't let him see how devastated she was at the thought of him getting married.

'My mother has already suggested a bride.'

'But…but you don't want to get married.'

'I know,' he said. 'But it's my father's dying wish. I have no choice but to consider it.'

Dell dropped her hand from his arm and stepped back, staggering a little at the pain his words stabbed into her. She struggled for the right words to show her sympathy for the situation he found himself in without revealing her hurt that he would be so insensitive as to discuss a potential bride with her.

'An arranged marriage? Didn't they go out of fashion some time ago? And what has that got to do with me?'

'Not an arranged marriage. I would never agree to such a thing. But if I chose to get married to fulfil my father's wish, the obvious bride for me is you.'

CHAPTER FIFTEEN

DELL STARED AT Alex, scarcely able to believe she'd heard his words correctly. '*Me!* Why would you say that?'

'You know how much I like and respect you, Dell. That's the first reason.'

Why did *like* and *respect* sound like the booby prizes? She wanted so much more from Alex than that. Not *love*. Of course not love, it would be way too soon for that even if insurmountable barriers didn't stand in their way. She was certainly not *in love* with Alex. A crush on her boss didn't mean she was in love with him. Of course it didn't. But she would like some passion and desire to sit there alongside *like* and *respect*. Especially if it was in regard to marriage— though this didn't sound like any marriage proposal she'd ever heard about or even imagined.

'And the other reasons?' she said faintly.

'My mother, my aunt, my cousins—even my father—assume because you're pregnant that I will do the honourable thing and marry you.'

'*What?*' The word exploded from her. 'You can't possibly be serious.'

Alex looked down into her face. Even in the slanted

light from the *taverna* she could see the intensity in his black eyes. 'I'm very serious. I think we should get married.'

Dell had never known what it felt to have her head spin. She felt it now. Alex had to take hold of her elbow to steady her. 'I can't believe I'm hearing this,' she said. 'You said you'd never get married. I'm not pregnant to you. In fact you see my pregnancy as a barrier to kissing me, let alone marrying me. Have you been drinking too much ouzo?'

'Not a drop,' he said. 'It's my father's dying wish that I get married. He's been a good father. I haven't been a good son. Fulfilling that wish is important to me. If I have to get married, it makes sense that I marry you.'

'It doesn't make a scrap of sense to me,' she said. 'You don't get married to someone to please someone else, even if it is your father.'

Alex frowned. 'You've misunderstood me. I'm not talking about a real marriage.'

This was getting more and more surreal. 'Not a real marriage? You mean a marriage of convenience?'

'Yes. Like people do to be able to get residence in a country. In this case it would be marriage to make my father happy. He wants the peace of mind of seeing me settled.'

'You feel you owe your father?'

'I owe him so much it could never be calculated or repaid. This isn't about owing my father, it's about loving him. I love my father, Dell.'

But you'll never love me, she cried in her heart. How could he talk about marrying someone—anyone— without a word about love?

'I'm so sorry, Alex, about your father's illness. But perhaps the shock of his sad news has skewed your thinking. Perhaps it has even…unhinged you,' she said. 'Who would think such a sudden marriage is in any way reasonable or sensible?'

'My family would not question marriage to you. In fact I believe they think us getting married is virtually a *fait accompli*.'

Dell was too astounded by his reasoning to be able to reply. She fought to keep her voice under control when she did. 'What about me? Where do I fit in this decision-making process? Aren't I entitled to an opinion?'

He put up his hand to placate her. 'You're right. I'm sorry. It seemed like such a good idea and I've rushed things. You know often my best decisions are made on impulse.' She had become so knowledgeable about his business dealings she had to admit the truth of that.

'This is my life we're talking about here, Alex. I deserve more than a rushed decision.'

'When it comes to your life, I think you'll see it makes a lot of sense,' he said.

'Please enlighten me,' she said. 'I'm still not convinced I'm not dealing with an idea sprung from grief-stricken madness.'

He shook his head but it was more a gesture of annoyance that he should be so misunderstood than anything else. 'Let me explain my perfectly sane thoughts,' he said.

'I'm listening,' she said, intrigued.

'You help me with this and there are benefits to you. You'll be able to stay here to have your baby, surrounded by people who will no longer be strangers. I have dual nationality so you would be the wife of a Greek citizen. Your baby will have a name. And I will support him or her until he or she is twenty-one years of age. You wouldn't have to ask your parents any favours or perjure yourself to get government social security. In fact you would be able to enjoy the rest of your pregnancy and after the birth without worrying about money or finding a place to live. And I imagine it would be somewhat satisfying to stick it up the BX.'

His last point dragged a smile from her. Clever Alex with his charisma and business smarts made the crazy scheme seem reasonable. But there must be more to it than that, an ulterior motive.

'It would also get the media off your back regarding Mia,' she said. 'Quite the fairy-tale romance. The press would lap it up. The story would make great publicity for your new venture.' She couldn't keep the cynical note from her voice. 'I suppose you've considered that angle.'

Alex stilled. 'Actually, I haven't. You can't honestly think that's a consideration?'

'I'm hardly privy to your thoughts,' she said.

'My only motivation here is my father's happiness while he's battling cancer. Since Mia's death I've done my best to make reparation to the people I harmed with my aggressive business techniques and ruthless selfishness. People like you. I'll never get the chance to make amends for my behaviour towards Mia and I'll live with that for the rest of my life. But I can try to make up for it with my father by getting married so he can dance at my wedding before he dies.'

If Alex had said just one thing about how fond he was of her, and for that reason if he was going to have to marry someone he would want it to be her, Dell would probably have burst into tears and said she'd do it. But he didn't. So she toughened her attitude.

She remembered how she'd felt when he'd kissed her at the Parthenon. How exciting it had been, how happy being in his arms had made her. How she'd ached for more.

'You say it wouldn't be a real marriage. I guess that means no...well, no sex.'

'That's right,' he said, so quickly it was hurtful. 'That wouldn't be fair to you when our bargain would have an end.'

As if it wouldn't be fair to bind her to a sexless, loveless union with a man who even now in this cold-blooded conversation made her long to be close to him—both physically and every other way. It would be a cruel kind of torture.

'What do you mean "our bargain"?' she asked. Thoughts about his proposition spun round and round in her mind.

'This would all be done legally. I would get my lawyers to draw up a contract setting out the terms and conditions. How you and your baby would be recompensed. The marriage would be of one year's duration.' His face contorted with anguish. 'Less if...if my father were to die before then.'

A great wave of compassion for him swept through her. He had been through so much. 'Oh, Alex, is it that bad?'

Her instinct was to comfort him, to put her arms around him, to try and take some of his pain for herself. But she kept her hands by her sides. This was not the moment for that.

He nodded, seemingly unable to speak. 'It seems so.'

They were already standing very close to each other without being conscious of it. The nature of the exchange of conversation needed to be for their ears only. A cool breeze ruffled her hair and made her shiver.

He put his hand on her shoulder. In the semi-light he looked more handsome than ever, more unattainable. The stronger his connection to his family grew, the more Greek he seemed to become. 'Please, Dell. I think we've become friends of a kind. If you don't want to agree to this for the very real benefits to you, can you do it as an act of friendship? I'll make sure you won't regret it. Please say yes. Please marry me. There isn't anyone else I'd rather be getting on board with this than you.'

Was that a subtle reminder that he was so determined to do this that if she said no, he'd find another woman who would jump at the chance to be the make-believe bride of multimillionaire Alex Mikhalis?

Could she bear it if he married someone else?

She took a deep breath. 'Yes, Alex, I say yes.'

His sigh of relief was audible, even on the beach with the muted music and chatter coming from the *taverna*, the swish of the small waves as they rolled up onto the tiny pebbles on the beach. 'Thank you, Dell. You won't regret this, I promise you.'

Already she knew she would regret it. Everything about the arrangement seemed so wrong. On top of that, she was tired of putting on her fluffy-chick face, of pretending she was happy when she wasn't. Now she had signed up for a year of pretending that she didn't care about the man who was going to be her fake husband in a marriage of convenience.

'I guess I'd be working for you, still. A different job. A new contract.' She tried to sound pragmatic, to justify the unjustifiable.

Alex frowned. 'I hadn't thought of it like that.'

'It might make it easier if we did.'

'Perhaps,' he said, sounding unconvinced. He took a step closer.

'But right now I need you to kiss me.'

'What?'

His gaze flickered over her shoulder and back to face her. 'You can't see from where you're standing but there are interested eyes on us. In theory I just proposed to you and you said "yes". A kiss is appropriate.'

Appropriate? When was a kiss *appropriate*? Obviously in this alternate universe she had agreed to enter the rules were very different. That didn't mean she had to abide by them.

She looked up at his dark eyes, his sensual mouth she ached to kiss in an entirely inappropriate way. 'I've got a better idea. *You* can kiss *me*. And you'd better make it look believable.'

Dell was challenging him. Alex had been exultant that she had acquiesced to his admittedly unconventional plan. But it seemed Dell and acquiescence didn't go hand in hand. Somehow, in a contrary kind of way, that pleased him. Dell wouldn't be Dell if she rolled over and did just as he commanded.

It made him want to kiss her for real.

Her eyes glittered in the soft half-light, tiny flecks of gold among the green. Her lips were slightly parted, a hint of a smile lifting the corners—halfway between teasing and seductive. 'What are you waiting for?' she murmured.

He was very aware of their audience. The family members who must have watched her seek him out on the beach. They stood inside the doorway some twenty metres away, obviously thinking they couldn't be seen, but the lights from the *taverna* highlighted their shapes. It appeared the group had gathered hoping, perhaps, for proof that he and Dell were a couple. He would give them that proof.

He pulled her to him and pressed his mouth to hers with a firm, gentle pressure. In reply, Dell wound her arms around his neck to pull his head closer, her curves moulded against him. Her scent sent an intoxicating rush to his head—the sharpness of lemon and thyme soap mingled with her own sweet womanliness. It was a scent so familiar to his senses he was instantly aware of when she entered or left a room. She kissed him back, then flicked the tip of her tongue between his lips with a little murmur deep in her throat. Surprise quickly turned to enthusiastic response as he met her tongue with his, deepening the kiss, falling into a vortex of sensation.

Alex forgot he was on the beach, forgot they had an audience, forgot everything but that Dell was in his arms and he was kissing her. This was no meandering journey between gentle kiss of affirmation and one of full-blown passion. It raced there like a lit fuse on a stick of dynamite. Lips, tongues, teeth met and danced together in an escalating rhythm. Desire burned through him, and her too, judging by her response as that little murmur of appreciation intensified into a moan. He groaned his own want in reply, pulled her close, as close as they could be with their clothes between them. He could feel the hammering of her heart against his chest. His hands slid down her waist to cup the cheeks of her bottom; she pushed closer as she fiercely kissed him.

'Get a room, you two.' Cristos's voice, in Greek, pierced his consciousness.

Dell pulled away. 'What was that?' Her cheeks were flushed, her breath coming in gasps, her mouth pink and swollen from his kisses.

Alex had trouble finding his own voice, had to drag in air to control his breathing.

'My cousin trying to be funny,' he said.

She looked up at him, her breasts rising and falling as she struggled to get her breath. 'Alex...that was—'

'I know,' he said, not certain of how it happened, knowing what it meant for their bargain, realising he had lost control and that he had to take back the lead.

Her eyes met his as a shadow behind them dimmed their brightness. 'We can't do that. A kiss like that wasn't what you'd call *appropriate*. It wasn't fair. Not when I—'

When she *what*? Alex wanted, needed, to know what she meant. Because at that moment when she had moaned her desire something had shifted for him. Something deep and fundamental and perplexing. He had to know if she had felt it too.

But there was no chance to ask her. Because then his family, headed by his parents, were spilling out of the *taverna* onto the beach and surrounding them with exclamations of surprise and glee and, from his mother, joy.

'I knew from the moment I saw them together, they

were more than friends,' he heard Aunt Penelope explain. Not explain—*gloat*.

He looked down at Dell, who looked as though she had been well and truly kissed. In a silent question, he raised his brow; she affirmed with a silent nod.

He put his arm around her. It wasn't difficult to fake possessiveness. 'Dell has just agreed to marry me,' he announced.

There was an explosion of congratulations and laughter. He looked up to see mingled pride, relief and love on his father's face.

'Thank you, Dell,' Alex whispered to her. 'I won't forget what you're doing for me and my family.'

Her face closed. 'It's just a business arrangement between us, remember,' she whispered back, being very careful she wouldn't be overheard.

So she hadn't felt it. He knew he had no right to feel disappointed. Nevertheless, his mood darkened but he had to keep up with the momentum of excitement as he and Dell were swept back into the *taverna*.

The third time someone wished them *'I ora I kali'* Dell turned to ask him what it meant. 'It means, "May the wedding day come soon",' he replied. 'And we need to have it as soon as possible. My father needs to get back to Sydney to continue his treatment. Is that okay with you?'

She shrugged. 'You're the boss. But of course it's okay with me. The sooner the better really.'

'You have made me very happy, son,' his father said when he reached them. 'Dell, welcome to our family.'

That made it worth it.

His mother burst into tears. 'Of joy, these are tears of joy,' she said, fanning her face with both hands.

'Dell, I've heard so many good things about you I feel I know you already.' She gave another sob. 'And my son looks so happy. Happier than since…well, you know what happened.'

Dell looked to him for help, started to stutter a response but he was saved by his cousin Melina who had helped him with her contacts in Athens. She picked up Dell's left hand. 'Show us your engagement ring, Dell,' she said.

A ring.

He hadn't thought of that.

It was immediately obvious that Dell's hand was bare. She shot a look of panic to him.

'This all happened very quickly,' he said. 'I will be—'

His mother saved him by sliding off a ring, sparkling with a large diamond, from her own left hand and handing it to him. 'Take this. Your father bought it for me for our anniversary a few years back. Our own engagement ring is something much more humble, bought when we were both students.'

She shared a glance of such love with his father, Alex felt stricken. Was faking his own marriage really the way to do this? But there was no going back now.

He took the ring and slid it onto the third finger of Dell's left hand. Her hand was trembling as she held it up for his family's inspection. There was a roar of approval. 'I will get you your own engagement ring, of course,' he said to her.

'That would be the height of hypocrisy and totally unnecessary,' she murmured, smiling for their audience as though she were whispering something romantic.

'You can give this ring back to your mother when our agreement is over.'

To anyone but him, who had got to know her so well over the last weeks, Dell seemed to accept the exuberant hugs and congratulations with happiness and an appropriate touch of bewilderment at how fast things had moved. However he noticed signs of strain around her mouth, a slightly glazed look in her eyes that told him how she was struggling to keep up the façade.

He did the only thing he could do to mask her face from his family. He swept her into his arms and kissed her again. And again for good measure because he didn't want to stop.

Dell was tired, bone weary. Her face hurt from so much forced smiling and acceptance of congratulations. Aunt Penelope's birthday party had turned into a shared celebration to include an informal engagement party for her and Alex. She felt ill-prepared for the wave of jubilation that had picked her up and carried her into the heart of his Greek family.

She had long realised the truth that Greek people were among the most hospitable in the world. Their generosity of welcome to her now stepped up a level because she was going to be part of the family. There was a certain amount of unsaid *I told you so* that, even in her fear of saying the wrong thing and inadvertently revealing the truth about her engagement, made her smile.

One thing came through loud and clear—Alex was well loved by everyone. She heard of his many acts of quiet generosity, the hard work he'd put into family projects. Even the children, who were very much part of the celebration, seemed to adore him, flocking around him. He leaned down to listen very gravely to what one little cherub with a mop of black curls and baby black eyes was saying to him. The toddler could have been his own son. Her heart turned over and she felt very strongly the presence of the baby in her womb. Should Alex have thought more about this plan before sweeping her up into it? Should she have done the sensible thing and said *no*?

It also became obvious how deeply worried his family had been about him. His father, George, explained how, after the siege in Alex's restaurant, he had feared his son had been heading for a breakdown. How desperately concerned he and Eleni, his wife, had been about him. How happy they were that their son had found some measure of peace back in the homeland of his grandfather's family. 'And now this, the best news we could have.'

Eleni patted her hand. 'To marry into a big Greek family can be overwhelming, I know. I will do anything I can to help you. Will your own mother be here?'

Her own parents. What would she say to them? More secrets and lies 'I'm not sure they'll be able to make the wedding at such short notice.' Her astute mother would realise immediately all was not as it should be. It wasn't a real marriage; she was tempted not to tell her parents about it at all.

'That would be a shame,' Eleni said, trying to hide her obvious shock that the bride's mother would not be in attendance.

Dell tried to play it down. 'Did Alex tell you I've been married before? I'm divorced. It's why we want to have a very simple civil ceremony.'

'He did mention it,' Eleni said. 'But it is his first wedding. I can't understand why he wants so little fuss made.' Dell wasn't surprised by the familiar female gaze as it dropped to her middle. 'Although we do understand the need to get married quickly.'

Dell refused to bite. 'George's treatment. Of course, I understand you need to get back to Sydney.'

Just then Aunt Penelope bustled up to take Dell's arm. Dell was immediately aware of an unspoken rivalry between Penelope and Eleni of the *I found her first* variety. Penelope pointed out that the matter of her wedding dress needed immediate attention. A lovely gown was not something that could be made overnight. Dell needed to think about it straight away. And her friend, a dressmaker, happened to be a guest at the party; she should meet her now.

'I'd thought I'd buy a dress off the rack in Athens,' Dell said, casting a helpless call for intervention to the more sophisticated Eleni.

Aunt Penelope didn't miss a thing. 'Ah, you think a village dressmaker could not make you the kind of wedding dress you want? My friend used to work in a bridal couture house in Athens. You show her a picture in any wedding magazine or on the Internet and she can make it for you.' As she led Dell away she added in a low murmur, 'My friend will help you choose the best style to accommodate your bump and allow for the dress to be let out if we need to do so in the days before the wedding.'

Dell stared at Alex's great-aunt, not sure what to say. Penelope laughed. 'You won't be the first Mikhalis bride to have a baby come earlier than expected after the wedding.'

Later, when she and Alex grabbed a quiet moment together Dell told him what had happened. 'Why didn't anyone tell me Aunt Penelope used to be a midwife? She told me she has delivered hundreds, maybe thousands, of babies and that she knew immediately I was pregnant that first day I went to the doctor. How are we going to tell them that the baby isn't yours?'

'We won't,' he said as he got swept away from her by the men to take part in the traditional male dances, some of them unique to these islands, that were an important part of any celebration.

As she watched Alex, as adept as any of the men in the dance, she knew she was there in this happy celebration under completely false pretences. Alex's motivations were worthy but how would these warm, wonderful people feel when they found out they'd been fooled?

Secrets and lies.

The most difficult secret for her to hide was her growing feelings for Alex and the most difficult lie was one she had to tell herself—that she didn't wish, somewhere deep in her heart, that this engagement party and the wedding that would follow as soon as they could arrange it were for real and she really was his much-loved bride.

CHAPTER SIXTEEN

To GET MARRIED in a hurry in Greece involved more paperwork than Dell had imagined, especially when Alex was being wed to a divorced foreigner. Then there had been issues with the venue. In Australia, you could get married anywhere you wanted by a civil celebrant. Not so in Greece. For a civil ceremony there was no choice but to get married in a town hall. The paperwork had been pushed through, expedited by the right people, so they were able to get married. But no one in Alex's family had been happy at the prospect of what they saw as a bland, meaningless civil union.

Before Dell knew it the ancient, tiny white chapel on Kosmimo had been re-consecrated and, two weeks after their impromptu 'engagement', she and Alex were getting the church wedding his family had clamoured for.

This was her not-for-real wedding day and she was feeling nervous. She had not spent much time alone with Alex in the past two weeks. The day after the party for Aunt Penelope, she had moved off Kosmimo and back to the villa. Her morning sickness was practically gone—though the weariness persisted—and the daily boat trips to the island and back to Nidri were bearable. Alex's family didn't think it appropriate they should be living on the island together so close to the wedding.

Dell might have put up an argument about that but in truth it was a relief. She hadn't been able to endure the close proximity to Alex sharing the pavilion with him. It was torture wanting him, knowing she couldn't have him.

She'd repeatedly reminded herself that the marriage was just a business deal. Another employment contract signed with the hospitality tycoon. It was the only way she could retain some measure of sanity among the excitement generated by his family, as they planned the wedding of their beloved son, nephew, cousin, to the Australian girlfriend they had given their seal of approval.

No one seemed to think it was unusual that the engaged couple had so little time together. George and Eleni had moved on to Kosmimo into one of the finished guestrooms. Understandably, Alex wanted to spend as much time as he could with his parents. Dell was always included and she did her best to be affectionate with Alex without anyone suspecting that her edginess was anything but pre-wedding nerves. She tried to hold herself a little aloof from George and Eleni because she really liked them. They were every bit as intelligent as her parents but in a warm, inclusive way. Losing them at the end of the year as well as Alex would be an added level of pain; the thought of losing George earlier was unbearable. Thank heaven she'd agreed to help Alex in his audacious plan.

She didn't have to feign interest in Alex's parents' stories and reminiscences of him as a little boy and rebellious teenager. She lapped up every detail and realised her obvious fascination with everything to do with her husband-to-be was noted and approved. George and Eleni, Aunt Penelope and Uncle Stavros made their delight in his choice of bride only too apparent. If Alex's kisses, staged in sight of some observant family member, got a tad too enthusiastic she was only too happy to go along with them. All in the interests of authenticity.

Two days ago, while working alone with Alex in their office on Kosmimo, she had felt a bubbling sensation in her womb and cried out. Alex had jumped up from his desk and rushed to her. 'What's wrong?' he'd said.

Then with sudden joy she'd realised. 'It's the baby moving inside me.' She'd put her hand on her small bump, waited, and felt the tiniest ripple of movement. 'My baby is kicking, I think.' She'd forgotten all about the complex layers of her relationship with Alex and just wanted to share this momentous discovery with him.

Alex had stood in front of her and she'd realised he was lost for words, a gamut of emotions rippling across his face. She'd been amazed to see shyness and a kind of wonder predominate. 'May I…may I feel it?' he'd finally asked.

Silently she'd taken his hand and placed it on her bump, her hand resting on top of his. The little tremor had come again. Then again. Alex had kept his hand there. When he'd spoken, his voice had been tinged with awe. 'There's a little person in there. Maybe a future football player with a kick like that.'

She'd smiled through sudden tears that had threatened to spill. 'Yes. There really, truly is. My little boy or girl. The baby I've wanted for so long.' Happiness had welled through her. The moment with Alex had been a moment so precious, so unexpected that she'd found herself not daring to say anything further, not wanting to break the magic of it.

Alex had been the first to end the silence between them. His hand had slipped from her bump and he had taken both her hands in his. 'Dell, I know this is something that I—' he'd started. But she never heard what he'd intended to say as the man tiling the kitchens had knocked on the door with a query for Alex.

The by now familiar shutters had come down over Alex's eyes, he'd dropped her hands and stepped back to turn and deal with the tiler, leaving her confused and shaken.

Now she stood at the entrance to the little chapel, in the most picturesque setting she could imagine near the edge of a cliff with perfect blue skies above and the rippling turquoise sea below.

The ceremony was to be a contemporary one, in recognition of the Australian background of both the bride and groom. But there would also be the traditional Greek Orthodox wedding service. She had been walked up from the resort to the chapel by her attendants, Alex's two sisters and his cousin Melina from Athens. His sisters had flown in yesterday from Sydney, husbands and children in tow. Aunt Penelope had organised dresses for all three as well as Melina's sweet little daughter, who had walked ahead strewing rose petals.

It was purely a Mikhalis family occasion and Dell was okay about that. This wasn't about her. It was about Alex and his love and loyalty for his father and her chance to help him right one of the wrongs he imagined he'd caused people close to him.

So here she was, surrounded by so much goodwill and happiness it was palpable, like a wave rushing through the wedding party and guests and whirling them around in its wake. But it was based on a false premise: that she was about to become Alex's loving wife and the mother of his child.

She was a fraud.

Could it be any wonder that, as she took her first steps over the threshold of the chapel, she was the most miserable she had ever been in her life? Her happy-chick face was threatening to crack from overuse. She took a deep breath to try and control her fear of the wrong she was about to do to this family and it came out as a gasp. Immediately friendly, comforting hands were upon her, patting down and soothing what they so obviously saw as a case of bride-to-be jitters.

She couldn't do this.

Then another step took her inside and she saw Alex waiting by the side of the small stone altar that had been festooned by his family with flowers. Her heart seemed to stop. He had never looked more handsome, his black hair and olive skin in striking contrast to his white linen suit. But it was the look of admiration and pride on his face as he caught sight of her that set her heart racing. It wasn't *love*, she knew that, but it was enough to let her decide to rip off that mask she was so weary of wearing and show him how she really felt. Later, she could put it down to what a good actress she had been on the day.

But right now she was going to let the truth shine from her eyes.

She loved him.

The person she had lied to the most was herself. Because she loved Alex Mikhalis with all her heart and soul and she could no longer deny it. She realised this was a make-believe wedding and nothing more would come of it but she was going to behave as though this were her real wedding.

To pretend just for this day there was love and a future.

She smiled back at him, a tremulous smile that she knew revealed her heart completely without artifice. Their gazes connected and held and there was no one else in that tiny church but her and the man she loved. But she could not tell him how deeply and passionately she felt all those things a make-believe bride should not feel for her pretend husband. There would be heartbreak enough when their contract came to an end—one way or another.

Dell in her wedding dress was so breathtakingly beautiful that Alex found himself clenching his hands by his sides in an agony of suppressed emotion. He wasn't aware of anyone or anything else. Not his father and his cousin Cristos by his side. Not the priest behind them. Not the tiny church filled with his Greek family and friends, the scent of roses and a lingering trace of incense, the sound of the sea breaking on the limestone rocks beneath. All his senses were filled by the beauty of the bride walking slowly towards him. *His* bride.

She was wearing an exquisite long dress of fine silk and lace, deceptively simple, cleverly draped to hide the secret everyone seemed to be only too aware of. Her hair was pulled back from her face and entwined with flowers at the nape of her neck and he knew the gown swooped low at the back and finished with a flat bow. She carried a bouquet of white roses and tiny white daisies, the traditional gift of the groom to his bride. Pearl earrings from her new mother-in-law hung from her ears.

He knew the whole wedding was a sham, although created with the best of intentions. But suddenly he ached for this marriage of convenience to be a marriage of the heart. For Dell to be his wife for real. As she took her place next to him and the traditional crowns connected by ribbons were placed on first her head and then on his, the realisation hit him.

She was his wings.

Dell was the one who would help him soar back into the full happiness and joy of life. Without her he would still be grounded, plodding along looking backwards and sideward, sometimes forward but never up to the sky where he longed to be. But he couldn't soar to great heights unless she was by his side. He needed her. *He loved her.*

How blind he'd been, how barricaded against ever finding love, ever thinking he *deserved* love that he hadn't seen it when love had found him. When had he fallen for her? At Bay Breeze when she'd been so kind at a time she'd had every reason to hate him? Or the day she'd zoomed up on her bike so full of life and vitality shining her own brand of brightness into his dark, shadowed life? Whenever it had been, he realised now that the job offer, the move to Greece had all been an excuse to have her nearby.

He had to tell her how he felt.

How ironic they were repeating vows—in Greek

and in English—to bind their lives together. Desperately he tried to infuse all his longing and love for her into their vows, hoping she would sense it, wanting this to be the one and only time he ever made these vows. Vows that made her his lifetime partner. When they were pronounced man and wife he kissed her with a fierce longing surely she must have felt. Then searched her face for a hint of returned feeling, exulting when he saw it, plunging into despair when he realised it could be all part of the game of pretence he had lured her into playing.

But telling her how he felt wasn't possible in a snatched aside between the rounds of congratulations and the endless photos. Then when they walked down the hill to the new resort he had created with her, where the party was to be held, they had to face the reception line that saw them individually greeting their guests.

He felt a pang of regret and sorrow when he realised she had none of her own family and friends there. She had point-blank refused to involve them in what she called the big lie. In all conscience he had not attempted to convince her otherwise. Now he wished he had done what he had wanted to do in the interests of authenticity—gone behind her back and invited her parents and Lizzie and Jesse. Because he didn't intend for her ever to have another wedding—this was it, for him and for her. He had every intention of claiming her for his bride for real.

After the feasting and the speeches, and before the dancing would begin, he managed to lead her out to the marble balcony that looked out over the sea. When a guest with a camera tried to follow them out he gestured for her to leave him alone with his new wife. He and Dell watched her depart and saw her tell others that the bride and groom needed some time together.

Alone with her, Alex found himself behaving like a stuttering adolescent. 'It went well,' he said. Of all things to come out when he had so much he wanted to say. Life-changing words, not inane chit-chat.

'Yes,' she said with a wistfulness he hadn't seen before in her and that nourished the glimmer of hope he'd felt at the church. 'I... I think we managed to...to fool everyone.' Fool them? Fool *him*? 'We both put on quite an act.' *An act?* Was that really all it was for her?

'Dell, did you...did you find yourself during the ceremony wanting...?' Where were his usual eloquent words when he wanted them?

Her brow pleated in a frown. 'Wanting what?'

Wanting our vows to be real. The words hovered on his tongue. But she seemed so cool and contained. What would he do if she denied any feeling for him? He had a year to convince her. He shouldn't rush into this—it was too important for him to get wrong. 'Wanting your family to be there?' he finished lamely.

There were shadows behind her eyes when she looked up at him. Her mouth twisted downwards. 'No, I didn't. There are going to be enough people disappointed and hurt when they find out the truth of what this wedding meant—or didn't mean. I don't want my side dragged into it.'

Her voice wasn't steady and he realised how difficult the deception was for her honest nature, how, although his father was beaming with happiness, perhaps his plan had not been in Dell's best interest. But how very different it might be if their marriage was for real. He had the crazy idea of proposing to her in earnest out here on the balcony. Going down on bended knee. But he thought about it for a moment too long.

She turned away from him, her shoulders slumped before she pulled them back up straight. 'We'd better get back to our guests. Act Three of this performance is about to start—the dancing.' Then she turned back, lifted her face to his in the offer of a kiss. 'We'd better do what our guests will expect us to do, Alex, a husband and wife alone together for the first time.'

When her cool lips met his, he knew she was pretending and he didn't like the feeling one bit. As she moved away he saw the moment she pasted a smile on her face and forced a brightness to her eyes he knew she didn't feel. Making her his bride for real might be more difficult than he had anticipated.

CHAPTER SEVENTEEN

LEAVING HER DISASTROUS encounter with Alex on the balcony, Dell retreated to the bathroom—the only place she could get a few moments to herself. She splashed her face with cool water, being careful not to damage her make-up. There would be more photos to come and she still had to play her role of the happy bride.

Back in the beautiful little church on the clifftop, there had been no need for her to pretend. After the fervent way Alex had repeated his marriage vows, not taking his eyes from hers for a second, her heart had done a dance of joy, convinced he might feel towards her something of what she felt towards him. And that kiss... He had really taken the invitation to kiss his bride to the extreme. Her toes in her kitten-heeled satin shoes curled at the memory of it. No wonder the congregation had applauded them.

But on the balcony his stilted conversation had proved anything but satisfactory. How foolish she had been to let the romance of an extravagant wedding catch her off her guard. And yet... For a moment she'd been convinced he had something important to say. Maybe he had thought it was important to talk about the fact her family wasn't there. But was it because he'd thought it mattered to her or because it might make people question the authenticity of their marriage?

She closed her eyes and let a wave of weariness wash over her. Actually, she'd let her personal feelings overcome her business sense. When her carefully worded press release went out announcing Alex's marriage and the news got out, people might question the lack of participation by her family in the wedding. She'd have to think of a way to explain it. So maybe that was what Alex had been trying to say. But she felt too tired to worry about that just yet. Not just tired. Unwell. She smoothed back her hair from her face and prepared to return to the fray.

Then the cramp hit her. And another. She clutched her stomach protectively. Saw her face go white in the mirror.

Please, not that, not now.

But when she went into the stall to check, there was blood.

Dell rested her face in her hands. Her baby was kicking. She'd allowed herself to believe everything was all right. This couldn't be happening. She couldn't get up, couldn't move, frozen with terror and disbelief and grief.

She didn't know for how long she sat there. But there was a knock on the door. 'Are you all right in there, Dell?'

Aunt Penelope. The woman who had been so good to her since she had arrived in Greece. She was a midwife. Aunt Penelope would know what to do. Dell opened the door.

'The baby?' the older woman asked.

Dell nodded. And let herself be looked after by her new family who weren't really her family at all.

Alex was talking to his cousin Melina about her four-year-old daughter who was their delightful flower girl. He hadn't even known Melina had a child until quite recently. Melina was explaining when his father interrupted them. Alex knew something was wrong when his father tapped him on the arm and took him aside. Dell needed to be taken to hospital urgently. She wasn't well and there was a chance she could be miscarrying. He heard the cry of anguish before realising it was his.

But his father told him he needed to be strong. How much had he had to drink because his speedboat was the fastest way to get his wife off the island? Fortunately all he'd had was a flute of champagne.

His wife.

Alex found Dell surrounded by the women in his family. His aunt, his mother, his sisters. She looked ashen, her eyes fearful, her hair falling in disarray around her face, stripped of her wedding gown and wearing the white dress with the blue tie she'd worn when he'd first kissed her in front of the Parthenon.

But when they saw him, the women stepped back so he could gather her in his arms. She collapsed against him and he could feel her trembling. 'Alex, I'm scared.'

'I know you are, *agapi mou*,' he said, scarcely realising he had used the Greek endearment for *darling*. 'Try not to worry. We're getting you to the hospital as fast as we can.' He knew how important this baby was to her. He would do anything he could to help her.

Alex murmured a constant litany of reassurance as he picked Dell up and carried her out of the building and down the steps leading to the water. But still he hadn't told her how much he loved her.

She protested she could walk but he wasn't taking any chances. He carried her to the dock where his boat, and the boats that had brought over the guests, were moored.

Then the women took over again as he took the wheel, released the throttle and pointed the boat towards Lefkada. People were worried about the baby. He was too. Since the day he had felt it move the baby had become real to him. But he was racked with the terrible fear that something might happen to Dell. He had a sickening sense of history repeating itself. Would he lose Dell as he'd lost Mia with her believing he didn't care about her?

The next morning, Dell lay drowsing in the hospital bed, hooked up to a number of monitors. She felt a change, sensed a familiar scent. When she opened her eyes it was to see Alex sprawled in a chair that had been pulled over by her bedside. He was still wearing his wedding suit, crumpled now, and his jaw was dark with stubble. Even dishevelled he was gorgeous. He wore a wide gold band on his right hand in the Greek manner. The ring that was meant to bind him to her.

Her ring—his mother's ring—was sitting tightly wrapped in her handbag inside the hospital cabinet. She would never wear it again.

'You're awake,' he said, his voice gruff.

'Yes,' she said.

'I didn't think you were ever going to wake up.' She hadn't been asleep the entire time. But she'd requested no visitors. Not even her husband. Until now.

He went to kiss her but she pushed back against her pillow to evade him. 'No need for that. There's no one here we need to fool.' Was that hurt she saw tighten his face? Surely not. She wanted his kiss, *ached* for his kiss. But she needed to keep her distance more.

'I'm sorry about our honeymoon,' she said. 'Have you managed to cancel the booking?' For appearances' sake, they had planned a short break in the old port town of Chania on the southern island of Crete.

His dark brows drew together. 'Why would I care about that when I'm worried sick about you? I haven't slept for fearing something would happen to you. And the baby.'

His reference to the baby surprised her. 'I'm okay,' she said. 'I don't want a fuss. I'm not miscarrying.'

He let out his breath on a great sigh of relief. 'Thank God. Are you sure about that?'

'Yes,' she said. 'But I need to stay in bed for a few days.'

She didn't want to discuss the intimate details with him. They hadn't been intimate. Hadn't made this baby together. It was nothing to do with him. As he'd made so very clear on several occasions.

He leaned closer to her. She could smell coffee on his breath. Noticed his eyes were bloodshot. 'Do you have to stay in hospital?' he asked. 'Or can you come home to Kosmima? I can organise nursing care for you.'

Home. The island wasn't home for her. Much as she had come to love it.

She took a deep breath to steady herself, braced herself against the pillows. 'I'm not coming back to Kosmima, Alex. Not today. Not ever.'

She expected him to be angry but he looked puzzled. Which made this so much harder. 'You want to go back to the villa? Why? That's not part of our agreement.'

'Not the villa. I'm going back to Sydney.'

'What?' The word exploded from him.

Slowly she shook her head. 'I can't do this, Alex. I'm reneging on our agreement. I'm sorry but I just can't live a lie. Your family are so wonderful. Aunt Penelope has been like a mother to me. Your mother too. I... I've come to love them. But I'm an imposter. A fraud. They're all so worried about me losing this baby because they think it's yours. Can you imagine how they will feel when they find out the truth?'

'But we're married now.'

'In name only. It's not a legal marriage.' She couldn't meet his eye. 'It...it hasn't been consummated, for one thing.'

'That could be arranged,' he said slowly.

She caught her breath. 'I know you don't mean that,' she said.

'What if I did?'

'I wouldn't believe you,' she said. 'You've never given any indication whatsoever that...that you wanted this marriage to be real.'

'Neither have you,' he countered.

'Why would I?' she said. 'This...this marriage is a business arrangement. I've signed a contract drawn up by your lawyers.'

'A contract you would be breaking if you went back to Sydney.'

'I'm aware of that,' she said. 'But the consequences of staying with you are so much greater than anything you could do to me by pursuing the broken contract. So sue me. I have nothing.' She displayed empty hands. 'The marriage isn't registered yet. If a marriage in Greece is not registered within forty days, it becomes invalid.'

He didn't say anything in reply to that. His expression was immeasurably sad. 'So it comes full circle, does it, Dell?' he said finally. 'Are we enemies again?'

How could he be an enemy when she loved him so much her heart was breaking at the thought of not being with him? But she couldn't endure a year of living with a man she loved so desperately in a celibate, for-convenience marriage. And then be expected to walk away from it with a cheque in her pocket, never to bother him again.

'Never an enemy, Alex,' she said with a hitch to her voice.

'So why this desire to run away to Australia? Surely it's not just about my family. So we keep to our deal and we break up after a year. Divorce happens all the time.' He shrugged. 'They'll get over it.'

She glared at him. 'You don't get it. You just don't get it, do you? You can't just play around with love, anyone's love.' *My* love.

Her voice was rising but she couldn't do anything to control it. A nurse came into the room. 'Are you okay, Mrs Mikhalis? Is something upsetting you?'

The nurse looked pointedly at Alex, who stood glowering by the chair. But Dell was too stunned at the way she'd so matter-of-factly referred to her as *Mrs Mikhalis* to really notice.

Alex towered over the hospital bed, over the hapless nurse. 'I am her husband and the father of her baby. I am not *upsetting* her. I'm here to take her home. To the people who love her.' Now he completely ignored the nurse, rather turned to face Dell. 'To the man who loves her.'

The nurse knew exactly when to exit the room quietly.

Dell pushed herself up higher in the bed. 'Was that "the man who loves her" bit for the benefit of the nurse, Alex?'

He came closer to the bed, took both her hands in his. 'It's purely for your benefit. I love you, Dell. I have for a long time. It just took me a while to wake up to it.'

'Oh, Alex, I love you too.' She gripped his hands tight. 'I... I thought I had a silly crush on you but... but it was so much more than that.'

'Aunt Penelope, the family, they saw it before we did,' he said.

He leaned down to kiss her, tenderly and with love. The same love she recognised now from his kiss in the church. Her heart started a furious pounding.

'Alex, the wedding. The vows. You meant every word, didn't you?'

'Every word. I was hoping you would recognise that.'

'I meant every word too,' she breathed. He kissed her again.

'That means we really are married,' he said. 'Registered or not. I want to take you home with me where you belong.'

'But what about the baby? You said you could never take on another man's child.'

He frowned. 'Somehow, I have never thought of the child as anyone's but yours,' he said. 'Then when I felt your baby move beneath my hand, I realised it didn't matter who was the sperm donor. The father will be the man who welcomes it into the world, who loves its mother, who truly *fathers* it, like my father fathered me.'

'That's quite a turnaround,' she said, a little breathlessly. 'Do you really believe that?'

'Our little flower girl today, you know she is adopted?'

'No, I didn't know that.'

'Neither did I, until Melina happened to mention it today. I was in Sydney at the time. She said she loved her little girl the minute she first held her in her arms. Her husband felt the same.'

'She's a very loved child, that's obvious,' Dell said thoughtfully.

'That she is. So why would I not love your child, Dell? I love you so that's halfway there. I guess I won't know how I feel exactly until I see him or her but I guess no parent does. I'll be there at the birth if you want me to and be involved from the very beginning.'

Dell put her hand protectively on her bump. She smiled. 'He or she—I hate saying *it*—just gave me a hefty kick. I think he or she is listening and giving his or her approval.'

Alex smiled too, his eyes lit with a warmth that thrilled her. 'I think the baby is telling me to take you home and love you and make a happy life together.'

'That baby has the right idea,' she said.

She swung herself out of bed so she could slide more comfortably into his arms. 'We're already married so I can't really ask you to marry me, but I think I will anyway. Alex, will you be my husband for real?'

'So long as you'll be my wife,' he said.

She laughed. 'I think we both agree on that. I love you, Mr Mikhalis.'

'I love you too, Mrs Mikhalis,' he said as he kissed her again, long and lovingly.

CHAPTER EIGHTEEN

One year later

DELL RELAXED BACK in the shade of the pavilion near the swimming pool and watched as her husband played with their daughter in the water. Litsa squealed in delight as Alex lifted her up in his arms and then dipped her into the water with a splash. 'We'll have her swimming before she's walking,' he called.

The baby gurgled her delight. At just six months old, she was nowhere near talking but she was very communicative, as she'd been in the womb. She and Alex had had endless fun making up meanings for her bump's kicks and wiggles.

Dell waved to her precious little lookalike. Litsa had been born with her mother's auburn hair and creamy skin but with brown eyes. People often remarked that she had the best of both her and Alex. Husband and wife would look at each other and smile. Alex had legally adopted Litsa. They would choose the right time to one day tell her about her biological father.

Alex need not have worried about bonding with the baby. As he'd promised, he'd been there at the birth and had adored his daughter at first sight. So had Dell.

Motherhood was everything she had dreamed of. Even more as she was enjoying it buoyed with the love and support of the husband she grew to love more each day.

She and Alex had debated whether or not to move back to Sydney but had decided to stay in Greece, at least in the short term. Pevezzo Athina had been such a success that it was already completely booked out for the season and beyond. They still lived in the pavilion but Alex had started building them a magnificent new house out of sight of the resort but within sight of the little church where they'd married and Litsa had been christened. Her blog had taken a slight change in direction but had not lost her any readers—rather she had gained them.

The best news was that Alex's father, George, had gone into remission and was a devoted grandfather when he visited Greece, which he did more often. He and Eleni even talked of buying a house nearby when they retired and living between both countries.

Much to Dell's surprise her mother had become the most doting of grandmas—after she'd got over the hurt of being excluded from the wedding. When Dell had taken her into her confidence and explained why, her mother had forgiven her. She'd surprised Dell by telling her that she and her father had always disliked Neil but hadn't wanted to criticise their daughter's choice of husband. When they'd flown to Greece to meet their new son-in-law, her parents had given their full approval. Alex had taken to them too.

There was a friendly rivalry between her mother and Eleni over who would spend the most time in Greece with their granddaughter. When the grandmothers had met after Litsa's birth, they'd realised they'd met each other before at a pharmaceutical conference and a genuine friendship had formed.

Who knew? Dell now mused. She would have to figure out a time to tell both the grandmas her news at the same time.

Alex gave Litsa a final plunge in the pool and swung her up into his arms to a peal of baby giggles. As her husband walked out of the pool, his lean, powerful body glistening with water, Dell felt the intense surge of love and desire she always felt for him.

'Are you feeling okay?' he asked. 'Need more dry crackers, more lemonade?'

'Ugh,' she said. 'No, thanks.'

No one had been more surprised than Dell when she'd fallen pregnant. For so long she'd thought herself the problem in her battles with fertility. Turned out she'd been married to the wrong man. Or that was what Alex said anyway. She could only agree.

* * * * *

If you've enjoyed this book, look out for
THE BRIDESMAID'S BABY BUMP
by Kandy Shepherd. Available now!

If you want to treat yourself to another
second chance romance, look out for
A MARRIAGE WORTH SAVING
by Therese Beharrie.

"I want to be with you, Jody. And not just as a friend."

"B-but I..." God. She was sputtering. And why did she suddenly feel light as a breath of air, as if she was floating on moonbeams? "You want to be with me? But you don't do that. You've made that very clear."

"You're right. I didn't do that. Until now. But things have changed."

"Because of Marybeth, you mean?"

"Yeah, because of Marybeth. And because of you, too. Because of the way you are. Strong and honest and smart and so pretty. Because we've got something going on, you and me. Something good. I'm through pretending that we're friends and nothing more. Are you telling me I'm the only one who feels that way?"

"I just..." Her pulse raced and her cheeks felt too hot. She'd promised herself that nothing like this would happen, that she wouldn't get her hopes up.

She needed to be careful. She could end up with her heart in pieces all over again.

* * *

The Bravos of Justice Creek:
Where bold hearts collide under western skies

THE LAWMAN'S CONVENIENT BRIDE

BY
CHRISTINE RIMMER

MILLS & BOON

First Published in Great Britain 2017
By Mills & Boon, an imprint of HarperCollins*Publishers*
1 London Bridge Street, London, SE1 9GF

© 2017 Christine Rimmer

ISBN: 978-0-263-92296-7

23-0517

Our policy is to use papers that are natural, renewable and recyclable products and made from wood grown in sustainable forests. The logging and manufacturing processes conform to the legal environmental regulations of the country of origin.

Printed and bound in Spain
by CPI, Barcelona

Christine Rimmer came to her profession the long way around. She tried everything from acting to teaching to telephone sales. Now she's finally found work that suits her perfectly. She insists she never had a problem keeping a job—she was merely gaining "life experience" for her future as a novelist. Christine lives with her family in Oregon. Visit her at www.christinerimmer.com.

For every brave soul
who dares to love again.

Chapter One

Sheriff Seth Yancy worked hard for his community. He lived to serve the citizens of tiny Broomtail County, Colorado, and he would do just about anything for his constituents.

But a bachelor auction?

No way would he agree to be a prize in one of those. Being raffled off to the highest bidder was beneath his dignity. Plus, he would have to go out with the winner. Seth hadn't gone out with anyone in almost four years. And way back when he did go out, it hadn't been with a woman from town—or anywhere in Broomtail County, for that matter.

He was single and planned to stay that way. Dating someone who lived in his community, well, that could get messy. Seth didn't do messy. As sheriff, he tried to set a good example in all aspects of his personal life.

And that meant that when the president of the library association asked him to be a prize in her upcoming bachelor auction, Seth went right to work gently and regretfully turning her down.

He sat back in his new leather desk chair in his brand-new office in the recently opened Broomtail County Justice Center on the outer edge of the small town of Justice Creek and said, "The last Saturday in May? I'm sorry, Mrs. Carruthers. That's a bad day for me." It wasn't really a lie, he reasoned. Because if he said yes to the woman in the guest chair across from him, it *would* be a bad day.

"Call me Caroline." She crossed her slim legs and folded her hands on her knee.

"Sure, Caroline. What time did you say the auction was?"

"We're planning an all-day event in the park. But you would only need to be there between, say, two and four."

"Two and four," he repeated, stalling a little, as though he really did want to help her out. And he did. Just not for this.

Caroline beamed at him from behind her cat's-eye glasses. "So then. We can count on you as one of our bachelors. I'm so pleased."

"Hmm. Hold on, now. I'll have to check." He clicked the mouse on his desktop and made a show of frowning at the screen. "I'm sorry, but between two and four is impossible." It was an outright lie this time. And Seth did not approve of lying. But to get out of being raffled off like a prize bull, he would sink pretty low. "I just can't make it."

Caroline's sweet smile never wavered, though her eyes were a flinty, determined shade of gray. "Sheriff, I can't tell you how much it would mean to us if you could find a way to rearrange your schedule and say yes."

He cleared his throat, the sound downright officious even to his own ears. "I'm sorry. Really."

She adjusted her glasses, causing the beaded neck strap to twinkle aggressively. "Did I mention yet that the auction will help finance the library's new media center?"

"Yes, you did, and I—"

"It's a great cause. An important project. Children who don't have access to the internet need a chance to become familiar with the life tools others take for granted. And how many of our seniors wish they could broaden their horizons and move into the digital age? The center is so much more than just a bonus for our community. It's an out-and-out necessity."

"Yes, I understand that. But I really can't—"

"And it will take so little of your time, Sheriff. A couple of hours in Library Park the day of the auction and then one date with the lucky lady who bids the most for you. We've gotten Silver Star Limousine from Denver to donate a limo for your date. The winning ladies will each get a spa day at Sweet Harmony Day Spa. You'll be expected to pay for the date, of course, and I know you and the happy girl who wins you will choose something memorable and fun to do together."

"I understand, but as I keep trying to tell you, Caroline, I really can't."

"Oh, yes, you can." She blasted that smile at him, brighter than ever. "We all do admire the important work you do here. We're grateful for your service to this community."

"Well, thank you. I—"

"Of all the eligible bachelors in our county, I believe you are the most respected." Eligible? Seth might be single, but he was far from eligible. To be eligible, a man had to be willing to get involved in a relationship, and he wasn't. Caroline's gray eyes seemed to bore right through him. "Respected and so greatly admired. Word does get around. I've heard about your fan club..."

His fan club. He supposed that didn't sound so bad. At least she hadn't called them badge bunnies, which a lot of civilians considered cool police slang. Seth found the term sexist and objectifying—and, yes, he knew all about sexism. It was part of his job to know about it and to squelch it whenever it reared its ugly head. He didn't approve of terms that objectified anyone. And as for his "fan club," there weren't that many of them. But they were certainly enthusiastic, always dropping by to see him with baked goods and big smiles. Seth skirted a fine line with the women in question. He tried to be polite and appreciative while never letting any of them get too close.

If he gave in and said yes to the auction, one of them would probably "win" him. How awkward would that be?

He didn't even want to think about it.

And Caroline was still talking. "A tweak of your calendar, a few hours in the park and a date with a generous, community-conscious woman. Just one date. For the needy children who can so easily be left behind, for the seniors with ever-narrowing horizons."

He willed Garth Meany, the dispatcher, whose narrow back he could see through his inner-office window, to get a call—nothing too serious, a drunk and disorderly or someone creating a public nuisance. No one should get hurt. All Seth wanted was a chance to "notice" Garth on that call. He could bounce to his feet, mumble something about a "390" or a "507" that required his immediate attention—and hustle Caroline right out the door.

Unfortunately, it was a Tuesday afternoon in April, and the citizens of Broomtail County were apparently sober and behaving themselves. "Caroline, I'm so sorry, but I have another appointment in—"

"Just say the magic word, and I'll get out of your hair."

"But I —"

"Please." Now her eyes were huge and mournful behind the slanted, glittery frames. "Sheriff. We need you."

He opened his mouth to say no again. But Caroline looked so sad for all those disadvantaged children with no access to the internet, all those shut-in seniors who didn't even know how to send an email. He really did hate lying. And did she have to keep using that word, *need*?

Seth Yancy was a bitter man in many ways. His life hadn't turned out the way he'd once hoped it might. And the last few months, since the sudden death of his only brother, Nick, had been nothing but grim for him. Nicky was a good guy, the best. And way too young to die. It just wasn't right, that he'd been taken.

Too many were taken. And always the ones who deserved long, full lives.

But even though he'd been feeling more down than usual lately, Seth still liked to believe he was a good public servant, that when the people of his county needed him, one way or another, he would come through.

Caroline regarded him steadily, waiting for his reply.

And by then, for Seth, there was only one answer to give. "All right. I'll rearrange my schedule."

An hour later, Caroline was long gone, off to corner some other poor schmuck and badger him into making a fool of himself on the bachelor auction block. Seth was still in his office reviewing last month's budget overages, with the jail's operations report still to get through.

But enough. He was done for the day.

The budget and the reports could wait until tomorrow. After being bested by that Carruthers woman, he needed a fat, juicy steak and a twice-baked potato, and he knew where to get them.

The Sylvan Inn sat in a small wooded glen a few miles outside of town. At four thirty in the afternoon on a weekday, the parking lot had one row of cars in it—the row closest to the front entrance. Seth pulled in at the end of that row.

Inside, the hostess led him straight to a deuce by a window that looked out on a shaded patio. Perfect. He felt the cares of the day melting away.

Caroline Carruthers?

Never heard of her.

His waitress, Monique Hightower, appeared. Seth had known Monique for a good twenty years, at least. They'd attended Justice Creek High about the same time, with him graduating a couple of years ahead of her. She'd been working here at the Inn for a decade, maybe more.

"Hey, Seth. You're earlier than usual for a weekday." Monique refilled the water glass he'd already emptied and set the bread basket in front of him. "Everything okay?" Monique was a good waitress, but she talked too much. And she had a rep for being overly interested in other people's business.

He replied, "Everything is just fine, thanks," in a tone that discouraged further conversation. "I'll have the house salad with blue cheese, a Porterhouse, bloody, and a fully loaded potato." A beer would really hit the spot, but he was still in uniform. "And bring me a nice, big Coke."

Monique jotted down his order. "Be right back with your drink and that salad." She trotted off, blond cork-screw curls bouncing in her high ponytail.

She was as good as her word, too, bouncing right back over with a tall, fizzy Coca-Cola and a plateful of greens.

Seth buttered a hunk of hot bread and got down to the business of enjoying his meal. By the time the steak and potato arrived, he felt better about everything. The auction was almost six weeks away. He'd put it on his calendar, and he'd promised Caroline he would pose for a picture and work up a bio that would make the women of Justice Creek eager to bid on him. He wasn't looking forward to either activity, but as soon as they were accomplished, he could forget about the whole thing until he had to show up at the park the last Saturday in May.

"All done?" Monique stood at his elbow.

"Yeah. It was terrific, as always."

She took his plate. "Wait till you see the dessert cart. On the house for you, Seth."

"Thanks, Monique. Just the check."

And off she went, returning in no time with the bill. He gave her his credit card. Not three minutes after that, she set down the leather check folder on the white tablecloth. He put his card away and picked up the pen.

"So. Jody seems to be doing great, don't you think, all round and rosy?" It was Monique. For some reason, she'd remained standing right behind him.

He added the tip and scratched in his signature. "Jody?"

Monique leaned a little closer and spoke very softly. "Jody Bravo."

He remembered then. Jody Bravo. Pretty brunette. Daughter of Frank Bravo, deceased, and Frank's second wife, Willow Mooney Bravo. Willow Bravo was a piece of work. She'd carried on a decades-long affair with Frank while his rich first wife, Sondra, was still alive. Sondra had given Frank four children. Pretty much simultaneously, Willow had given him five. Including Jody, who owned a flower shop on Central.

Jody and Nick had been friends there for a while, at the end.

Monique said, "She's due next month, right?"

This was getting weird. "Due to...?"

"Have the baby, of course."

Evidently, Jody Bravo was pregnant. Given that she'd been a friend of Nicky's, he probably should have known that.

But why, exactly, did Monique Hightower think she ought to bring it up to him?

He dropped the pen on the open check folder. "Monique."

"Yeah?"

"Come on around here where I can see you."

She sidled into his line of sight looking uncomfortable now, giving him big eyes and a sweet never-mind of a smile. "So. Can I get you anything else?"

He hit her with his lawman's stare, dead-on with zero humor. "You went this far. Better finish it, whatever it is."

"Ahem." She slid a glance toward the kitchen, scoping out the location of her boss, no doubt. "I...thought you knew, that's all."

"Knew what?"

"Well, I mean that the baby Jody's having..." The sentence wandered off into nowhere.

"Go on."

"Well, Seth. It's, um, Nick's baby."

Nick's baby.

Seth heard a strange roaring in his ears, as though the ocean were right outside the window, giant waves beating on that pretty shaded patio. "Did you just say that Jody Bravo is having Nick's baby?"

Monique's curly knot of hair bobbed frantically with her nod. She leaned close and whispered, "I can't believe you haven't heard. I mean, I know he was your stepbrother, but you two were closer than most blood-related brothers. And it's not as if Jody's been keeping it a secret. Everybody knows that baby is Nick's, that it's a girl, due at the end of May."

The roaring of the invisible ocean got louder.

...it's a girl. Everybody knows...

Everybody but *him*.

Come to think of it, Nicky'd had a crush on that Bravo woman, hadn't he?

That was back in the late summer and fall, not long before Nick died. Nick had told Seth he had a thing for

Jody, but that Jody didn't feel the same, so they were "just friends."

Just friends. That had pissed Seth off. He'd wondered if that Bravo woman was leading his little brother on. After all, she had to be, what, eight or nine years older than Nick?

And Nicky had always been too easy, too tender and open, his big heart just begging for someone to break it. Maybe Jody Bravo had some idea that Nick wasn't good enough for her because he was a simple guy, happy to work the family ranch for a living, a guy who hadn't been to some fancy college.

If so, she was a fool. There was no man better than Nick.

And wait a minute. She came to the funeral, didn't she? Walked right up and shook Seth's hand, said how sorry she was.

But she didn't say a single word about any baby.

"Oh, look," Monique piped up nervously. "One of my other customers needs more coffee. Good to see you, Seth. Have a great day…" She was already bouncing away.

Seth let her go. He needed more information, but he knew better than to seek it from Monique. The invisible ocean still roaring inside his head, he rose, pushed his chair back under the table and headed for the door.

Once back in his cruiser, he started the engine and got out of there, turning back onto the highway going east, away from town. For a while, he just drove, tuning out the chatter on the scanner, willing his blood to stop thundering through his veins.

Had he planned to go home? Kind of. But he didn't. He blew right by the turnoff to the Bar-Y.

Maybe it wasn't even true. Monique was hardly a reliable source, after all; she could so easily be wrong about everything, or even lying.

But what if it *was* true?

Was that Bravo woman ever planning to tell him?

Halfway to I-25, at the small town of Lyons, he did turn the cruiser around. He went back the way he'd come. But he didn't take the turnoff to the Bar-Y then, either. He drove on past it and straight into town, where he found a parking place right on Central a few doors down from Jody Bravo's flower shop.

At twenty past six, he stood between the tubs of bright flowers and thick greenery that flanked the shop's glass door. His pulse thundering louder than ever, he went in. A little bell tinkled overhead, and Jody Bravo, behind the counter across the room, glanced his way.

Even with the counter masking her body from the waist down, he could see she was pregnant. And pretty far along, too. That belly looked ready to pop.

He let his gaze track upward to her face. Did she pale at the sight of him? He couldn't be sure. But she definitely looked wary, her soft mouth drawn tight, a certain watchfulness in her eyes.

"Sheriff," she said coolly. "I'll be right with you." And she turned a friendly smile to the older man she was waiting on. "Roses and lilies." She passed him a paper-wrapped cone full of flowers. "Excellent choice. I know she'll love them…"

Seth hovered near the door, not sure what to do with himself. Another customer came in, and he moved to the side to clear the entrance. And then he just stood there, surrounded by greenery, breathing that moist, sweet smell created by so many flowers and growing things pressing in close.

"Seth?" asked the Bravo woman as the second customer went out the door.

He realized he was staring blankly at a hanging basket full of cascading purple flowers. "Right here," he answered, though she was standing directly behind him and no doubt looking straight at him. He turned around and met those wary eyes. "We need to talk."

Resigned. She looked resigned. His certainty increased that Monique had not lied; that giant belly cradled his brother's child.

Nicky's baby. He didn't know what he felt. Joy, maybe. And something else, something angry and ready for a fight.

She said, "It's time to close. I need to bring in the stock from out in front and deal with the register."

"I'll help."

"No, it's fine. I can—"

"I said, I'll help." It came out as a growl.

She stiffened, but then she answered calmly, "Well. All right, then. If you'll bring in the flowers." She gestured at a section of bare floor space not far from the door. "Just put them there for now."

"For now?"

"I'll take them to the cooler in back later."

"As long as I'm bringing them in, I can take them where you want them to go." He put out a hand toward the glass-doored refrigerator full of fancy arrangements that took up much of one wall. "You want them in there?"

She bit her lip like she was about to argue with him. But then she said, "No, there's a walk-in cooler in back."

She pointed at the café doors near the check-out counter. "Through there."

"All right, then. I'll bring everything in."

They got to it. She turned off the Open sign and closed out the register while he carried in the tubs of flowers, trekking them through the inner door to the other fridge. Once all the tubs were in, she locked the shop door. There was an ironwork gate between her shop and the one next door, but it was shut, the shop on the other side dark and quiet.

She must have seen him glance that way. "My half sister Elise owns Bravo Catering and Bakery through there. She closed at six."

And so they were alone, with no chance of interruption.

He got to the point. "I heard a rumor that you're having my brother's baby."

He didn't know what he'd expected. Denial? Nervousness? An apology for holding out on him?

But all he got from her was the barest hint of a shrug, followed by a quietly spoken confirmation. "Yes. Nick was my baby's father."

The soft words struck him like blows. All at once, his ears were burning. His stomach clenched, and he really wished he hadn't eaten so much steak.

Sucking in a long breath through his nose, he accused, "You were at the funeral."

"Yes."

"You stepped right up to me. You shook my hand. You had to know there was a baby then."

"Yes, I did."

"But you said nothing." He gave her a look meant to make her knees shake and waited for her to explain herself. When she only regarded him steadily, he demanded, "What is the matter with you? Why am I the last to know? My brother has been dead for almost six months, and until Monique Hightower shared the news today, I had no idea there was a baby involved."

That seemed to get through to her. Scowling now, she whipped up a hand, palm flat in his face. "Don't you get on me, Sheriff. I thought you knew—and didn't care."

Didn't care? That knocked him back. He took a moment to gather his composure. And then he said, deadly calm, "You thought wrong. Did Nick even know?"

Slowly, she lowered her hand to her side. Her diamond-shaped face was all eyes at that moment, eyes of a blue so deep they looked black. Those eyes stared right through him. "He knew."

Seth couldn't help but scoff when she said that. "Oh, no. Uh-uh."

"Why even ask if you're not willing to accept my answer?"

"I guess I had some crazy idea you might tell me the truth."

"That *is* the truth."

"How long did he know?"

"I told him a few days after I found out myself. That was about six weeks before he died."

"I don't believe you."

Twin spots of color flamed high on her cheeks. "Keep calling me a liar, and I'm just going to have to ask you to leave."

Was he out of line? Probably. A little. But she should have told him that his dead brother had fathered a child. And that she'd told Nicky? He couldn't see it. "Nick was a stand-up guy. If he'd known there was a baby, he would have wanted to marry you. That was who he was, a simple man with a big heart and high standards, a man whose own natural father deserted him *and* his mother. Nick wouldn't do that. If he knew about that baby, you'd have a ring on your finger—and there is no way that he would have..." His throat locked up. He swallowed hard to loosen it and then tried again. "If Nick knew he was going to be a father, he would've told *me*."

Chapter Two

Jody Bravo stared at the shiny badge pinned to the starched khaki dress shirt right above Seth Yancy's heart and tried to decide what to say next.

Unlike Nick, who'd been lean and wiry, of medium height, Seth was a tall man, imposing, built broad and tough. Not as handsome as Nick, but a good-looking man if you liked them strong-jawed and dripping testosterone. He was one of those guys who looked like a cop in or out of his uniform, as if he'd been born to protect and serve and would do so whether you wanted him to or not. He wore his brown hair clipped short and his posture was ramrod-straight.

His anger with her? It came off him in waves.

Yes, she should have told him about the baby earlier. She supposed. In hindsight. But she found him so... forbidding. At the funeral, when she'd offered her condolences, he'd narrowed his eyes at her and muttered a grudging *thank you*. She'd read his attitude loud and clear; he couldn't wait for her to move on. So, yeah, she'd kept putting off telling him, kept asking herself why it even mattered if the step-uncle knew about Nick's baby or not? At the same time, she'd had some vague plan to go see him, have a little talk with him, eventually, when the moment felt right.

But the moment never felt right. Also, she really had wondered if he knew about the baby already and simply didn't care. So, yeah, she'd been struggling with a powerful desire never to have to deal with the guy in any way, shape or form.

But right now she just felt sorry for him. So what if he was acting like a first-class douche canoe with his judgmental attitude and insensitive accusations?

The man missed his baby brother. And he was hurt that Nick hadn't confided in him.

As for the marriage question, she didn't even want to get into that with him. But still. He was here and clearly he cared. She gave him the truth. "Nick did ask me to marry him. I turned him down."

"Why?"

She did know what he meant by the curtly uttered question, but she was feeling just snarky enough to ask for clarification anyway. "Why did he ask me, you mean?"

"Why did you turn him down?" He barked that one at her.

Stay calm, she reminded herself. "Nick was a wonderful guy. He deserved a woman who loved him with all of her heart."

His lip curled in a sneer. "And you didn't."

"You should stop talking," she said with excruciating sweetness. "Because I have to tell you, Seth. Every time you open your mouth, you give me a new reason *not* to be nice to you. I'm sorry Nick didn't tell you. But I was only three months pregnant when he died. I'm sure he thought he had plenty of time."

"Plenty of time. My God. Plenty of…" Seth shook his head. His upper lip was sweating.

Again, her exasperation with him faded.

Nick had told her all about the big brother he admired so much. He'd said Seth was the kind of man you wanted at your back in a tough situation, always cool and even-tempered, a man who kept command of himself and his emotions no matter how bad things got.

But right now, Seth Yancy was far from cool. He stared at a point somewhere beyond her left shoulder. It seemed to her he hovered on the brink of losing it completely.

Jody stepped forward and wrapped her fingers around his rock-hard forearm. "Seth."

He flinched and blinked down at her hand. "What?"

"It's okay."

"I don't…"

"Shh. Come on." She pulled him to a bentwood chair by the window, an old one she'd decorated by painting it with twining vines and little flowers. "Sit right here. Let me get you some water…" She gently pushed him down.

He resisted. "No. No, I'm all right."

"Humor me?" she coaxed.

Slowly, he sank into the chair. She let go of his arm—and he grabbed her hand. "Look. Honestly. I don't know what my problem is. I shouldn't have been so hard on you…"

"It's okay," she soothed.

"I apologize. I didn't know you were having Nicky's baby. I really didn't know."

"It's okay…"

He blinked and frowned up at her. "You keep saying that."

"Because I have this feeling that you're not hearing me."

He kept hold of her fingers with one hand and scrubbed the other one down his face. "I heard you."

Gently, she pulled free of his grip. "Stay here. I'll be right back."

Seth did what she asked of him. He sat there in that spindly chair until she returned with a bottled water. "Here you go. Drink." She pressed it into his hand.

He stared up at her, at her worried eyes and her serious mouth. "I'm not usually such a jackass."

Her mouth twitched in the beginnings of a smile she didn't quite let happen. "I really do understand. I'm sure it's a shock."

"I…"

She tapped the sweating water bottle. "It's nice and cold. Drink."

It wasn't a bad suggestion, especially given that his mouth felt like he'd just swallowed a bucket of sand. So he unscrewed the lid and put the bottle to his lips. He drank it down in one go.

"Better?" she asked.

"Yeah. Thanks—and I am sorry. I don't know what got into me."

"You're forgiven." She spoke softly. Her eyes were kind now.

He had a thousand questions to ask her. He hardly knew where to start. But what he did know was that he *would* be a part of Nick's baby's life. "I want to help. Any way I can."

"Well, thank you…" The words were right. Her expression wasn't. She bit the corner of her lip and fell back a step.

He wanted to grab her arm and pull her in close again. "What's wrong with my wanting to help?"

"Nothing. Nothing at all. It's very kind of you, and I appreciate the offer. Right now, though, there's nothing to help me with. I'm all set."

"Set? How's that?"

"Honestly, there's nothing more to do at this point. I've got everything handled. I have excellent insurance and I'm getting great prenatal care. I'm watching my diet, taking my vitamins. The baby and I are both in good health. The baby's room is ready. My sisters are all three helping out, planning to be with me through labor and delivery. I have full-time backup here at the store for those first weeks after the birth. My due date is a month and a half away, and I'm all ready to go."

"Well, great," he replied, though to him it was anything but. He needed to help her, and how could he do that if she had everything under control?

She added too brightly, "But I promise I'll be in touch as soon as she's born."

"It's a she?" he parroted blankly, remembering that Monique had said the baby would be a girl.

"Yes." Jody did manage a smile then. "Her name is Marybeth."

Marybeth. Nicky's little girl will be named Marybeth. "I still want to help."

"And you can."

"Tell me what to do."

A nervous laugh escaped her. "As I said, I can't think of anything right now, but you never know…" The way she was looking at him? Not good. Like she wished he would leave, and the sooner the better.

And he couldn't blame her for wanting him gone. He'd jumped down her throat, done a first-class imitation of an overbearing ass, when he should have been gentle and coaxing and kind.

He really ought to go. He should retreat and regroup— and do a better job of acting like a civilized human being the next time he talked to her.

So all right. Next time would be better. He bent to set the water bottle on the floor, lifted the flap on his right breast pocket and pulled out one of the business cards the county provided for him. "Got a pen?"

"Uh. Sure." She zipped over to the counter with the register on it and came back with a Bic.

He took it and jotted his private numbers on the back of the card. "Call me at the justice center anytime, for anything. And you can reach my cell and the phone at the ranch with the numbers on the back."

"I… Great. Thanks." She accepted the card and the return of her pen and looked down at him expectantly, waiting for him to get up and get out.

And he would. Soon. But first there were things he had to tell her, stuff she needed to know. "After we lost Nicky, I moved to the ranch."

"Ah. That's right. You used to live in…?"

"Prideville." The former county seat was a forty-mile drive from Justice Creek. "With the justice center here now, I wanted to be nearby anyway. And my dad retired to Florida a few years back. We've got a great couple, Mae and Roman Califano, out at the Bar-Y. They're good people. And they can run the place with their hands tied behind their backs. But I think it's important to have someone in the family living there."

"Yes. Yes, I can see that."

"You know how to get to the Bar-Y, right? You've been there, haven't you?"

"Yes. I have, a few times, actually—last fall, after Nick and I became friends. And I've met the Califanos, too. I liked them."

He tried not to stare at her belly. He had a yen to touch it, to see if the baby might give a little kick, provide him with tangible proof that Nicky's child lived.

But he knew he'd blown his chances for any belly-feeling today. "Just in case, I can jot down the address for you..."

"No. Really, I know how to get to the Bar-Y—I mean, if I need to get there." Her gaze shifted toward the door and then right back to him, as though she could hustle him out with the flick of a glance. He took another card from his pocket and held it out to her.

He watched a dimple tucking itself in at the corner of her mouth. "Seth." She held up the first card. "I already have one."

"Jody, I would really appreciate having your numbers, too." He said it hopefully, pouring on the sincerity, though as sheriff, he would have no trouble getting his hands on just about anything he needed to know about her. But it was better if she volunteered her contact information. That way when he called, it would be because she'd given him tacit permission to do so.

"Oh. Well, sure." She accepted the card, scribbled on the back of it and returned it to him.

"Great." He stuck the card back in his pocket. And then, reluctantly, he stood.

She flew to the door, turned the lock and pulled it open. "Thanks, Seth. I'm...glad you came by."

No, she wasn't. But it was nice of her to say so. "Call me. I mean it. Anytime."

"Yes. All right. I will."

He didn't believe her. But that was okay. If she didn't get in touch with him, he would be contacting her.

He was helping out whether she wanted him to or not.

"So will you call him?" Elise asked the next morning at the bakery. Three or four days a week, they shared breakfast at a small table tucked away in a corner. Bravo Catering and Bakery was already open. Jody would open Bloom in half an hour.

Jody leaned toward her sister across the table. "I have zero reason to call that man." She kept her voice low in order not to share her private business with every customer in the place.

Elise fiddled with her ginormous engagement diamond. She did that a lot, usually while smiling dreamily. She and Jed Walsh, the famous thriller writer, were getting married at the end of June. And actually, she was looking more thoughtful than dreamy right at the moment. "He's the baby's uncle, right? And he really wants to help. You said so yourself."

"There's nothing to help with. I'm so completely on top of this whole situation. You guys threw me three showers. There's nothing left to buy. The baby could come tomorrow. I'm ready to go. I mean, I have three birth coaches, present company included."

Elise gave a little snort. "You are so efficient I can't stand it. I get it. You've got this. It's all under control."

"As a matter of fact, it is. And I do."

"Kids do need family, though."

"Handled. We're Bravos. There are too many of us to count."

"Seth Yancy is your baby's family, too—and I can't believe I even have to remind you of that."

Jody stared into her steaming cup of rooibos tea. "Okay, Leesie. I get it. And I know you're right." She took a thoughtful sip. "I'll…reach out to him."

"You do realize you shudder when you say that?"

"I find him intimidating, okay? And the way he looks at me." She couldn't suppress another shiver. "Like I need a good talking-to, you know? Like I wasn't brought up properly and my moral compass is all out of whack."

Loyal to the core, Elise jumped right to Jody's defense. "Well, that's just rude. Maybe I should have a word with him."

Jody snorted a laugh. "Don't you dare—and really, he's not *that* bad. He was upset that I hadn't told him about the baby. And he was curt with me at Nick's funeral, but that's understandable. Nobody's at their best after losing a brother out of nowhere in a tractor accident."

"So. You'll give him a chance, then?"

"Yeah. Yeah, I will." But not until later. She had it all together this time around. She didn't need Seth Yancy's help.

True, he had a right to know his niece. And he would. After Marybeth was born, she would give him a call.

Elise said, "A week from Saturday Jed has to fly to New York for some publicity thing. He wants me to go."

"Can you afford to be away? Don't we have two parties that weekend?" Jody used the word *we* loosely. Her part would be minimal. Bloom would provide floral centerpieces for both events.

"They're just small dinner parties. Danielle can run them." Danielle was Elise's second in command at Bravo Catering.

"So go."

"I don't know. I want to be here for you, in case you need me."

Jody groaned. "Oh, please. I'm in perfect health. The baby is doing great, and I'm not due till the end of May. And if anything happened—which it won't—Nellie and Clara are a phone call away." Nell Bravo and Clara Ames were their other two sisters.

Elise fiddled with her ring some more. "I would be gone for four days, Saturday through Tuesday."

"Not a problem."

"It seems like a long time."

"Elise. Stop worrying."

"I'm trying."

"I've had no cramping, no spotting, not a single sign that the baby might be early."

"And besides, first babies usually come late, right?"

"Right." Jody tried not to look guilty.

Okay, so she had a few secrets. And somehow, she'd never gotten around to sharing them with her sisters, or anyone else in the family, for that matter—well, except for her mother. Somehow, Willow Bravo, of all people, had figured it out and shown up on her doorstep when Jody was six months along. As far as Jody knew, though, her mother had never told another soul.

And, no, Jody wasn't ashamed that she'd given her first baby up for adoption. All things considered, her choice had been the right one. And no one was going to judge her, anyway. She really ought to stop lying by omission and tell Elise and the rest of them the real reason she'd suddenly decided to spend several months in Sacramento at the age of eighteen.

But come on. It was thirteen years ago, which definitely put it into the category of old news. And she just didn't feel up to going into it now.

Kind of like she didn't feel up to reaching out to Seth Yancy...

On second thought, maybe there had been a little damage to her moral compass, after all.

"Jody?" Elise was watching her through suddenly worried eyes. "You okay?"

Jody pulled it together. "I am just fine. And *you're* going to New York with Jed."

The following Tuesday, Jody stood at the design station at Bloom. She was shaving the corners off a cube of floral foam when in walked the sheriff. Again.

Jody put down her knife with care. "Hello, Seth."

He took off his aviator sunglasses and his County Mounty hat and came right for her. "You never called." He set the hat on the counter and the glasses beside it.

Careful not to let anything spill on his hat, she brushed the shaved bits of foam from her hands. "There was no reason to call you. Everything is fine."

"You're sure?" He regarded her solemnly, with bleak concentration, as though if he stared hard enough, he could see inside her head and discover all the ways she wasn't taking proper care of herself.

Jody had a burning need to let out a long, exasperated sigh. Somehow, she quelled that. "I'm sure."

"Should you be on your feet so much?"

She was suddenly glad for the deep counter between them. He couldn't look down and see her slightly swollen ankles—which were nothing out of the ordinary for a woman in her third trimester. "Honestly. I'm taking excellent care of myself."

He sent a suspicious glance around the shop. "Those tubs of flowers outside are heavy. You should have help carrying them in at night."

She had a good answer for that one. "And I do have help. Plenty of it."

"How so?"

What? He had to have specifics as to her employees and the hours they worked? Fine. She would give him specifics. "I hired an extra assistant. I already have one who comes in to work with me on Saturday, runs the shop on Sunday by herself and picks up the slack whenever I need her. The new one comes in at two and stays through closing, Monday through Friday. And when the baby's born, she'll be here full-time for as long as I need her, and my original assistant will be working more, too." Was that enough information to end this interrogation?

Apparently not. "You were here on your own a week ago when we talked." It came out as an accusation with *How could you be so irresponsible?* implied at the end of it.

No way I have to explain myself to you. But then she went ahead and did it anyway. "The new girl called in sick that day. But she hasn't missed a day since. And if she can't make it, and the other clerk is busy, I have more people I can call."

"What about when you open up in the morning?"

"What about it?"

"Who carries all those tubs of flowers outside then?"

Seriously. Was this in any way his business? No. But if she told him to butt out, he might just decide to stick around and explain in detail all the reasons he had a right to cross-examine her. And what she really wanted was for him to go away. "For weeks now, my sister Elise or one of her clerks has been helping me open up every morning that I'm here on my own."

"I'd be happy to come by and pitch in."

"I... Thank you. I'll remember that."

"You still have my card with my numbers?"

Where had she put that? "I do. Yes. Of course."

"Jody." He gave her that laser-eyed stare again. "Did you lose my card?"

"No. Of course not."

"Show it to me."

She stood very still and reminded herself sternly that she was not going to start yelling at him. "I don't have it handy. Sorry."

The sheriff was not pleased. He pulled out a cell phone and punched some numbers into it. Her cell, in the pocket of her bib apron, blooped. "I've sent you my numbers. Again."

"Thanks." She knew she didn't sound the least appreciative, and by then, she didn't even care.

He took another of his cards from his breast pocket, grabbed a pen from the jar on the corner of the counter and wrote down all his private numbers all over again.

"Just to make sure you don't lose them this time." He held it out to her.

She didn't take it. "Seth, come on. You already put them in my phone."

"What if you lose your phone?"

"I won't." She folded her arms and rested them on her protruding stomach. "And anyway, I still have the first card you gave me. It's around. Somewhere." They glared at each other.

"I just want to help." He said it gently, but there was no mistaking the disapproval in his eyes.

And then the shop bell over the door jingled, saving her from saying something she shouldn't. Two well-dressed middle-aged women came in. "I have customers," she said with a blatantly unfriendly smile. "If you'll excuse me." She sidled out from behind the counter and made for the newcomers. "Hello, ladies. How may I help you?"

By the time she'd sold the women a mixed bouquet each, Seth had given up and left. She found the card he'd been trying to hand her on the design counter next to the partially shaved cube of foam. Shaking her head, she stuck it in her apron pocket.

And then she banished Seth Yancy from her thoughts.

Humming softly to herself, she went back to work arranging peonies, roses, green hydrangeas, maidenhair ferns and two gorgeous green-tipped purple Fiesole artichokes in a mercury glass compote bowl.

On Friday, Seth called her at home. He wanted to know how she was doing. She said she felt great.

He said, "If you need anything, you'll call me?"

"Absolutely," she replied and refused to think too deeply as to whether or not that was true.

A few minutes after she hung up, she got another call—this time on her cell. It was her sister Nell, who ran a construction business with their brother Garrett. Nellie wanted to fly to Phoenix that weekend for a home show. "Just checking in to be sure you're doing all right before I even think about deserting you."

"You're not deserting me. Nothing is happening here. Go."

"I might stay over until Tuesday or Wednesday. Visit with an...old friend."

"You know you sort of paused before the 'old friend' part, right?"

"What can I say? It's a business-with-pleasure kind of situation."

"Nellie."

"Um?"

"Have a fabulous time."

"I will—and you *would* tell me if there were any signs you're going into labor, right? Any spotting or weird cramping or if the baby had dropped?"

"Of course I would. My due date is four weeks out, and there's nothing to worry about."

Nellie started waffling. "You know, the more I think about it, four weeks isn't that far off. Anything could happen in the meantime."

"Nellie. Stop. There is nothing for you to worry about. And anyway, Clara's here if I need her."

"And also Elise," Nellie added helpfully.

Jody hesitated. She really didn't want Nell to talk herself out of the trip.

"Jo-Jo, you're too quiet."

So she confessed, "Elise is taking a quick trip to New York with Jed for some publicity event."

"You didn't tell me that Elise took off." Nellie said it in a chiding tone.

"She didn't. Yet. She's leaving tomorrow and will be back Tuesday and you'll be back Wednesday, and how many times do I have to tell you that I'm experiencing no signs of approaching labor, but if anything happens, I can call Clara. Or Rory." Rory McKellan was their cousin. "Or one of the guys if it comes down to it." They had five brothers and all of them lived in the area. Four of those brothers were either married or engaged to women Jody counted as friends. "There is no shortage of people I can call in an emergency."

Nell made a humming sound. "You really are sure about this?"

"How many times do I have to say it?"

Nell blew out an audible breath. "Sorry I got so freaky."

"Not complaining. I love that you care."

"I mean, you've had a textbook pregnancy, and you're healthy as a horse."

"Is this where I make a neighing sound?"

"Har-har. And it is your first baby and first babies—"

"Usually come late," Jody finished for her, wishing never to hear that particular phrase again.

"Love you, Jo-Jo."

"Love you, too. Call me when you get home."

"Will do."

She'd barely hung up when the phone blooped with a text. It was Seth.

You sure you don't need anything?

She actually chuckled as she texted back. Who are you and how did you get this number?

It wasn't easy, let me tell you. Call me. Anytime.

Absolutely. Will do.

The next day was Saturday. Nell flew to Phoenix and Elise and Jed took off for New York. Seth called that night. Just to check on her, he said. She told him yet again how well she was doing and he let her go.

Sunday, Lois Simonson, one of her two employees, ran the store all day. Jody stayed home and took it easy. She sat around in her pj's with her feet up and binge-watched the second season of *Outlander*—really, where was her own Jamie Fraser? She'd been waiting for him for most of her life. A couple of times she'd dared to hope she'd found what she was looking for.

Wrong on both counts.

And Nick? He'd been a sweetheart. But she'd known from the first that he wasn't the guy for her.

She put her hand on her giant belly and grinned to herself. She had Marybeth now. Her little girl would be enough for her. She would be a good mom and raise her child to know she could make anything she wanted of her life. And she would always have her sisters and her brothers and a network of in-laws and friends to count on and love.

Who needed a man?

Seth called that night, too. She grinned when she saw it was him. Was she kind of getting used to hearing his deep, careful voice?

Maybe. A little.

"What have you been doing?" he asked.

"Nothing. I have the day off, so I've been taking up space on the couch, watching TV."

"Good," he said. It was the first time she'd ever heard anything approaching approval in his voice when he talked to her. "And I know you're eating right. At least, that's what you tell me every time I call."

"Well, there was that carton of Ben and Jerry's Chunky Monkey and now it's gone. But otherwise, I had breakfast, lunch and dinner, and all three were comprised of heart-healthy, fiber-rich, nutritious ingredients. And you're kind of like an old mother hen, you know that?" There was a choked sort of sound from his end. "Seth Yancy, did you just almost laugh?"

"Me? Not a chance. Do you need anything?"

"Such as…?"

"Food. Supplies. Bottled water?"

"Are we preparing for the zombie apocalypse?"

"Just answer the question."

"No, Seth. As I keep telling you, I have everything I need, and if there's something I've forgotten, well, they have supermarkets now where I can pick up whatever I've run out of."

"You're being sarcastic."

"You noticed."

"And that reminds me. Should you even be driving?"

"Yes. I definitely should. And I do. Anything else?"

"Look. I'm trying really hard not to annoy you."

"I know that. And I thank you for it."

"I just want to—"

"—help. I know. And I appreciate it, Seth. But I've run out of ways to tell you that I am taking care of myself and there's nothing, really, to help me with."

He was so quiet she thought he'd hung up.

"Seth?"

"Right here. Okay, then. I'll check in tomorrow."

"Did I mention that the baby isn't due for weeks yet?"

"Yeah. Got that."

"So…are you planning to call every day?"

More silence. Finally, he asked, "Are you telling me not to?"

Yes! But somehow, she couldn't say that. Because it was so painfully obvious that he cared about his brother's unborn baby and he really did want to help. "No. It's okay." It came out sulky and grudging. "Let me try that again. I mean, thank you for, you know, being here. And I'll talk to you tomorrow, then."

"All right." Was that gravel-and-granite voice of his marginally softer? She couldn't be sure. "Sleep well, Jody."

She felt another smile curve her lips. "Good night, Seth."

Monday, he showed up at Bloom again just before closing time.

Jody was only too happy to introduce him to Marlie Grant, her second clerk and floral designer. Marlie, like Lois, had a talent with flowers and could be trusted not only to handle design and selling, but also to purchase stock from the wholesalers and flower farms nearby. Marlie took the last customer of the day, leaving Jody at the design station with Seth.

"I told you I had help," she said smugly as soon as Marlie was busy with old Mr. Watsgraff, who came in every Monday to buy a dozen white roses for his wife of forty-nine years.

"I'm staying to carry in the flowers." He made it sound like a threat.

"Fine. Help out. Be that way."

"You look tired."

She leaned toward him across the counter—as much as her giant stomach would allow, anyway. "Don't start in. Please."

Was that the beginnings of a grin tipping the corners of his bleak slash of a mouth? "Or you'll what?"

"I have an in with the sheriff's office is all I'm saying, so you'd better watch your step."

"Yes, ma'am." He said it quietly, and the sound sent a little shiver running down the backs of her knees.

She'd heard he had several feminine admirers in town, nice single women who often showed up at the justice center bringing cookies and wearing bright, hopeful smiles.

Until that moment, she'd never understood what they saw in him. Yeah, he was young to be sheriff. And hot and muscled up and manly and all that. But up till the last couple of check-in calls, she'd also found him overbearing and judgmental, which had pretty much made her immune to his fabled hotness.

But right now, when he almost smiled at her and then said *Yes, ma'am*, all teasing and low, well, she could see the appeal. A little bit. Maybe.

As soon as old Mr. Watsgraff went out the door with his cone of roses, Jody turned off the Open sign, and Marlie and Seth brought in the stock from outside.

He hung around until after Marlie left and then walked Jody out to her Tahoe in back.

"How about some dinner?" he asked, still holding the door open after helping her up behind the wheel.

She was actually tempted. But she was also uncomfortable with the idea. Would he ask her about Nick, want more details of their supposed romance, which had actually not been a romance at all? She wasn't ready to get into that with him and probably never would be.

"Thanks, Seth. But I just want to go home and put my feet up."

He gave a slight nod. "Well, that's understandable. I'll follow you, see that you get home safe."

"Seth." She looked at him steadily and then shook her head.

He gave it up. "Talk to you tomorrow."

"Good night."

He swung the door shut at last.

At home, she cooked a nice dinner of chicken breasts, steamed broccoli and rice, but when she sat down to eat, she just wasn't hungry. She felt at loose ends, somehow. Edgy, full of energy.

A little bit nervous.

She wandered aimlessly through her house, which she loved, a cozy traditional one-story, with a modern kitchen, a sunny great room and three bedrooms. Her father had made sure that each of his nine children were well provided for. Jody's trust fund had matured when she was twenty-one, and a year later, during the housing bust, she'd gotten an amazing deal on her place in a short sale. It was more house than she'd needed at the time, but she'd bought it anyway. Now it was worth three times what she'd paid for it, and with the baby coming, she was glad for the extra space.

In the baby's room, she lingered. She spent a half an hour admiring everything, touching the tiny onesies and the stacks of cotton blankets, hardly daring to believe that in a month, she would hold her baby in her arms. It was adorable, that room, if she did say so herself, with teal blue walls and bedding in coral and teal, cream and mint green. It had a mural of bright flowers and butterflies on one wall, and the whole effect was so pretty and inviting, all ready for Marybeth, even though she wouldn't be using it for a while. At first, she'd have a bassinet in Jody's room.

Eventually, she wandered out to the great room and tried to watch TV, but she couldn't concentrate.

She called Clara, who was down with the flu, of all things. Her husband, Dalton, had it, too, and so did their two-year-old, Kiera. Jody ordered her to get well, and Clara answered wryly that she was working on it.

After hanging up with Clara, she had the ridiculous desire to call Seth. But that would only encourage him, and that didn't seem right.

She went to bed at nine thirty and couldn't get comfortable, even with her body pillow to help support her belly and another pillow at her back. She was just sure she would never get to sleep.

But then the next thing she knew, she looked over at the bedside clock, and it was after two in the morning.

And something was…

She put her hands on her belly, felt the powerful, involuntary tightening, as though her body had a mind of its own.

"Dear, sweet God…"

With an animal growl, she threw back the covers and slithered to the floor, where she crouched like a crab on the bedside rug, groaning and huffing, fingers splayed over her rippling stomach as a second-stage contraction bore down like an extra pair of giant, cruel hands, pushing so hard she would have buckled under the pressure if she wasn't already on her knees.

She panted her way through it, and when it was over, she realized there was liquid dripping down her inner thighs. Her water had broken.

Her water had broken.

And Clara had the flu, Elise was in New York, and Nellie had gone to Phoenix.

But not to panic. Uh-uh. She'd done this before and she could do it again.

One hand still on her belly, she reached up and grabbed her phone off the nightstand. And then she just sat there, half expecting to wake up in her bed and discover that she really wasn't in active labor, after all; it was only a dream.

But then another one started.

Okay. No dream.

She used her phone to time that one as she squatted on the floor, moaning and grunting, the pain rising to a peak at thirty-two seconds, after which it faded back down. Once it was over, she estimated she had three to five minutes until the next one hit.

Time to find a ride to the hospital and then get in touch with her doctor—well, past time for both, actually.

But she refused to freak. Because there was nothing to be alarmed about. She was in labor, yes, but she had it under control. Her birth coaches might be unavailable, but at least there were plenty of people she could call. Even in the middle of the night, someone ought to be able to come pick her up and take her to Justice Creek General.

And if they weren't, well, there was always Uber. Or 911.

She brought up her cousin Rory's number and almost hit Call.

But then, for no comprehensible reason except that he kept insisting he really wanted to help, she scrolled down to Seth's cell number and called him instead.

Chapter Three

He answered on the first ring, sounding wide-awake—as though he'd been sitting up with his phone in his hand in the middle of the night, waiting for her to call. "Jody. What can I do?"

Her mind chose that moment to go blank. "I...need..."

"Anything. Yes." His voice was so calm, so even and strong. She felt she could reach right through the phone and grab on to him to steady herself. "What do you need?"

It was a simple question, and she had the answer ready. Except when she opened her mouth it was like pulling wide the floodgates on a full dam. "Elise and Nellie are out of town, and Clara's got the flu. I was going to call Rory, but then I thought of you and I..." He started to say something. But she didn't let him. She babbled right over him. "They all think it's my first and the first one always comes late, and I never corrected them, never *told* them. Because that's kind of how I am, you know? I keep too much to myself, I want to have it together and take care of business, and I end up pushing people away because I'm so self-sufficient. And now here I am on the bedroom floor, dripping all over the rug, without my birth coaches in the middle of the night. It's like I'm being punished by fate for lying to everyone about the first one, you know?"

"Jody."

"Um?"

"What do you mean, dripping?"

The note of alarm in his voice had her rushing to reassure him. "It's not that much. I exaggerated."

"You're not making sense."

"You're probably right."

"And, Jody, you said 'the first one.' The first what?"

"Baby," she blurted out and then slapped her hand over her big, fat mouth. Oh, God. She hadn't even told her sisters, and here she was, blathering it all out to Seth, who might want to help and all but still remained essentially a stranger to her.

"So," he tried again, clueless but still determined to stick with her and give her whatever she'd called him in the middle of the night to get. "Are you saying you feel guilty because—"

"Never mind. Doesn't matter. It's not why I called."

Dead silence. Then, "Okay. Let's go with that. Why did you call?"

Seriously? He really didn't know? "Seth, take a wild guess."

"I…" He was totally at a loss.

She was messing with him, and she really needed to

stop. "I'm in labor. I'm having my baby, like right now, tonight, and I wonder if—"

"Wait. What? Are you all right?" Now he really was freaked. "Is there bleeding? Do you need an ambulance?"

"No. Yes! I mean, I'm fine. There's no blood."

"But you mentioned dripping..."

"It's not blood—it's amniotic fluid. My water broke. It happens. You said you wanted to help, and I need someone to give me a ride to the hospital, and I thought—"

"Wait. You're not due for a month, you said."

"I'm at thirty-six weeks and going into labor now is perfectly normal."

"It is?"

"Believe me, if it wasn't, I'd have already called 911."

Another deep silence. And finally, "All right, then." His voice was dead calm again. Like he'd flipped a switch from frantic future step-uncle back to law-enforcement professional, a man with a job to do and no time to waste on the vagaries of human emotion. "Are you at home?"

"Yes."

"You didn't give me your address." She rattled it off. "Okay, then. Fifteen minutes, I'll be there. Did you call your doctor?"

"I will. As soon as I hang up and get through this next contrac—" A ragged yelp escaped her.

"Jody. Are you still with me?"

"Right here," she grunted.

"Are you okay?"

"Fine—except for, you know, having a baby."

"Tell me honestly. Do you need an ambulance?"

Given the pressure bearing down on her uterus, she

longed to scream, *Yes!* But she'd done this before. It felt normal, if having a baby could ever be called such a thing. "I just need a ride, okay? And I need a ride soon."

"I'm on my way."

Fourteen minutes later, she'd been through three more contractions, in between which she'd called her doctor, wiped up the dripped-on rug, put on a maxi-pad, yoga pants and a big shirt and carried her already-packed suitcase to the front door. Not bad for a woman in active labor.

She was crouched in the front hall, panting her way through the next contraction, when the doorbell rang. "It's open!" she shrieked and panted some more.

The door swung back, and she was looking at Seth's boots. "Jody? Are you—"

"Kind of busy here…" She waved a hand at him and went back to focusing on her breathing, on riding out the pain.

He came and knelt at her side until that one peaked and passed off.

Only then did she meet his eyes. "Thanks for coming." He wore jeans and a T-shirt and looked almost approachable.

She held out her arm. "Help me up?" He pulled her gently to her feet. She swayed against him for a moment. It was reassuring, leaning on him, such a broad, hard wall of a man. She could see the dark dots of beard stubble on his strong jaw, and he smelled clean and warm, like a just-ironed shirt. She was suddenly ridiculously glad she had called him. "Thanks."

"You ready?" He bent to grab the handle of her suitcase.

"Let's go."

Outside, he led her to the camo-green Grand Chero-kee parked at the curb. "Back or front?"

"What? You didn't bring the cruiser?" When he only looked at her patiently, she answered his question. "I'll sit in back. More space for rolling around in agony when the next contraction hits."

He got her settled in, tossed her suitcase into the passenger seat and climbed up behind the wheel.

The ride to Justice Creek General took seven minutes. She knew because she was timing contractions and the spaces between them the whole way.

At the hospital, they were ready for her. She'd preregistered and her ob-gyn, Dr. Kapur, had called ahead to say Jody was on the way. They put her in a wheelchair and rolled her to a birthing suite.

Seth followed her right in there.

"Thanks." She flashed him a pretty good imitation of a smile. "I'm good now. You can go."

"Someone should be here. I'll stay."

"But I can call—"

"It's almost three in the morning. I'm already here."

She would have argued with him, but she knew how much good that would do her. "You're staying no matter what I say, aren't you?"

"That's right."

A nurse came in and introduced herself as Sandy. She took Jody's vitals, waited out another contraction with her and then got a quick history. After that, she pulled a gown and a pair of canary yellow socks with nonskid soles from a cupboard.

"Your gown and some cozy socks." Sandy handed them over and pointed at a set of long cabinets tucked into the corner. "Your street clothes can go in there. Dr. Kapur should be in soon." She nodded at Seth. "Sheriff."

"Thanks, Sandy," he replied, as though he and Sandy were best pals and he had every right to be there. Apparently, Sandy was on the same page with him. She shot him a big smile and left them alone.

"You need help getting into that?" He gestured at the gown.

"No, thanks. Step out, please."

"If you need me—"

"Thanks. I mean that. Out."

He left and she changed into the gown and socks. Dr. Kapur came. She examined Jody and confirmed what Jody already knew. Just like the first time, her baby was coming fast.

Forty-five minutes later, Jody had flown through transition, and it was time to start pushing.

Somebody had let Seth back into the room. By then, Jody didn't even care. Pushing a baby out left zero room for modesty. And privacy? Forget about it.

She had the mattress adjusted to prop up her back, her gown rucked up high and her legs spread wide, her feet in the bright yellow socks digging into the mattress. Seth was right there. He gave her his hand to hold on to.

Okay, he was practically a stranger, but so what? He was there and he was strong and steady, and she could hold on to him, right now, when she needed him.

Dignity? Self-control? She had none. She shouted and swore and clutched Seth's hand for dear life.

Was it this bad last time? It must have been. She should have remembered that.

As Marybeth's head crowned, Jody shouted, "Never

am I ever having sex again! Never in this lifetime, no matter what!"

Dr. Kapur let out a soft chuckle and told her how great she was doing, that she should push just a little bit more, bear down just a little bit harder...

And she did and she felt it—the head sliding out. Moaning in agony, she looked down between her wide-open legs as Dr. Kapur freed Marybeth's little shoulders.

And that was it. Marybeth slithered out into the world.

With another long moan of exhaustion, Jody let go of Seth's hand and let her head fall back against the pillows.

When she looked again, Seth was down there with the baby. Dr. Kapur was checking her airways. Marybeth let out a soft cry—and then a louder one.

Dr. Kapur passed Seth the blood- and vernix-streaked baby. Seth took her, held her close, whispered something Jody couldn't hear.

And then Jody was reaching for her. "Please..."

Seth passed her over, laying her down on Jody's still-giant stomach. Jody gathered her in, kissed her sticky hair, her bloodstained cheek. "Hello, Marybeth. I'm so glad you're here..."

Seth stood close to the bed where Jody held her newborn baby.

The doctor got to work cutting the cord and stitching Jody up. Jody paid no attention to what was going on between her legs. She cuddled Marybeth close and cooed in her ear. The nurse, Sandy, approached the bed with a stack of clean linens.

Seth glanced down at the streaks of blood and white stuff on his arms. He could use a little cleaning up, too. "I'll be right back," he whispered to Jody. She didn't even look up.

In the suite's bathroom, he rinsed away the blood and the milky white goo that had covered Marybeth. With a wet paper towel, he rubbed the stuff off his T-shirt, too. He leaned close to the mirror, checking for more on his face and neck.

Seth stared in his own eyes and marveled at what had just happened in the other room.

Could a moment change everything? Seth knew that it could. A moment was all it had taken seven years ago in Chicago—a single moment to empty him out to a shell of himself.

And back there in the other room, it had happened again. He'd held Nicky's baby for a matter of seconds. Those seconds made up the moment that changed his world all over again.

In the space of that moment he saw his own emptiness, and he saw it filled with all he needed, everything that mattered, right there in his arms. Life. Hope. The future. All of it in a tiny, naked, squirming newborn baby still connected to her mother by a twisted, vein-wrapped cord.

As he'd held Marybeth for the first time, the past was all around him. And not just what happened in Chicago.

But also another moment years and years ago, the first time that everything changed.

He'd been fourteen that day, the day his dad brought Seth's future stepmom, Darlene, to the Bar-Y for the first time. She'd brought her little boy with her, too.

"Nicky," she'd said, *"this is Seth..."* Seth looked

down and saw the kid looking up at him through giant blue eyes.

At that time, Seth already considered himself a grown-up. He understood life and there was nothing that great about it. He sure had no interest in his dad's new girl-friend's kid.

But then the kid in question had held out his small hand.

Seth had taken it automatically, given it a shake and then tried to let go.

But Nicky managed to catch his index finger and hold on. *"Tet,"* he said proudly. It was as close as he could get to saying *Seth* at that point.

And that was when it happened, that was the first moment when everything changed.

As Nicky clutched his finger and Darlene chuckled softly, Seth felt a warm, rising sensation in his chest, a tightness, but a good tightness. He kind of liked the little boy and his pretty mother.

He slid a glance at his dad. Bill Yancy, always so sad and lonely and serious, was smiling, too.

What would it be like, to have a mom who made his dad smile, to have a little brother who called him *Tet*? Seth realized that he wanted a chance to find out.

As soon as Darlene and Seth's dad were married, Bill legally adopted Nick. Seth finally had a normal, happy, loving family. The years that followed were good ones. The best.

But eventually there was Chicago and the next big mo-ment, the one that added up to the death of his dreams. After Chicago, Seth had come home. He'd taken a job with the sheriff's office.

But really, he'd only been going through the motions

of living. And he only felt emptier with each new loss. Five years ago they lost Darlene to breast cancer. And then his dad, sad and silent and lonely all over again, had pulled up stakes and moved to Florida.

Seth had tried to stay positive. Two years ago, he'd run for sheriff and won. He'd tried to be proud of that, of serving his community and doing a good job of it.

But losing Nicky last November had been the final straw. Since Nicky died, Seth had greeted every empty day with bleak determination to get through it and on to the next one.

Until today.

Until he held Nicky's baby, and it came to him sharply that while Nicky might be lost, this tiny, living part of him carried on.

When Seth returned to the main room, the nurse was busy at the sink near the window. The doctor was gone. Jody looked up from Marybeth and into his eyes. "Thanks. For the ride. For being here."

"Nothing to thank me for. I'm right where I want to be."

Jody started to say something.

But the nurse stepped close again. "Let's clean that little sweetie up a little." She patted Jody's shoulder. "Then we'll help you with a shower and bring on the tea and toast."

Jody surrendered Marybeth reluctantly. She let her head fall back again and closed her eyes. A long, tired sigh escaped her. "I'm beat." She looked it, her brown hair pulled back in a saggy ponytail, bruised circles beneath the lowered fans of her eyelashes.

Seth wanted to reach out, to smooth the damp hair

that had straggled loose from her ponytail. He wanted to take her hand again, to reassure her that he was good with this, with Marybeth, with all of it. That he was there for Jody to hold on to. And he was. All the way. Because being there for his brother's baby meant being there for Jody, too.

He lifted a hand toward her, but changed his mind and let it drop to his side without touching her. She looked peaceful, her head on the pillow, eyes still closed, that back-talking mouth of hers soft now, lips slightly parted. Resting. Jody deserved every second of rest she could get. He would stand watch over her, back the nurse off until she woke up.

"You should go now," she said softly without opening her eyes.

He didn't answer her.

Death had stolen Nick's right to be there for his baby. But Seth was very much alive. And whether Jody Bravo liked it or not, Seth was stepping up to give Marybeth anything—and everything—she might need.

He was going nowhere. Marybeth's mom might as well start getting used to having him around.

Chapter Four

"She is so beautiful," Elise whispered. She cradled Marybeth close and smoothed the blanket around her sleeping face. "When can you go home?"

"They're keeping us overnight. Barring complications, Dr. Kapur will release us tomorrow morning."

Elise, who'd had Jed drive her straight to the hospital from the airport, looked faintly alarmed. "What complications?"

Jody waved a hand. "There are none. Relax. It's just to be on the safe side. Both Marybeth and I are fine."

"I'm so glad. And I can't believe we all three managed to be unavailable just when you needed us."

"It happened." Jody poured herself some water from the pitcher on the bed tray and took a long sip. "And it all worked out."

"But we were supposed to—"

"Leesie, Marybeth is fine. I'm fine. You are not to feel bad about it."

"But I do. I should have been here and I—"

"Stop. How was New York?"

"Amazing. Do you need me to make some calls?"

"All done. I'm covered at Bloom, and every Bravo for miles around knows about Marybeth. Three of our brothers and their wives have been by already—oh, and Rory and Walker, too."

"You are a marvel."

"Well, I had help. Seth made most of the calls for me." Seth had left twenty minutes ago, just as Elise was arriving. Jed had gone off to get some coffee, giving the sisters a little alone time.

Elise's mouth curved in a soft little smile. "Aren't you glad you reached out to Seth?"

"Yeah. He's been great. The guy won't *stop* helping me. I keep telling him he can go."

"And now he has."

"Not for long. He'll be back at six or so, he said."

Elise frowned. "Is that okay with you?"

"It's odd. I mean, already, I'm kind of used to having him around. And he really does seem to want to be here. He's in insta-love with his niece."

Elise rocked the pink bundle gently from side to side. "Well, and who wouldn't be?"

"And he really seems to want to help. Plus, when they brought in the birth certificate he was all over it, making sure I put Nick down as Marybeth's dad."

"And here you thought he didn't even care," Elise chided.

"Yeah. I got it way wrong on that score. And I guess,

well, I don't think it hurts if he wants to be involved. Do you?"

"Of course not. But the real question is, how do *you* feel about it?"

Jody stared out the window at the thick green branches of the fir tree just beyond the glass. "It's strange, how easy it would be for me to start to count on him. He's bossy, you know? But now I'm getting used to him, he's somehow bossy in a good way. He knows what he wants and he really does try to do the right thing. And I have no problem pushing back at him when I don't like what he's up to."

Elise wore her dreamy look suddenly. "Oh, I get that. Jed's the same way. There's Jed's way and the wrong way. Most of the time he's right, but when he's not I have to stand my ground with him. And that's okay with me. Kind of keeps me on my toes." Marybeth let out a whine. "She's waking up. Look at those eyes. Gorgeous…"

"Bring her here. I'll nurse her again. I'm supposed to practice every chance I get."

Elise brought her over and settled her in Jody's waiting arms. She pushed her gown open and Marybeth rooted around, finally latching on, but not for long. After only a minute or two, she popped off the nipple and started fussing again, little, cranky bleats of sound.

Jody felt a sudden spurt of anxiety, a sense of complete incompetence. She forced herself to take a slow breath and let it out by degrees. This was new territory—she had to remember that. She'd never nursed her little boy, hadn't even let herself see his tiny face. They'd taken him away as soon as he was born. Her breasts, swollen with milk that wouldn't be used, had ached for days afterward…

"Jody? You okay?"

She blinked and shook her head. "Yeah. Sorry, faded out there for a minute."

Elise laughed. "Well, you did just have a baby. It's possible you're a little tired."

Marybeth cried louder. Jody switched her to the other side. She latched on again. That time she stuck with it awhile. Jody looked down at her little mouth, her tiny nose. *Please, God, let me do this right...*

Eventually, Marybeth fell asleep again.

Elise took her and tucked her in the bassinet. Jed came in. They visited for a few more minutes, and then he and Elise left.

The afternoon passed slowly. More family and friends came to see Marybeth, including Nell, who'd hopped a plane from Phoenix as soon as she heard the baby had been born. She said she was ready to come home anyway. Her hookup with that old friend hadn't worked out, after all.

Nell didn't stay long. Nobody did. They just wanted to check in, see the new mom and make a fuss about the baby. They all offered to be there to drive Jody and Marybeth home the next day. She thanked them and told them she'd call them if she needed a ride.

The nurses served dinner at five. Jody ate with one hand, Marybeth cradled in the other. The baby was fussing a lot, nursing fitfully but not really settling in about it. Around five thirty, she finally closed her eyes and slept again. Jody kissed her pink forehead and tucked her back into the bassinet. A few seconds later, her cell vibrated on the bed tray.

It was her mom, calling from Hawaii. In recent years, Willow Bravo spent most of her time on vacation.

"Hi, Ma."

"Darling, I got a message from Seth Yancy that you had your baby. How are you doing?"

"My baby is beautiful and healthy and we're both fine."

"I can't wait to meet her. Give her a kiss from her grandma?"

"I will."

"And so...you're on good terms with the sheriff?"

Was she implying that Jody had been on bad terms with Seth before now? With Willow, it was hard to tell. "Yes. Well, he recently found out that he was going to be an uncle. He got in touch. We...got to know each other a little. And then I went into labor last night and needed a ride to the hospital."

"What about your sisters?"

"Long story. But anyway, Seth drove me here and then stuck around to help."

"And you are *letting* him help. This is a first."

Jody felt her stomach knot up. "Passive-aggressive much?" She was careful to speak just above a whisper in order not to wake Marybeth.

"It's only an observation," Willow answered, her voice downright gentle. "You've always been so independent—that's all I meant. It's rare for you to let someone close, especially in this sort of situation."

"What sort of situation do you mean, exactly?"

"Jody. I only mean you've never had much contact with Sheriff Yancy until very recently. This is a challenging time for you, as it is for any new mother. Usually, when things are tough for you, you don't want anyone close enough to see your weakness, especially not a man you don't know all that well."

"I'm not weak."

Willow chuckled. "You're making my point for me. You realize that, right?"

Okay, so her mother could sometimes be way too perceptive. Jody tamped down her defensiveness. "Seth is a good guy, and he's already crazy about Marybeth."

"I'm glad," said her mother in a neutral tone. Apparently, she really didn't want to fight, and Jody probably ought to stop being annoyed with her just on principle. "And I'm here if you need me."

Right. In Hawaii, Jody was careful *not* to say. And then she felt guilty for even thinking that. Willow *had* flown to Sacramento all those years ago because she was worried about her older daughter. When she'd discovered Jody's secret, she'd stayed long enough to meet the childless couple who would be taking the baby. Jody had called her when she went into labor, and Willow had flown right back to her side, staying with her through the birth and recovery. So really, Willow *had* been there when Jody needed her.

"Thanks, Ma," Jody said and found that she meant it. "And when *are* you coming home?"

"Right away, if you need me."

"No, really. I'm doing fine."

"A few weeks, then."

"All right. Have a great time."

"I will. And I…"

"What, Ma?"

"I wasn't the most attentive mother. I realize that." It was only the truth. For the first eighteen years of Jody's life, Willow was laser-focused on getting her lover, Jody's father, to divorce his first wife and make Willow his bride. "But I do love you, darling," she said. "Very much."

"And I love you." It was true. Willow could get on her last nerve, and Jody hated that her own mother had spent a couple of decades trying to steal another woman's husband. But she'd worked past that bitterness, mostly. And her siblings and half siblings had, too.

They chatted a little longer about inconsequential things, and then Willow said goodbye.

Seth returned a few minutes later wearing jeans and a different T-shirt. He had an overnight bag in one hand and a pie in the other.

Jody's heart kind of lifted at the sight of him. She realized she'd been waiting for him, that she'd wanted him to come back, that he made her feel safe and cared for. And she liked that—though she'd always been a person who insisted on taking care of herself.

Her pleasure at seeing him was probably some weird postpartum reaction. She decided not to analyze it too deeply. "Oh, look. You brought me a pie. Key lime?"

He almost smiled. "How'd you guess?"

"I'm a girl who knows her pies. One of your admirers made it, am I right?"

He half scowled as he set the pie on the low cabinet near the door. "They're very nice women. And how did you know about them?"

"Seth. Everybody knows about your fan club. It's a thing. People find it charming that the sheriff has lots of female admirers."

He cleared his throat officiously. And his ears were pink, which she was coming to realize was the way that he blushed. Seth Yancy, a blusher. She loved that. "You're grinning," he grumbled. "Why?"

"You really want to know?"

"Never mind." He set his bag down on the floor

near the cabinet and approached the bassinet. "How's our girl?"

Our girl. Should it bother her that he thought of Marybeth as partly his?

Well, if it should, it didn't. Not really. Instead, she found his claiming of her daughter charming. Like his fan club and the cute way he blushed.

"Jody?"

"Um?"

"How's she been?" he whispered, bending over the sleeping Marybeth.

"So far, so good. A little fussy. Everybody says she's gorgeous."

"Because she is." Reluctantly, he straightened. "I want to pick her up."

"Don't you dare. Let her sleep. And you'll get your chance before you know it. It won't be long before she's awake again, believe me." He was looking at her so... steadily. "What?"

He took the chair by the bed. "You look tired. Did you get any sleep?"

"Please. People in and out constantly. Marybeth fussing. Trying to learn how to nurse her. It goes on..."

He peered over at the baby again. "She seems peaceful now."

"Let's enjoy it while it lasts. And I have to ask, what's with the overnight bag?"

He glanced at it as though he hadn't noticed until now that he'd carried it in with him. "Oh, that. I talked to the nurse a few minutes ago."

"About?"

"I had to promise her some of your pie, but they'll be bringing in a cot for me in a little while."

She knew she absolutely, positively ought to draw the line at this. "You think you're sleeping in this room with me?"

His big shoulders slumped. "Look. All right. If it's too much, I can camp out in the waiting room."

"Seth. Marybeth is fine. You should just go home."

A muscle twitched in his rocklike jaw. "It's just one night. I'll feel better if I'm here. They won't let me have a cot out in the waiting room, but I'll just sleep in a chair out there..." And he looked at her through those gorgeous eyes that were a warm brown with golden flecks near the iris. Oh, God. He was so working her. "I want to be here in the morning. I want to take you back to your house, help you get settled in..."

Before she could make herself form the word *no*, there was a tap on the door.

An orderly stuck his head in. "We have your roll-away."

And just like that, it was decided. Seth jumped up to help, and Jody didn't say a word to stop him.

It wasn't so bad, having him in the room with her through the night. He made himself useful, getting up more than once to quiet the baby when she cried, even changing her diaper twice. And the next morning, he went to Jody's house to pick up a few things for her while she waited for Dr. Kapur to release her and Marybeth.

He came back with the car seat, which he'd correctly installed in the passenger-side second-row seat of his big Jeep. He'd even figured out how to put in the soft newborn insert so that Marybeth fit in there just right, all cozy and safe.

He helped Jody up into the passenger seat and then

he drove them home. Once there, he took charge, getting Jody and the baby all comfy in Jody's room. By then it was almost noon. He made sandwiches and heated up some canned soup and ate lunch with Jody before heading off to the sheriff's office to get a little work done.

At six thirty, he returned with takeout from Romano's— best Italian in town.

"Seth, you don't have to bring food. My sisters are handling all the meals for the first few days. Elise dropped by while you were at the justice center. She brought her famous roast chicken and browned potatoes."

"Great," Seth replied as he loaded lasagna onto plates for them. "We'll have the chicken tomorrow night."

He also brought a foil-wrapped pan of sinfully delicious Samoa cheesecake bars that someone in his fan club had whipped up for him. Jody ate three of those.

"Don't bring any more desserts into my house," she grumbled as she reached for that third bar. "Or I'll never lose this baby weight."

"Whatever you say, Jody." Already, she knew what he meant by that. She could dole out instructions to her heart's content. And he would go ahead and do things his way.

That night, he slept on the blow-up bed in her tiny third bedroom. She shouldn't have let him. But he asked her so nicely, and he was so great with Marybeth. In the morning before he left, he made her oatmeal with raisins and honey.

It was nice, having him fix breakfast and put it in front of her.

"Thanks, Seth. I know I keep saying that, but you really have gone above and beyond."

He sent her an oblique glance. "I want to ask you something, but I don't want to piss you off."

She enjoyed a bite of oatmeal. "I'm worn-out and cranky. You know that, right?"

"I think that any way I answer that is going to be wrong."

"What I meant was, good thinking on the part about not pissing me off." To that, he shrugged and sipped his coffee, and she was suddenly sure that, whatever it was, he'd decided not to ask. That was when she realized that she *wanted* him to ask. "Go ahead. What is it?"

"About you and Nicky..." He dipped up a bite of the hot cereal and brought it to his mouth. Once he'd swallowed, he muttered gruffly, "What happened with that?"

Ugh. He was such a straight-and-narrow kind of guy. She doubted he was going to think much of her answer. "How about this? I'm not mad at you for asking. And I want you to try not to get mad when I answer."

She expected him to waffle on that. But he only said, "Deal."

So she told him about that night in August. "I hadn't been out with anyone in a while—a few years, as a matter of fact."

"Why not?"

No way she felt up to going into all that right then. "Do you want to hear about what happened with your brother or not?"

He saluted her with his coffee mug. "Sorry. Go ahead."

"I decided I needed to get out more, have a little more fun in my life. So on a hot night last August, I went to Alicia's." The roadhouse was out on the state highway, about five miles from town. "I had a great time. Danced a lot. Drank too much. And met your brother, who was sweet and charming and a really good dancer. Things just…took their natural course. We got a room in the motel across from the roadhouse and spent the night together."

He was watching her too closely.

Her throat felt tight, and she gulped to loosen it. "And, yes, we used condoms. And it was just that one night."

Seth sat back in his chair. The room was too quiet. She almost wished Marybeth would wake up and start crying. She could go soothe her baby and stop talking about Nick.

But Marybeth slept on. And Jody continued, "I liked him a lot. But honestly, he was too young for me. And I don't mean just in years. He was…such a sweetheart. So open and true. I felt a thousand years old around him."

"Why? You're not *that* much older."

Jody chuckled. "Thanks. I think." She fiddled with her spoon. "As for why, it was just the way I felt, that's all—older than Nick in a thousand different ways." Yeah, there was more to the why of it. But all that was another story, *her* story, a story she didn't feel like sharing. "Nick wanted to go out with me and I was flattered, but I knew it wasn't going anywhere. He was a good guy, though, and we became friends. We'd hang out together here. And at the ranch. But we never got romantic again."

Seth sat forward. "He didn't tell me about the baby. But he did say he wanted for there to be more with you."

"Well, that wasn't happening. Not for me. And when I found out I was pregnant…" That had been awful. The stick had turned blue, and she'd had to face the fact that she'd done it again.

"When you found out you were pregnant, what?"

"Come to think of it, didn't we cover that already— on the first day you came into Bloom to ask me if my baby was Nick's?"

"You mean, that you went to him right away with the news?"

"Yeah. He wanted marriage. I didn't. But we agreed we would learn how to be parents to our baby without being married. And then, way too soon, he died."

"And...that's it? That's all of it?" He glowered at her.

At least, she thought he was glowering. "Yeah. That's all—and remember, you said you would try not to get mad."

"I'm not mad."

"Well, Seth. You *look* mad."

"I miss him, that's all." His voice was like gravel rubbing on sandpaper, and those gold flecks in his eyes shone extra bright. "He and his mother were the heart of our family."

Jody felt the pressure of tears at the back of her throat. "I'm so sorry," she whispered. It sounded limp and inadequate, but what else could she say?

He pushed his chair back and picked up his empty bowl. "Thanks. For telling me. You finished?"

She passed him her bowl.

That evening at six thirty, he appeared on her doorstep again.

She was way too glad to see him. He made her life easier, putting the dinner on, washing up afterward, bringing amazing baked goods that she really should stop eating. He was always ready to help with the baby.

And there was just something so rock-solid about him. He was too serious, and half the time she just knew he was thinking unflattering things about her. But still, he made her feel safe and protected, as though nothing could go too far wrong as long as he was nearby. Already, they seemed to have fallen seamlessly into a daily routine.

The next morning, Friday, he made breakfast again. And when he left for work, she found herself wondering how she would get along when he stopped coming back.

Marybeth fussed constantly. To Jody, it seemed she must be hungry, though Jody's milk had already come down. It was whitish in color, no longer the yellowish colostrum babies got the first few days after birth. So the milk was there, but Marybeth just didn't seem to be getting enough.

Jody called the nursing coach that Dr. Kapur had recommended. The coach, Debbie, came out to the house and worked with her, giving her pointers on how to make sure Marybeth latched on properly, showing her the best nursing positions, helping her set up her rocking recliner with pillows and everything she needed close by for convenience and ease. So she would be relaxed, so Marybeth would feel safe and cozy and keep at it long enough to fill her little tummy.

Debbie's visit didn't help. That weekend was awful. Marybeth cried all the time, and Jody tried not to cry right along with her. Jody's breasts felt knotted and achy with milk, and she was already considering pumping and then feeding Marybeth her breast milk in a bottle.

But Debbie had urged Jody to give it time.

"Marybeth is doing fine," Debbie had said. "Sometimes it takes several days before mother and baby get comfortable with the nursing process."

Jody wasn't comfortable. And judging by all the wailing, neither was her baby girl. Still, she stuck with it, but she worried constantly that her baby was starving. Plus, the endless crying made her want to scream.

She was supposed to be doing it right this time.

And she wasn't. Her little baby was miserable and Jody was, too.

Thank God for Seth. He continued to sleep on the blow-up bed in the spare room. Both Saturday and Sunday, he went off to the justice center, but only for a few hours each day. Sunday, he drove out to the Bar-Y, too—and came back with a big suitcase full of his clothes.

The sight of that suitcase really lifted Jody's spirits. If he was bringing more clothes, then that meant he intended to keep camping out at her house for a while. Right?

Was it wrong to be ridiculously happy about that?

Really, she ought to tell him he didn't need to spend every free second helping her take care of her baby, that he should go home to the Bar-Y and relax at night instead of walking the floor with a squalling newborn.

But she told him no such thing. Instead, when he showed up with that suitcase, she gave him the old dresser in the spare room and told him the closet in there was his, too.

And then Marybeth started crying.

Seth put off unpacking to settle her down. By now, it seemed to Jody that Marybeth only stopped crying when Seth rocked her in his big arms.

Monday morning when he went out the door headed

for the sheriff's office, she almost grabbed his arm and begged him not to go.

After he left, Clara, who'd recovered from the flu by then, stopped by. Marybeth bawled through her visit. Clara held her anyway and said she was beautiful and reassured Jody that everything would be fine.

But everything wasn't fine. Marybeth was suffering, probably starving.

That afternoon, Jody called the nursing coach again. Debbie showed up a half an hour later. She gave Jody a few more tips for soothing Marybeth and then ran through the nursing pointers a second time, adding some relaxation exercises for the stressed-out mom to do while the baby napped. As if.

Debbie said the baby was healthy, and there was nothing to worry about. She asked for a quick run-down of Jody's diet and then declared that Jody hadn't mentioned any foods or beverages that might affect Jody's breast milk and be irritating to Marybeth's delicate system. Debbie wanted to know how many wet-diaper changes Marybeth needed in a twenty-four-hour period. When Jody said four or so, Debbie said that was normal.

Next they talked about Marybeth's poop. Because when you had a little baby, poop mattered. Debbie said one bowel movement a day at this point was normal, too, that Jody just needed to keep working with the process and give it a few more days. Things would settle down. Debbie guaranteed that.

"And call anytime." She gave Jody a blithe smile as she went out the door.

"I will." Jody nodded obediently while screaming inside.

Marybeth did go to sleep eventually. Jody put her in her bassinet and turned on the monitor. In the great room, she tried a few of her new relaxation exercises. Did they help? Not really. That Marybeth might wake up any minute and start crying again kept her on edge.

So she gave up trying to relax and checked in with Lois at Bloom to make sure everything was on track there. When she hung up with Lois, she took a load of laundry from the dryer. A single cry erupted from the baby monitor as Jody started to fold a tiny pink polka-dot shirt. Clutching the shirt to her chest, she held her breath and waited, praying Marybeth would just go back to sleep.

But the cries continued, getting louder and more insistent.

Jody tossed the little shirt in the laundry basket, grabbed the basket and took it to her bedroom. She emptied the pile of laundry on the bed, dropped the basket on the floor and bent over the bassinet.

"Shh, now. It's okay…"

Marybeth screwed up her red face and wailed all the louder.

Jody picked her up and carried her to her nursing chair.

After Marybeth had nursed, Jody burped her, changed her and even sang to her. That seemed to work, which completely surprised Jody, who couldn't carry a tune if her life depended on it. But Marybeth seemed to like the sound of Jody's voice. She settled down and relaxed against Jody's shoulder.

For a little while.

By six, she was fussing again, and Jody couldn't wait for Seth to arrive.

And by quarter of seven, when he still hadn't shown, she wanted to knock herself out with a hammer. Anything to get away from her little baby's misery and her own complete failure to be the mom she had promised herself she would be this time.

Last time, she'd done what she had to do. She'd given up her little boy. But this time, with Marybeth...

This time was her second chance.

And this time, she'd been so certain she was going to do it right.

But she wasn't doing it right. It wasn't working out. It was all going wrong.

Seth finally appeared at twenty after seven with a giant bag of Romano's takeout in one hand and a clear plastic cake caddy containing a gorgeous chocolate cake in the other. Jody wanted to shove the baby at him, grab the cake and run howling out the door.

Instead, she held her crying child on her shoulder and followed him to the kitchen, where he set the food on the counter and explained, "I'm sorry I'm late. Little family dispute. The parties involved demanded to talk to the sheriff personally before they would put down their weapons."

"Weapons!" Jody repeated in alarm, causing Marybeth to cry louder. Jody lowered her voice. "They had weapons?"

"Don't get excited. I drove out there. We talked. They put away their guns and agreed to get some family counseling. Crisis resolved." He stepped to the sink to wash his hands.

Jody experienced a moment's relief that no one was hurt. But Marybeth just kept on crying—louder than ever if that was even possible. Jody's frustration and hopelessness came flooding back. In a second or two, she would break, blow it completely, collapse to the floor wailing as loud as the baby.

Seth said the magic words. "Here. Let me take her."

The tears were pushing, demanding she let them flow. Her throat ached with the effort to hold them back. *Failure*, mocked an evil voice in her head. *You're a pitiful excuse for a mother.*

Seth was watching her. Even with her vision blurred by held-back tears, she could see his concern. Clearly, he got that she was losing it. "Jody." He put up both hands and patted the air between them, and she felt worse than ever. The poor guy not only faced angry families with guns at work, he came home to Marybeth's incompetent mom having a meltdown. "Jody, it's okay..."

"No, Seth. No, it is not okay." She had to get out of there. "Just take her. Please." Lifting Marybeth off her shoulder, she handed her over.

Seth took her in those big, gentle hands of his. As soon as he had her, before he could say one more word, Jody whirled on her heel and ran for her room, where she swung the door shut harder than she should have and gave the privacy lock a vicious twist.

Alone at last.

Sagging back against the door, she willed herself to pull it together.

But the tears kept pushing. They were going to get out. She just couldn't keep swallowing them down.

Letting her knees buckle, she sank to the floor and slammed both hands over her mouth, as if that could keep the tears from escaping.

It couldn't. *She* couldn't.

So she leaped to her feet again and marched to the bed. Shoving aside the tangle of unfolded laundry, she threw herself down with a hard, hopeless sob.

Chapter Five

It took Seth a while to get Marybeth settled. He walked a path from the kitchen to the great room and back again, bouncing her just a little with each step, creating a rhythm, a combination of movements, that usually worked to quiet her down.

As he walked her, he rubbed her tiny back, stroked his hand over the peach fuzz on her little head and whispered to her. He called her his girl, the best girl, the sweetest girl around.

The crying got weaker, then became intermittent, interspersed with hiccups. Slowly, the hiccups stopped, too.

Finally, with a tired little sigh, she went quiet.

A few cooing sounds, another sigh…and silence.

He carried her to the room he slept in and shut the curtains to block out what was left of the daylight. Then

he put her down on her back on the blow-up bed, arranging pillows on either side of her to make sure she
couldn't somehow wiggle over near the edge.

She was sleeping peacefully, innocent as an angel.

Now, to find out what was up with Jody.

The three bedrooms in the house were grouped together on a small L-shaped hallway off the front entry.
He left the door open to his room. If Marybeth cried,
he would be able to hear her. Jody's room was only a
few steps away.

He tapped on her door. "Jody?" No response. He tried
to decide whether to knock again or leave her alone. But
then the door slowly opened.

Puffy eyes and a red nose gave her away. She wasn't
crying now, but she had been.

"You okay?"

"Not really." She smoothed back her tangled hair
and slid a glance over his shoulder, toward the other
two bedrooms. "Is she…?"

"Sound asleep. I put her on my bed and boxed her in
with pillows. She's never been in that pretty room you
made for her, right?"

Jody sniffled. She rubbed at her nose with a wadded-
up tissue. "Right."

"So I didn't put her down in there."

"Um. Okay."

"I thought maybe if she woke up in a strange room,
she might be scared or something."

Jody made a strangled sound—a wild laugh, maybe.
Or a tortured sob. He couldn't really tell which. "You're
amazing, you know that? You're ten times the mother
I'll ever be."

He had no idea how to respond to that, so he went with, "You're a fine mother."

Apparently, his reply amused her. She let out a tight little laugh—which was great, he decided. He would take amusement over a breakdown any day. She asked, "And you've determined this, how?"

He didn't even have to think it over. "You're here for her. You want what's good for her. It's obvious you love her and will do anything for her."

"It is?" Her voice was so small. Lost-sounding.

He knew she needed comforting. And he was there to do whatever she and Marybeth needed. He held out his arms. "Come here."

She didn't even hesitate, only swayed toward him with a sigh. He gathered her in. They stood there in the open doorway to her room, arms wrapped around each other. He breathed in her coconut-and-vanilla scent from the lotion she used on Marybeth and tried not to think too hard about how good her body felt pressed close to his.

"I should pull myself together," she mumbled against his shoulder. "But you're kind of good to lean on."

"Lean all you want. Whenever you need to." He rubbed his chin against her silky hair, realized that was going a bit far and stopped.

"I was so sure," she whispered, pressing herself even closer against him, her voice low enough that he could barely make out the words. "I had it all planned. I was going to do it right this time around."

He remembered what she'd blurted out concerning first and second babies the night Marybeth was born. It was probably none of his business. Unless she needed to talk about it. In that case, he was more than willing to listen.

Stroking a hand down her back, he echoed, *"This time around.* Meaning there was a time before?"

Jody lifted her head from his shoulder and looked up into his stern, square-jawed face.

What was it about him? At first, she'd only wanted him to leave her alone. But now she couldn't even imagine how she would have survived the past week without him. She couldn't wait for him to show up at the end of each day. It meant so much to know he was right there in the spare room every night, ready to pitch in whenever she needed him.

She held his gaze. "You already know there was a time before."

He answered with a slow nod. "You want to tell me about it?"

Did she? "Yeah. And to work up the courage, I'm going to need cake. Lots and lots of cake."

He lifted a hand. His fingers ghosted down her temple and guided a stray curl behind her ear, the light touch warming her through and through. "You have to eat your lasagna and Caesar salad first."

"Oh, now. There's a real hardship."

He actually smiled then, and it looked really good on him. "Excellent. We have a plan."

With a lot more reluctance than she wanted to admit to, she pressed her hands to his broad chest and stepped back. His arms dropped away. She went to the nightstand and got him the baby monitor. "The receiver's already in the kitchen."

He took it and turned for his room.

* * *

Jody ate her dinner and had her cake. By the time they carried their plates to the sink, she was half hoping Marybeth would wake up and give her an excuse not to rehash old news.

But her daughter slept on.

They went into the great room and sat on the couch together—Jody at one end, Seth on the other. She tucked her stocking feet up on the cushions and tried to decide where to start.

Seth waited, not pushing her.

Finally, she began, "During my last year of high school, I got pregnant by my high school sweetheart..." At three months along, right after graduation, she'd finally worked up the nerve to tell him. "He went ballistic, accused me of trying to pass some other guy's baby off as his. And then he packed up and moved to Indiana. He was already registered at Notre Dame for the fall."

Seth muttered something under his breath.

"What?" she asked.

"Never mind. Go on."

She pulled a throw pillow from behind her back, braced it on the sofa arm and leaned her elbow on it as she explained how crazy things had been with her family then. "My dad's first wife, Sondra, had just died. The day after the funeral, he married my mother and moved her, Nell and me into the mansion he'd built for Sondra. Elise still lived there at the time and so did her best friend, Tracy, who'd been taken in by Sondra when Tracy's parents died. Elise was reeling from the loss of her mom—and then in moves her dad's husband-stealing new wife and two of the kids she'd had by him."

"Bad?"

"Unbearable. We're all close now. We've put all the old garbage behind us. But at the time, Elise and Tracy hated Nell and me, and we hated them right back. We all resented my mother for being a total home wrecker. There were fights, screaming matches. I only lived there for two months and then I moved out again. I told everyone I couldn't take all the drama…"

"But really, it was because of the baby?"

"Yeah. But I didn't tell anyone—not anyone in my family, not any of my friends. I just couldn't deal with talking about it, somehow. I was eighteen, so nobody had to know." She'd found an adoption agency who tracked down her runaway boyfriend in Indiana. "My ex-boyfriend signed off all rights to the baby. Then the agency found me the Levinsons, a really wonderful couple in Sacramento. The Levinsons paid all of my expenses. They flew me to Sacramento and put me up in my own apartment. I had all the money I needed for living expenses during the remainder of my pregnancy. They also made sure that I had the best prenatal care."

"Nobody in your family wondered why you'd suddenly moved to California?" He sounded skeptical.

"It was a hard time for the family. My half siblings were totally pissed off at how my dad married Willow so fast and installed her in Sondra's house. None of us—meaning my mother's kids—liked it, either. My moving to Sacramento for a while didn't even make the radar with them. Except for my mother. She's usually the definition of self-absorbed, but somehow she figured it out. I was six months along when she showed up on my doorstep. She didn't give me a hard time, just wanted to know how I was and insisted on meeting the Levinsons. She's never told anyone, as far as I know."

"It's a secret, then—from everyone else in your family?"

A curl of defensiveness tightened her belly. "It's just... It's never been something anyone needed to know."

"That wasn't a criticism." He looked at her so levelly, and his voice was kind. "I just needed to know if the information is confidential."

"I *am* going to tell them. One of these days." She glanced toward the unlit fireplace and tried not to feel like crap about everything.

After a minute or two, he nudged her along. "So... you had the baby?"

She just wanted this sad, old story over with. "Yeah. A little boy. The Levinsons took him right away. I didn't want to see him or hold him, you know? Didn't want to take any chance of getting too attached. The Levinsons and I agreed *not* to keep in touch. When he's eighteen, if he chooses to, he can contact me. I moved back home a few weeks after the birth. That should have been the end of it. But then, about two years ago, I couldn't take it anymore, wondering. Worrying that I'd done the wrong thing, that maybe he was unhappy, maybe he needed me."

"You got in touch with the couple who adopted him, after all?"

She shook her head. "I didn't want to freak them out, get them scared that I had changed my mind. I just wanted to know for sure that he was all right. So I hired a private investigator. He worked up a detailed report, including pictures of the Levinson family with my little boy, whose name is Josh. I could see from the photographs that he's happy. There was one of him hugging his mother in the front yard..." The pointless tears blurred her vision again. She dashed them away. "All that to say that I believe Josh Levinson is doing just fine."

Seth grabbed the box of tissues from the coffee table. He held them out to her.

She took one and blew her nose for the umpteenth time that evening. "And now..."

"Yeah?"

"Well, the plan was that this time, with Marybeth, I would do it right, you know? I would keep my baby and have it all handled. I would be calm and relaxed and completely on top of things."

"That's a tall order."

"A lot of women manage it."

"Jody, you're doing fine."

"But Marybeth seems so unhappy. I mean, am I starving her? It seems like she's hungry all the time. So far it just feels like I'm getting everything wrong." She lowered her head and tore at the soggy tissue in her hands.

"Hey." Seth's hand settled over hers, so warm, slightly rough, wonderfully soothing.

She looked up on a ragged breath and met those surprisingly soft brown eyes of his. Had she expected him to judge her?

Maybe. A little—after all, he was such a straight-and-narrow, upstanding sort of a guy.

But Seth didn't judge. "Your high school sweetheart was clearly no hero, and you did what you had to do at the time. You even checked back later to make sure the child was all right. And you're not getting it wrong now. Marybeth is healthy. She's going to be fine. You need to stop being so hard on yourself."

Jody sniffed. "Thank you." She probably shouldn't have, but she let her body sway toward him.

He didn't pull back. On the contrary, he wrapped those big arms around her and gave her a hug. For a lovely, lingering moment, she leaned into his solid strength, breathed in his clean scent and allowed herself to feel completely safe and protected.

And then a series of fussy little cries started up from the baby monitor.

"Shh," he whispered, his breath warm against her hair. "Maybe we'll get lucky and she'll go back to sleep."

"We can hope." She shamelessly indulged herself and snuggled in closer.

But the cries from the monitor only increased in length and intensity. Reluctantly, Jody pulled free of his embrace. She dabbed up the rest of her tears.

"I'll get her," he said.

She managed a smile. "You're the best. But it's definitely my turn."

It really helped, Jody realized, to confide in Seth, to let him reassure her and comfort her.

Within the next couple of days, the nursing seemed to go better. Marybeth still cried, but not nearly so much. She finally seemed to be getting enough milk.

By the end of that week, Jody knew she should tell Seth he didn't need to stay over anymore, that she could manage just fine on her own. But Sunday was Mother's Day, the biggest flower-selling day of the year—with the possible exception of Valentine's Day.

When she mentioned the crushing workload at Bloom over that coming weekend, Seth took family leave from the justice center. He looked after Marybeth full-time on Thursday, Friday, Saturday and Mother's Day, so that Jody could run between the house and Bloom getting ready for the big day and then selling flowers like crazy when Sunday finally came.

She promised herself that on Monday, once the Mother's Day push was over, she would sit down and have a talk with Seth. She would tell him how much she appreciated all he'd done and suggest that the time had come for him to move back to the ranch.

But Monday came and went. Somehow, she never quite got around to reminding him that she didn't need him living in her spare room anymore.

So he continued to show up every evening bringing wonderful baked goods from his fans at the sheriff's office and spelling Jody with Marybeth. He went back to the ranch once or twice a week to check in with the couple who took care of the place. But he lived at Jody's, essentially. And she just let him.

Because he took such good care of her little girl—and of Jody, too, to be honest. She counted on him more than she should have. Her life went so smoothly when he was around.

And sometimes, in the evenings while Marybeth slept, they would stream a movie together or just sit and talk about nothing in particular—like what went on at the sheriff's office and how his dad liked living in Dunedin, Florida, and how her mother had seemed driven to travel constantly since her father had died.

So yeah. When he left, she would not only miss his help with Marybeth, she would miss his company, too.

Elise, Nell, Clara and her half brother Darius's new wife, Ava, all stopped by that week. When they teased Jody that the sheriff had fallen for her, she shook her head and explained how Seth just needed to be there for Nick's little girl.

By then, Jody was taking Marybeth with her to Bloom for a few hours each day and feeling more and more confident that she hadn't turned out to be a complete failure at motherhood, after all. Really, it wasn't fair to Seth the way she kept taking advantage of him. The guy had his own life. How could he get out there and live it when he spent every spare moment with her and her baby?

Friday morning at breakfast, she made herself broach the subject. "Friday already," she said, going for a light touch. "Can you believe it?"

He sent her one of those looks. Like he could tell from her voice that she was probably up to something. "I've noticed it generally comes after Thursday."

"What I meant was, maybe you want a night off for once. You could catch a movie, go out for a beer…"

He frowned and then he shrugged. "I can watch a movie here with you, and there's beer in the fridge."

Okay, so much for the offhand approach. She wiped her mouth with her napkin. "Fine, Seth. I'll be more direct."

"Good idea." He watched her, those gold-flecked eyes wary.

"You've been here every night since we brought Marybeth home from the hospital…"

He set down his coffee cup. "You want me to get my stuff together and go back to the ranch, is that it?"

"No, I… Seth, I love having you here. I honestly do.

You're incredible with Marybeth and you're always so helpful, and I enjoy your company, too."

"So what's the problem, then?"

"Nothing. There's no problem. It's just, well, you've been beyond wonderful, but you have your own life and I have mine. We can't just go on like this, with you living in my spare room indefinitely."

"Why not? I like it here. I like everything about living here. I like helping out, being with Marybeth. And as you said, you and I get along great."

"But I—"

"Wait a minute." Now he was scowling. "Is it that you're afraid people will talk?"

She laughed. She couldn't help it.

His scowl deepened. "Why is that funny?"

"I don't know. I mean, who even worries about stuff like that anymore?"

His ears turned red. "I do. And if it bothers you, I—"

"Seth. Any possible gossip about you and me is not a problem for me, I promise you."

"Do you want me to pay rent, then?" Muscles bulged and knotted as he lifted an arm to rub the back of his big neck. "Because I'm happy to pay rent. In fact, I've been thinking I really should contribute. How about six hundred a month? Would that be enough?"

"Don't be ridiculous. Of course you're not paying me rent. You buy most of the food. You take care of the baby. You cook. You clean." She flopped back in her chair and folded her arms across her stomach. "Oh, Seth. Rent? Excuse me? Uh-uh. No way."

He got up, got the coffeepot and poured himself another cup. She watched him and tried not to think about how much she would miss him when he was gone, miss these ordinary moments—having breakfast together, watching him get up for more coffee, admiring the way he filled out his uniform both going and coming.

Yeah, okay. So what if she was perving on him? She might have sworn off sex and men, but there was no law against enjoying the view.

He sat back down. "All right. You like having me here. I make things easier for you, and you and I get along. You've refused my offer of rent and you say you're not worried about what people might say. So then, if none of those things are a problem for you, why *do* you want me to go back to the ranch?"

She gave up and admitted the truth. "I don't."

He got that look men too often get when confronted with the workings of a woman's mind. "Then, Jody, why are we talking about this?"

"Because… I don't know. I feel that I'm taking advantage of you."

"You're not. Can we consider this subject closed? Please."

"But…don't you want, you know, your freedom? Your independence? You're a single guy, and you ought to be enjoying yourself."

"Enjoying myself doing what, exactly?"

"I don't know. Playing poker with the guys? Going out with superhot women? Staying up all night?"

The corner of his stern mouth twitched. For Seth, the slight shift in expression was almost a grin. "I can stay up all night here. And I do. Whenever Marybeth won't go to sleep."

"Oh, you are just hilarious," she said with a sneer.

He knocked back a big slug of coffee and set the cup down harder than he needed to. "Look. Poker, sex with strange women and staying up all night have never been things that held much appeal for me. I'm a family guy, but my chance for getting married and having kids… well, that didn't work out for me."

"Hold on. Didn't work out? What does that mean?"

He rubbed the back of his neck again. "There was someone, once. Her name was Irene Vargas. She died."

When had that happened? She'd never heard a thing about it. "Here in Justice Creek?"

"No. Before. Years ago. In Chicago. I went to college there, and then I went to work for Chicago PD."

"Wait. You fell in love in Chicago and she died?"

"Yeah."

"Oh, Seth." What was it about him? He was so straight-up, so serious, so emotionally guarded. He wouldn't give his heart easily. That he'd loved someone and lost her—that would have cut him so deep. "I don't know what to say."

He made a gruff, throat-clearing sound. "There's nothing *to* say."

Oh, yes, there was. She wanted to know about it—about Irene, his lost love. All the details. Everything. But he was wearing his blank-eyed, watchful, lawman stare, and she knew he'd already revealed more than he wanted to. Still, she couldn't stop herself from suggesting, "I just meant, how are you going to find someone else if you're hanging around here all the time?"

"I'm not looking for anyone else."

"But—"

"Look, Jody. You're on your own and so am I. We get along and we both love Marybeth. I would rather be here than anywhere else. If you don't mind me being here, would you please not tell me that I should go?"

Okay, she got the message. He really wanted to be here. And *she* liked having him here. Win/win. Right?

Too bad warning bells had started ringing in the back of her brain. Because she liked having him here a little *too* much, now, didn't she? He was kind and smart—and funny in his dry, serious way. He took really good care of her daughter and of her. Add to all that the undeniable fact that he looked way too good in his uniform...

If she let him keep staying here, who knew what unacceptable emotions might creep up on her? He could be dangerous to her, to her heart that had already been broken and broken again, thank you very much.

And yet...

He loved her daughter, and he was a rock, right there when she needed him. She owed him for all the ways he'd come through for her since the night Marybeth was born.

At this point, she just couldn't bring herself to insist that he go. "All right, then, Seth. You're welcome to stay. We'll just take it day by day. If one of us starts to feel differently about this arrangement, we'll reevaluate. How's that?"

His hint of a smile went full out, and her silly heart did a somersault in the cage of her chest. "Thanks, Jody. You've made me a happy man."

Chapter Six

All that day and into the evening Jody couldn't stop asking herself, *Am I falling for Seth?*

Uh-uh. No way.

It was only that he'd turned out to somehow be the perfect man for her at this point in her life. All hot and hunky—and his idea of a great time was changing diapers and sleeping on her blow-up bed.

Was that even normal?

The guy really needed to get out more.

And seriously. Given the circumstances, of course he would start to seem like the guy for her. He adored her child, treated Jody like a queen and lived in her house with her, ensuring that she got an eyeful of his broad chest and fine butt day in and day out.

No, she decided late that night as she sat in her nursing chair with Marybeth in her arms. She wasn't falling for Seth. She was just grateful to him. Grateful and appreciative of his many wonderful qualities.

As any woman in her position would be.

The fourth Tuesday in May, Jody packed up Marybeth and all her baby gear and drove to Bloom at nine thirty in the morning. Marybeth behaved like an angel that day, so Jody stayed on past her usual few hours. Customer traffic was high for a Tuesday, with steady sales all morning and into the afternoon.

At four, Marybeth cooed from her carrier on the design counter as Jody filled a large Murano glass vase with purple irises and red tulips for a regular customer.

Marlie, at the register ringing up a sale, looked up when the entry bell chimed. "I'll be right with you…"

"No hurry," said the customer. She was probably around Jody's age, slim and attractive, with gorgeous, long ash-blond hair. She spotted Jody right away. They shared a smile, and the woman wandered over to the design counter.

"What a darling baby," she said. As if on cue, Marybeth cooed and waved her tiny hands.

Jody chuckled. "She can be an angel, absolutely. You have kids?"

"No." The blonde looked kind of wistful. "Still single, no babies." And then she asked much too casually, "Are you Jody?"

Jody clipped the stem of a tulip at a slant and tucked it into the arrangement. "That's me."

"I'm Adriana Welch. I moved to town from Colorado Springs a couple of years ago."

"Welcome to Bloom, Adriana. What can I help you with?"

"Well, I'm just…having a look around—and this little beauty is Marybeth, right?"

By then Jody had zero doubt that Adriana was after more than a bouquet of flowers. She stuck another tulip in the vase. "How did you know my baby's name?"

Spots of color flamed on Adriana's smooth cheeks. "Well, I know Seth. I met him a few months ago, right after they opened the justice center here in town. I went into the sheriff's office to take care of an overdue speeding ticket, and there he was. He's such a great guy. So steady and kindhearted, with that dry sense of humor…"

So. A card-carrying member of the Seth Yancy fan club. Jody should have guessed. "Did you make the key lime pie? Amazing. Or the double-chocolate cake? Unbelievable. Or wait. How about those deep-dish oatmeal chocolate bars? I have to tell you, at this rate I'll never lose the baby weight."

"I made the cake," Adriana confessed.

Jody groaned just thinking about that cake. "So good. I'll have you know you caused an orgasm in my mouth."

Adriana laughed. "Well, that is the goal." And then she raised a hand and wiggled her fingers. "Sheriff Yancy fangirl—I'll just go ahead and admit it."

Jody felt a little stab of annoyance at this pretty woman who baked a killer chocolate cake and also appeared to be a very nice person. Was it jealousy?

Absolutely not. Jody refused to be jealous of someone just because that someone had a crush on Seth. That would make no sense at all.

Well, not unless Jody wanted Seth for herself.

And she'd already come to the firm conclusion that she did not. The entry bell chimed again. A customer left with the arrangement Marlie had just rung up. Three women came in. Marlie went to help them. Adriana leaned closer and pitched her voice lower. "I know I'm being kind of pushy, but I really have to ask…"

Jody added another iris to the vase. "Go ahead."

"Well, Seth makes no secret of how much your baby means to him. He has pictures of her on his phone, and he's been showing them off." Jody wasn't surprised. He'd been snapping photos all weekend: Marybeth on her play mat, Marybeth in her bouncy chair, Marybeth in her newborn-size purple plastic bathtub. In the bathtub shot, he'd sworn she was smiling. Jody hadn't had the heart to tell him it was probably just gas.

"Yeah." Jody cut a generous length of cobalt blue grosgrain ribbon. "He loves his girl, no doubt about that."

"But is he…?" Adriana paused, apparently in search of just the right words. "I heard he's been staying at your house to help out since the birth?"

Jody nodded as she wrapped the ribbon around the neck of the vase. "He's been terrific. I don't know how I would have managed without him."

"But, um, are you two a couple—and, God, I hope it's not too tacky of me to ask?"

Jody tied the bow and fluffed it. "No. It is not the least tacky." Did she sound sincere? She hoped so. Because it wasn't tacky. It was up-front and honest. Not to mention brave. "And Seth and I are *not* a couple. He's just doing what he can for Nick's daughter."

"He's such a good man." Adriana said it with feeling.

"Oh, yeah." *Not jealous. Uh-uh. No way.* "The best."

"And I ask because, well, you know, Library Celebration Day is Saturday."

"That's right." Between having a baby and running her business at the same time, Jody had forgotten all about the event. "It's an all-day thing in Library Park, right?"

"Right. And in the afternoon, the library association is running a bachelor auction. Several local single guys have volunteered to go on the block, including Seth."

No way did that sound like something Seth would agree to. "If you win, what do you get?"

"A date with the bachelor you outbid everyone else for—and I think I heard your brother Garrett got roped into being auctioned off, too." Garrett was second-oldest of Jody's three full brothers and the only one currently unattached.

And Seth's involvement in such a non-Seth-like activity was starting to make sense now. "Roped into it, huh?"

"Pretty much. Have you *met* the president of the library association? Nobody says no to Caroline Carruthers."

Jody knew Caroline. And Adriana was right about her. "So, bottom line, Seth is on the bachelor auction block Saturday, and you want to bid on him?"

Adriana blushed and beamed. "Oh, yes, I do. And I'm not the only one who'd like to win a night out with Seth—I mean, as long as he's not taken."

Jody had a totally contrary urge to put on her meanest face and order the blonde to back off. But that wouldn't be right. Seth was not hers and never would be.

"Jody?" Adriana prompted hopefully.

And Jody made herself say it. "He's not taken."

"But are you sure?" Adriana didn't look convinced.

"Seth Yancy is a free man," Jody insisted with a firm nod. "Go for it. And good luck."

That night at six thirty, Seth used the key Jody had given him to let himself in. The house smelled of something good for dinner. It was great to be home.

Not home. Jody's house, he sternly corrected himself.

He was kind of having trouble lately remembering that he didn't actually live here, that he was only staying temporarily, until Jody decided it was time for him to go.

He hoped she'd let him stay on indefinitely, but he knew that eventually she would want her privacy and the use of her spare room again. She would send him back to the ranch where the Califanos had everything under control and he had the main house all to himself.

Seth loved that old house. Yancys had been born and raised in it for four generations. But with only him living there, the place echoed with emptiness.

Unlike Jody's house, which smelled like dinner and made a man feel welcome, made him feel as though he was part of a family, after all. And he was. Marybeth was his family. Jody, too, when you came right down to it. She and Marybeth were a package, and he was just fine with that.

"I've got stew ready in the Crock-Pot. Hungry?" she asked when he entered the kitchen and went straight to the sink to wash his hands.

"Yeah. Smells good."

She'd already set the kitchen table. He got himself a beer, and they sat down.

"I talked to my dad today," he said as he smoothed his napkin on his lap and reached for his fork. "He wants to fly out for a visit the first week of June. He can't wait to see Marybeth."

"First week of June would be great."

"He would stay at the ranch. But he's pretty excited about being a grandpa, so you'd better expect to have him underfoot a lot around here."

"I'm looking forward to getting to know him."

"Good, then. I'll tell him."

They both got to work on the stew. Seth was just getting that prickly feeling under his skin that she had something on her mind when she said, "Adriana Welch stopped by Bloom to see me today."

He swallowed the hunk of meat he'd just stuck in his mouth. It went down hard. He had no idea why he felt suddenly on edge. Yes, Adriana was one of his supposed fan club, but what could she possibly say to Jody that could get him in trouble? "She's a nice woman, Adriana."

"Yes, I thought so, too…"

That. Right there. The way her voice trailed off at the end. What did that mean, exactly?

He asked with great caution, "And she came by to see you, why?"

Jody sipped her ice water and set the glass down just so. "She and several other women plan to bid on you at the bachelor auction Saturday."

The bachelor auction. A raw litany of bad words scrolled through his brain. He'd been trying not even to think about Saturday. It was coming up way too fast.

Jody added, "Adriana wanted to check with me first, though, to make sure you're not taken."

"Taken," he repeated blankly. And then he said it again, this time as a question. "Taken?"

"Well, Seth. You've been living in my house for weeks. It's natural that your admirers would start to wonder if you and I are doing more together than looking after the baby."

Seth drank some beer—a big gulp of it, as a matter of fact. "I hope you set her straight," he said. And then as soon as the words were out, he wanted to snatch them back. Because he honestly wouldn't mind in the least if people thought he and Jody were together.

If he and Jody were together, he would never have to go back to living alone. He could be with her and Marybeth, have a permanent place with them. Every day that passed, he wanted that more.

"I told her not to worry, that you definitely weren't taken."

"You encouraged her." It came out sounding like an accusation—which he supposed it was.

"Yes, I did. It's the truth. You're *not* taken. And besides, you want women bidding on you, the higher the better."

"No, I don't."

"Well, you should. It's for a good cause."

"I don't like it, Jody. I never liked it. That Carruthers woman just wouldn't take no for an answer."

"Seth. Come on. It'll be fun."

"No, it won't."

She made a low, teasing sound in her throat. "You know what you sound like?"

"Don't tell me."

But of course, she did. "An overgrown baby. Pull up your big-boy pants and stop with the tantrum."

He gave her the kind of look he usually reserved for repeat offenders. "I am a grown man. Grown men do not have tantrums." She just shook her head and ate more stew. And he couldn't stop himself from asking, "Will you be there?"

She frowned. "For the auction? I wasn't planning to, no."

He wanted that, he realized. He wanted her there. A lot. "It's a whole-day thing. With booths, games, food, music. The auction is from two to four. You could bring Marybeth. You'll have a great time."

Her mouth was twitching. He failed to see what was so all-fired amusing. "Seth, the last thing I need is to bid on a bachelor—and you'd better not be working up to asking me to bid on *you*."

Why not? That sounded like an excellent idea to him. He could give her the money. She could win him, and he wouldn't have to go out with Adriana or some other nice woman he had zero interest in romantically. It wouldn't exactly be fair play. But the library would still get the money, and that was the goal.

However, the way she was looking at him, he knew she wouldn't go for that. So he fibbed, "No way would I ask that of you."

She didn't believe him. He could see it in those fine blue eyes. But she played along. "Good."

"I just need a little moral support from my two favorite girls, that's all. Caroline Carruthers wouldn't take no for an answer, and now I'll be going out with some woman from town, and the truth is, I have a firm rule about that."

"What rule?"

"I don't date local women."

"Why not?"

He didn't want to get into it. But somehow, he found

himself telling her anyway. "Because I know it's never going to go anywhere with anyone, so to date someone in my county is just going to lead to trouble in the end. I don't want things to get messy. I'm the sheriff, after all."

She sat back and folded her arms. Not a good sign. "How 'bout this? Maybe if you took a chance, went out on a limb and spent an evening with a nice woman, you might change your mind and realize you would like to get something going with her, after all."

"I won't. That isn't going to happen."

She put both hands to her head, as though this conversation might possibly cause her brain to explode. "Seth. How can you be so sure?"

"I have no interest in a relationship. I'm the sheriff, and it's on me to set a good example—which means *not* leading innocent women on."

Jody outright scoffed at him then. "Oh, come on. It's the twenty-first century. Not a trembling virgin in sight."

Now he felt kind of insulted. "I wouldn't encourage a virgin—especially not a trembling one."

"Great, then. Because Adriana seems confident and savvy to me. She's not going to expect anything beyond a nice evening out with you if she wins a date with you— and I'm betting the rest of the women who might bid on you are the same, right?"

He didn't want to answer her. He knew it would only get him deeper into this uncomfortable conversation that he didn't want to be having in the first place.

"Right?" she demanded again.

He gave in and said it. "Right."

"So then, I can promise you that none of them will

expect a lifetime commitment because you took them out."

"I just don't believe in any of that."

She looked at him sideways. "Um, any of what?"

"Dating someone when I know it's not going to go anywhere."

Jody sat forward again, picked up her dinner roll, tore it in half and then dropped it back to her plate. "It doesn't have to go anywhere. I mean, come on. You don't have to be married to have a good time with someone."

He opened his mouth to backpedal a little, but ended up blurting out the bald truth about himself instead. "I'm not after a good time with someone. I don't believe in sex outside of marriage—or without love, at least. Preferably both."

Jody gaped. "I don't know where to start. By *a good time*, I don't necessarily mean sex. But as long as we're going there, you've never *been* married. Have you?"

"No, I have not."

Her head went back and forth, and her eyes were wide as dinner plates. "I know I shouldn't ask..."

"No, you probably shouldn't." He drank some beer.

And she asked anyway. "So you've never had sex with anyone?"

He could simply refuse to answer her. But over the past weeks something of a bond had grown between them. He felt a need to make her understand. "I've had sex, yes—with women I wasn't married to. When I was younger I didn't always live up to my beliefs."

She clapped both hands to her mouth, as if trying to keep the next question from getting out.

A hard sigh escaped him. "Go ahead. Ask."

She dropped her hands. "What about Irene, in Chicago?"

He almost just told her to mind her own business. But the bond he felt with her tugged at him. He lived in her house, and he understood that if he wanted to *keep* living there, he needed to make an effort to get along with her, to communicate. "Yes," he said. "Irene and I were lovers. I was in love with her. I'd asked her to marry me and she'd said yes. I already *felt* married to her."

"And after you lost Irene?"

"There's been no one. Except myself, I guess you could say."

"Wait a minute. Not a single date? You didn't meet someone for coffee? Nothing?"

"There were dates, yeah, after I'd been back here in Colorado for a couple of years. I'm human, after all." He watched her sip that weird herbal tea she liked and waited for a teasing remark concerning his humanity or lack thereof. But no. She was quiet, her gaze locked with his over the rim of her mug. So he continued, "I went out with a few women I met online."

"I'm guessing these were women who didn't live in Broomtail County?"

"You're guessing right. I took them to dinner and maybe a movie and then I took them home. But I knew it wasn't going anywhere, that I was kidding myself and wasting their time and mine. I didn't want sex with a stranger. And I didn't want a relationship. So after a while, I stopped looking, online or otherwise."

"How long since you returned to Colorado from Illinois?"

"Seven years."

"Oh, Seth." She said it way too softly. Too...tenderly.

"What?" he demanded in a growl.

"I can't decide if I'm sad for all you've missed out on—or in awe of you for having principles and managing to stick by them for seven long years."

"Awe. I'll take awe."

She laughed. And then he laughed, too, of all things. The sound was pretty rusty. But still, it felt good.

They picked up their forks and started eating again. Neither of them spoke for several minutes.

He scooped up the last bite of his stew. As soon as he'd chewed and swallowed, he took another stab at getting her to be there Saturday. "Please, come to the park for the auction."

She looked up from mangling her dinner roll. "It's not going to be that bad. And it's only one date."

"You sound like Caroline Carruthers," he grumbled. And then he leveled his gaze on her and willed her to give in. "Please, come. I want a friend there."

At 1:45 on Saturday afternoon, Library Park was packed.

People wandered from booth to booth, buying T-shirts, books and library paraphernalia, handmade crafts and art by local painters and photographers. Kids played tag between the trees. There was a food pavilion—a giant white canopy over rows of picnic tables, food carts surrounding the covered tables. Under another wide white canopy beside a portable stage, a six-piece band played country rock.

Jody, in jeans and a Bloom T-shirt, black Chucks and a Broncos hat, pushed Marybeth in her stroller and made a mental note to find out if this would become an annual event. If so, next year, she'd see about getting Bloom involved somehow.

"Darling!"

Jody glanced back and saw her mother, gorgeous as always in black capri pants, an off-the-shoulder lace-work shirt and sexy wedge sandals, coming toward her. "Ma!" She wheeled the stroller under a tree, out of the way of the crowd.

"It's so good to see you." Willow took her by the shoulders and air-kissed her cheek, bringing the scent of sandalwood and tropical flowers, a fragrance that some shop in Paris made just for her. "I flew in this morning, and Estrella said the magic words *party in the park* and *bachelor auction*." Estrella Watson was the Bravo Mansion's longtime housekeeper. "Well, I had to see for myself—and what have we here?" Willow dipped to a graceful crouch beside the stroller. "Hello, beautiful. It's me, your grandmother, who completely adores you." Marybeth was having another good day. She waved her hands at her grandma and cheerfully cooed. "She's perfect. I have a few little treasures for her. I must drop by with them. Soon."

"Anytime. I'm at the shop a few hours a day, but the times vary. Just call my cell first."

"I will." Willow swept upward again. "You look well. A little haggard."

Gee, thanks, Ma. "I keep busy."

"Don't wear yourself to a nub, now."

Jody tried not to grit her teeth. "Ma, I will do my best."

"Excellent. So. Are you here to nab yourself a bachelor?"

"No."

"I hear Caroline Carruthers managed to round up the hottest, most successful single men in town—including your brother Garrett," Willow added with pride.

Jody was stuck back there with her mother talking about hot men. Did Willow plan on bidding? Eww. "Uh, yeah. Garrett's on the block, all right."

"I hope some lovely girl wins him. It's about time he settled down."

"Ma. It's for a good cause, but come on. Nobody's ending up married to Garrett because they 'won' him at the library auction."

"Honestly, Johanna." Willow hit her with her given name though she preferred Jody, and Willow knew it, too. "You have zero romance in your far-too-practical soul."

"You may be right." Romance hadn't exactly been good to her so far.

Willow said, "The bachelors have been all over the park today, chatting up women, introducing themselves." Jody tried not to wince for poor Seth. He would just love wandering the park, instigating teasing conversations with random women. Not. Her mother asked coyly, "So, how many bachelors have you met so far?"

"Marybeth and I just arrived." In order to support Seth, who wouldn't shut up about it until Jody agreed to be there when the bidding started.

"Did you at least check out the list of prospects and their bios on the library website? Your sheriff is included."

"He's hardly *my* sheriff."

"Well, he was there for you, right, the night Marybeth was born?" Before Jody could answer her, Willow whipped out her tablet phone and stuck it in front of

Jody's face. "Look." Handsome male faces scrolled up the screen. A picture of Seth went by. He looked manly and determined, a ray of light glinting off the badge on his uniform shirt. "See anything you particularly like?"

Laughing in spite of herself, Jody slipped her hand under the visor of her cap and covered her eyes. "Ma. Stop. Now."

Willow lowered the phone and heaved a sigh so loud it could be heard over the band wrapping up a cover of Sam Hunt's "Make You Miss Me."

"I worry you'll never find what you're looking for, darling, that's all."

Jody stared into her mother's beautiful sea green eyes and reminded herself that Willow just wanted the best for her. "Thank you. But I have everything I need, and I'm happy. I truly am."

Willow made a show of pressing her lips together. "This is me keeping my mouth shut—and look." She pointed at the stage where Caroline Carruthers had stepped up to the mic. "The auction begins."

Caroline spread her arms wide and announced with enthusiasm, "Welcome, everyone, to our first annual Library Celebration Day!" Jody clapped good and loud with everyone else. And then Caroline launched into a spirited speech, starting with how happy she was to see such a crowd on this beautiful May afternoon. She ran down a list of the latest improvements at the library, encouraging everyone to come often and use all the library's services. She reminded them all about the silent auction just waiting for more bids under a nearby canopy, then announced the total donations so far, mostly from people giving money online. She thanked a few donors and volunteers specifically for their generous and ongoing support.

Then she leaned close to the mic and mock-whispered gleefully, "And, yes, ladies and gentlemen, it's that time at last. Fifteen of Justice Creek's best-looking and most eligible single guys are stepping into the spotlight today, offering fifteen fortunate and generous women the chance for the date of their dreams. I present to you...the bachelors of Justice Creek!"

The band played "Fever," and out they came, most of them good-naturedly strutting, some even busting Magic Mike–like moves. They wore tight jeans, cowboy boots and snug, muscle-showcasing T-shirts printed with library-themed humor: "Reading is sexy" and "Meet me in the stacks" and "I read past my bedtime."

Two of the bachelors were firefighters. They wore yellow helmets and red suspenders. Garrett, who ran Bravo Construction, wore a tool belt. Seth had a badge pinned over his heart as did a guy she recognized from Justice Creek PD. The guy from the police department even had handcuffs clipped to his belt. He was one of the better dancers, and he really got the crowd whooping and cheering.

Seth didn't dance. He walked in and stood at the end of the line of men. And she had to hand it to him. He looked dangerously hot not doing anything, just standing there in jeans that hugged his hard thighs and that tight black T-shirt that clung to his chest like it was in love with him. No wonder the women couldn't quit baking him pies.

Jody knew he was looking for her. She watched those eagle eyes scanning the crowd. She gave him a hint of a nod when he spotted her and felt a certain lovely warmth low in her belly at the way his hard face softened when their gazes met.

Her mother leaned close. "Okay, Johanna. There's more than love for Marybeth going on with you and Seth Yancy."

"Mind your own business, Ma," she replied out of the side of her mouth.

"You know I'm bound to find out anyway."

She would, of course. That Seth spent all his free time at Jody's place was no secret. Jody went ahead and admitted, "He's been helping me out."

"Helping you out, how?"

"You name it, he helps with it. We've become friends, I guess you could say. And since we brought Marybeth home from the hospital, he's been staying at my house nights, in the spare room."

"No." There was far too much breathless glee in that single word.

Jody looked her mother square in the eye. "Yeah."

That silenced Willow—at least for now.

Caroline went down the line, spending a minute or two with each bachelor, getting their names, their ages, their occupations and their interests. Then the men filed offstage, and a couple of guys brought on a podium. A rangy older man in a cowboy hat came on. Caroline introduced him as the auctioneer. He moved behind the podium. The band played "Let's Get It On" and out came the first bachelor.

The bidding began.

It was actually kind of exciting. And a lot of fun. The guy from Justice Creek PD was third to last and brought nine hundred bucks, which had everyone hooting and hollering in glee. Garrett was next. He had that killer smile, and he joked about his tool belt and what good care he took of his tools. A nice bidding war ensued over him. He brought twelve hundred, the best price so far.

And then there was Seth. He strode onstage to "Pour Some Sugar on Me," not even cracking a smile. How did he do it? He walked straight and stood proud and somehow the temperature in the park rose by ten degrees—or was Jody the only one who felt the heat?

Caroline had questions on cue cards from the ladies in the crowd. Seth answered them straight-faced, big arms folded across his powerful chest.

The bidding commenced. A lot of women joined in, Adriana Welch leading the pack. She topped each competing bid.

Seth stood mostly unmoving through the process, wearing his sternest, most sheriff-like expression, not friendly at all, yet somehow so…magnetic. He was like some giant tree that begged to be climbed. Every woman in that park seemed to feel the power of his uncompromising stare. Didn't they?

Jody certainly did.

And he kept looking at her, glances that burned right through her. She knew what he was doing. That man was willing her to save him from Adriana and the rest of them. But Jody stood firm. It wasn't her job to rescue him, and it wasn't going to kill him to spend an evening out with someone like Adriana, someone pretty and fun.

Or so she kept telling herself every time she almost let her hand shoot up to join in the bidding war.

And not because he willed her to, either. Not to save his fine butt from the women who adored him.

Uh-uh. Not to help him out.

But because she wanted to—wanted to place the

winning bid and get all those other girls to back the hell off. Wanted to stake her claim and make sure everyone knew that he belonged to her.

Which he did not. Not in any way.

What was the matter with her? This could be a problem and she knew it. She never should have let him talk her into coming to the park today. She should have stayed home, not let herself get involved in any way.

Jody held her arms down tight to her sides and set her mind firmly on not raising a hand, no matter what. All she had to do was last until the auctioneer banged his gavel on the podium and shouted, *Sold!*

And then her mother leaned close. "Win that man," Willow commanded. "Or I'll do it for you."

Jody sent her mother her best arctic glare. "Ma. Don't you dare."

Willow did dare.

She lifted her shapely arm, snapped her perfectly manicured fingers to get the auctioneer's attention and took the next bid.

Chapter Seven

Adriana countered Willow's bid. Another woman countered that.

And Willow bid again.

A lot of people knew Willow Mooney Bravo. They knew the story of Willow and Frank and Frank's first wife, Sondra. To most longtime residents of Justice Creek, Willow was considered nothing short of a home-wrecking femme fatale.

Jody wanted to sink right through the grass to the center of the earth as all around her and her baby and her infuriating mother, people snickered and stared and a few of them even whispered to each other. They laughed and they clapped. Jody knew what at least a few of them were wondering: Had bad Willow Bravo suddenly decided to put a move on hunky, upstanding Sheriff Yancy? What would she do to him? Something ruinous, wicked and wild, no doubt.

The last to drop out against Willow was Adriana. Willow topped her final bid by shouting, "Fifteen hundred!" It was two hundred dollars higher than Adriana's bid. Everybody clapped.

The auctioneer pounded his gavel and asked Adriana for fifty bucks more. She shook her head. "Going once," warned the auctioneer. "Going twice..."

Seth had relaxed since Willow started bidding—oh, he was still standing there with his arms crossed and his legs braced apart, his expression carved in stone. But after living with the guy for weeks, Jody could read him pretty well. She saw the twitch at the corner of his mouth that gave away his effort not to smile.

Apparently, he'd figured out what her mother was up to, that Willow was set on winning him for Jody. And being won by Jody was what he'd been after all along.

Because they were good buddies, Seth and Jody. Because he could count on her not to try to put a move on him. With Jody, things wouldn't get "messy."

For some reason, that he was so pleased with her mother's machinations annoyed Jody no end. If she was going to win the guy anyway, she would damn well make it happen herself.

Jody stuck up her hand.

The whole park seemed to go absolutely still. Silence echoed in the balmy air.

The auctioneer pointed his gavel at Jody. "Fifteen fifty." He aimed the gavel at her mother. "An even sixteen?" Willow gave a tiny shake of her golden head. The auctioneer scanned the crowd. "Do I hear sixteen? Ladies? Don't miss out! Going once, going twice..." The gavel went down. "Sold to the lady in the Broncos cap for 1,550 dollars!"

The crowd went wild, clapping, laughing, whistling. Throwing their hats in the air.

"Attagirl." Willow patted her shoulder. Jody turned to say something sarcastic, but her mother had already set off through the crowd.

Caroline Carruthers called, "Winners, congratulations! Come on up here and claim your men!"

There was more hooting and hollering. That last burst of sound finally woke Marybeth up. She started to cry.

Jody pushed the fussing baby forward toward the stage. When she got there, Seth could soothe Marybeth. After all, she'd paid fifteen fifty for him. He could at least make himself useful.

Seth was waiting for her, looking way too pleased with the way things had turned out. He jumped down off the stage, took the stroller with Marybeth in it and hoisted it up there. Then he reached for Jody.

She shook her head. "I'll take the stairs."

But he grabbed her by the waist and lifted her anyway.

As her feet left the ground, she clutched his giant shoulders and let out a shriek. "Seth, put me down!"

And he did—on the stage, which brought another loud flurry of applause and laughter from the crowd. Then he jumped right up beside her, grabbed her hand and raised it high. "Smile," he commanded. "Give the folks a wave."

It was done. She'd won the guy. Might as well give the crowd what they wanted. Jody smiled and waved, which caused more clapping and stomping and catcalls.

When Seth finally let go of her hand, he bent right down to Marybeth, lifting her so gently out of the stroller and up to his shoulder. The ripple of applause increased again, but Marybeth didn't seem to care about all the noise now. She snuggled right in.

They joined the other bachelors and their dates. Caroline thanked the crowd and the auctioneer. She congratulated the winners and reminded them of the table under the tree where three library-association ladies waited with open cash boxes and credit-card readers to take the money the winners had bid.

To a final round of applause, the group on the stage disbanded. Seth put Marybeth back in the stroller long enough to get her down off the stage.

Jody jumped down after them. "If you'll take the baby for a minute, I'll settle up with the library ladies."

Marybeth had started fussing the minute he put her back in the stroller, so he scooped her up again and cradled her close. The crying stopped.

"I'll take care of the money," he said. "It's only fair."

Jody made a show of rolling her eyes. "What in the world has fairness got to do with this?"

He leaned closer, and she got a tempting whiff of his manly, clean scent. "Come on, Jody. I know your mom forced your hand. Let me pay for this. I want to."

"Ah, but see, *that* wouldn't be fair." She poked him in the chest with a finger. It was like poking a boulder. "I won you. I'll pay for you."

He shook his big head and patted the baby on his shoulder. "There's no making you see reason when you get that stubborn look."

"It's settled, then. Watch the baby. I'll be right back."

"I'll go with you, at least."

Together, they headed to the long table under the tree. Jody pulled her credit card from her cross-body bag and waited her turn to pay. Seth, at her side, held Marybeth in one arm and pushed the stroller with his free hand, making himself useful as he always did. The guy was way too easy to have around.

Jody tried to keep in mind all the ways he irritated her. Didn't work. Her frustration with the situation had faded to nothing.

Seth was happy and so was Marybeth. It felt great to be out in the sun on a beautiful day. Yeah, he'd just cost her more than fifteen hundred bucks. But hey. It would go to a good cause.

At the front of the line, she offered her credit card to the lady from the library association. "I won the sheriff." Beside her, Seth actually dared to chuckle, and she had to stop herself from poking him in the ribs with an elbow.

But the library lady shook her head. "Your bid's been paid."

"By who?"

The library lady peered at her list. "Mrs. Franklin Bravo."

Ma. She should have known.

Jody turned and glared at Seth, who was actively grinning. Seriously, the man never cracked a smile, but today he couldn't stop smirking. "What are you going to do if my mother wants her date with you?"

His grin vanished. She found his look of bewildered surprise way too gratifying.

But then the library lady piped up with, "Are you Johanna Bravo?"

"Yeah. So?"

"It says here that you are the holder of the winning

bid. Mrs. Bravo has only paid it for you. The date with the sheriff is yours."

Jody whipped her head around to find Seth starting to smirk again. "Wipe that smile off your face," she commanded. He tried to look innocent, but didn't succeed. She turned back to the lady behind the cash box. "As you just pointed out, *I* won the sheriff. I want to pay for my prize."

"I'm so sorry," said the library lady. "But this bid is already paid. It's a donation freely given. We don't refund donations."

Jody tapped her Chuck Taylor. Damn her mother anyway. Willow just *had* to have the last word.

And really, Jody should have been happy with Willow paying up. Her mother had a lot more money than Jody did. Plus, Jody had only won Seth because her mother had manipulated her into it. It could definitely be considered fair that Willow should pay.

Beside her, Seth cleared his throat.

She froze him with a glance. "Shh. I'm thinking." And that was when the solution came to her. She gave the library lady a gracious nod. "All right, then. I'd like to make a donation for 1,550 dollars, please."

As the library lady's eyes lit up, Seth growled, "Jody..."

She shushed him again. Yes, shushing was rude, but she didn't feel like listening to him tell her what to do. "It's tax deductible," she muttered, as if that explained everything. "And it's for a good cause."

"Oh, yes, it is!" chirped the library lady as she accepted Jody's credit card.

Once Jody had signed for the money and received her tax-deductible receipt, her Silver Star Limo voucher and gold-embossed coupon for a full day of pampering at Sweet Harmony Day Spa, Seth suggested, "Why don't we hang around for a while, get something to eat and enjoy the band?"

"Oh, right," Jody scoffed. "Now the auction's over and you don't have to worry about one of your admirers putting a move on you, you're feeling good."

He didn't even pretend to deny it. "Hey. Got me there. Let's get a hot dog."

"Why not?" Marybeth seemed content. If she got hungry, Jody had pumped milk that morning and had a bottle ready to feed her.

They stayed for two hours. Jody devoured a chili dog and a tall lemonade, and they made the rounds of the craft, art and book booths, meeting up with Clara and Dalton and their little girl, Kiera, for a while and later running into Jody's half brother James, his wife, Addie, their seven-month-old, Brandon, and Addie's grandfather and her grandfather's girlfriend, too. They all sat together at a picnic table to catch up.

More than one of the other women who had bid on Seth stopped by to congratulate Jody on her win, Adriana among them. She leaned close to Jody and teased, "We all knew there was more going on with you two than you admitted the other day."

Jody played along. "It was the tight T-shirt. I realized I *had* to have him."

Seth, sitting next to Jody feeding Marybeth her bottle, heard what both women had said.

He knew Jody was joking, but her response pleased him anyway. Somehow he kind of liked the idea of Jody laying claim to him. He liked just about everything right at this moment.

Was this happiness? It sure felt like it.

Seven long years had passed since he last felt this way, felt that the world had more good in it than evil, that today was a fine day and tomorrow would be great, too.

He looked down at the baby he held in his arms. She waved her little fist and made soft smacking noises as she sucked on her bottle. That feeling happened in his chest, a good kind of tightness, a warmth. A rightness. He'd only truly loved a few people in his life: his dad, his stepmother, Nicky and Irene.

And now there was Marybeth. There had been too many losses. But Marybeth made up for a whole lot of loss.

Beside him, Jody laughed at something her brother James had said. Seth liked Jody's laugh. It was low and rich and real. It reached down inside him and stirred things up. At first, he'd fought that stirring. But sometime in the past week or so, he'd given in and let himself be stirred.

He liked a lot of things about Jody. She was smart and beautiful and easy to be around. She didn't take any crap from him, and he admired her for the way she stood up for her beliefs. He'd also grown to respect her. Slowly, he'd come to appreciate her ingrained integrity. Yeah, she'd made some choices he would never have made. But she owned her mistakes, took responsibility for her actions.

He fully understood now why Nicky had fallen for her.

And as for himself? He'd finally faced the truth.

He was attracted to her. He couldn't deny it anymore, didn't want to deny it.

They were compatible, him and Jody. They worked well together. He'd lived in her house for three and a half weeks and their lives just naturally seemed to fit together like the parts of a well-oiled machine. They never argued over household stuff. They both just kept at it till everything that needed doing got done. They picked up the slack for each other.

They were a good team.

And lately, in the past few days anyway, maybe longer, he kept finding himself thinking that they could have a good life together, raise Marybeth together, be a family, even have more kids...

That night, when Jody dropped down beside him on the sofa in the great room after putting Marybeth to bed, he muted the basketball game and asked, "So where do you want to go for our big date?"

She made a sound of amusement low in her throat. "What date? I want you right here doing what you always do, rocking the baby, changing the diapers, bringing the baked goods and the takeout for dinner—and washing up the dishes afterward."

Actually, he loved the sound of that. "Whatever you want from me, Jody, it's yours."

She drew up her bare feet and crossed them on the cushions. "Wow. That was downright affectionate."

He wanted to touch her—that silky brown hair, the curve of her cheek. Yeah, he still loved Irene and that was forever. After losing her, he'd known that he would never get married.

But now there was Marybeth, and she changed how

he looked at things. He and Jody could make a good life together—good for each other, good for Marybeth. "Ever been married?"

She grabbed a throw pillow and bopped him on the shoulder with it. "Really? Suddenly you want to talk about my past relationships?"

He picked up the remote again and turned the game off. "What's wrong with that?"

"I don't know. It just seems…un-Seth-like, somehow. I mean, you're always willing to listen when I need to talk something out, and I appreciate that about you. But you're not exactly one of those guys who *asks* for it."

"Look. I like you."

"Um. I like you, too?"

He almost laughed. She did that to him. Made him want to laugh again. "Do you *really* like me, Jody?"

She hugged the pillow to her chest. "Of course I do."

"Good. Ever been married?"

"Never."

"Serious relationships?"

She hugged the pillow tighter and tipped her head to the side, studying him "You honestly want to know." That time it wasn't a question.

"Yes, I do."

She tipped her head the other way and stared at him some more. Then, finally, she gave it up. "No, I have never been married. After my father carried on a quarter-century-long affair with my mother while still married to his wife and then my high school boyfriend dumped me because I was having his baby, I had some serious trust issues when it came to men, I guess you might say."

"Understandable."

She put the pillow in her lap and fiddled with the fringe on it. "After I came back from Sacramento, I went to CU for a business degree. And I went a little wild in college. I had more than a few lovers. But there was nobody serious. I wanted things casual. I didn't want to get too close." She slanted him a wary look. "Don't get judgy, now."

He hadn't been judging her. Had he? "What makes you think I'm judging you?"

"I know how you are, Mr. Straight-and-Narrow."

"Jody. Come on. I told you I had some wild years myself."

She laughed then. "Point taken. So, I kept things casual, but I *was* looking."

"For?"

"A good guy, a trustworthy guy. When I was twenty-three, I found that guy. Or so I thought. His name was Brent Saunders. Brent was an insurance adjuster here in town. He was also kind and gentle and thoughtful. I just knew I had found what I was looking for. We were together for four years."

"What went wrong?"

"Brent was never quite ready to talk about marriage. At first, that worked for me. I wanted to take my time, to be sure it was the real thing with him. We'd been together about eight months when he told me he loved me. I said I loved him, too. After that, he was always saying it. But he never said a word about forever. After two years together, I told him my goals, which included marriage and children—marriage to *him*, I hoped."

"So then, he finally proposed?"

"Not a chance. Brent was vague on the marriage thing. He loved me more than his life, he said. But why rush into anything? We had plenty of time. After four years together, I finally admitted to myself that Brent and I were going nowhere. I broke it off. Three months later, he eloped with the receptionist at his office. They moved to Seattle soon after."

"What a jerk. Not to mention, a fool."

"Thank you. I mean, he could've had *me*."

"He was an idiot."

She hugged her pillow again. "You're kind of a hard-ass, Seth."

"Me? No. I'm gentle. Trustworthy. Thoughtful, too."

She snorted a little as she stifled a giggle. "What I meant is that being a hard-ass is only on the outside. Deep down you're a softy. And sometimes you do say just the right things."

"I say what I really think."

"Mostly. Except when you put on your Mount Rushmore face and say nothing at all."

"Sometimes less is more when it comes to talking."

"Said no woman, ever." Her cheeks were pink, and those blue eyes gleamed. And her mouth. He liked the shape of it, the pretty dip of the Cupid's bow on top, the softness below.

He wanted to kiss her. But he held himself in check. For now. "But about Brent…"

She cocked an eyebrow. "Yeah?"

"It must be a relief that you never said yes to that bozo."

"Well, he would've had to ask in order for me to say yes to him, but you're right. It worked out for the best."

"And after Brent the bonehead?"

"Hmm. Brent the bonehead. Catchy. I like it."

"After Brent…?"

"After Brent, I seriously considered swearing off love and romance for good. I was twenty-seven when I broke it off with him. I decided to focus on my business, on my family and friends. It was fine for a couple of years. And then I started feeling that I was missing out on the most important things. I still didn't know if I would ever find *the* one. But I kind of started thinking I needed to get out and try to meet up with guys again. And then, one night last August, I decided to get out and party. I went to Alicia's."

"And you met Nicky…"

"Yes, I met Nick."

"No one since that night with him?"

She met his eyes steady-on. "No one. Somehow, I always get it wrong, romance-wise, and I've kind of made peace with that. I've got Marybeth now. She and I are a family."

He resisted the urge to correct her, to say that he was part of her family, too. He wasn't. Right now, they were connected through Marybeth. Right now, they were friends. As she and Nicky had been.

Seth wanted more. How to get her to give him more, that was the question.

Jody said, "So. Now you know way too much about me. And I still don't really understand what happened in Chicago, how you lost Irene."

Irene. No way did he want to talk about Irene. Ever.

But if he wanted a chance for a future with Jody, he was going to have to answer her questions, lay it out for her, say what had happened and how.

He admitted, "I don't even know where to start."

Jody reached out and touched his shoulder, a little pat of reassurance. He wanted to grab her fingers, pull her toward him, hold on tight and not let go. But then she took her hand back and wrapped it around her pillow. "Tell me about her. Just start with the easy stuff. Was she tall? Petite?"

"Tall," he said. "Irene was tall, with black hair and eyes to match…" His voice deserted him.

Jody helped him out again. "Serious? Playful? Intellectual? Shy?"

"She could talk to anyone. She was outgoing. And happy, a happy person." Something had eased inside him. It wasn't such a hard thing, to talk about her, about the woman who had been everything to him.

"What kind of work did she do?"

"Irene ran a diner called the Olympia. She'd pretty much grown up there, she and her older sister. But by the time I met her, she was running the diner alone. She couldn't stand to see anyone hungry. I used to tease her that she gave away more meals than she sold."

"She was generous."

"Yeah. Generous to a fault. Her mom had died when she was sixteen, and once her mom was gone, her dad started drinking too much. The older sister got married and moved to Kansas City, so Irene took over the diner. Then her dad died, and she was on her own. The Olympia was two blocks from Chicago Lawn Station, where I worked. That's how I met her. I went in for a ham on rye with mustard, and it was love at first sight."

"Really?" Jody was smiling. "You. In love at first sight…"

He offered a shrug, muttered, "What can I tell you?"

"More. Just…more."

"I asked her out."

"And?"

"She said yes. Six months later, I asked her to marry me. She said yes to that, too. I was the happiest man alive. We were planning a June wedding. She gave up her apartment and I gave up mine, and we got a larger one together. I was about to make detective, and life couldn't have been better…"

Jody asked, "Did she ever come to Colorado?"

He shook his head. "No. We kept planning a visit. But somehow, it never quite worked out that we could both get away at the same time." They should have *made* time; he saw that now. Because you never know when you're going to end up out of time.

"And then?" Jody softly prompted.

All of a sudden, his throat felt like he had something stuck in it. He coughed into his hand to loosen the tightness. "It was a Friday morning in April. I was off-duty, and Irene's head waitress was opening the diner for her. It was raining, a sleety, slushy kind of rain. And we were out of coffee. I said I'd make a run to the corner store. She wanted to go with me. So we went together, sharing her umbrella, running through the freezing rain…"

Irene had been laughing, he remembered, when he pulled open the door for her. She had a great laugh, full out and full of life, and there were drops of rain caught in her black hair as she lowered her umbrella.

"Seth?" Jody was waiting.

He got on with it. "There was a guy. A guy in a Dracula mask holding a .38 on the woman behind the counter." A soft gasp escaped Jody. And suddenly, the words were surging in him, pushing to get out. He couldn't get it over with fast enough now. "I saw what was happening as the guy turned and pointed the revolver at Irene. I shouted, 'Down, Irene!' The guy in the mask swung the gun on me, which was exactly what I wanted him to do. I had my service weapon in a shoulder holster under my jacket. It wasn't the greatest neighborhood, and people knew I was with CPD, so I was in the habit of carrying even in civilian clothes. He turned on me and I went for my weapon, knowing I would probably take a hit, but with a minimum of luck I could get in a good shot even if I went down. But Irene. Irene didn't get down. She cried out, 'No!' and she threw herself in front of me."

Jody made a strangled sound. And once again, the words had backed up in his throat.

He had to force himself to finish it. "The shot stopped her heart. She died giving me just enough time to pull my weapon and kill that sucker as the woman behind the counter pulled hers and shot him, too."

"Oh, Seth." Jody clutched her pillow, eyes wet and glittering, tear tracks down her cheeks.

"She was…everything. My life." The words sliced like razor blades in his throat.

It made him furious. Furious and sick at heart, to remember. Looking back, he could see all those separate moments that had led to her death. All the seemingly meaningless decisions that he might have made differently. If he'd bought coffee the night before. If he'd insisted on going to the corner store alone. If he'd entered the store first, if he'd pushed her down instead of *telling* her to get down.

Jody was watching him. And she knew him well enough now to get where his mind was tracking. "It wasn't your fault. Objectively, you know that. Right?"

"It doesn't matter."

"That's a lie. Come here."

He regarded her warily. "Why?"

"Because I want to hug you. I want to grab you and hold you and tell you it will be all right."

What possible good could a hug do? "But it's not all right."

"I can see that." She just kept watching him from her end of the couch.

And then he was moving, scooting her way, not even knowing he would go to her until he was halfway there. She held out her arms, and he went into them, into her softness, into the scent of her light, fresh perfume and a hint of vanilla from the baby lotion. Twining those slim arms around his neck, she guided his head down into the crook of her shoulder.

It felt good there, in her arms. It felt right. She stroked her fingers through his short hair. He let out a long breath and gathered her closer.

What was it about her? The feel of her body drained the tension right out of him. He could hold her forever.

Hold her, and more.

She stirred him, always had, he realized now. It was partly that cool way she looked at a man, that stubborn streak that rubbed him all wrong at the same time as it excited him. From the first time he noticed her, late last summer when she and Nicky became friends, he'd felt the pull toward her.

And resented it powerfully.

Now he didn't have to resent his desire for her. Now he had plans for her and for him and for Marybeth's future. Now it was only fitting, only right, that he should want this contrary woman.

But then she framed his face between her soft hands and made him look at her. "I'm not buying your crap,

Seth." She gazed way too deeply into his eyes. "It does matter that you know Irene's death wasn't your fault. If you blame yourself, you need to stop. Blaming yourself for something you didn't do is really bad for you, for your spirit. For your heart. For your soul."

How did she do it? The woman could stir his anger as easily as soothe him. He took her by the waist and pushed himself back from her, retreating to his end of the couch, where he glared at her and she stared right back at him, refusing to let him intimidate her.

Finally, he gave it up. "All right. It wasn't my fault. Happy now?" It was a taunt, pure and simple.

But Jody refused to be baited. "After a story like that, it would be pretty hard to feel happy. But I'm glad you told me. You've let me know you a little better, and that's good." She caught her plump lower lip between her teeth, and her eyes were deep as oceans. "Seth, I hate that you lost her. I really do."

He didn't need anyone's pity—nor did he deserve it. "I didn't protect her."

"Keep talking like that." Her voice had gone flat. "I'll hit you with my pillow again."

"It's a fact. I didn't."

She puffed out her cheeks with a hard breath. "On second thought, I won't hit you. I don't need to. You're doing a great job of beating yourself up all on your own."

Okay, so she had a point. There was nothing to be gained by getting bogged down in placing blame and should-have-beens. "Let me try again. I do know it wasn't my fault. But that doesn't change the fact that Irene died for me, and I'm not okay with that. I'll never be okay with that."

* * *

Later that night, sitting in her comfy recliner by the window nursing her baby, Jody couldn't help dwelling on what Seth had told her.

She'd wanted to know what had happened to Irene. Now she did. It didn't feel all that great to know, actually.

But it did help her to understand Seth better. She ached for what he'd suffered. And he couldn't hide the fact that he wasn't over his lost love yet—that Irene still owned his heart.

Jody had to watch herself with him. She really needed *not* to go getting ideas about the two of them getting closer.

He'd loved one woman, loved her completely. And he hadn't been with anyone since that awful rainy morning in Chicago. He wasn't going to suddenly decide to try again just because Jody might have foolishly developed a crush on him.

They were friends. Friends united in the shared goal of giving Marybeth the best that life had to offer. Friends and only friends.

She wouldn't go getting her hopes up that there might be more.

Monday night at dinner, Seth said, "I got us a table at Mirabelle's for seven Saturday night. Why don't you call and set up your day at the spa for Saturday? And give me the limo voucher. I'll call them and reserve a car for Saturday night."

"Mirabelle's?" It was a new restaurant in town, a small, cozy place with white tablecloths and crystal chandeliers and a chef from New York. Everyone said the food was really good and the service impeccable.

"I heard it was good," he said. "Would you rather go somewhere else?"

"I just didn't know we were doing that."

"Doing what?"

"Going through with the date."

He set down his fork. "We're doing it." His voice was deep and rough, and his velvet-brown gaze caught hers and held it.

It just wasn't fair that the guy was so damn hot. *Not happening*, she reminded herself. *Don't get ideas.* "What about Marybeth?"

"It's only a few hours. Get a sitter. Maybe one of your sisters or maybe your mom?"

"Ma? Please."

"She did raise five children, didn't she?"

"She's probably off on her next cruise already."

"A babysitter, Jody. I'm sure you can find one."

"But Marybeth is barely four weeks old."

"Jody. We're going. Stop making excuses."

"And a day at the spa, too? I don't have time for that."

He ate two bites of his pork chop before he spoke again. "I'll look after Marybeth while you're at the spa. But get a babysitter for Saturday night or I'll get one for you. We're going to Mirabelle's."

She sagged back in her chair. "Why are you so determined about this?"

"Because I want to take you out."

"But...you don't go out, remember? There's no point because it can't go anywhere. Not to mention, I live in Broomtail County, and what if it got messy with me?"

"Too late." He was almost smiling. She could see that

increasingly familiar twitch at the corner of his mouth. "It's already messy with you."

"I am not joking, Seth."

"Neither am I. I want to be with you, Jody. And not just as a friend."

"B-but I…" God. She was sputtering. And why did she suddenly feel light as a breath of air, as if she was floating on moonbeams? "You want to *be* with me? But you don't do that. You've made that very clear."

"You're right. I *didn't* do that. Until now. But things have changed."

"Because of Marybeth, you mean?"

"Yeah, because of Marybeth. And because of you, too. Because of the way you are. Strong and honest and smart and so pretty. Because we've got something going on, you and me. Something good. I'm through pretending that we're friends and nothing more. Are you telling me I'm the only one who feels that way?"

"I just…" Her pulse raced and her cheeks felt too hot. She'd promised herself that nothing like this would happen, that she wouldn't get her hopes up.

She needed to be careful. She could end up with her heart in pieces all over again.

"Jody, please go out with me Saturday." He gazed across the table at her, so solid and manly and *real*. The guy who had come for her when she needed him, the man who'd had her back ever since the night her baby was born.

"I…" Where were the words? She had no words.

He pushed back his chair and came around the table toward her. When he reached her side, he held down his hand.

Her heart had come all undone somehow. It bounced

around in her chest like a rabbit on steroids. She put her hand in his. His big, hot fingers closed around her cool ones.

And then he was pulling her up out of the chair. Her napkin drifted to the floor. She made no effort to catch it.

He caught her face between his hands, the hands that had held hers when she was in labor, the hands that could always soothe Marybeth. She stared up at him, mesmerized, as his mouth came down to hers.

His lips were soft. So warm. They felt like heaven on hers, brushing back and forth.

And then settling. Claiming.

She opened on a sigh and let the kiss deepen. His fingers trailed up to her temples, fingertips gently stroking into her hair.

This. Oh, dear, sweet heaven. This.

This was magic. So beautiful and right. And she wanted more of it. More of *him*. She'd taken two big chances in love and both times she'd lost out.

But didn't they all say that the third time's the charm?

What about Irene? warned that wary voice in her head. *He's still not over her.*

Maybe not. Maybe he would never get over Irene. Anything could happen. It could all go so wrong.

But what if this time, it went right instead?

She would never know what she might have had if she didn't take a chance.

"Jody..." He breathed her name against her mouth. "Say you'll go out with me."

She wanted to. So much.

And really, why not?

Right now, at this moment, all he'd really asked for

was that night out she'd won at the bachelor auction. One evening with just the two of them, no dirty diapers, no crying baby to distract them from each other. She didn't have to make a big deal about it. She could just say she would go out with him, take things one step at a time.

He took the kiss deep again, deeper than before. She opened and let him all the way in. His arms came around her, pressing her closer, flattening her breasts against the hard slab of his chest. The scent of him swam around her, so delicious, so right. His tongue explored the secret places beyond her parted lips.

He made her feel cherished. And desired. He...why, he *wanted* her. He really did. The way he kissed her left no doubt on that score. Against her belly, she could feel his arousal. There was heat, real heat, between them. Heat and hunger, too.

How long had it been for her, since a kiss felt this good?

Too long, definitely.

And beyond the building heat, there was the rest of it. The rest of *them*, of Jody and Seth, together. Because they were partners, she realized. And had been for a while now.

Whatever happened in the future, their bond had been established in the birthing suite at Justice Creek General. And it had only grown stronger with every day that passed.

You never knew how things would turn out. You could go to the corner store for coffee and lose it all.

So as long as she was breathing, with strength in her body and hope in her heart, a woman needed to explore all the possibilities.

He lifted his head and his eyes met hers. "Please, Jody. Come out with me."

"All right," she said. "Mirabelle's. Saturday night."

Chapter Eight

Clara agreed to watch Marybeth that Saturday night. She came nice and early and listened attentively to each and every one of Jody's detailed instructions concerning baby care.

Jody knew she was overdoing it. Clara had a two-year-old of her own. She'd changed a thousand diapers and heated up more than one bottle of breast milk. Still, it was Marybeth's first time with a sitter and the first time Jody had left her for an evening. Clara seemed to understand that Jody needed to tell her a bunch of stuff she already knew.

At a quarter of seven, Seth herded Jody out the door toward the limo waiting at the curb. Clara stood in the doorway waving goodbye, a perfectly content Marybeth cradled in her arms.

Mirabelle's, on Grandview Drive, was exactly as

advertised, intimate and so pretty, each table a little oasis of candlelight. The glassware sparkled, the silver gleamed, and a single, perfect orchid on a delicate stem grew from a tiny green ceramic pot. It was still daylight when they got there. Their table had a view of the pale moon suspended above the mountains. The moon glowed brighter as the sky darkened.

Jody had a glass of white wine in honor of the occasion, and they shared an appetizer of poached shrimp with avocado, cilantro and lime. Seth looked way too handsome in his crisp white shirt and gray jacket.

He said, "I like that red dress."

It was simply cut, sleeveless and formfitting. "I was lucky I managed to get it zipped up."

The gold streaks in his eye glowed warmer than ever. "You only had to ask. I would've helped."

Her breath got all tangled up in her throat, and she felt the blush as it colored her cheeks. "You really are flirting with me, aren't you?"

He leaned closer. The light from the antique chandelier overhead cast his eyes into shadow. "You want me to stop?"

It seemed a bad idea to be too truthful. But she did it anyway. "No. No, I don't want you to stop."

He raised his glass of very old whiskey. She tapped it with her wineglass.

The waiter came back a little while later. They ordered salads and entrées. It was all delicious. He wanted to know about her spa day. She said she'd had everything—hair, nails, hot rock massage. She didn't mention the full-out Brazilian. They were only at the flirting stage, after all, and she hadn't been freed up for sex from her doctor yet, anyway. At this point, her going Hollywood was definitely TMI.

However, that she even teased herself with the thought of mentioning it over dinner said a lot more about where this thing with him was going than she was strictly comfortable admitting to herself.

In so many ways he was so rigid, so...traditional. Would he be that way in bed, too? Stiff in a bad way.

She grinned to herself at her little private joke.

And he was watching. "Tell me?"

She shook her head slowly. He had the grace not to push.

When the waiter offered dessert, Jody shook her head. "This dress is tight enough as it is, thank you."

But Seth ordered the chocolate mousse cake anyway and then insisted she have a bite. Or three.

"Will you ride out to the ranch with me?" he asked as they crossed the dark parking lot toward the waiting limousine.

She realized that she wanted to go with him out to the Bar-Y. She wanted it a lot, which kind of surprised her. It wasn't as if she'd never been there before.

Mentally, she calculated how much time she had. They'd spent an hour and a half over dinner, so she had three and a half hours left, max, before she would have to nurse or pump again. So there was time. And Clara should be okay with it. Her sister had urged her to stay out for as long as she wanted; Dalton was looking after their little girl, Kiera, and expected Clara to be gone late.

"I'll have you back with Marybeth by eleven," he promised.

She had her arm in his, and she leaned a little closer to him, into all that heat and strength. "Sure. I'd like to go out to the ranch."

The ride to the Bar-Y took under twenty minutes. It was almost full dark by the time they arrived.

Someone had turned on the porch light of the main house. As the limo rolled to a stop in the light's golden glow, a black Lab ran across the yard from the foreman's cottage. The dog sat obediently by the rear door until the driver pulled it open and Jody got out.

"His name's Toby," said Seth, coming around from the other side of the limo as she bent to pet the dog. "But it looks like you and Toby have already met."

"Once or twice." She let Toby swipe a few kisses on her chin as Seth told the driver what time to come back for them.

The limo sailed off back down the driveway, and Roman Califano, tall, white-haired and whipcord lean, in faded Wranglers and a worn chambray shirt, came out the front door of the cottage. "Seth!" He waved.

Seth waved back and Roman started for them, so Jody and Seth met him in the middle of the yard. She greeted Roman.

He gave her his shy smile. "Good to see you, Jody."

Seth said, "Dad'll be here Monday."

"We're looking forward to it. Mae'll fix his room up nice and make sure the fridge is full." Roman congratulated Jody on her baby and added, "Don't be a stranger. You bring that little one out to meet Mae soon, you hear me?"

"I promise," she said.

With Toby at his heels, Roman headed back to his

place. Seth led Jody up the steps of the two-story ranch house.

Inside, it was as she remembered, the rooms large, the furniture of good quality, but worn. The formal dining room and living room flanked the entry from which stairs led up to the bedrooms on the second floor.

"Nicky ever show you around the upstairs?" he asked.

She shook her head. "We always hung out down here."

"Come on. I'll give you the tour. All this will be Marybeth's someday. You might as well have a look at what belongs to your little girl." He started up the stairs.

Jody was too stunned to move. "You're not serious."

He stopped three steps up and faced her again. "What? You don't want to see the second floor?"

"No—I mean, yes, I do want to see the upstairs. But…you're leaving the ranch to Marybeth? Seriously?"

"Who else would we leave it to?"

"I, well, I just had no idea, that's all."

Looking down from the third step, his hand on the polished wood banister, he studied her face. "Sorry. I guess I just assumed you knew."

"Um, no. I had no clue. I, well… It's wonderful. Thank you—I mean, on behalf of Marybeth."

"Nothing to thank me for." He ran his palm downward along the banister and then back up, as though enjoying the smooth surface of the polished wood. "My father already turned the place over to Nick and me equally back when he moved to Florida, so as of now, with Nick gone, half of the Bar-Y is already Marybeth's. When I go, Marybeth will be the sole Yancy heir. My father's completely on board with that. It's what Nick would have wanted, and it's what I want, too—and you're looking at me like I just sprouted horns and possibly a forked tail."

She laughed at that, the sound a little tight, uncomfortable to her own ears. "It's a surprise, that's all."

He came back down to stand with her at the foot of the stairs. "I suppose you want to know what, exactly, your daughter will be inheriting."

She stared up at him and realized she was happy in that moment, glad that he'd insisted they should have their night out. "Yes. I would love to hear all about the Bar-Y."

He launched into the particulars, his voice rich with pride. "The Bar-Y is 3,500 acres. We've got 1,530 cow-calf pairs, fifty other cows and eleven bulls. We have six horses right now, quarter horses, mostly. There's the ranch house, the bunkhouse, the foreman's cottage, plus a number of outbuildings in good repair and several corrals. We maintain our equipment and our roads. We also own water rights, irrigation systems and 112 miles of fence."

"Well," she said, for lack of anything better. "Marybeth will be so pleased."

He gazed at her steadily, his expression thoughtful now. "Kind of sprung it on you, huh?"

"Yeah. But I'll manage to get over the shock somehow."

"You're not upset with me?"

"For what? My daughter's the heir to a working ranch. It's a lot to take in, but in a very good way."

There was a moment. They gazed at each other. She had the strangest sense that she belonged right here. In this house. With this man.

"The upstairs?" he asked.

She put away her crazy fantasy and replied, "Absolutely. Can't wait to see it."

Up the stairs they went. He showed her the rooms. The master had a walk-in closet, a good-size bathroom and big windows looking out over the backyard. The three other bedrooms shared the hall bath, which was bigger than the master bath, with subway tiles running halfway up the walls and a gorgeous old claw-foot tub.

Downstairs, he took her back through the family room and into the kitchen, where he pulled open the door of the old white fridge. "I have apple juice, Dr Pepper and beer."

"Water?" she asked, her throat gone suddenly scratchy, her eyes burning a little as she thought of Nick, of the first time she'd stopped by to visit him here. He'd offered her the same choices: juice, pop or beer.

Seth shut the refrigerator door and turned to her. He saw her face, and his mouth tipped down in concern. "What is it? What'd I do now?"

"Nothing. You've been wonderful." She bit her trembling lip. "It's just… I haven't been here since a couple of days before Nick died."

His craggy face softened. "It's hard sometimes, huh?"

"Mmm-hmm. And a lot harder for you than for me, I'm guessing."

A floor plank creaked once, a strangely lonely sound, as he closed the distance between them. He put his hands on her shoulders. Her breath caught at the contact. "I'm glad you were with him, that you were his friend. It used to make me mad, that he was so crazy about you and you didn't feel the same."

"I noticed that—and *used to*, meaning you don't feel that way anymore?"

His gaze held hers, steady. Sure. "Now *I* want you. And I'm a guy. A possessive guy. I like it better if I don't have to deal with the possibility that you're still carrying a torch for my brother."

Now I *want you...*

She stared up at him, not sure how she felt. Was this thing with him moving too fast? Probably. Confusion tangled her thoughts. She should tell him to back off. But what she *should* do and what her heart and body yearned for were two completely different things. "I'm not in love with Nick." It came out slightly breathless. "I never was."

"I know. You made that painfully clear that first day I cornered you at your flower shop. And as of now, well, even if you were in love with Nicky, I would get past it."

She wasn't following, exactly. "Past it?"

"I would learn to deal with it if I had to, if you *had* loved Nicky that way—even if you still loved him, I would accept that. I would get over it and move on." His hands glided inward, until his rough palms rested in the twin curves where her neck met her shoulders. A rush of heat blew through her, settling low. "Because I think we could be good together, you and me." His thumbs caressed her, burning twin paths of sensation on either side of her throat.

His brushing touch felt so good. She had to swallow a moan—and then he swooped close and kissed her, a long kiss, slow and deep. Her knees went to jelly. She was lucky she didn't melt to the floor.

By the time he came up for air, all she could do was

gape at him, stunned. And then she made herself ask, "What about Irene?"

He answered without pause, his voice rough as a stretch of bad road. "Irene is gone. Same as Nicky's gone. Deal with it."

"It's not the same. You just said it yourself. I was never in love with Nick. I haven't spent seven years not even letting myself look at another man."

His hand moved down her arm in a slow caress. He caught her fingers. "Let's go outside."

"You're changing the subject."

"That's not necessarily a bad thing."

Was he right? Was she making a big deal out of nothing? She didn't think so. But...

She pulled her hand from his.

His amber gaze turned pleading. "Jody. Don't say no without hearing me out."

"I don't remember there being a question."

"I'm getting there."

She closed her eyes, swallowed. Her mouth and throat were dry as dust. "Water. Please."

He seemed to shake himself. "Yeah. All right." He took a glass from a cupboard and filled it from a pitcher of ice water in the fridge. She drank it down. "More?"

"No, thanks. That'll do it."

He took the glass and put it on the counter by the sink. She watched him move around the empty kitchen, and a strange calm settled over her.

She wanted him, too. She wanted him with her, wanted him at her side, helping her raise her daughter, his niece—and his heir, of all impossible things. She wanted him in the living room at night, waiting for her on the couch while she put Marybeth down to sleep.

She wanted him across the table from her in the morning. And at night for dinner, the two of them sharing the events of their separate days.

And while she was adding up all she wanted from him, she might as well be honest with herself. She wanted him in her bed, too. She wanted him in all the ways a woman can want a man.

And she wanted him more than she'd ever wanted any man before.

Was this love, then? Had love found her for real at last?

Of course not. Talk about getting ahead of herself. And what did she know about real love, anyway?

She'd thought she'd loved Dean, the high school sweetheart who walked out on her. And Brent, who married someone else as soon as they broke up. She'd been so wrong. On both counts.

"Outside?" Seth's hand brushed hers again.

She realized she wanted that, the feel of his hand around hers, encompassing. Undeniable. She accepted his touch, weaving their fingers together that time.

"This way." He took her out the glass doors in the family room, down the back steps to the unfenced backyard, pulling her onward beneath the brightening stars, across the open space, into the trees. It wasn't long before the trees gave way to a clearing, where the crescent of moon shone down and the stars were a million pinpricks in the dark fabric of the night.

A large, flat-topped boulder poked up from the tall, silvery grass in the center of the treeless space. Seth led her to it and pulled her down beside him.

"It's a pretty spot," she said. Beyond the tops of the surrounding trees, in the far distance, the mountains reached for the moon. Everything was silvered in star-light.

"It's *my* spot, my secret place, the place I used to come to be alone. To think. To plan my life. To get over the hard things."

"Hard things like...?"

He turned her hand over and idly traced the lines of her palm with his index finger, his touch warm, gentle. Right. "My mom left when I was still in diapers, ran off with some drifter who came through looking for work. My dad used to tell me that she would come back. She never did. For years after that, until my dad met Dar-lene, he was a distant man. He took care of business, went through the motions of living, but something was missing. The sadness in him went clear to the bone."

"You were lonely as a boy," she whispered.

"Yeah." He gave her hand a squeeze. "I was five or six when I wandered out here for the first time. From then on, I spent a lot of time here, sitting on this rock." He tipped his head back and stared up at the stars. "Until I was ten or so, when I came here I would wish for my mom to come home like my dad kept promis-ing she would. And then I heard the hands talking one day, about how my dad wouldn't give up waiting for a woman who was never coming back. I finally accepted that the hands had it right. By then, I just wanted to get away, be a lawman, fight for right and justice." He chuckled, a sound without much humor in it. "I didn't know how I would do that, exactly. My dad expected me to follow in his footsteps. Being the only Yancy after him, it was my duty eventually to run the Bar-Y. But then along came my stepmom, and my dad was happy again. Plus, there was Nicky, a Yancy to run the ranch…"

"So you got to go live your dream, after all."

He raised his hand, palm out. She pressed hers against it, palm to palm. A delicious shiver traveled up the inside of her arm, into her chest and straight to her heart.

"I'm talking too much," he said.

She slipped her fingers between his and held on. "No, you're not. I like it, sitting here on your special rock in your secret place, learning more about you."

He shifted then. Moving with surprising grace for such a big man and still holding her hand, he slid off the rock and sank to his knees in front of her.

Jody blinked down at him. There was only one reason she could think of for him to take a knee. "What's going on, Seth?"

"I want you, Jody."

Omigod. Had she had any idea he would do this? No. Not a clue. She needed to slow him down. "Seth, I don't think—"

"Wait. Let me finish."

She almost objected again. But then she didn't.

Because deep in her wild and still-hopeful heart, she *wanted* him to finish.

"I want everything with you," he said. Her heart pounded so hard, and her blood raced through her veins. She thought she would faint.

But she didn't faint.

And he had more to say. "I want to take care of you, make things good for you, help you raise Marybeth."

A sound escaped her, not a word, more of an audible sigh.

And he kept on. "I've been so sure for so long that I would never have a family of my own. But I was wrong. You did that, Jody. You and Marybeth. You gave me hope again. You gave me something so good to come home to at night. I'm like my dad—I get that. I need family or I'm dead inside. And you, Jody, you and Marybeth, you are my family. I want to marry you, Jody. I want the world to know that you're mine and I'm yours."

Oh, how did he do that? How did he know to say such beautiful things?

And he wasn't finished yet. "And I'm hoping, maybe, in a few years, if you're willing and it works out that way, there could be more children. I would like that, if we had more kids. But don't get me wrong. If it's only the three of us, that's okay with me. You and Marybeth, you're plenty. You're all that I need." He reached into the inside pocket of his jacket, and when he pulled his hand out, she saw he had a ring, a gorgeous vintage oval-shaped diamond with smaller diamonds glittering on the white gold band. "It was my stepmother's." His eyes shone so bright in the moonlight. "I...hope it's okay."

Jody gasped. "Seth. It's beautiful."

"Say yes to me, Jody."

The absolutely crazy, insane truth was that she wanted to say yes. She *longed* to say yes.

Still, she tried to hold on to her scattered wits, to carefully examine the exact words he had said. The word *love* had not been among them. She knew why, too. He'd *had* love, true, lasting love, and that wasn't what he offered her.

He was, however, offering her forever. A real commitment. He wanted a life with her, just as she wanted one with him.

He was no Dean. He was nothing like Brent. And he wasn't dear, sweet Nick, either. Nick had been wrong for her, too innocent, too young.

But Seth?

Seth was so exactly right. With his rough edges and his bossy ways, his deep need to protect, his limitless tenderness with her little girl.

His unswerving devotion

Seth understood her. She'd told him her sins and the secret of her lost little boy. He saw the whole of her.

He *wanted* the whole of her.

Forever. She could have that with him. It wasn't perfect. But what in life ever was?

The moon bathed his upturned face in silver. "Jody. Dear God. Say something, please."

"I…" It was all she could manage. There was more, so much more she should be saying. But somehow, her thoughts refused to organize themselves into actual sentences.

"Damn it, Jody." The mild swearword shocked her. Seth never cursed. And then he was rising, sweeping to his feet, pulling her up and into his hard arms, yanking her good and close. "Say yes." His head swooped down. He took her lips in a searing kiss that left absolutely no doubt about the chemistry between them.

Heat sang beneath her skin. She wanted to pull him down in the silvery grass, rip off all his clothes and hers, as well, to lay claim to his big body, right here and now, make him hers in the most fundamental way. So he would know that even if he had to save his heart for the woman who'd died so he would live, she, Jody, owned the rest of him. His body was hers.

But then he lifted his head, and she was gazing up into his shadowed eyes. "Say yes to me, Jody."

He was the man she wanted. And *he* wanted *her*. He wanted to be with her, to take care of her little girl.

They had a true and powerful bond, even if neither of them was willing to call it love.

It was just so right with him, so good. With him, she had everything she'd given up hope of ever finding with a man. And if he saved his words of love for the woman he'd lost so tragically, well, it wasn't as if that woman would ever return to take him back.

"Jody?" He sounded worried now.

And wait.

Hold on a minute.

Really, she needed *not* to get carried away. She should slow this down, take more time. They didn't have to rush into forever. Forever would be waiting for them when they were ready.

But then again, she longed to say yes to him. It burned inside her, the need to accept what he offered her. They were so good together. And she wanted what he wanted, a life together—the two of them and Marybeth. She wanted to live the little fantasy she'd had back there in the front hall of the ranch house, in that moment before he led her up the stairs.

And words of love or not, now that he'd made what he wanted clear and it turned out to be exactly what she wanted, well, her answer really wasn't going to change, was it?

"Say yes," he whispered, prayerfully now.

That did it. She simply could not deny him. Couldn't deny her own hungry heart.

She reached up her left hand and laid her fingers along the side of his face. "Yes."

He made a low sound, desperate and tight. "What was that you said?"

"I said yes, Seth."

He grabbed her hand, pressed a kiss to her fingertips and then slipped that beautiful diamond ring on her finger. "Yes." He kissed her fingers again, breathing the word against her skin. "You just said yes."

She laughed then—at the wonder in his voice, at the look of joy and surprise on his face. "Yes, I did. Let's get married as soon as possible."

And he picked her up and spun her around, right there in the silvery starlight, in the center of the beautiful clearing he'd considered his secret place when he was a boy.

Chapter Nine

They were married right there at the Bar-Y a week later.

Seth's dad, Bill, holding Marybeth in his arms, stood up as Seth's best man. Jody had no attendants, but her sisters were there, her mother and her brothers, too. Once you added in wives, husbands, fiancés, children, employees and various other friends and associates, it was a pretty good-size group for such short notice.

There were plenty of flowers from Jody's shop, and Elise and her crew provided most of the food—but not the wedding cake. For that, Adriana Welch had outdone herself, baking three triple-decker chocolate cakes at Jody's request.

Pastor Jacobs from Elk Street Community Church officiated. Jody wore a retro tea-length blush-pink dress with a fitted bodice and a full skirt, which she'd bought at the local bridal shop, Wedding Belles. She carried a bouquet of bright pink peonies. Her hair was piled up loosely under a short veil.

Elise stepped up and took her bouquet for the vows. A few minutes later, Seth slipped the wedding band that matched her gorgeous engagement ring on her finger.

The minister said, "Seth, you may kiss your bride," and her new husband lifted her veil. Then he cradled her face in his big hands and pressed his warm, soft lips to hers. He kissed her slowly, taking his sweet time about it.

Friends and family pressed in close, but Jody forgot all about them.

There was only the two of them, Jody and Seth, married. Sharing their first kiss as husband and wife. He let his wonderful hands stray down to her shoulders and lower, gathering her close to him, wrapping his arms around her nice and tight as he went on kissing her. She could have stood there in her pink dress with her mouth fused to his into the next century and beyond.

But then Marybeth, in her grandpa's arms, let out a high trill of sound that could have passed for a laugh.

The baby's seeming mirth was contagious. Someone giggled. And then someone else chuckled.

Against her lips, Seth whispered, "More on this later."

And then she was laughing, too.

Pastor Jacobs presented them as Mr. and Mrs. Yancy, and it was official.

She'd married Seth Yancy.

The party lasted until long after dark. When all the guests had finally headed home, Elise's crew stayed to clean everything up. Seth, Marybeth and Jody returned to her house in town. Bill was staying at the ranch house, and Jody and Seth wanted privacy for their wedding night.

The ride back to town was a quiet one. Marybeth snoozed in her car seat. Jody stared out the windshield at the clear, starry June night and tried to ignore the fluttery sensations in her stomach and her ongoing state of near-breathlessness.

She'd been to see Dr. Kapur on Thursday. It was full speed ahead in terms of her sex life with her new husband. She'd had a contraceptive shot that was already working, and she and Seth had discussed protection. Due to their mutual long-term abstinence, they'd agreed that no condoms would be necessary tonight.

It kind of amazed her that she would now have a sex life again after so long. There had only been Nick, that one time, in four years.

And what about Seth? In terms of abstinence, he put her to shame. She slid him a glance. In the dashboard light, he looked so stern and composed.

He must have felt her gaze on him. "What? Say it."

She gulped. Hard. "Just thinking…"

"About sex, you mean?"

A wild, nervous laugh tried to burst out of her. She held it back, but it got away from her and came out as a goofy, snorting sound.

He nodded. "Yeah. I can't wait, either." And then he reached across, took her hand and kissed the back of it. "You're beautiful. And I'm the luckiest guy in the world to be married to you."

At the house, Jody left Seth in the great room with Marybeth.

"I'll be right back," she promised. "I'm just going to change out of this dress."

Just like that, she was gone. He patted Marybeth's tiny back and kissed her temple and thought about how he'd wanted to be the one to take that dress off of his bride. But Marybeth was hungry now, and that made her fussy. It was his job to keep her happy while Jody put on something more nursing-friendly.

"I'll take her now." Jody emerged from the bedroom hallway wearing a loose-fitting blue robe. She took the baby from him and disappeared back down the hallway.

He went to the kitchen, where he got down the whiskey and poured himself a stiff shot. Knocking it back in one go, he put the shot glass down hard. Then he wandered over to the breakfast nook and stood staring blankly at his own shadowed reflection in the window that looked out over the dark backyard.

Married. To Jody. He could hardly believe she'd said yes, given him permission to be with her. To be a father to Marybeth. Now he would never have to move out and leave them.

He would have it all, after all, though he'd long ago given up the last hope of such a thing. He wanted his new wife. Wanted her bad. Wanted her way outside the scope of the boundaries he'd set on himself since the loss of Irene.

And by some miracle, by a chain of impossible events that included not only the birth of his niece but also the loss of his only brother way too soon, he would have her, have Jody. She belonged to him now. As did Marybeth. No one and nothing could take them away from him.

Except death, which came for everyone eventually.

But he'd already put up with more than his fair share

of death, hadn't he? With just a minimum of luck he and Jody would have years and years together before they'd be facing that again.

Eventually he left off staring blindly into space contemplating his shocking good fortune. He went to the spare room where he changed from his dark suit to track pants and a T-shirt. Only then did he join his bride and Marybeth in the master bedroom.

"She's finished," Jody whispered from her recliner by the window.

Seth took the drowsy baby in his arms.

Jody held up the baby monitor, and he took it from her.

In the spare room, he put the monitor next to the blow-up bed. Then he burped and changed Marybeth. She was asleep by the time he positioned the pillows around her. He stood back for a moment to look at her, so sweet and peaceful, his now to love and protect.

In the master bedroom, Jody had already turned back the bed. As he stood staring at the snowy-white sheets, hardly daring to believe that in the morning he would wake up in that bed with her, he heard the bathroom door open behind him.

He turned. She stood in the doorway in a white, filmy bit of cobwebs and lace and nothing else. He could see the soft, womanly shape of her beneath the robe that wasn't really a robe at all. Her dark brown hair, warmed with red glints in the light from behind her, was loose on her shoulders. And her blue eyes were enormous, trained on his face.

"Jody." It came out like a prayer. Thankful. Sincere. And rough with yearning, too.

Her bare feet whispered across the rug and then she

was in front of him. He smelled her perfume, a little flowery, but also dark, like spice and sex. He wanted to grab her, yank her close, put his mouth and his hands all over her.

And yet there was a certain reverence within him, a reluctance to be as rough as his need for her demanded. "I'm afraid to touch you. Afraid I might…"

Her sweet mouth trembled on a smile. "Shatter into a million overexcited pieces? If so, I know the feeling."

"I was thinking more that I might hurt you. But yeah. What you said? That, too."

"Seth." She reached up a hesitant hand. Her finger brushed down the side of his throat, stirring sensations. Heat. Hunger. The promise of this night, of all their nights to come. "You won't hurt me." And then she went on tiptoe.

Her lips brushed his, back and forth.

Until he couldn't stand not to hold her good and tight in his arms. He grabbed her close.

She came up against him with an eager moan, and he claimed the kiss from her, deepening it, owning it. Her mouth opened beneath his, making way for his tongue to sweep in and taste the sweet and the salt of her. Her arms slipped up over his shoulders to encircle his neck. He felt her soft, full breasts pressed to his chest. He felt…

Everything, every curve, every inch of silky, cool skin, even the parts that were covered by that little bit of nothing she'd put on in the bathroom. He felt her all through him, in his blood, to the bone, her breath in his mouth and the warm satin of her hair against his cheek, the scent of her darker now, richer than ever. To him,

she smelled like pure sex now. And he was rock hard
and ready, aching to fill her.

"Yes," she whispered. "Seth..."

"Can't wait." He groaned the words against her
parted lips.

"Yes," she said again, encouraging him when en-
couragement was the last thing he needed. "Oh, please.
Everything..."

"Everything." He gave the word back to her as he
took her down across the bed.

He should have been slow—he knew it. Slow and
seductive and gentle and teasing.

But it had been so long and he ached so bad.

And she wasn't helping him to keep control.

"Now," she commanded, grabbing for his T-shirt,
dragging it up and over his head. "Right now." She
shoved at the track pants. He helped her, barely getting his erection free of the elastic waistband before she
was pushing the pants over his hips and on down his
thighs. He kicked to get out of them. They went over
the side of the bed.

"Seth. Oh, my. All these muscles. And this..." She
wrapped that cool, smooth hand around him. "Amazing."

"Jody. Jody, no!" He grabbed for her wrist.

She gave a low, needy moan that reached down inside him and stirred him all the hotter. "Let me..." And
she tried to lower that smart mouth of hers onto him.

He couldn't let her do that. He would lose it completely if she did.

But then, well, it kind of looked like he would lose it
anyway. He drove his fingers into the thick fall of her
hair and grabbed on to keep her from taking him in.

"Ouch!" she cried.

"Sorry." He pulled her head up to him and kissed her lips, smoothing her hair as he did it, trying to soothe the pain that he'd caused. "Sorry, baby, but you were going to make me lose it…"

"So lose it." She made a low, growling sound. "I can't wait."

"Slow down…"

"No. Uh-uh. Later for that…"

He gave up trying to control it—control her. She was totally wild, and who was he to hold her back? He let her do what she wanted.

And what she wanted was frantic and beautiful, embarrassing and awkward and fine.

She grabbed that froth of cobwebs she was wearing and pulled at it until she got it above her waist.

He made the mistake of looking down then, getting an eyeful of all that womanly softness.

Bare. She was bare down there, completely revealed to him. The sight shocked him with a jolt of pleasure so strong, he almost erupted into climax right then and there.

"Jody!"

And she laughed, the sound naughty and bold and completely without shame, as she yanked the filmy nightgown over her head and tossed it away. "You like it?"

He pushed her gently to her back and rose up over her. And then he couldn't stop himself. He had to touch her, to feel the smoothness, to cup that bare mound and then to slide a questing finger along her slick, wet, unprotected folds. "Beautiful…" He groaned. He really was going to lose it, and she wasn't even touching him.

But she saved him from completely humiliating himself, saved him by wrapping one leg around him and then the other, by taking him in her hand again and guiding him into place.

He cradled her head on the pillow between his two hands. "Look at me while I come into you…"

The blue eyes, shining so bright, stared straight into his as he pushed in, as he tried with every ounce of will and restraint he had in him to take it slow for both their sakes. She'd had a baby not six weeks before, after all. He needed to be gentle with her. He needed to take care.

But she only smiled her naughty, knowing smile at him and wrapped her legs tighter around him. He sank into all that hot, wet softness.

It was sheer heaven, the best place a man could ever be.

"Kiss me, Seth."

Oh, and he did. He kissed her slow and deep and thoroughly, somehow managing to hold himself still for her, letting her find the pace and the rhythm that worked for her, though no way, at this point, would he be able to take her to the peak. This had to be way too fast for her.

But apparently, it was how she wanted it. She'd set this frantic, headlong pace—and not for herself.

For him.

She'd made this rough magic for him.

It didn't last long. He *couldn't* last long.

"Jody. I can't hold back…"

"Good." Her mouth slid away from his. She pressed her soft cheek to his beard-scruffy one. "Don't hold back." She breathed the command into his ear. "I don't want you to hold back…"

And that did it. His climax plowed through him, undeniable, unstoppable, painful in the best way, and mind-blowing, too.

His head filled with the scent of flowers and spice, he surged into her so hard and deep. And she took him, rode it out with him, murmuring heady encouragements, her soft hands stroking his back, her legs wrapped so tight around him, the whole of her claiming him, branding him as hers.

"Mrs. Yancy, that was not how I planned it," he confessed a few minutes later as they lay side by side. She had her hand on his chest, her head on his arm. He nuzzled her tangled hair and breathed in the sweet scent of her girlie shampoo.

"Mr. Yancy, that was perfect and don't you dare say otherwise."

He nipped her temple with his teeth. "Perfect for me, maybe."

She laughed, a low, sexy laugh that had him thinking he'd be ready to go again in no time. "There will be plenty of time for me. After all, we have a lifetime, right?"

"Yeah. Yeah, we do…" He touched her pink nipple.

"Careful," she warned.

"I don't mind."

"Sure?"

"Positive." He wanted to touch every inch of her. He cradled her breast in his hand and rubbed the nipple until a few drops of milk appeared.

"There's a towel." She kissed his shoulder. "In the nightstand drawer…"

He pulled the drawer wide and took out the hand

towel she'd stashed there. But then, after wiping up the moisture, he couldn't resist causing more, wiping that up, too, then dropping the towel in easy reach as he ran his fingers down the center of her, dipping one in at her navel, loving her softness, marveling at the silky texture of her skin.

And not only the look and feel of her, but the way she was as a woman, so open. Honest and lacking in pretense.

He'd liked that about her from the first, even when he'd been angry at her for not marrying Nicky, and for not seeking him out to tell him about the baby after Nicky died.

There were no coy games with Jody. She didn't open up easy, but when she did, she gave her all. She was strong and smart and serious. But with that edge, too, that sharp sense of humor, that toughness that came from the hard knocks she'd taken, the hard choices she'd had to make.

She fit him. Fit him in every way, including this. Fit him even better than Irene had…

Seth closed his eyes. Where had that disloyal thought come from?

"Seth?" Jody took his face between her hands. He opened his eyes reluctantly. She searched his eyes. "What is it?"

"Nothing," he whispered and kissed her.

"But…"

He kept on kissing her, nipping at her lips a little, spearing his tongue in, tasting all the slick, tempting places beyond her parted lips, until she went pliant and willing again.

"You went away there for a moment," she whispered.

"Right here," he replied and meant it. "Right here, with you, on our wedding night."

She smiled at him then, a glowing, open smile.

He returned to the pleasure at hand, tracing circles on her hip bones as she sighed and lifted toward his touch. *Mine*, he thought, as he went lower, down to where she was bare for him. He dipped his fingers in, loving the feel of her, wet and so willing.

She whispered his name, eased her legs wider. He deepened the caress, sliding two fingers in and then three, bracing up on an elbow so he could watch her face as she came apart for him that very first time, her mouth a soft O, her eyes glazed with pleasure.

"Seth." She wrapped her hand around his neck and pulled him down for a long, sweet kiss.

For a while, they drifted together, lazy and easy, whispering about nothing, sharing slow touches. Until she reached down between them again.

"Uh-uh." He took that naughty hand of hers and the other one, too, and raised them both above her head. "Keep these clever hands above your head. This time's for you."

"But I already—"

"Shh." He kissed her mouth, firm and quick. "I mean it. No hands."

Jody surrendered control.

Reaching, she found the top edge of the mattress and took hold. She let him do what he wanted with her.

And, oh, it was glorious, to be at his command. Those knowing fingers of his, warm and just rough enough, glided over her, stirring every last hungry nerve, making her body hum with need and yearning.

He bent close and he kissed her. Endless, arousing kisses that wiped her mind free of all rational thought. Kisses that began on her lips and then went lower.

And lower...

She looked down at him as he kissed her where she wanted him most. Her hands gripping the mattress for all she was worth, she lifted her body eagerly toward that wet, intimate caress.

He wasn't shy. He used his lips and his tongue and even his teeth to drive her higher. And those knowing fingers, too, he put them in play, until all she could do was moan his name and rock frantically, bucking her body to get closer to him.

And closer still...

And then at last, when he moved up her body again and she felt him, right there where she burned for him, pressing inside, she had no words fine enough for how good it felt.

It was exactly right, the way he came into her, slow and firm and steady, the gold in his eyes molten, his mouth swollen from kissing her, whispering her name rough and low. It was everything she'd given up hope of ever finding.

He was everything.

This man. A real man, her husband now. A man who shared his hardest secrets and listened when she told him hers. A loyal man who took care of her and her baby. A man who knew all the right ways to make her body burn.

She lifted her legs, wrapped them around him. It wasn't enough. "I need..."

Somehow, he knew. "Your arms, Jody. Put your arms around me now."

"Yes. Oh, Seth…" She let go of the mattress then and grabbed for him, twining her arms around him, too.

His big body pressed her down, and she pressed up to meet him. She held him so tight as he rocked into her, pushing her closer to the edge of sheer bliss.

Until, with a sharp cry, she went over, every nerve shimmering, a spiral of sparks and wonder lighting her up from inside as her climax burned through her.

And truly, she didn't mean to say it. She wasn't *going* to say it.

After all, he'd made it more than clear that everything he had was hers.

Everything but that.

But something broke with her climax, just broke wide open. And the truth she'd been denying came pouring out.

"I love you," she cried as her body pulsed around him. "Seth, I love you so much!"

Chapter Ten

He didn't say it back to her.

He didn't acknowledge the words, either.

Instead, he held her close. He kissed her endlessly. He treated her so tenderly, carrying her into the bathroom a little while later, filling the tub and sharing a lazy bath with her, then taking her back to bed.

Marybeth woke them at a few minutes after three in the morning. He went to get her. Jody nursed her there, in the bed, and then Seth carried her off to the spare room again, to change her and put her back down to sleep.

Jody lay alone, waiting for him, trying not to think too much about the three little words she'd said to him, about how he'd behaved as though she'd never said them at all.

What had she expected? For him to say them back to her?

No. She'd had zero hope that she'd get words of love from him. Because, even though they'd never actually discussed it, they were both clear on the love issue. She, Jody, had forever with him. They belonged to each other now.

But love?

Well, it wasn't exactly that love didn't enter into it.

It was only that he'd given his love already. He had to keep something just for Irene.

Jody reminded herself that she needed to be at peace with that. She'd known how it was with him when she said yes to him.

The next day, they went back to the ranch to spend some time with Bill, who was head-over-heels for his new granddaughter. They stayed for lunch and dinner, the men talking beef prices, alfalfa yields and fence repair. Jody puttered around the big, dated ranch house kitchen with Mae Califano. A grandmother several times over, Mae was as tall and lean as her husband, with thick gray hair and a ready smile.

Around seven that night, Jody, Seth and Marybeth returned to town.

Seth put Marybeth down in the spare room again and then came for Jody in the great room, scooping her up in his arms and carrying her straight to bed. He made love to her slowly the first time and hard and fast later. She reveled in every kiss, every lingering touch.

And she was careful not to let herself say her love out loud again. There was simply no point in going there. Again, she reminded herself that she'd said yes to him knowing that his heart was taken. She had no right to turn around and demand what he couldn't give.

She'd made her peace with the situation.

Or so she kept telling herself.

Monday at breakfast, Seth said he wanted to adopt Marybeth.

Jody wasn't surprised. "I think that's wise. My brother James is in family law. How about if I call him? I'll get us an appointment as soon as possible. We can get the process started."

Seth had just lifted a spoonful of oatmeal to his lips. He set it back in the bowl without eating it. "You're serious? Yes, you'll let me adopt her. Just like that?"

"What? You think I should argue with you about it?"

He knocked back a gulp of coffee. "I kind of thought I would have to convince you."

"Seth. If anything ever happened to me—"

"Don't even think it." He had visibly paled.

Her heart warmed. No, he wouldn't say he loved her. But she did matter to him. She mattered in the deepest way.

She made her tone softer. "I'm only saying that you're the one I would want for Marybeth, the one to stick by her, to look after her. You're already the dad that she needs. No matter what happens, you need a legal claim on her, too. I also think it's what Nick would want, to have the big brother he loved so much take care of his little girl."

Seth shoved his chair back hard enough that it went over with a crash.

"Seth!" Jody gasped as he rounded the table toward her. "Seth. What in the...?"

He grabbed her hand and pulled her up from her chair, sending it over backward, too. "Jody." He wrapped those big arms around her. "Jody…"

"What?" She stared up at him, bewildered.

"You amaze me, you really do."

She laughed then. "That's me. I aim to amaze."

His mouth swooped down and covered hers in a mind-bending, beautiful, never-ending kiss. He braced one arm at her back and bent to slide the other arm behind her knees.

"Seth!" she cried again, as he scooped her high against his chest and carried her to their bedroom, where he made fast, hot love to her, leaving her breathless and panting for more. They rested for a little while, and the second time was slower and infinitely sweet.

The next day, Tuesday, they visited Calder and Bravo, Attorneys at Law, to take the first step toward making Seth Marybeth's legal dad.

A week later, on Monday, Bill returned to Florida. By then, Jody and Seth had already established a pattern for their daily lives. They stayed at the house in town during the week and went to the ranch on Saturdays and Sundays. The house in town was close to both Bloom and the justice center, so very little time had to be wasted driving back and forth to work. On the weekends, Seth could concentrate on whatever needed his attention at the ranch.

Jody loved the old ranch house. She wanted Marybeth to have a lot of good memories there, and she was already making plans to update the kitchen and redo the bathrooms—well, except for the big one upstairs with the claw-foot tub. That was perfect as it was.

The day after Bill left, Jody took Marybeth and met Elise for breakfast at the bakery.

"At last," said Elise. "You, me and morning coffee. Just like old times." From her stroller, Marybeth made a cooing sound. "I think you have the perfect baby."

"As of this moment, yes, I do. Let's savor the joy."

They talked about Elise's wedding, which was less than two weeks away now, with the ceremony to be held at Elk Street Community Church and the reception afterward at Justice Creek's famous and purportedly haunted Haltersham Hotel.

"So…" Elise swallowed a bite of blueberry muffin. "Married life? Good?"

"Crazy wonderful." *Except I said I love him and he didn't say it back.*

Not that she was letting herself dwell on that.

"I mean, you and Broomtail County's favorite lawman?" Elise widened her eyes and threw out both hands. "Whoever would have guessed? Except, when I see you together, it's so obvious. It's like you were meant for each other. Everyone says so."

"Everyone?"

"Clara, Nellie—me, of course." She added their sisters-in-law: "Addie, Chloe, Paige, Ava…"

"Seriously? You've all been discussing my relationship with Seth?"

"Of course. I mean, it happened pretty fast, but we all agree you're a great match. Seth is so self-contained, you know? And so are you. It's always been like pulling teeth to get you to admit when you're upset about something."

"Oh, come on. I'm not *that* bad."

"Yeah, you kind of are. But it's okay. We love you,

anyway. And I have to tell you, before you and Seth got together, he always seemed so unhappy, so depressingly grim. Polite and helpful, with a good head on his shoulders, the kind of guy you would want to have around to take things in hand during a natural disaster. But so stern. So serious. But then, last week at your wedding, I had a few minutes with him. He was charming and friendly. And, Jody, when he looks at you…" Elise fanned herself. "Whew. That guy is wild for you."

Not wild enough. The thought rose unbidden. Jody pressed her lips together to keep from saying too much.

But she must have given herself away. Elise leaned closer. "Jody, what's the matter?"

No. Bad idea to go there. What was Elise going to tell her that she didn't already know? Jody relaxed her shoulders, looked her sister straight in the eye and replied, "Not a thing. Why?"

"I don't know. For a moment there, I thought…"

"What?"

"There's really nothing bothering you?"

"Honestly. No."

Did she feel bad about lying to her sister? A little.

But really, how could it be lying when she *was* fine? She just needed to keep things in perspective, that was all.

But it ate at her, just chewed away at the edges of her happiness. She loved her husband, and she wanted him to love her back. And sometimes, when he kissed her or looked at her across the breakfast table in the morning, or asked her how her day had been when he got home from the justice center, she would know in her heart that he *did* love her. That, as fast as it had happened between them, from the night Marybeth was born until their marriage five and a half weeks later, she owned his heart as he owned hers.

That it was only the words he couldn't give her. Because he owed them to Irene and Irene alone.

Which, increasingly, pissed her the hell off.

She found herself understanding her mother better, of all things. Understanding what it was to love a man beyond all reason and know that he belonged to another. No, it wasn't the same, what her mother had done, fighting tooth and nail for all those years to steal another woman's husband.

It wasn't the same.

But still, Jody felt a certain kinship with her mother—or wait. Maybe it was Sondra Bravo Jody understood better now. She'd always wondered why Sondra never kicked Frank Bravo out on his sorry ass and filed for divorce.

Now she kind of got it. It was just possible that Sondra had loved Frank Bravo as passionately and possessively as Willow did. Sondra couldn't have her husband all to herself, but she clung to what she could have of him, anyway.

"What is going through that mind of yours?" Seth asked. He stood over her as she sat on the back steps at the house in town. It was nine at night and he'd just come out the sliding door after putting Marybeth to sleep in the spare room. They'd been married for two and a half weeks.

For a moment, Jody just sat there, facing away from him, staring off toward the back fence. Was this it, then, his invitation to talk about what she'd said on their wedding night?

She knew it wasn't.

"Why do you ask?" she said without turning.

"You've been kind of quiet all evening, that's all."

Jody turned and looked up at him, feeling that now-familiar ache of longing under her breastbone, wanting to get honest with him and at the same time just... not ready.

Not ready to go there, not ready to lay her heart on the line and then have to face the painful things he might say when she did.

She chose the coward's way. "I've been thinking we should go ahead and start putting Marybeth to sleep in her own room."

His bare feet brushed the porch boards as he came and sat beside her. He had the receiver for the baby monitor in his hand, and he set it on the next step down.

She waited for him to call her bluff, to insist that she get straight with him, tell him what was really on her mind.

He did no such thing. Instead, he wrapped his big arms around his spread knees and stared up at the night sky. "I thought you wanted her in the bassinet with us."

She studied his profile, his strong nose and hard jaw, the manly jut of his Adam's apple. A hint of his aftershave came to her, and a shiver of desire hollowed her out down low. "Seth. She's never in the bassinet with us. She's been sleeping in the spare room ever since we got married."

He slipped her a glance. The promise of the night to come thickened the air between them. Suddenly the little problem of loving him when he couldn't love her back seemed to matter a whole lot less than it had a minute before.

"We make a lot of noise," he said.

"Exactly. And I'm thinking we'll probably continue to do so."

"As long as I have anything to say about it, we will." He was looking straight at her now, a look that stole her breath and made her acutely aware of her blood as it pulsed through her veins.

"And that reminds me…"

"What?" He reached over and ran the backs of his fingers slowly down her bare arm. Nerve endings flashed and sizzled in response to that light touch.

What were they even talking about? *Focus.* "I want to fix up the room she's been sleeping in at the Bar-Y, too." The room was directly across the hall from the master bedroom, a nice, sunny space that faced the front yard. "I want to get her a crib there, paint the room in little-girl colors, set things up right for her there, too, so I don't always have to be hauling all her stuff back and forth."

"No problem." He slipped those caressing fingers under her hair and clasped the back of her neck. Better than a giant slice of Adriana Welch's chocolate cake, the feel of his hands on her flesh. "So, you're fine, then?" He pulled her in to him.

"Never better," she whispered as his mouth came down on hers.

And it was true, at that moment, as his fingers slid up into her hair, cupping the back of her head, holding her steady while he plundered her mouth.

It was true, as he slipped his other hand up under her tank top, clever fingers closing on her breast, kneading it until she moaned and felt her milk come in.

She pushed at his giant shoulders and looked down

at the dark spot on her shirt right over the curve of her breast. "Look what you did."

The hand in her hair slid lower. His fingers were warm on her nape, firm on her shoulder, arousing as they glided down her bare arm until he had hold of her hand. "Come inside with me. You can get out of that wet shirt."

She didn't argue. She might not have his love, but she owned that big body of his. When she held him in her arms, he belonged only to her

He scooped up the baby monitor and rose, pulling her up with him, leading her back inside and straight to their bedroom. He set the monitor on the nightstand and got right to work getting her out of her clothes.

In about thirty seconds flat they were both naked, shirts and pants and underwear a tangled pile around their bare feet.

And then he grabbed her close again and put his mouth on hers, reaching down, those amazing hands curving under her bare bottom, lifting her.

With a moan of pleasure, she curled her arms around his neck and hitched up her legs to encircle his waist. His fingers moved, inching inward. And then he was touching her, opening her, readying her, his erection already hard and thick against her belly.

A cry escaped her. He drank it in—and then, out of nowhere, he broke the kiss.

She glared at him, wanting more. More kisses, more caresses, more of this wild beauty that pulsed between them. "What?" she demanded.

"You," he answered rough and low. "Everything."

Still standing, with her all wrapped around him, he slanted his head the other way and kissed her some more. She kissed him right back, heedless of their clothes trampled under his feet as his fingers worked their heady magic at her wet and eager core.

She was ready, beyond ready. Hooking her legs tighter around him, she lifted up and away to try to get him in place and take him inside.

He only chuckled and pulled her back to him, good and tight against his muscled heat, trapping his hardness between their bodies again. "Kiss me some more, Jody. Let's make it last…"

Jody held on. She kissed him forever as he went on touching her, driving her higher, making her burn.

Until she went over the edge of the world for him, letting her head fall back, whimpering at the ceiling, holding on to him for dear life as completion sang through every nerve.

Only then, so gently, did he lower her to their bed, only then did he come into her, gliding home to fill her. She sighed in pleasure as she took him in.

Once there, he stilled for a sweet, endless moment. And then he rolled them so she was on top, her legs folded on either side of him. "Ride me, Jody. Take me there."

She was only too happy to comply. Bracing her hands on his chest, she pushed her body up to a sitting position. It was so good this way—well, every way was good with him. But she loved looking down at him, watching the wonder and excitement on his face as she moved on him, rocking him slow and sweet. And then harder. Faster.

Until he lost it completely, grabbing her hips and pulling her down tight to him, spilling into her as he chanted her name.

Later, when he slept beside her, she reminded herself again of how good they were together, how she loved the life they shared.

And what were those three little words, really? Nothing but a certain arrangement of sounds.

No, he hadn't said them. But if she only stopped yearning for them, she could more fully appreciate all that he gave her, all that he was.

They shared so much. It should be enough.

She needed to remember that.

That following Saturday Elise married Jed. She had her three sisters, four sisters-in-law and her cousin Rory for her bridesmaids. Her lifelong friend, Tracy Winham, was her maid of honor.

The ceremony was at four with the reception at five thirty and expected to go well into the night. To start the day off right, Elise and her bridesmaids met at ten in the morning at Elise's favorite salon for hair and makeup.

Originally, Jody had planned to opt out of everything but the ceremony and maybe an hour or two at the reception afterward. She had Marybeth to consider. But Mae Califano volunteered to come in from the ranch and watch the baby at the house in town. That way, Jody could run home and nurse every four hours or so—or find somewhere private to pump if she had to.

It all went off beautifully, Jody thought. Elise wore a full-length white dress lavish with beads and lace and a cathedral-length veil. Flowers from Bloom filled the church. The bridesmaids wore teal blue satin, each in a different style. Annabelle Bravo, their brother Quinn's six-year-old, was the flower girl. Annabelle's best friend, Sylvie, carried the rings. Both Sylvie and

Annabelle wore fairy princess costumes complete with jeweled tiaras and filmy wings.

Elise and Jed had written their vows. An audible sigh went up from the guests when Jed confessed that he'd finally found happiness the day Elise knocked on his front door. He had more to say, all of it beautiful, full of love for his bride. He held Elise's hands and he looked in her eyes, and he promised to love her forever.

As Jed said his vows, Jody's sisters and sisters-in-law glanced out at the pews, looking for their husbands to share a quick glance of love and belonging. Jody did the same, her gaze seeking Seth.

His eyes were waiting. He gave her a slow smile. All that they had together—the passion, the mutual respect, the tenderness, the love for Marybeth—it all seemed to shimmer in the air between them.

It was a good moment. She turned back to the bride and groom reassured, somehow, that what she had with Seth was as real and as lasting as what Elise had with Jed, what Clara shared with Dalton, what Sylvie's mom, Ava, had with Jody's half brother Darius.

After the ceremony, there were pictures. When the photographer finally let them go, Seth drove Jody back to the house. They checked in with Mae. Jody nursed Marybeth, and then off they went again, this time to the hotel.

The weather was perfect, a little warm maybe, but not too bad. Snowy-clothed tables set with silver-rimmed china waited on the terrace, where dinner would be served. Cocktails, champagne and appetizers came first as everybody met and mingled. Then they settled in for the meal.

At seven thirty, the guests gathered in the ballroom

to watch the bride and groom share their first dance. After that, they could stay inside for more dancing or return to the terrace to visit without having to compete with the band.

The photographer called the wedding party together again— this time on the terrace as the sun began to set.

After that second round of pictures, Jody rejoined Seth in the ballroom. He tugged her close to his side and nuzzled a kiss against her hair. "Let's dance."

"You dance? Somehow, I never pictured you as the dancing type."

He gave her that slow smile of his. "I'm full of surprises."

"It's a fast one," she teased. "You sure?"

"I think I can manage to shuffle around."

Actually, that he was game for a dance delighted her. She followed him out onto the floor and they danced around each other like everyone else was doing.

After three fast dances, the band played a slow one. Seth pulled her close. She went happily into his arms, leaning her head on his shoulder as they swayed to that Ellie Goulding ballad from *Fifty Shades of Grey*.

What was it about him? In his arms she felt cherished and completely at home.

He rubbed his hand gently at the small of her back, sliding it up, stroking her hair, then caressing his way back down again, reminding her of what would happen between them that night when they were finally alone.

What she felt for him was like nothing she'd ever known before. She kept waiting for loving him to somehow become more ordinary, something accepted, like breathing. Something she could do without even having to think about it. It would be so much easier to love him that way.

He cradled her closer still. The woodsy scent of his aftershave seduced her. His lips brushed her temple.

Longing filled her.

All she wanted was everything. Was that so unreasonable?

She stifled a desperate laugh at the absurdity of her overwhelming desire, a laugh that could too easily have become a sob.

Truly, she only wanted what she'd given up hope of ever finding. Forever *and* his heart, too. Funny, that she'd had the words of love from Brent, but he never would give her forever.

With Seth, it was the other way around. Would she ever in her life manage both at the same time?

The truth she kept denying rose up within her. Really, this wasn't working.

It wasn't getting any better for her. She couldn't do it any longer, couldn't just wait around and hope that she would stop obsessing over loving him—or that he would somehow see the light, get past the awful events of seven years ago and openly return her love. She was going to have to figure out a way to make peace with herself, a way to somehow ease this awful feeling of being all bottled up inside.

She really did need to talk about it with him.

She needed to tell him she loved him—tell him calmly this time. Face-to-face. So he would have to acknowledge it, so he wouldn't be able to lie to himself that she'd only gotten carried away during a mind-blowing orgasm.

The song came to an end. They swayed to a stop.

She lifted her head from his shoulder and looked up into those warm amber eyes.

He gazed at her so tenderly. "My beautiful bride." And he tipped up her chin and brushed a kiss against her lips.

That did it.

The words rose up, demanding release. And she let them out for the second time. "I love you, Seth. I'm *in* love with you."

Chapter Eleven

His face went blank and his ears turned red.

Her heart shriveled to a dried-out raisin inside her chest.

And then, a moment later, he pulled it together. "Jody," he said, rough and low. Kind of chiding. As though she had wounded him by saying such a cruel thing. "Jody, you know that I care for you deeply, too."

I care for you deeply.

Ugh. Just…ugh.

Something clicked within her. A certain calm descended. "This isn't working for me. We have to talk about this."

He actually winced. "Now?"

The sense of calm deserted her as fast as it had come. Fury swept through her, heating her cheeks, making her heart race. It would have been much too satisfying to call him a bad name and run from the ballroom.

However, he did have a point. Elise's wedding was hardly the time or the place.

"You're right," she said. "We'll talk later." A fast song began. "For right now, keep dancing..."

It was after one in the morning when Jody thanked Mae and walked her out to her pickup.

Back inside, she could hear Marybeth starting to fuss.

Seth appeared from the great room holding the receiver for the baby monitor. "I'll get her."

"No. She'll want to nurse. I'll do it." She turned for the baby's room. Seth had moved her recliner in there.

She'd just settled in with Marybeth at her breast when he stuck his head in the door and asked, "Want me to change her?"

Jody shook her head. "I'll do it. Go on to bed."

He hovered there in the doorway, his tie undone, his eyes both wary and worried at once. All man. *Her* man—well, mostly. "Jody, I..."

"It's late," she whispered. "Get some sleep. We'll talk about it tomorrow."

He started to speak again, then seemed to think better of it. Tapping a palm on the door frame, he turned and disappeared down the hall.

A half an hour later, she settled her sleeping baby back in her crib, turned off the little lamp by her nursing recliner and tiptoed out into the hallway. The master bedroom door was open, but the light was off.

She actually dreaded going in there, but she made herself do it. Seth was already in bed, facing the far wall, the covers pulled up over his big shoulders.

Jody undressed in the bathroom. When she slid under the blankets with him, he didn't move.

Carefully, she settled on her side facing away from him, closed her eyes and waited for sleep to come and take her away from this too-quiet, dark room where the man she loved slept with his back to her.

In the morning, they ate breakfast in silence. She fed Marybeth and he changed her.

He had the whole day off, and so did she. They'd planned to head out to the ranch, but when he asked if she still wanted to go, she shook her head. "As soon as Marybeth goes to sleep, we'll talk. Then we'll see."

"What do you mean, we'll see?" He seemed angry, suddenly.

Well, too bad if he was upset. She wasn't all that happy with the current situation, either. "I mean, let's talk first before we decide what to do with the rest of the day."

"Jody—"

She showed him the hand. "*After* Marybeth goes to sleep."

Seth resented each minute as it ticked by. He didn't want to do this. They didn't need to talk—not about this. Not about love.

He'd thought Jody understood him, that she knew exactly where he came down on the question of love. But apparently, he'd gotten it all wrong.

By ten, Marybeth had conked out on her play mat in the great room. Seth carried her to her room.

When he came back out, he closed the door. Jody was the most reasonable woman he'd ever known. He didn't think things would get heated. But on the off chance that they did, well, no need to scare the baby.

Jody was waiting for him on one end of the sofa in the great room, looking way too good in skinny jeans that hugged every curve and a snug pink T-shirt, her bare feet up on the cushions, tucked to the side. He took the other end of the sofa.

For several awful seconds they both sat silent. Should he speak first?

He had no idea what to say. Whatever he came up with, he was just about certain she wouldn't like what he said.

Finally, she took the lead. "We never actually talked about love that night you asked me to marry you. We should have."

And he should keep his mouth shut now. He knew that. But he didn't. "Jody, I honestly thought you understood my position."

"I know. I thought I understood it, too. I thought I accepted it."

She did? "Then why are we doing this?"

She stiffened at his harsh tone. "You are not a stupid man, Seth Yancy. I know that you know what the problem is." She spoke each word way too clearly, like she was biting them off with her teeth. And then she paused for a very slow breath. "Love is important, Seth. Love matters. I love you."

I love you. It was the third time she'd said it. Every time she said it something happened inside him, a sense of triumph, a hot and wild spurt of pure joy—followed immediately by a hard slap of shame.

She said, "When I accepted your proposal, I knew I didn't have your love. I knew then as I do now that you feel you owe your love to Irene, because of what happened. Because she gave her life for yours. Is that wrong? Tell me if I've got it wrong."

He looked away. It hurt to hear her say it out loud like that. "If you understand, then why are we talking about it?"

"Because I *need* to talk about it. Because it's a hard thing, a really painful thing. And the hard and painful things are the ones we need to talk about the most."

He wasn't so sure about any of that—at least, not when it came to this particular hard, painful thing. And the more he thought about it, the more he hated the way she'd said the truth right out loud like that. Yes, he owed his love to Irene. But it sounded all messed up, somehow, when she put it in words. "It's just how it is, that's all."

She brushed his shoulder, so lightly, a touch that burned him to the core. "Look at me, please."

He made himself meet her eyes.

She scanned his face as if seeking points of entry. "I'm sorry, Seth. I misled you. I misled us both."

He didn't get it. The plain fact was that if anyone had done any misleading, it had been him. Because she was right. The night that he proposed, he'd never once said straight-out that his love was not included. Saying it out loud very likely would have been a deal-killer, and he'd known that at the time. He should be ashamed of that. And he was. Not ashamed enough to have done things differently, though.

He wanted her too much, needed her, really. With her, he had everything he'd never thought to have again. He would have done worse than just misleading her to get a yes out of her that night.

She said, "You're a wonderful man, and we fit together, you and me."

"Exactly."

"We're suited to each other. The way we are together, the way our lives mesh, I never thought I was going to find that with a man. I mean, with you, doing everyday things is...fulfilling. Exciting. Just all-around *right*. So I wanted you, wanted to be with you. I couldn't wait to be your wife."

Cautiously, he suggested, "All that sounds really good."

She nodded. "It *is* good."

"And it's the same for me. I don't see the big problem."

"The problem is that I said yes too soon."

"No. Not true."

"Yeah. I wanted everything you offered me, the two of us together, building a good life, raising Marybeth. And maybe other babies if it worked out that way. I still want it all, Seth. Everything you offered me. That isn't going to change." She reached out—and hesitated just before she touched him. Her hand fell to her thigh.

"Jody—"

"Wait. Please. The truth is, I want what we have, and I'm happy. But I want your love, too. I can accept that Irene will always have a claim on your heart. I respect that. I think that's beautiful and right. But you have to make room for me in there, too. That's what marriage is. We stood up together in front of Pastor Jacobs and promised to love and honor each other. *Love*, Seth. It was right there in our wedding vows."

He didn't know what to say to her. "Jody. I told you. I do care for you."

Her lip curled, and not in a smile. "Okay, now you're starting to tick me off."

"What? I don't—"

"Don't give me that *I care for you* crap, Seth. I know that you *care* for me. You *care* for me in a thousand ways, and I love every one of them. But your *care* for me is not what we're talking about here."

"I just…" He stood. "I can't talk about this anymore. There's just no point."

She tipped that beautiful face up to him, her soft mouth set. "You may be right."

He didn't like the sound of that. "What are you saying?"

A frown creased the smooth space between her eyebrows. "I don't know. I'm not sure."

"Jody, dear God in heaven. What we have is good."

She rose, too, unfolding those fine legs to stand and face him. "I know it is, Seth." Her voice was soft now, almost tender. "I love you. I do."

There it was again—a flash of heat, a stab of shame. "We'll be all right."

"I don't know."

"You don't know? Why are you talking like this? You're my wife. Of course you know. We'll work it out. That's what married people do." Or what they *should* do, anyway.

Now he was thinking of his mother, all those years ago, running off with some drifter and never coming back. Not a lot of working-things-out going on there.

Jody said, "I would like you to give what I've said some serious thought. It might not hurt to find someone to talk about it with."

He glared down at her. "Someone to talk with?"

"That's right. I think talking to someone else about this could be a good thing for you."

How was this happening? The whole world was spinning right out of his control. "A psychiatrist, is that what you mean? I don't need a shrink."

"If you're uncomfortable with a professional, maybe call your dad or talk to Roman or Pastor Jacobs..."

His dad. She wanted him to call his dad about this? Not happening. And Roman? Even worse.

As for Pastor Jacobs...

No.

Just no.

"I'll think about it," he said. And he would. Way too much. Not that thinking about it would have him running to Pastor Jacobs to spill his guts. When a man had problems, he worked them out himself.

And for now, well, he didn't need to stand here and listen to her hint that she might be planning to leave him. "Is that all, then?"

"Think about what I've said. Please?"

He couldn't take anymore. He had to get out of there. "I'm going out to the Bar-Y. You coming?"

"No. You go ahead." She speared her fingers in her silky hair and raked it back from her forehead. "I could use a little time to myself, anyway."

Jody cleaned the house that day. She did laundry. She roasted a chicken with new potatoes for dinner, though she had her doubts that Seth would return for the meal.

But he did return.

And when he came back, he was calm and so kind. He praised the meal and talked about the new tractor he and Roman were thinking of buying. He took over with the baby the way he always did, changing diapers, walking her, whispering to her, cuddling her while he watched the Rockies game.

In bed, he pulled Jody close. She went to him with a yearning sigh. She gloried in his kiss, in his every caress. Their lovemaking was urgent and better than ever.

Afterward, he held her close. She tipped her head back and kissed him. "I love you," she said and prayed that a miracle might happen, and he would say it back to her.

Or at least, that he might be willing to talk about the problem some more.

Her prayers were not answered.

He said, "Good night, Jody." And he reached over and turned off the light.

Monday was more of the same. He was attentive and warm to her at breakfast. When he got home that night, he was helpful and kind.

They reached for each other when they went to bed. He entered her slowly. The heat between them burned high. It was heaven, just to be held in his arms.

But when she told him she loved him, he did not say it back—or even acknowledge that she'd said it at all.

Same thing on Tuesday. A whole lot of mutual civility between them, but every word felt empty. He was in the same room, but a million miles away from her.

That night, she went to bed early. When she got up to feed Marybeth, he was sleeping beside her, a big lump under the covers, facing the wall.

Wednesday, it got worse. They didn't talk. He ate breakfast, carried his dishes to the sink and left her there to finish up her bacon and eggs alone.

The distance between them was growing. She had to do something.

That night, at dinner, she said, "I've been thinking about what we discussed on Sunday…"

He put up a hand. "Don't go there, Jody. There's just no point."

Tears scalded her throat and burned behind her eyes. But she'd be damned if she let them fall.

Uh-uh.

She finished her dinner in silence, put the dishes in the dishwasher and went to bed early again.

Thursday, she met Elise at the bakery for breakfast. They talked about the honeymoon Elise and Jed were planning. As soon as Jed finished the novel he was working on, they would fly to Paris for three weeks.

Elise sensed that things weren't right with Jody.

"You know you're going to need to talk about it eventually," Elise said as she cut her muffin into quarters and then blotted up the crumbs with her fork. "Whatever it is, I'm here and I'm listening."

Jody cut a bite of her cinnamon coffee cake and then didn't even feel like eating it. She felt so low, she had trouble pretending that nothing was wrong. "I can't talk about it now, but you're the best and I love you."

"When you're ready, let me know. I'm here."

"I know. And I will." She hoped it wouldn't come to that. But things weren't getting any better between her and Seth. At some point, she was going to need to talk it out with someone. Elise would most likely be the one.

Or maybe Nellie. Or Clara. Or Ava or Rory.

Actually, it cheered her up just to think of her sisters, of all the women of her family by blood and by marriage. When she needed them, they would be right there.

As fed up as she was with Seth, she ached for him that he seemed to have no one he would tell his secrets to.

He used to tell them to her.

But since she wouldn't stop repeating her unbearable words of love to him, he was telling her nothing.

Nothing at all.

And she, well, she totally resented this crap he was giving her.

He had it all wrong. And he had to know that. What man did that? Told a woman she could have everything from him, all that he was and all that he owned.

Just not his love.

That hurt. It was a blow straight to her heart. And every time she said she loved him and got nothing back, he just drove the pain deeper.

The pain made her angry.

And she was mad at herself as much as at him. She *had* known where he stood on the question of loving that night he asked her to marry him. She'd known, but she'd said yes, anyway. She really was a complete fool when it came to love.

It had to stop. They needed, somehow, to work it out.

But again that night, they slept turned away from each other, each clinging to their separate sides of the bed.

Friday night it was the same.

Saturday, she took Marybeth and went to Bloom for a few hours. When she got back to the house, he was still at the justice center. He showed up at a little after one and went straight to the spare room to put away his service weapon and badge in the safe he'd installed there.

A few minutes later, he appeared in the great room, where Jody was folding laundry, with Marybeth in her bouncy seat on the floor. He picked up the baby and patted her back. She cooed in contentment that Daddy was home.

"I'm going out to the Bar-Y," he said. "Will you come with me?" He looked so tired. She ached for him.

And for herself. "Sure." She planned to go into Bloom the next day for a couple of hours. "I'll need my own car, so I'll follow you in the Tahoe."

At the ranch, he went off with Roman to look for a missing calf. She hung out with Mae. They all had dinner together, and then Mae and Roman went back to their house across the yard.

By eight, Marybeth was asleep in her freshly painted and furnished room. Seth sat in the family room staring at the TV.

And Jody?

She just couldn't take it anymore. Not one more night marooned on her side of the bed. Uh-uh. Not doing that.

In the big master bedroom that looked out on the backyard, she got out the suitcase she'd stored in the closet a couple of weeks before and filled it with random items of clothing she'd been leaving at the ranch since she and Seth got married. There were a few things in the baby's room she needed, too, but she would grab those just before she went out the door.

She rolled the suitcase into the family room. Seth glanced over and saw her.

The suitcase got his attention. He pointed the remote. The TV went dark. "Jody," he said wearily. "What are you doing?"

"This isn't working." She launched into the little speech she'd been rehearsing as she packed. "I think we need a break. I'm going back to the other house, and I want you to stay here. For a while. Until we find a way to work things out."

He stood and demanded, "You're leaving me?" He took a step in her direction.

She put up a hand and he stopped. "No, Seth. I'm not leaving you. I told you, I'm taking a break."

His eyes burned right through her. "Leaving won't solve anything."

"Maybe not. But I'm not spending another night with you like this. I'm going to put this suitcase in the Tahoe and then get Marybeth—and don't worry. I know you'll want to see her. So I'm thinking you can stop by a few hours a day at the other house. Call me tomorrow. We can work that out."

He moved a step closer. "This isn't right."

"If you take another step I'm going to say stuff you won't like."

He froze. "Jody. Don't go." And then he did what she'd warned him not to. He took another step and another. Until he was standing right in front of her, smelling of soap from the shower he'd taken before dinner—soap and that woodsy aftershave of his. And man.

All man.

Her man that she desperately needed a break from.

She swallowed hard and glared up at him. "I warned you."

And then he made it worse. He lifted his big hand and cradled the side of her face. His touch burned as hot as his gaze on her. "Jody..."

She knocked his hand away and jumped back. "You need to do some thinking, Seth. You need to decide if you're going to be mine or not. I know you loved her. And I know your guilt runs bone-deep, that she died and you weren't able to save her. But this thing you have, this *rule* you have about not having any love for me, about saving all your love for her? It's a rotten rule, Seth. And I'm not going to live my life with some bad rule of yours sucking all the joy from every moment we have together."

"Jody, stay."

"No."

"Jody, please." His voice was so gentle now. Full of love—or whatever it was he felt for her that couldn't be love because he loved a dead woman and not her.

"Uh-uh. Not like this." Bracing herself against the temptation to soften toward him, she rolled the suitcase around in front of her, making it a barrier between them.

"Walking out on me solves nothing."

"Maybe not. But I need to go."

"Jody, you said it yourself. You knew the situation when you married me. I want you. I *like* you. I'm happy with you—or I was, until just lately. We can have everything together. Why can't you see that?"

"What I see is it's *not* everything if your love gets saved for her."

"Jody, be reasonable."

"Reasonable? Forget that. I'm not feeling reasonable, and I'm also not through. It's…it's ridiculous, is what it is. You've, what? Had your great love and you can't love again? Please. It's what I said. It's crap, as big a bunch of crap as your other rule about not dating women from town. And you know what? I might have put up with it. I might have let it go, gotten over it, given you time to come to trust and believe in what we have together, given you time to finally let her go—but no. You had to make it crystal clear that you're *never* getting over her. You had to be sure I understood that twenty years from now, I'll be loving you with everything I have in me to love—and you'll still be cutting me out, telling me you *like* me and *want* me and I'm *yours*, but as for loving me? So sorry, Jody. Out of luck there."

His ears were bright red, and his face had gone ghost pale. "That's not fair."

"Fair?" She leaned over the suitcase to wave her hand in his face. "Oh, come on. You don't even want to start lecturing me about what's fair. I waited my whole life for you, and if you think I'm settling for less than all of you, you need to think again." She grabbed the handle of the suitcase and turned for the door.

He didn't try to stop her.

Which was just as well. She'd said all she had to say to him. For now, she just needed to throw the suitcase in the Tahoe, grab the baby and return to the empty house in town where she could nurse her broken heart in peace.

Chapter Twelve

For the past few days, Seth had believed that it couldn't get any worse between him and Jody.

But now she'd taken Marybeth and returned to town without him.

Yeah. Okay, he got the picture now.

It not only *could* get worse. It just had.

And she'd left in a fury. Had she been careful driving home? He shut his eyes to block out the sudden graphic image of her Tahoe wrapped around a tree.

He made himself wait a half an hour before he called to be sure she'd gotten back to the house safely.

"I'm fine," she said, her voice flat, disengaged. "Thanks."

"I…left my badge and the Glock in the safe there."

"Come and get it tomorrow. And anything else here you need."

You. I need you and I need Marybeth. "Can I see Marybeth, too?"

"Of course. Three o'clock?"

"I'll be there."

"See you then." And before he could think of what to say to keep her on the line, she was gone.

He stared at the TV for a while and then went upstairs to face his bed without her in it.

The next day crawled by. It seemed like three o'clock would never come.

He knocked on the door of the house where he used to live like some stranger come to visit. She answered with Marybeth in her arms. He stood there and stared at her, at her blue eyes that saw too much, at her mouth that he wondered if he'd ever get to kiss again.

She stepped back to let him in and then handed him the baby. Marybeth made a small, happy little sound.

"How've you been, sweetheart?" He kissed her fat little cheek, and she cooed as he laid her against his shoulder. The pain and lack that had dogged him all day eased a little.

"I have a few errands to run," Jody said. "I'll be back in two hours."

Wait. She was leaving? "You don't have to go."

Her mouth tightened. But all she said was "I just fed her. See you." And she grabbed her purse and phone from the table by the door and left.

When she got back she wanted to set a regular time for him to visit.

How about every night, all night, and mornings and weekends? How about you just let me come home?

But of course, that wouldn't fly, so he asked for evenings. He could come over from the justice center once he was done for the day before heading back to the ranch for the night.

"Eat before you show up," she said. "Please."

That cut him deep. "You don't even want to eat with me?"

She took a slow breath before she answered. "The whole point is to have a break. People taking a break don't eat together."

He couldn't resist a show of sarcasm. "I didn't know there were rules for this."

"Well, there are. Just like *your* rules about loving— or *not* loving, as the case may be."

About then, Marybeth must have picked up the tension between them. She started to fuss.

Jody said, "Let's not stress out the baby. See you tomorrow night."

She opened the door for him and ushered him out.

The next night he brought dinner with him anyway, in spite of her *rule*. He offered to share. She just picked up her phone and purse and said she'd be back in a couple of hours.

It went the same on Tuesday night. She left as soon as he arrived and shooed him out the door the minute she got back.

By Wednesday, he was starting to wonder why he didn't just go ahead and say it to her. Would that be enough for her, if he just said, *I love you*?

Unfortunately, he knew he couldn't do it—or at least, that if he did manage to choke the words out, he would only sound like a bald-faced, despicable liar. And that would only make her all the more determined to keep on as they were.

As they were? It was awful. He couldn't believe he'd lived like this for all those endless years. He wanted his wife back, wanted his *life* back, the life he'd created with her, the life with laughter and honest talk between them, with great sex and her soft, curvy body in his arms while they slept.

By Friday afternoon, it was so bad he was starting to admit that maybe Jody was right.

He had a problem, one he hadn't made himself solve for seven years. The problem had worked for him. It was an excellent and effective way to punish himself for what had happened to Irene.

But then along came Jody. And now, when he punished himself, he was hurting her, too.

He needed to talk to her about it.

But when he picked up the phone, he set it right back down. Because just admitting he had a problem wasn't enough.

What was she supposed to do with that information? It still remained *his* problem to solve.

She'd said he should talk to Pastor Jacobs or a therapist or maybe his dad. What were they going to tell him that he didn't already know?

As he picked up the phone again, he realized it was time to find out.

Jody wanted Seth back.

Every time he showed up at the door, it got harder not to throw herself into his arms.

Still, she held out, held back. She reminded herself of

the hardest truth: it wasn't going to work if she couldn't have his heart.

Friday night, he seemed different, somehow. Quieter, more at ease. He didn't bring dinner to share, didn't try to get her talking the way he'd done every other night that week, didn't offer to take the Tahoe in for service the way he had two days before.

He took Marybeth from her arms and asked, "So, where are you off to tonight?"

"Dinner with my sisters and Rory at the Sylvan Inn." She'd set up the meeting and would pick up the check. "I'm going to tell them about my little boy."

He studied her for a moment, his expression hard to read—accepting maybe? Even pleased? "Why now?"

"I don't know. It seems like it's about time, that's all."

He gave her a slow nod, but didn't say anything else.

She caught herself about to lean up for a kiss. "Well. See you in a while."

"Take your time. I'll be here."

An hour and a half later, Jody sniffed back tears as the waitress—not Monique Hightower, thank God— set three gorgeous desserts and a handful of spoons on the table. She then poured them coffee, served Jody tea and left them alone.

Nellie dug right into the tiramisu. "I can't believe that *Ma* knew."

Jody sniffled. "Yeah, it's scary when you think about it. She's a lot more perceptive than she lets on."

Clara handed Jody another tissue. "You all right, Jo-Jo?"

"I'm still sad about it. I always will be." Jody blew her nose. "But I really do feel I did the right thing."

Across the table, Elise dabbed at her eyes, too. "I get why you didn't tell us then. Some of us were downright evil at the time." She pointed her thumb at herself and pulled a long face.

"You weren't *that* bad," said Nellie. Elise shot her a look, and Nellie relented. "Okay, you were pretty bad."

They all laughed through their tears.

And then Rory said, "I know you're going to work it out with Seth."

Nell tasted the lava cake. "I still don't get what the problem is." Jody had only said that they were having issues, taking some time apart. "What *issues*, exactly?"

Clara reached over and ran a hand down Nell's fabulous auburn hair. "I don't think we're getting details, honey."

Nellie wrinkled her perfect nose at Clara. "Hey, a girl can hope."

"And we're here for you, remember that," said Elise. "Anytime. Whatever you need."

A chorus of agreement went up from the others.

Jody wiped her eyes again. "I hit the jackpot when it comes to sisters, that's for sure. Cousins, too." She gave Rory a wobbly smile and raised her teacup high. "And here's to our sisters-in-law." They all lifted their cups. "To Addie and Ava, Chloe and Paige."

Nellie tried the crème brûlée. "Omigod. This is the best. Pick up your spoons, my sisters. You need to taste this, and I need *not* to eat it all myself."

"How'd it go?" Seth asked, turning off the TV and rising from the sofa.

"It was good. Really good. It feels right that I told them."

"I'm glad." He picked up his phone from the table at the end of the sofa. "Tomorrow I've got some things I have to deal with."

Things he had to deal with? What did that even mean?

Not that it was any of her business. They were taking a break from their marriage. That meant neither of them had to explain their activities to the other.

A break from their marriage?

Who'd come up with that brilliant idea?

Oh, right. *She* had.

He added, "So I think I'll have to skip the visit tomorrow. Unless you need me to—"

"No. No, really. That's fine. Sunday at three, then, same as last week?" Had they only been doing this for a week? It seemed like a lifetime to her.

"Three's good." He turned for the door.

She followed him to her small square of entry hall. "Good night, then."

"Night, Jody." He went out the door.

She shut it behind him and leaned back against it with a heavy sigh.

Seth was waiting on the front steps of the ranch house at 2:15 p.m. the next day when the rental car rolled into the yard. He got up and went down the steps.

The blue sedan pulled to a stop, and the trunk popped open. Seth grabbed the small suitcase from inside as Bill Yancy got out and shut the door. Roman's dog, Toby, came bounding over.

Seth's dad bent to greet him. "Hey, Toby. How's my good boy?"

The dog panted and wiggled in delight as Bill scratched him around the ruff of the neck.

Seth said, "Long flight just for a conversation."

His dad rose to his height. "I'm retired. I can go where I want when I want. And some conversations oughtta be had face-to-face." He reached out his arms. Seth put down the suitcase and went into them. They slapped each other on the back and stepped quickly apart.

From the porch of the foreman's cottage, Mae called, "Hey, Bill!" Seth's dad waved, and Mae whistled for Toby, who barked once and ran back the way he'd come.

Seth picked up the suitcase and led the way inside.

Two hours later, Bill was all settled in one of the rooms upstairs. He'd had a little nap and a sandwich. It was a sunny day. Seth got a couple of cold ones from the fridge, and they went out to the back porch, where they sat in the pair of black walnut rocking chairs that Seth's great-grandfather had made back before he died in the Battle of Belleau Wood during World War I.

"Where even to start?" Seth took a long pull off his beer.

His dad didn't say anything. Bill Yancy had always known how to wait.

Finally, Seth started talking. He talked about Irene, about her death, about the promise he'd made himself that there wouldn't be anyone else for him. "But then along came Marybeth. And Jody. And everything changed." He spoke of his happiness. And the words of love he felt he couldn't give his wife. "And now she's gone. We're taking a break, she says. She's not going to take me back until I can say I love her and mean it."

"Well, *do* you love her?"

Seth opened his mouth, then closed it and shook his head. "I don't mean no. I just mean..." Seth swore. It was one of those words he never let himself say, but the moment seemed to demand that word, somehow. "I don't even know what I mean."

Bill sipped his beer. The old rocker creaked as he leaned back. "I'm going to tell you something now."

Seth slanted his dad a look. "Something helpful?"

"Well, that's my hope. And while I'm telling you, I want you to think how I always said that above all, a Yancy is loyal."

"You've always been that, Dad, loyal to the core."

"Yeah." Bill didn't sound especially pleased with the fact. "I fell in love with Darlene when you were seven years old."

Seth took a moment to let that sink in. "But you never brought her home until I was fourteen. I was fifteen when you married her."

"That's right. By the time I brought her and Nicky to meet you, I had been in love with her for seven years. I met her first when she worked at Ames Bank, before she got that waitress job at the diner. I used to go in that bank and make extra deposits and withdrawals just to see that smile of hers."

Seth had started to catch on. "But you were still thinking my mother would come back."

"That's right." Bill rocked and the old chair creaked. "Carlotta had run off when you were barely walking. I should have divorced her by the time I met Darlene. But no. I had my ingrained Yancy loyalty to live by. I was a married man, and it was my duty to wait for my wife to come home. Then came the day that Darlene asked me out. I passed her two twenties and a deposit slip across the counter between us and she gave me that beautiful smile of hers and said, 'Bill Yancy, let's go to the movies, just you and me. What do you say?'"

Seth swallowed hard against the lump in his throat. "I miss Darlene."

"Son, you are not alone—and where was I? Ah, yes. Darlene asked me out and that scared me to death, I wanted it so bad. But by then, I'd been telling myself for six years that Carlotta would come home. I'd never gotten a divorce. I *was* a married man. I told Darlene I couldn't. And then I turned around and left that bank and never went back. I started banking at Wells Fargo, and I set my mind on not thinking of Darlene Sampson's beautiful smile ever again. Four years after I ran from the bank where she worked, I heard she started going out with Kirk Couch. I knew that guy was trouble and I didn't like it, but I was a married man and had no right to say anything about what Darlene Sampson did. And then she went and married Kirk. And then he left her, ran off just like Carlotta had done to you and me, left her with a sweet little boy and nothing much else. I got my divorce then, and Darlene got hers. The rest you pretty much know."

Seth didn't much like the comparison his dad seemed to be making. "My mother walked away from us and never looked back. Irene died saving me. No way is that the same."

"Course it's not. Your Irene and Carlotta were nothing alike. But you and me? You not only got that Yancy look from me, you got that sense of loyalty so strong it can lead you astray if you're not careful."

"Loyalty is a good thing, Dad."

"I can't argue that point. What I *can* say is that I

threw away seven years of happiness because I wouldn't stop clinging to something that was long gone. I think about that, son. I think about it a lot. Seven years I lost in misery, seven years I could have been spending with my beautiful Darlene. Yeah, I think about Nicky, too. That without my pigheaded foolishness and those seven years wasted, we wouldn't have had Nicky, and I can't imagine a world that never had Nicky in it. But still. Darlene's gone now. And the hard fact is that I could have had seven more years with her if I'd only had my head on straight. What will you be thinking when Jody is gone?"

"Damn you, Dad. Don't say stuff like that."

Bill stopped rocking. "Tell me, Seth Patrick Yancy, is Irene Vargas ever coming back?"

"Of course not."

"Do you think she died so that you could be unhappy?"

"What are you saying?"

"Irene died so you could live, boy. Think about that. Think about what she gave for you. Think about Jody and Marybeth, who are living and breathing and in need of your love and tender care. Ask yourself if the way you're behaving honors a fine woman's sacrifice."

Bill left the next day.

Seth walked him out, put the suitcase back in the trunk of the blue sedan and closed the trunk lid. He went around to the open driver's-side window. "I wish you'd stay."

"Not this time."

"Think about coming back home to live, Dad."

"I like Florida. The blue, blue sky. The palm trees

and white sand beaches with the waves sliding in. And it's been easier, not to be where everything reminds me of Darlene."

"You might change your mind, though. We miss you here."

"I gotta admit, I've always been a family man. You work things out with Jody, I might be tempted to come on home and practice bein' a grandpa full-time."

"I love you, Dad. Thanks."

Bill gave a quick nod. "Proud of you, son. Never forget that." And then he started up the car.

Seth stood back to watch his father drive away.

Five minutes later, the blue sedan was long gone, and Seth was still standing there in the yard beside the cruiser he'd driven home the day before. He was thinking about Jody, about all the things he needed to say to her. He was hoping he could somehow make her see that he was finally ready to be the man she needed him to be.

It was one of those Sundays.

Lois was on the schedule for that day, but she had some weird virus and called in sick. Jody called Marlie and got lucky there. Marlie went in to open up.

But then Bloom's Sunday delivery driver, Bobby Krebstall, didn't show up. When Marlie tried to call him, he didn't pick up and didn't call back.

So at ten thirty, Marlie called Jody, who packed up a fussy Marybeth and drove to the shop, where she discovered that Bobby, who'd worked the day before, had driven the delivery van home. So, not only no driver, but no van to deliver the orders in.

Bobby was so done working for Bloom. Jody tried

the two drivers they used during the week, but neither could come in that day.

It could have been worse, she reminded herself as she sat in the office in back nursing Marybeth and hoping the baby would stop fussing so much. There weren't that many deliveries, and she could make them in the Tahoe.

At two thirty that afternoon, Marybeth was crying in her car seat, and Jody had one more delivery to go. Sweet old Mr. Watsgraff and his wife were celebrating their fiftieth anniversary. They lived in a small, new development not all that far from the turnoff to the Bar-Y. Mr. Watsgraff wanted the usual white roses, but this time he'd ordered three dozen and sprung for a gorgeous Tom Stoenner art glass vase.

All day, as she'd alternately soothed her unhappy baby, helped Marlie in the shop and headed out to make deliveries, Jody had kept thinking she ought to call Seth and warn him that she might be late to meet him at the house. Actually, he would have come to her rescue in a New York minute and appeared at the shop to do Marybeth duty for as long as she needed him if she'd only asked him.

But she didn't like asking him for things. She didn't like how damn wonderful he was with her, with her baby—okay, fine. *Their* baby. After all, he would be Marybeth's legal father as soon as the adoption went through.

But whatever she called him vis-à-vis Marybeth, she *didn't* want to call him on the phone and admit that she needed him. She wanted *him*, all of him, damn it, including his stubborn heart and those all-important three little words spoken out loud and clear and without hesitation.

However, she didn't have what she wanted, and she was starting to fear that she never would. She'd made her big stand, and they were living separately. And as far as she could make out, he still felt he owed his love to a dead woman.

Marybeth yowled.

"It's okay, sweetheart." She sent a quick glance over her shoulder at the sobbing baby. The car seat was pointed backward, but Jody could clearly see her baby's red cheek and angry, open mouth and her little fist waving. "It won't be long now. Mommy just has this one more delivery, and then I'll take you home to Daddy."

Marybeth only wailed louder.

Jody gritted her teeth and turned onto the street where the Watsgraffs lived.

She parked in the Watsgraffs' driveway, leaving the windows down a crack so the baby would have fresh air for the three minutes it took to carry the flowers inside. At 2:35, she set the vase full of roses on the Watsgraffs' dining room table. Mrs. Watsgraff was teary-eyed. Mr. Watsgraff beamed.

Jody wished them the happiest anniversary ever and got the hell out of there.

In the Tahoe, Marybeth was still crying. Jody opened the door behind the passenger seat and leaned in to check her diaper. Dry. As a rule, Jody tried not to depend on pacifiers. But some days, well, what was a harried mom to do?

She got one out of the pocket of Marybeth's diaper bag and slipped it into the baby's crying mouth.

Marybeth blinked in what truly did look like outrage. And then she opened her mouth wide. The pacifier dropped out. Jody tried to poke it back in again, but her baby was having none of that.

In the end, Jody gave up and stuck the pacifier back in the diaper bag. "Just a few minutes longer, sweetheart," she coaxed. "You'll be with Daddy. You'll feel better then."

Marybeth cried all the louder. Again, Jody considered calling Seth to let him know she could be late. But then, if she got on the road immediately, she could make it in time.

Jody shut the door and went around to the driver's side. She climbed behind the wheel and got going, observing the speed limit until she left the Watsgraffs' development, but pressing the gas a little harder than she should have once she got out on the open road.

She was maybe ten minutes from town and making great time when a lovely thing happened. Marybeth stopped crying. Jody glanced at her in the rearview mirror. She was sound asleep, her little head turned to the side, looking exhausted and adorable, a shiny bubble of drool on her pouty rosebud mouth.

Jody started to smile—but then through the back windshield she saw the flashing lights.

"Crap." She'd only been going a few miles over the speed limit. Some days a girl just couldn't catch a break.

The cop behind her turned on his siren, too.

"You have got to be kidding me..."

The siren wailed louder.

"Fine," she muttered. "All right. I'm pulling over." She slowed, steered to the shoulder and stopped.

Behind her, the siren wound down to nothing, but the lights kept on flashing. Tires crunched gravel as the cruiser slid in behind her.

She didn't realize it was Seth until he emerged in his khaki uniform, aviator sunglasses and Smokey the Bear hat. He shut the cruiser's door, adjusted his sunglasses and came right for her.

She rolled down her window but stayed in the car. Wasn't that what you were supposed to do when an officer of the law pulled you over—even if the officer in question just happened to be the guy you were married to?

He leaned in the window, bringing that infuriatingly wonderful scent of soap and man. "Going a little fast there, young lady."

She took off her own dark glasses and tossed them on the passenger seat before hitting him with a look cold enough to freeze the testicles off a polar bear. "Is this supposed to be funny?"

"Not wise to use that smart mouth on an officer."

God. That sounded downright dirty. What did he think he was doing, anyway?

She turned her gaze straight ahead and told herself things could be worse. At least Marybeth hadn't started screaming again. Yet. "It's been a hellacious day, Seth. I was hurrying to get to the house in time to meet *you*, in case you've forgotten. And I'm not in the mood for—"

"Ma'am. I want you to step out of the car."

Wow. Had he lost his mind? It seemed increasingly possible.

"You do remember that you were coming to see Marybeth at three?"

"I remember. Step out of the car, miss."

"What is the matter with you?" She pushed the words out through clenched teeth.

He moved back from the door a step and crossed his arms over his chest. "I'm not going to ask you again."

Ha. As if there had been any *asking* going on. "Fine. You want to play it that way?"

"Oh, yes, I do. Ma'am." What was up with him? The way he called her "ma'am"?

It made her think of tangled sheets and his big hands all over her. "Have you gone insane?"

To that, he said nothing, just waited there with those arms she wanted wrapped around her crossed over his chest, his badge glinting aggressively in the hot afternoon sun as more than one car whizzed by not six feet away, the occupants watching wide-eyed through their side windows as they passed.

He still wasn't budging. She supposed she had to do something. "Fine. You want me out?"

"That's right. I want you out."

"Well, you got it, then. I'm getting out." She shoved open the door, swung her shoes to the gravel and jumped to her feet, grabbing the door as she did it, slamming it shut good and hard in her fury—and then wincing as she realized she'd probably startled her poor baby awake.

But no. Marybeth slept on.

And her husband had definitely lost his ever-loving mind. He stood silent and still as a statue. Beneath the wide brim of his hat, the lenses of his dark glasses reflected her own distorted image back at her.

She lit into him. "What is the matter with you? You can't just come after me in your cruiser. Seth Yancy, this is harassment, pure and simple. You should be ashamed of yourself."

Once again, he said nothing. But he did move at last.

He took off his hat and his sunglasses and set them carefully on the Tahoe's hood.

Only then did he speak. "It's not harassment, Jody." Now his voice was quiet. Tender, even. Really, what was going on here? None of this made sense. "I promise you it's not."

She glared at him sideways, totally lost as to what he was up to and also unwilling to back down. "Oh, yeah, well, if not harassment, what is it, then?"

What he said next almost buckled her knees. "This is me trying to find the way to tell you that I'm hopelessly in love with you."

She made a noise then. It wasn't a word, exactly. It was more a cry of pain and longing.

"Jody?" He looked suddenly terrified. "Jody, are you okay?"

She blinked at him owlishly. "Um. Yes. I think I am, yes."

"You sure?"

"Well, if I'm not I definitely could be. Now, where were you? Please, go on."

And right there, on the side of the road a little more than halfway between the Bar-Y and their hometown, Sheriff Seth Yancy dropped to his knees. "I love you, Jody." He stared up at her, and there was no mistaking the truth in his eyes. "Forgive me, Jody. Take me back. Make my life worth living. Please."

She gaped down at him. "I don't... What are you...? Seth." Her throat burned and her vision blurred with tears. "Oh, God. Seth."

"I've done what you asked for. And what you asked for was right. I talked to my father, and he made me see that we don't honor the dead if we refuse to be all we can be for the living. I love you, Jody. Let me give you my all. Let me be just for you—you and Marybeth and any other little ones that God might be willing to give us. Give me one more chance. You won't regret it. That is my promise. I swear that to you. That is my vow."

She blinked away the blinding wet heat of her tears and looked down at his upturned face, saw the truth in him, saw that somehow he had done it, put his guilt and his pain behind him enough to reach out for her at last. "You, um, ahem. Would you get up, please?" She offered her trembling hand.

He took it, strong fingers closing around hers, the wonder of his touch arrowing straight to her heart. "Jody." He swept upward. And he touched her face, a caress both reverent and full of tender care. His fingers brushed the curve of her cheek, and everything within her cried out in joy. "You are my love, Jody. You are my everything."

Another cry escaped her. She held out her arms.

That did it. He grabbed for her and yanked her close, wrapping her up in his heat and his strength and, at last, the miracle of his love. "One more chance..." He pressed his lips to her hair.

"Yes. Oh, yes. Oh, Seth. Thank God."

"I love you, Jody."

"And I love you."

And he lifted her chin and he kissed her, right there on the side of the road with several good citizens of Broomtail County rubbernecking the sight as they rolled by in their cars.

He kissed her and then he kissed her again. And then finally, when the baby woke up with a cranky little cry, he let her go and ushered her back into the Tahoe, opening the door for her, gently shutting it once she'd settled into the driver's seat.

He took his hat and sunglasses off the hood and then leaned in the window as she hooked up her seat belt and started the engine. "I'll follow you home."

"Yes." She glanced over her shoulder at her baby. Marybeth was quiet again, staring dreamily into space, her little fist stuffed in her mouth.

Seth said, "Keep to the speed limit, now."

"Yes, Sheriff. I will."

"I'm letting you off with a warning this one time. But I'll be keeping my eye on you."

"I will behave, Sheriff. I will be good."

"I intend to hold you to that."

"I expect nothing less," she replied. "And you'll see. I keep my promises. I will not disappoint you. We're going to have a great life together, you and me."

His stern mouth twitched at one corner. "Something tells me we're not just talking about speed limits here."

"Something tells you right. We're talking about everything."

"Now, there's a tall order."

"Everything, Seth. All that we have together, all that we are and all we will be. I love you, and it's everything to me that you can finally say you love me, too."

He leaned even closer. His mouth brushed hers. "I do love you," he whispered. "So much. With all my heart."

"See you at home," she whispered.

He straightened with a slow nod. "See you at home."

Epilogue

A year after Seth declared his love for his wife on the side of the road, Bill Yancy returned to live at the Bar-Y. A year after that, Jody was pregnant again.

In February of the following year, as a blizzard turned the world to white outside the ranch house windows, Jody had her baby right there at home without the aid of a single medical professional.

But Seth was with her through it all, the same as he'd been when she had Marybeth. More than once, he said how much he loved her as he fed her ice chips, rubbed her back and reminded her to breathe. She said she loved him, too.

But having a baby? If she'd only remembered how bad labor was, she'd have stopped with Marybeth. And when it came time to start pushing, she clutched his hand so hard the bones ground together, and she swore never in her life to have sex with him again.

Downstairs in the family room, Marybeth climbed into her beloved grandfather's lap. "Mommy sounds really mad, Pop-Pop."

Bill guided her head to rest on his shoulder and stroked her shining golden hair. "She's not mad, Bethie. She's just having a baby. She will be fine."

"You promise?"

"Oh, yes, I do."

"She sounds like she's crying, too, like she might have a bad owie."

"Could be. But she's a tough one, your mommy. And your little brother will be here before you know it."

Marybeth's half brother was born twenty minutes later. They named him Nicolas, after the uncle he would never get to meet.

Two years after that, Jody had a little girl, Darlene. And three years after that, another boy. They called him Patrick.

That same year, Josh Levinson, twenty years old and a sophomore at UCLA, asked to meet his birth mother. Jody and Seth welcomed him at the Bar-Y. Having grown up an only child, Josh was excited to discover he had four half siblings.

And at the age of forty-three, seven years after he married the mother of his brother's child, Seth Yancy remained sheriff of Broomtail County. He still had a flock of pretty admirers who showered him with baked goods and bright smiles.

Jody had no problem with any of those women.

She knew his heart belonged to her.

* * * * *

MILLS & BOON®

Cherish™

EXPERIENCE THE ULTIMATE RUSH OF FALLING IN LOVE

A sneak peek at next month's titles...

In stores from 18th May 2017:

- **Behind the Billionaire's Guarded Heart** – Leah Ashton
  and **Wild West Fortune** – Allison Leigh
- **Her Pregnancy Bombshell** – Liz Fielding
  and **A Conard County Homecoming** – Rachel Lee

In stores from 1st June 2017:

- **A Marriage Worth Saving** – Therese Beharrie
  and **Honeymoon Mountain Bride** – Leanne Banks
- **Married for His Secret Heir** – Jennifer Faye
  and **Falling for the Right Brother** – Kerri Carpenter

Just can't wait?
Buy our books online before they hit the shops!
www.millsandboon.co.uk

Also available as eBooks.

MILLS & BOON®

EXCLUSIVE EXTRACT

Miranda Marlowe has just discovered
she's pregnant with her boss's baby…

Read on for a sneak preview of
HER PREGNANCY BOMBSHELL

Tomorrow she would go down to the beach, feel the
sand beneath her feet, let the cold water of the
Mediterranean run over her toes. Then, like an old lady,
she would go and lie up to her neck in a rock pool heated
by the hot spring and let its warmth melt away the
confused mix of feelings; the desperate hope that she
would turn around, Cleve would be there and, somehow,
everything would be back to normal.

It wasn't going to happen and she wasn't going to
burden Cleve with this.

She'd known what she was doing when she'd chosen
to see him through a crisis in the only way she knew
how.

She'd seen him at his weakest, broken, weeping for
all that he'd lost, and she'd left before he woke so that
he wouldn't have to face her. Struggle to find something
to talk about over breakfast.

She'd known that there was only ever going to be
one end to the night they'd spent together. One of them
would have to walk away and it couldn't be Cleve.

Four weeks ago she was an experienced pilot working

for Goldfinch Air Services, a rapidly expanding air charter and freight company. She could have called any number of contacts and walked into another job.

Three weeks and six days ago she'd spent a night with the boss and she was about to become a cliché. Pregnant, single and grounded.

She'd told the border official that she was running away and she was, but not from a future in which there would be two of them. The baby she was carrying was a gift. She was running away from telling Cleve that she was pregnant.

She needed to sort out exactly what she was going to do before, have a plan firmly in place, everything settled, so that when she told him the news he understood that she expected nothing. That he need do nothing…

Don't miss
HER PREGNANCY BOMBSHELL
by Liz Fielding

Available June 2017
www.millsandboon.co.uk

Copyright ©2017 Liz Fielding

CP0517_2

Join Britain's BIGGEST Romance Book Club

- **EXCLUSIVE** offers every month

- **FREE** delivery direct to your door

- **NEVER MISS** a title

- **EARN** Bonus Book points

Call Customer Services
0844 844 1358*

or visit
millsandboon.co.uk/subscriptions

CB3

MILLS & BOON®

are delighted to support
World Book Night

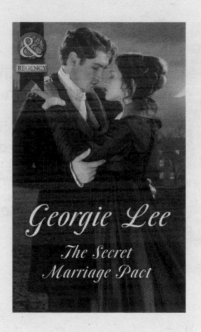

World Book Night is run by The Reading Agency
and is a national celebration of reading and books
which takes place on 23 April every year. To find
out more visit worldbooknight.org.

THE READING AGENCY